Legacy Earth

Mick MacNeil

Published by Mick MacNeil, 2021.

LEGACY EARTH

First edition. December 25, 2021.

ISBN: 978-1777158156

Written by Mick MacNeil.

Table of Contents

The Quickening 1

The First Awakened | Maricel: Artifacts Specialist........ 4

First Steps 12

The Buzz 15

She could sense more than see more was going on around her. She sensed an increase in noise from daytime. It was faint and indefinable and did not come near her. It clearly suggested to her she was not exactly alone. What Maricel didn't know was a growing population of small nocturnal creatures was moving into her area. Tiny rodents and insects were bringing life to the silence. She watched in amazement as tiny, winged creatures banged against the glowing orbs of street lamps. A soft buzzing around her ears reminded her of the bee. The sound was fainter but somehow more persistent. When it stopped, she felt movement on her neck, then a brief, sharp feeling of itchy discomfort. Reflexively, she brought her hand to her neck, slapping at the source of the discomfort. 20

Death and Itching...22

Seasons..26

Something New 33

Scout...36

Time to Move On 47

Raphael: Hunter, Weapons Expert, and Tactician | Survey 57

Guardian..65

An Unexpected Terror.....................................71

The Hunt 79

Jolinda: Healer, Pharmacologist, Medical Technician, Physician | First Things 87

Mewser 93

Forestman and the Elvin 105

An Eventful Storm 127

Slow Recovery 133

Patah: Psychological and spiritual analyst and counselor | A Flawed Legacy 138

Beginning the Quest 144

Illusory Human 151

Systematic Search 158

What Sort of Creature? 173

Ending Evil 179

The Chase 182

Shattered Peace 374

Super Computer 377

Overture 385

This book is dedicated to my mother who loved to tell stories and taught me the joy of story telling

The Quickening

It was a scene of unimaginable darkness. Had we been there, you and I, we would, from our vantage point, have been struck by the total absence of light and the complete silence, the lifelessness of it all. Oh, if we had a light, we would have seen trees laden with leaves and fields of grass, but while at first glance it would seem to indicate life, we would have quickly realized it was an illusion. The trees, the grass, the entire world was lifeless and while filled with things we would recognize as elements of life, the utter stillness, the absolute silence and the total darkness would inform our senses but for ourselves there was no living thing. The vista for as far as one could tell was dark and silent and lifeless. Since no one was present in the darkness complete, there was no vista. Then from our imagined viewpoint on an airless hill, intense patches of purplish, pink light grew and spread rapidly to cover our entire view would dazzle us. Had we been in a spaceship not too far away we would have seen the light envelop the orb on which in our imagination, we had been standing. Looking outward into the surrounding space, we would have observed pockets of the same phenomena occurring for far as the naked eye could see. Back on our imagined viewpoint, we would be overwhelmed by a change as unimaginable as the lifeless stillness we had encountered just moments before. Then as we watched, the purplish pink light would vanish and we would be surrounded by the subtle sound of animals, the thrumming of insects and the humming ticklish breeze ruffling the grass and leaves. In the east, a bright shiny orb would appear a rising above a distant and verdant horizon, and we would discover ourselves in a warm summer morning surrounded by life.

While we were not really there to experience it, it was the very thing to happen. It happened because the time of mankind is now passing. The last remnants of humanity, to us, god-like creatures, were on the verge of transmutation into pan-dimensional beings, in which the last remnants of humanity would be shed. Before leaving their humanity behind, they had decided they would leave a legacy to their human origin. They would revitalize the long-dead sector of the Milky Way Galaxy holding within its burnt out and scattered particles, their original home, the tiny planet of earth and the cold and lifeless ash once Sol one, a G type star called the sun, once warming the tiny Solar System from whence they had sprung.

They had decided their legacy would be built around the period when early humans had first begun to move beyond the limits of their tiny world and stood on the threshold of space. God-like, but not gods, those about to shed their last traces of humanity, searched everywhere to gather the elements to provide authenticity to their re-creation. Working with what they could find, or they could understand, vast as it was, these majestic beings revitalized the stars and planets around their early home, and reinstituted life as it would have been around the 21st century. Their creation, like the environments they sought to recreate, like all creation, was imperfect. They rebuilt the 21st century with broad strokes spreading over 500 or more years. With the countless eons having passed, it was good enough.

As they left this phase of existence behind, they were certain their progenitures would, as they had, make the necessary corrections.

The First Awakened
Maricel: Artifacts Specialist

Coffee!

Maricel sat up quite suddenly, tearing the gossamer fabric enclosing her from head to toe. "Man," she exclaimed. "I really need a coffee!"

Those may well have been the first words ever to be spoken in this new world. Apart from the fact these words were quite problematic. Not only did they startle Maricel who had spoken and heard words voiced out loud for the very first time, it also brought with it puzzlement. Maricel did feel the need for something, something she termed, "coffee."

What Maricel found puzzling was whatever this thing called coffee was she wanted some, but at the moment, had no idea what to look for and where she would find some. Looking around Maricel could see she was surrounded by a large number of bizarre looking devices. To her surprise, she discovered almost instantly she was able to know what the device was called, what its function was and how to use it. This she found quite intriguing because she was sure she had never seen any of these things ever before. Among these artifacts surrounding her, she found several she could use to make coffee. She chose the one she recognized as being easy and interesting to use.

The next step was to figure out what coffee was. There, on a higher shelf, she spotted a container with the word coffee written on the side, three times in fact, in languages she knew as plain Earth Standard, Assianangle, and Mars Basic. Reaching up she brought it down and read the directions on the side in all three languages. While she couldn't quite figure out how she knew what it said, she realized she already understood how to work the coffee maker. She just needed to find something called a coffee dipper or tablespoon. It took a few minutes rummaging through the smaller items and some of the containers. Within minutes she was in the process of brewing coffee. When she turned the coffee maker on it started immediately. The on button glowed a soothing shade of blue. There was a gurgling sound as the water began to drip through. Although at the moment it held no significance for her. There was no identifiable power source for the coffee maker; no wires, no plugs, and the necessary water was there without her having to pour it and without a hose connection to bring it in. At the very instant, the first brewing was done the machine was ready to go again. Although she wasn't nearly as surprised by this as you or I might have been, had she checked out all the other electronic devices, she would have found none had a connection to a power source. Still, if she were to turn one of them on it would have started instantly. Of more concern for Maricel at the moment was to find something called a "cup." The first mouthful was hot and shocked her. This was a new and unexpected effect causing some of the hot liquid to fall from her mouth and land on her foot introducing her to a new and somewhat unpleasant sensation. Still, she had to admit there was something pleasurable about the hot liquid as she swallowed it. The coffee done, Maricel took a moment to look around. She stopped in front of a reflective surface to gaze at the strange figure looking back at her. She recognized a fair looking face seeming to fit the term pretty, bordered by long red hair barely covering her ears and rested partly on her shoulders and back. Two perfect green eyes were centered by a pleasantly perky nose sitting above full lips and completed by a well-formed chin. She could see the body was still draped with strands of thin gossamer fabric that a few minutes earlier had covered her completely. The shape was slim, the breasts firm, the legs long and shapely. This was the body of an athlete. The age appeared to be somewhere between 20 and 30 years old while the reality was it been in this life for just a few minutes. Something she might at once understand but still find hard to resolve. It only took a beat for her to recognize this was an image of herself reflected back from the shiny surface. She began to pull off the pieces of gossamer fabric still clinging to her. Then she stopped, realizing she should retain some sort of covering as she had no real idea of what she would encounter as she began her journey of discovery.

She would follow the directions of her mind and put on one of those outfits she knew instantly were hers to wear, hanging on hooks fastened to the wall. First, however, she wished to rid her body of all traces of the gossamer webbing.

Scanning the crowded room, she saw an open doorway through which she could identify items designed for personal hygiene. Among these was a small plastiglass enclosure. Maricel immediately knew this was a vapor cleanse shower. She stepped in and pressed the one button on the wall. With a gentle whirr, the door shut behind her and for a brief second, she felt a sensation of panic. The panic quickly passed as she was engulfed in a warm, fragrant vapor. While novel for Maricel it didn't seem outside the realm of normal but for those living in the early 21st century of origin earth except for a few sci-fi buffs they would not recognize such a device. For several moments Marcel stood enraptured by the warm fragrant pulsations with delicately moving across her body. As quickly as it had begun it ended. The surrounding mist vanished, and the door opened with another gentle whirr. She stepped out feeling incredibly refreshed and made her way to the wall where the clothing hung. While the items all appeared similar she chose one outfit the color and feel of which, appealed to her eye and to her touch. In short order, she donned a one-piece form-fitting outfit covering her from neck to ankle.

There were a number of pockets as well as fabric and metal attachments near her waist which she knew would allow her to carry any necessary utensils she might need to help her in her exploration while keeping her hands free. Lastly, at her feet she found what she instantly knew were boots, a soft pliable leather-like material made them easy to put on encasing her feet in comfort. A small knife was sheathed against the outside of her right boot.

She began to gather the tools she somehow knew she would require to help her in her explorations. While she was still dogged with a sense of uncertainty about everything, she did seem to know a lot. Her name (–name?), was Maricel and she seemed to have some kind of innate expertise regarding artifacts dating from some mysterious era extending from the early part of something she knew as the 19th century to the late in the 25th century. She was certain this referred to a period of time, a concept she was just beginning to feel comfortable about.

She really had no idea where she actually was or even when she actually was. Most of the artifacts in the room seem to be primarily late 20th and early 21stcentury but some were clearly older and others of far later times. For Maricel, however, they were all items of the present time. It was just some were clearly more technically advanced. Those labels late 19th-century late 20th century early 25th century really meant nothing to her. For her they all belonged to right now and which was all she decided she really needed to know. Maricel spent some time going through all the items in the room. There were quite a number of items and devices. Most we're kitchen devices, toasters, four kinds of coffee maker, three microwave ovens varying in technological sophistication, and grinders. There were sealers as well as a wide variety of useful food management utensils. There were also numerous personal devices such as; electric toothbrushes, a whole range of different kinds of razors, and hair drying and manipulating devices. While thorough the collection was quite random is if whoever put them there had only a vague idea of what they actually were. Eventually, she checked out everything. Although she could swear with absolute certainty she had never seen any of these items before she knew them all, their function and how they worked. This was a mystery Maricel felt had to be solved. She needed to know what she was, where she came from, how she got here and of course how she knew so much about all of those devices. She had read all the labels in Earth Standard, Assianangle, and Mars Basic but learned nothing more than what she had already known. She would discover, even as she gained answers to her many questions not all questions were answerable.

She checked the piece of furniture on which she had awakened. It was a body shaped pod around which hung the remnants of a fine cloth like material having recently covered her entire body. It didn't seem much like what her mind told her a bed was. She reached down to touch the delicate material, this time with the purpose of understanding rather than trying to remove it. This was different from what she sought to do in the shower.

It felt as if it were hardly there. She had a sense this was far different from the fabrics making up the articles of clothing she had found or, for that matter, any of the other objects she found in the room. It was a body shaped pod around which hung the remnants of a fine cloth like material which recently covered her entire body. Had she a term for it, she might have thought it was almost biological, more akin to a delicate skin. It seemed in some odd sense alive unlike the fibrous material it first appeared to be. She touched it. At her touch, it began to shrivel and then disappear leaving no trace. Whatever it was, its job was done.

For a brief moment, Merisel had the uncomfortable feeling it had been a part of her and was it her fate to shortly follow it into nothingness. No, she could feel the life force coursing through her body. There was a sense of strength, a vitality making it clear to Maricel she was not going to shrivel up and dissolve into nothingness. She felt this in a way convincing her there was timelessness to her. She had much to do, and far to go.

In the same way, she had an instinctive awareness her knowledge was almost mystical and valuable. She was certain there was more to this place than a room full of useful but redundant artifacts. Knowing this she now felt the necessity to figure out her next step. Looking around the room, she saw an indentation in the smoothness of the surrounding wall.

The indentation was a rectangular shape higher than it was wide. Above it was an illuminated sign showing symbols in Mars basic, Earth Standard, and Assianangle. Each of these symbols she recognized as meaning "exit" or "the way out". Since she somehow understood the symbols for each of the three languages, any one of them would have been enough but redundancy appeared to be a necessary component of this room.

She walked to what she immediately identified as a doorway to take her out of the chamber. As she approached it seemed to come to life with a gentle hum and began to slip to the side. She could see it was an access to another room-like space. Not far beyond this doorway she could see a colorless wall. She wondered if she should go through.

Unsure of what to do next, she took a step back and immediately the door closed with the mechanical sigh. She stepped forward and it began to open again. She stepped back and it closed. She repeated this several times with the same result. It was exactly the result she expected but was still delighted to observe.

A sense of caution had overridden her first impulse. She decided before she go out on the town, she would need things to bring with her when she left the room. Almost without thinking, she circled the room once again, this time picking up various objects the first being a backpack where she could place the rest of the items she had selected. While she wasn't exactly sure of why she had selected what she did, she had a feeling of certainty these things would be valuable to her as she set out on her first exploratory journey into unknown territory.

The pack fit naturally to her back and the lightweight metal staff she had picked up was both walking stick and weapon should she require one. Gathered and ready she approached the door; paused to let it open, then stepped through the opening into a hallway.

First Steps

The walls were painted a virtually colorless neutral shade. A strip of solid softly lit material ran along the length of the walls where they met the ceiling. It lit the corridor in one direction, extending into dimness. In the other direction, Maricel noted a different kind of light far along the passage. Instinctively, she headed towards the brighter light. She was filled with an almost paradoxical sense of contentment and of fear. At one level, she knew she was doing what she was supposed to do, on another level, she felt a strangeness, an overwhelming uncertainty of what she might encounter. This she realized was all new to her. She remembered nothing beyond the moment, not so long back; when she had awakened with a craving something called coffee.

So now she knew what coffee was, but it and all the other knowledge she had didn't help her remember why she was here. Still engulfed by the contradictory senses of contentment and fear, she made her way down the hall. The floor was soft beneath her feet. As she approached the light a new sensation, a sense of anticipation came over her. She could feel whatever she was about to begin, it would be the beginning of something tremendous, something wonderful, something important for which, she had been created. Her feeling of excitement crescendoed as she approached the opening marking the end of the corridor.

Gazing through the opening she was presented with a wonderful and intriguing Vista. There was such richness, colors of green and brown, gray paved streets, Maricel saw strange multihued vehicles frozen in place, and a sense of distance briefly overwhelmed her.

She stood, awestruck at the entrance into this incredible vastness. Then she stepped through the doorway. There was no portal to push, only a slight tingling in her nerve endings as she passed where the corridor and outer world met. For several moments, she stood outside the door mesmerized by her surroundings. Briefly it all appeared to her to be a complete sensory jumble of colors and images.

Having stepped beyond the doorway and out into the world, Maricel was exhilarated. The air was warm and fresh. She sucked it greedily into her lungs, chuckling as she exhaled. Above her, she could see a brilliant blue screen with tiny white puffballs drifting across it. Sky and cloud, although she knew the names, were concepts unfamiliar to her. In one direction, there was a verdant expanse dotted with towering pieces of greenery. What vague grasp of the concept of grass and trees she had begun to consolidate in her mind, theory and experience meeting.

As she was pondering the idea of the natural environment, words such as park, woods, recreation, flashed into her mind informing her that despite her knowing, there was much uncertainty. She did know about buildings and streets and could recognize the different vehicles edging them; trucks, cars, bicycles, jet boards, ornithops. Just as with the devices where she awakened, she immediately understood the purpose, function, and operation of each. Maricel knew if she boarded or entered one, she could start it up and direct it off the curb and into the street without any difficulty. But, right then, she was more interested in enjoying the air, the blue sky above and the warmth and light emanating from the bright golden yellow sun dominating the sky. She followed the walkway gazing with wonder at all she could see in the shop windows along her route.

Many items she saw, Maricel recognized immediately, such things as clothing, machines designed to take pictures, machines designed to show pictures, machines to warm and cool things were oddly familiar. What she didn't recognize immediately were liquids in bottles and strangely attractive small items she instinctively recognized as food. She saw many things through the shop windows; cleaning robots, companion robots, tool robots designed for repairing vehicles and some designed for household repairs. Everything she saw enthralled her.

Maricel was relishing the physical activity; the movement of her body, the lifting, and lowering of her feet in a stride carrying her so very quickly and so very smoothly along the walkway between the windows and the stationary vehicles. For quite some time, she continued along the street examining all the windows along one side of her path and the varied and multicolored vehicles edging the other.

The Buzz

Feeling the warmth of the day and the sweetness of the air she felt she could have gone on and on. It was then she heard a sound she knew didn't come from her, not the sound of her step or her breathing.

The sound came from somewhere beyond her. It was a buzzing, and it was growing louder. Maricel stopped quickly looking for its source. She saw as it flew past very close to her head, a tiny yellow and black creature. In amazement, she watched the tiny creature buzz past her to land on a vividly colored object above a green stem embedded in a container of earth. This she knew was part of the natural environment. The thing growing in a planter sharing it with several others of its kind, Maricel knew immediately to be a flower. The flying creature was called a bumblebee. The bee fascinated her, and she watched it closely, wisely staying enough out of range to avoid being struck by it should it come in her direction.

She loved how its fans, its wings, worked and the little black legs it danced around on as it gathered to them a powdery material from the center of the blossom. The buzzing was exquisite, and she basked in the sound just as she had the sunlight and the fresh warm breeze. The bee, finished its task, flew off, it's buzzing fading as it disappeared toward the greenery across the street.

Maricel was sad to see it go and watched until it vanished from her sight. Only then did she become aware she and it were the only living things in the entire landscape. Maricel was now conscious her surroundings were lifeless except for herself and the bee. She understood she had been excited by the simple presence of one tiny living creature.

Once it had disappeared from sight, it was as if a dark cloud came over Maricel. Although bright and clear as ever, she was saddened by the lifelessness of her surroundings. The plants were, she knew, alive but unlike her and the bee, they were fixed and quiet, their lives being lived in stately immobility. Already Marissa was feeling the first tinges of loneliness.

After this, she explored more methodically. She climbed into a nearby car, a Studebaker Lark, whatever those words meant, and turned the key already in the ignition. She pumped the accelerator and the car roared into life. It was interesting, but she wasn't prepared to go too far from where she started, so she turned it off and got out.

She wandered the street a while longer eventually opening the doors of some of the shops for a closer look at what they held. Things she knew to be magazines showed images of those looking similar to her. Some images showed groups of those much like her. There was, she felt, a rightness to this. This view of so many others like Maricel had her wondering where they could be.

Meanwhile, in the forests, in the fields, in dark alleyways, lakes and rivers and ponds, the process of procreation was well underway. In less than a day, earth's lesser creatures were multiplying, their numbers growing exponentially. As the first day made its way to its end, the silence still prevailed. Marisol was beginning to grow weary and felt the need to return to the room where she had awakened.

Shortly later she was returning through the portal to the now familiar enclave filled, as it was, with artifacts, foodstuffs, and for Maricel, a lonely sense of security. To fight the feeling of loneliness,

To escape this feeling of loneliness, Marcel immersed herself in experimenting with her amazing knowledge of all those things she found around her. She began dropping into the surrounding shops, and while finding no one there, busied herself testing everything she could: Cameras, TVs, robots, in fact, anything she knew to be neither too complex nor too time consuming. Later, she would put them to the test as well. Everything, she noted so far worked just as she had expected it would.

The T.V.s she found quite interesting, especially the holographic ones, however, the productions were, in almost every case, limited and fragmentary. Still, she was able to spend a few moments around what at least gave the visual impression of being very much like herself. Time and time again she would believe she was beginning to figure out what was happening in what she was watching, when, without warning, it would fade into a colorful vision of meaningless static and then some other unrelated scene would appear.

The language spoken in these scenes appeared to randomly skip from plain Earth Standard to Assianangle and Mars Basic and just as often into those mysterious languages she barely understood; English, Russian, Spanish, Chinese. There were so many and her understanding so limited. Often only fragments of words or phrases were intelligible to her.

While trying to interpret the languages presented on the screens or in the holoframes was difficult, some of the other sounds such as the music frequently accompanying many of the images were delightful. Even tiny snatches of melody were riveting. It made her smile and want more. She found some music players and surveyed the limited supply of actual discs, tapes, flash drives, and a variety of other storage devices on which music could be found. The music was generally fragmentary, but sometimes she would find extended pieces. There were symphonic passages and pop songs reflecting a wide range of instrumentation and vocal effects. At times, she found her body moving with the rhythms of the different melodies.

On one occasion, she felt moisture coming from her eyes as a particular piece of music seemed to underscore her loneliness and made her feel sadness. Just as she had first awakened with a craving for coffee, some strains of the music made her aware she craved companionship.

She had no idea if there was anyone else like her anywhere, and even if there was, she knew the world was large. She had taken a Gyrocopter up and surveyed as far as she could from altitude, checking out the more interesting sites and although sometimes she thought she saw signs of things moving below, she could never be certain. She felt herself to be a solitary living thing immersed in a world without life except for a tiny bee's brief intrusion into her life then vanishing without a trace.

As she broadened her investigations through the streets among the buildings and the greenswards, she found much to delight and distract her, but at the end of the day, she would return to her room, hungry and tired with a feeling she couldn't quite identify, and sadness would often embrace her as she fell off to sleep. She would, however, sleep soundly and dreamlessly from sundown until dawn, a clear indication daytime was her time to explore. After many days of exploration, of hours watching fragments of movies, plays, and documentaries and of listening to snatches of music, she found herself more restless at night and often difficult to fall asleep.

Night on the Town

One night Maricel had fallen asleep, only to find herself awake long before sunrise. Although aware she hadn't slept very long, she didn't feel the least bit tired. She could not resist an eagerness to be up and decided since she was no longer able to sleep, she would go for some fresh outdoor air. Stepping out, she was surprised to discover a coolness in the air she had not encountered during the day. Street lamps lit the silent streets, casting shadows and blanketing everything with ominous undertones.

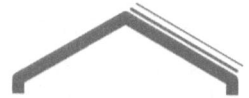

She could sense more than see more was going on around her. She sensed an increase in noise from daytime. It was faint and indefinable and did not come near her. It clearly suggested to her she was not exactly alone. What Maricel didn't know was a growing population of small nocturnal creatures was moving into her area. Tiny rodents and insects were bringing life to the silence. She watched in amazement as tiny, winged creatures banged against the glowing orbs of street lamps. A soft buzzing around her ears reminded her of the bee. The sound was fainter but somehow more persistent. When it stopped, she felt movement on her neck, then a brief, sharp feeling of itchy discomfort. Reflexively, she brought her hand to her neck, slapping at the source of the discomfort.

Death and Itching

The light from the street lamps revealed a tiny, dark blob in her palm. A feeling of dampness accompanied it. This was the first meeting of mosquito and human on legacy earth but far from being the last. What Maricel didn't yet know, this particularly adventurous flying insect would be joined by countless others of its breed. Not quite yet, however, for this was the first encounter, and for a great many more days, it would be the last.

One thing had changed irrevocably. With the slap, death had been introduced to Maricel's world. The tiny clump of crushed matter in her hand did not regain form, nor would it. A second generation mosquito had somehow been carried far from its birthplace in a distant swamp to meet a human revealing a series of firsts one being the surrender of its life in the encounter.

The site of the discomfort on Maricel's neck began to itch. This annoyed her enough to decide she had had enough of the night world and returned to her room. There she checked the site of the itch with a mirror. She saw a tiny reddish colored bump in which the itch seemed to center. She found dragging her fingernail over it provided some relief. Although she felt some concern, after all this was a first for her, the itch was slight. She went to her sleeping area and lay down. The itch was soon forgotten. Then, it was morning, and the itch was gone. "Perhaps," thought Maricel, "it was a dream."

When she examined her neck, she discovered a greatly reduced version of what she had seen in the night. It was much smaller, and the color was closer to of the rest of her skin. There was no itch and by the end of the day, no sign of the tiny creature's invasive attack. While it was gone completely, Maricel's curiosity was aroused. She decided she needed to study the 'dark time', to investigate the sources of those sounds she had heard the previous night. She was also beginning to develop a sense of wariness. She knew she needed to be careful because if something the size of the bee, or even larger could attack her out of the dark the consequences could be more serious than a short-lived itch. Still, the sounds and activity of the night drew her.

After several silent days, she decided she would check out the nighttime streets again. This time, she would cover as much bare skin as possible to avoid even an annoying itch like earlier one. Once again, Maricel set out into the evening. She found the slightly cooler air refreshing. The shops, with their windows lit up, seemed to be there just for her. When she entered a doorway, interior lights would come on. When she approached a particular display, the lights would brighten in intensity.

As she explored further she encountered many new and interesting sites; bridges over a slow-moving river, elaborately lit buildings, walled parks, and gardens. Everything was open to her. She explored buildings filled with paintings and statues. She made her way through other buildings filled with books, some of which she took home with her. Although most were incomplete, she found with very few exceptions she could comfortably read the words. From awakening, she was fluent in Earth Standard, Assianangle (a historical language of old earth) and Mars Basic. A few of the books, she discovered were in other languages. Some were quite strange and some she could almost understand, but the meanings of the words and symbols were obscure. These were written in languages with mysterious names were known to her; Chinese. English. French, Spanish, Russian. Eventually, she would come to recognize, if not quite clearly understand books written in a vast variety of languages. More importantly, she came to realize copies of all these books could be found in the three main languages in which she was most fluent.

She quickly came to realize while there was a certain glamor to the night, the best time for any extensive exploration was during the day. Night seemed to create an enclosed border to the world. Daylight pushed those borders back opening things up. Daytime provided Marcel unlimited perspective to explore her world yet limited to the large and architecturally diverse city in which she had awakened.

She developed a routine in which her explorations would carry her further and further from her home. Eventually, she established stations where she could spend the night if too far to get home easily or too late to return before dark. These locations contained everything she required. She found well-stocked apartments providing sleeping quarters, plenty of food and water and many different city views. Despite this, she still preferred to return to the location where she first awakened and would do so whenever possible.

Seasons

As the days and nights unfolded, she began to notice something different. On her trips outside what she identified as her home with its little circle of shops and the small park edging it, the air seemed to be cooler, and the darkness lasted longer. One time while traveling several way stations from her home, Marcel encountered tiny cold, white flakes drifting through the air. On another occasion, it covered the ground. The covering was light and easily disturbed. She never encountered more than this. Eventually, the days seemed to stay light longer, and the air grew warmer. The jackets she had found on those longer colder nights were no longer necessary.

Not many days later, she found her home was an important place where she needed to go for refuge from the heat of the day. Inside the buildings she visited, she found the air always comfortable. neither too hot nor too cold.

There was always plenty of food available in the kitchens and on the counters of the places she visited. Frequently she would find "heat and eat" packages, food inside a box that would cook itself when the tab on the end of the box was pulled. Within seconds it could be taken out plated and fully cooked. The plates were invariably throwaway, vanishing when dropped in any garbage bin.

Maricel found stoves and microwaves, dishwashers and well-stocked pantries and refrigerators ready for use in almost every building or house she entered. In every case, she left them as she found them. As the days drifted by, Maricel visited and explored the many local sites; museums, art galleries, factories, apartment buildings and stately mansions.

On one of her expeditions, she had discovered a large mall. She was fascinated by it and found herself returning to it regularly. She was often amazed at how much she recognized and at her understanding of exactly how things worked. She had explored most of the mall when she decided to enter the darkened location at one end of the enormous building. It was called a cinema. Along the walls, she saw what she recognized as ticket vending machines, video game consoles, and even some mechanical games. She tried some of the games. They were interesting and she knew she would eventually return and try them all in the coming days.

Walking through the wide, reception area she came up to one of the ticket machines. She could see it listed the names of what it said were movies currently being shown in the theatre complex. A rectangular button with the instructions "push for ticket" was lit up just to the side of each movie title. She randomly pushed one. With a whirr and a click, a small sheet of thick paper with printing on it came out a slot just below the list of names, another sign just above it flashed off and on saying, "take ticket". She had not expected this and watched as a small rectangle of paper with printing on it fluttered to the floor. She stooped to pick it up, reading the print informing her in three basic languages and the more obscure English to proceed to Theatre 5. Then she heard a musical chord from behind her and turned to see an illuminated sign also in 4 languages telling her to follow the arrow to Theatre 5. Down a short hallway she could see sets of doors, the third one on the left was lit up with a sign informing her this was the entrance to Theatre 5.

Approaching the doorway, she saw another sign stating: "please seat yourself". As she entered, a large wall screen the seats were facing, suddenly lit up to show a stylized picture of a cell phone covered by a red circle with a diagonal line through it. Then, she heard a loud human voice speaking the words printed under picture of the cell phone. She didn't know what language she was hearing but she knew it was telling her: "the feature will be starting shortly. Please take your seats and refrain from loud talking. Be sure your cell phones are turned off so as not to disturb your fellow members of the audience.

Astonished, she sat down in the nearest seat as the room filled with music and new patterns began to appear where the large picture of the cell phone had been Maricel laughed quietly to herself because she had no cell phone and there weren't any fellow audience members. Words and symbols began to scroll across the large area of the wall Maricel understood to be a movie screen. She was fascinated watching the screen changing. Then she was looking down on a city from somewhere high above. There was some movement in what appeared to be a small park or green space. She held on tightly to the armrest as the screen made her feel she was falling towards it.

This was a day of firsts for Maricel as the screen resolved itself into a view from ground level bringing into focus something she had not seen in any of her travels, life-sized human beings interacting with each other.

Although looking somewhat like versions of herself, they appeared more youthful and each one was dressed differently riding along the park path on wheeled boards she recognized as "skateboards". There were four of them, one clearly female and they were bantering with each other as they rode along. Maricel found herself enthralled by the dialogue and the visual of the people themselves. This was all new to her. As Maricel watched, the four board riders made a sudden stop. The faces of two of them grew to fill the screen a look of horror on their faces. While never having seen such an expression before, she immediately recognized the look. The next thing she saw was a fifth human, a body sprawled on the ground. Then, as if by magic, people in blue uniforms and military style hats were surrounding it, keeping people back. Another person not in uniform was taking pictures of the body as two others also without identifiable uniforms pushed their way through the gathering crowd.

They were wearing some kind of card on a ribbon around their necks and the ones in blue stepped aside to let them approach the photographer and the body. The one with the long blond hair spoke to one of the men in blue. "What did you find?" she asked. "Well, ma'am," responded the uniformed man, "Forensics isn't here yet, but I would say it looked as if the body was completely drained of blood. No sign of the blood though, except for a drop or two at two tiny wounds on the neck."

"What are you thinking?" laughed the other non-uniformed person. "You think our perp is a vampire?"

The two men in blue and the longhaired blond joined in the laughter. The blonds face grew larger on the screen, "Oh, oh," she said, looking straight at Maricel, "better start sharpening up the wooden stakes..."

The screen changed completely and the words, "Night of the Vampire" in Earth Standard, Assianangle, and the odd, obscure language of English again, flashed across it, in large, letters and symbols appearing to be dripping red. The screen went dark, and a voice said, "Our feature is about to begin."

A different set of words and symbols in the same languages filled the screen and another of what Maricel recognized as a moving picture began. The movie was hard to follow. It was clearly a patchwork and in a very short time the cycle repeated. Maricel sat and watched those repeating fragments of film several times. She was amazed and overjoyed at the crowd and group scenes. So many people like her, together, talking...laughing.

Leaving the theatre, she could not get these images out of her mind. The vague sensation having haunted her since she first woke up in this world came rushing home to her. She wanted to be with people! To this end, Maricel returned to the cinema regularly. Sometimes she went in the evening and sometimes she went during the day.

There were a number of different fragmented motion pictures and Maricel found she preferred the family scenes. Group scenes with ten or more happy, laughing people gathered together. Her favorite was a movie depicting a birthday barbecue. There were so many people; laughing, talking, playing and being silly.

While these were her favorites, she loved all the movies. No matter how much she enjoyed them, she found when she left the cinema she felt melancholy. She had no one to meet with or to talk with or to share a laugh.

Many nights after spending hours in a movie theatre or two, Maricel would leave the mall and gaze up at the darkening sky. She would watch stars beginning to appear, those countless tiny pinpricks of life arrayed before her in a celestial pattern no one from the twenty-first century would recognize. On many an evening, she would look up at the moon. During its waning and waxing, she could see tiny clusters of light glowing ever so faintly from the hidden portion. Often, she wondered if it was where the birthday barbecues were; the place where people were gathered together to share pleasure and enjoyment in each other's company. Despite the vast range of technical and natural knowledge she had awakened with, she did not have a clear sense of how large the world was. She had no idea if there was another like her anywhere.

A layer of sadness hung over her as she continued to explore and encounter the novelties of her empty city. She was still able to put away the feeling of sadness in her explorations maintaining the level of interest and curiosity she had felt from the start. One late evening after spending most of the day checking out the mall shops and their inventories and trying out all the theatres in the cinema, Maricel stepped out of the complex to find a layer of something white seeming to cover everything. She knew the name, snow and had seen it before, so she had little fear and reached out to touch it. As she knew it would be, it was cold and when she raised her hand for a closer look, she could see it turning to a clear liquid. She knew the clear liquid was water. She brought it to her tongue confirming it, indeed, was water.

From somewhere in the back of her mind sprung a complete explanation of the white substance. When the air grew cold, it reached the point where rain crystalized, and particles came together to produce this snow. The explanation could not match the wonder she felt at the sight of it. On her way out that morning she had noticed the air was quite cool and there was dampness in the air. In fact, she had to go back inside to find a warmer jacket. She knew these were the ideal conditions for snow. She could see the source of the snow, a gathering of clouds drifting off in the distance. Although cold, the sky above was clear, and the moon and stars seemed brighter than she had ever seen.

Something New

Walking towards home she encountered something she hadn't seen before. There were animal prints in the skiff of snow covering the sidewalk. She could see several tiny sets of prints and one set significantly larger. She assumed the nighttime noises she often heard might be related to the makers of these prints.

The area where Maricel had awakened was relatively temperate and snow covers, even light ones, were rare. On those few occasions when snow did cover the ground, she could see the prints of tiny animal paws. She also noticed one set of larger prints, suggesting an animal about knee high. While the tiny prints appeared to her to be random she was surprised to find the larger set of prints showing up close to wherever she was in her explorations. After seeing this, she began to be more aware of her immediate surroundings as she walked the streets on her exploratory outings. Sometimes she would detect movement out of the corner of her eye. When she turned to look, she could see nothing.

As time passed, she began to sense more than see the presence of a four-legged creature moving furtively on the edge of her sight. Whatever it was, it seemed to stay just out of reach, but was always there, following her on her walkabouts. It never threatened, never made a sound, just kept pace with her while remaining hidden in the shadows.

Maricel didn't find herself feeling threatened by her invisible tracker. In fact, she looked forward to the mysterious presence and would have missed it if it wasn't there ready to follow whenever she stepped out. Checking around outside her home building, Maricel found evidence something, most likely her follower, was staying as close to her as it could without showing itself. There were small signs, nest areas near her door, footprints and overturned refuse cans where Maricel had tossed left over bits of food. The creature, itself, whatever it was, while too shy to show itself had somehow secretly attached itself to her.

The light skiffs of snow revealed the creature was nesting closer and closer to the exit door of her building. It had yet to pass through the phased doors into the building and there was never any evidence it had nested near any other phased doors or attempted to enter them. The many phased doors through which Maricel could pass with nothing more than a light tingling sensation except for the one at her building never showed signs of being closely approached. Although she suspected the sensation passing through the doors might be enough to put off a smaller creature, it was unlikely to hold back anything trying with purpose, to get in. The fact nothing had tried was both a relief and a concern for Maricel.

She was glad her home seemed safe from unwanted visitors but wondered about the timidity of her follower. The phase doorways were the common main entrances to the larger buildings and malls. They held the weather at bay and was important when the air was especially cold. While her invisible companion had nested closer and closer to the door, the sites were always tight to the wall or in the shelter of planters or other places where it could curl up as small as possible to conserve heat.

As she went about her exploration Maricel would drop into a nearby kitchen and grab something to eat. Often, she ate while walking and she would discard what she could not eat in the receptacles marked 'trash'. Given time, these receptacles would break down and eliminate anything thrown into them. Checking, Maricel learned anything she put into these receptacles would be gone by the next day.

Returning from some shorter expeditions while a fine layer of snow covered the land, Maricel would see her invisible companion's paw prints at the edge of one of the lower height bins. These were bins where she had often deposited her leftovers. While she could see no leftovers in the bin, she did see evidence some of the bits of food had been removed from the bins and mostly eaten. The invisible follower was eating her leftovers.

Seeing this, Maricel began to leave small caches of foodstuff beside the trash bins. Inevitably they were gone when she returned to inspect them. If there was snow, the familiar paw prints surrounded the place where she had placed the food caches. Without snow, she would not see any footprints, but the food could not be seen as well. Clearly, her invisible companion had eaten it.

Scout

The creature, a young Labrador Retriever, would watch the two-legged being with a sharp sense of longing. Still a pup, it was too frightened to get close but equally frightened to get too far away. It sensed something about the larger creature that seemed familiar. Its presence was comforting, something it had not felt for some time. The dog wanted to approach, but wariness based on earlier experience prevented.

The young lab, we'll call him Scout, the name Maricel will call him, had come by his wariness through a tragic series of events.

His sire and Dam had met each other shortly after generation. They had found a home and an unlimited supply of food in a small farming community. They were the only residents. They had no concept of the future, for them, it was only themselves and the moment. In due time, they had a litter of pups. Scout was one of the six newborns.

As he began to grow, he was quite different from his siblings. While they stayed close to their parents, he was curious and adventurous. On many occasions, he left his dam and littermates to explore, sometimes getting lost for hours and often risking his life in the woods and around the small buildings edging the open farmland of his home.

On one particular occasion, Scout had found a tiny space through which he could enter one of the buildings. The scents were delicious and intriguing, and he lost himself in exploring this delightful odor rich environment. A loud roar shocked him back to a broader awareness. At first, he thought there was something in the building with him, something threatening him. The light in the room was dim, but bright enough for him to detect anything in there with him. He could see he was alone. The roar had come from somewhere outside, somewhere very nearby. When Scout heard the familiar sound of his parent's angry and terrified barking, knew where the roar had come from. It was outside, whatever this roaring creature was, and it had found his family's home. Scout made his way to the tiny space through which he had got into the building. He looked through the gap and could see some distance away where his parents were defending their home shelter from a strange and very large creature. It stood on two legs as it lunged at the two adult dogs, I reached out with long fur covered arms completed by hand like appendages completed by large, taloned claws with which it swiped at the rapidly attacking and withdrawing dogs. A grin of long white fangs snapped beneath a ferocious muzzle. Scout's parents fought hard to protect their litter. The clawed arm struck his mother tearing open her stomach and tossing her aside. As Scout watched, the air was filled with the sound of pain. He could hear above the barking of his father, the squeals of pain and howls of agony from his mother and siblings. He watched as his father leaped for the throat of the creature only to be brushed aside by a large furry forearm. His father quickly regained his footing and attacked again and again until the creature's teeth and claws ripped his flesh. His father was able to avoid serious damage from the vicious creature, but each time he attacked, his movements were slower as he fought exhaustion until the creature was able to catch him with its powerful arms and threw him, huge claws ripping off strips of flesh as he flew into a tree... His father screamed in pain as his spine snapped. Then there was silence except for the grunting and shuffling of the huge creature. The beast spent some time among the remains of Scout's family while a terrified Scout remained silent and hidden. We watched the creature as if finally lumbered off, but it wasn't until the next morning a still frightened Scout was able to leave his hiding spot. He approached near to where his family had made their den and where the huge creature had viciously attacked and killed them all. He could not bring himself to get too close to what to his eyes were nothing more than several piles of bloody flesh and bones. He could still smell the scent of fear and warning from the remains. The parting message of his parents, contained in their death scent was clear. Scout turned away from the carnage without a last look backward and began a long journey. A journey consisting of cowering beneath buildings and bushes, of eating little but the occasional insect coming too near until, nearly starving, exhausted and sore, he had followed a series of ravines into the heart of a large city where Maricel lived. There, for the first time in many weeks it saw another living creature. It was the first he had seen since the beast killed his family.

He was wary of this new creature, but sometimes, it would leave food around. He would follow keeping close enough to find the food scraps the creature dropped. He made every effort to keep out of sight. He developed a growing awareness the two-legged creature knew of his presence. Since it offered him no harm and seemed to be leaving more food behind for him, he chose to stay nearby. Scout was becoming comfortable staying close to the mysterious creature.

Maricel, too, grew used to having the small creature nearby. As days passed, it was becoming a more visible companion, sometimes stepping out of the shadows to accept the food offerings, but still holding back from getting too close. Scout was longing for the company. It had been an important part of his early days with his family.

Scout understood this two-legged creature would not be as vicious as the one that slew his family. This one seemed satisfied to let him stay nearby and even provided food. His dog memory of the vicious killer of his family struggled with his desire for company preventing him getting too close.

Maricel found herself looking for the elusive creature. First thing when leaving her building, often throughout the day, she would look around in hopes of catching sight of her distant companion. Sometimes she would set down food and stand off some distance to watch the stealthy approach of the young dog to the food. It was amazing how it would warily watch her and cautiously examine the food, bolt it down and then back off into concealment. As the days passed, the distance between the two grew slightly less, but Maricel could tell the small creature was ready to bolt. It was apparent to her despite the maintained distance, a comfort level between the dog and Maricel was developing. It had not yet come to mutually trust, but Maricel felt confident this little beast was not a danger to her. Although she fed it and encouraged it to come closer, wariness lingered on both their parts.

On one of her expeditions taking her farther afield than usual, she came across a cinema not a part of a huge mall. It was a dual theatre cinema, the kind of cinema that in the original 21st century would show independent and cult movies with a small but faithful following.

In Maricel's world, like every other aspect she had encountered, it seemed more of a prop, set to enhance the feeling of the city. Inside, while everything about it was new, it held an aura of age and long use. The posters framed against wallpaper and the fully loaded snack bar exuded a much-used tackiness. The prop builders had clearly done their best to be faithful to the sketchy bits of information they had about the early 21st century.

In one of the two theatres, fragments of a movie were running and there, Maricel discovered just what her distant companion really was. The fragment of film focused on an animal almost a twin of her companion. A voice-over spoke in English, a language she had grown to better understand. The language she now knew as one of the root languages of both Earth Standard and Assianangle. They were distant from English and other root languages, but she was able to detect enough similarities to learn English well enough to follow movies and read some of the books she had found.

The voice spoke in gentle tones, "The Labrador Retriever is a great companion, loving and faithful." Pictures flashed across the screen of the dog, the twin of her wary companion, walking beside a human. In another fragment a similar dog was in a park chasing a circular object in another the Labrador Retriever was lying at a human's feet. The human was seated, book in hand, in a large comfortable chair in front of a large fireplace. She wondered if she could get close to her very distant companion as the person in the last movie fragment, and form as close a friendship with it as the fragments of motion picture suggested.

While she was uncertain just how to draw the pup closer, this would be taken out of her hands. The dog had been her faithful companion for so long she expected it to always be nearby. So, at first, she didn't notice when it wasn't there. Its bed near the door hadn't been used for several days. Scout had a habit of arranging the blankets she had left for him into a circular nest, but Maricel could see it had been blown open by the wind and not returned to a nest. Immediately she realized she hadn't seen the dog for several days. She wasn't really sure how many. She found herself worrying and although she tried to tell herself it was fine and had likely found new things to explore and might just reappear someday, she couldn't help but include a search during her daily explorations.

When several days had passed with no sign she was about to give up. A feeling of deep sadness came over her as she made her way along the edge of the park remembering the small black pup peeking out from among the trees. She was so deeply lost in her reverie she almost missed the unusual sound, a faint crying, coming from deep in the park. Suddenly her focus shifted from her thoughts to the faint sounds of fear and pain. She began to search the park to find the source of the mournful crying.

She came to a culvert encased by high walls. The soft pleas of a hurt, terrified animal emanated from it. Climbing down into the culvert on a three-rung ladder bolted into the concrete, Maricel found the young dog. It was huddled against the wall behind some rocks licking at its paws. Seeing her, the pup tried to get up and move away but its paws were obviously hurt and there was really nowhere it could go. It stared at her, in its eyes a resigned look of fear mixed with hopefulness.

Maricel approached slowly, extending her arms, holding out some dry meat she had brought with her. She moved slowly and cautiously so as not to spook the dog. It shrunk back against the wall; its eyes fixed on the food in Maricel's hand. Scout was famished and the appeal of the food was insistent.

His hunger was struggling to overcome his fear as he allowed Maricel to approach until she was holding the meat under his nose. He reached out and gently took the piece of dried meat from her. Despite his hunger and the taste of the meat starting him drooling, Scout did not eat it until Maricel had backed off. A patient Maricel sat on one of the rocks waiting for it to swallow. She offered some more dried meat and the dog gratefully accepted. He was very hungry, but as he ate, he kept a wary watch on Maricel.

He might have felt a growing bond of trust with this two-legged creature, but it was a creature also walking on two legs he had seen tear apart his sire and dam and his littermates. This one might appear to be different, with its shiny skin and its gentle fragrant scent unlike the rugged fur and strong odor of his family's killer.

Having fed several pieces of dried meat to the dog, Maricel slowly backed away. The young dog attempted to rise to its feet only to squeal in agony as it set its weight on its left front leg and quickly sat back down. "let me see that leg," Said Maricel.

These were the first words ever spoken to the pup and he cocked his head to one side, pain now mixed with curiosity. The sound was soft and gentle. There was no threat in it, but as Maricel approached, the pup pressed back against the wall trying to make himself smaller. It tried to push itself back with its left front paw, squealed with pain and stopped short. "It's OK," said Maricel softly, "I will help you."

She reached out and gently took hold of the sore paw. Startled, the dog accepted the touch. It reminded him of his mother, licking him as he pressed against the warmth of her body. He had felt safe then and now, some of the same feeling came over him. He let her turn the paw revealing a broken nail and a crack in the pad of the paw which had an ugly red and white sheen. Maricel reached carefully into her bag with her free hand and came out with a tube of cool antibacterial unguent. She spun open the cap, still holding the turned paw and squeezed some of the cream onto the injury.

Within seconds, the pup's pain was gone, and a pleasant warmness came over the wound and it began to close. The broken claw was less painful, too. The pup felt more relaxed than he had been since the moment he had stepped away from his mother to explore the nearby buildings. He did not resist when Maricel bundled him up in her arms and made her way out of the culvert. While still feeling a trace of fear, the young dog was overcome with a sense of joy and gratefully licked the nearest of the hands holding him. He barely noticed the slight tingling as Maricel carried him through her doorway and took him to her rooms.

She set him down on the rug and brought him a bowl of water he immediately began to lap up. She opened some tins of food from the supply she had gathered. The dog ate and drank with gusto then closed his eyes and drifted off to sleep. Maricel sat on the edge of her sleeping pod intently watching the small creature as it slept. She sensed no threat from it just as it had sensed no threat from her.

She lay back on her bed and drifted off to sleep. There would be time to become better acquainted. Perhaps as in the fragmentary movie she had seen, this young Labrador would become a regular companion for her. It was amazing how quickly the relationship between Maricel and the Labrador pup grew. The wariness and shyness vanished within a few days and a bond of trust and affection began to develop. On her explorations, the dog remained at her side taking regular jaunts ahead to check things out but always returning. The first time the dog had walked away from her, Maricel felt a moment of panic. She worried the dog might be going back to its earlier ways. A wave of relief washed over her when the Lab returned and stayed with her. Maricel was developing the comforting knowledge her newfound companion would never get very far from her. However, a nose, obviously more sensitive than Maricel's would call him to investigate the new and amazing scents that abounded. He would check out the source of any sounds he heard. It would most often be a small mammal or a newly arrived bird. He would bark a greeting, or perhaps a warning but never went beyond that. Having made his statement, he would return to be with his companion.

It occurred to Maricel the dog's forays away from her made it something of an advanced scout, checking out any potential surprises that might lay ahead. He would then return confidently to its human friend to lead her towards or away from whatever it found. Because of his tendency to scout ahead, Maricel began to call him "Scout" and, he began to respond to the name. Maricel called him to her, knelt down and scratched him behind the ears. "I'm going to name you "Scout" if it's alright with you." She said.

Scout responded with a brisk wag of his tail and snuggled his nose under her arm. A sign, she felt, was his approval of the name.

So, it was Maricel, and Scout formed a partnership. Accompanied by Scout, Maricel felt more confident exploring farther from home. Many a night, she and Scout would find a room or an apartment in which to spend a night as they moved farther and farther afield. They shared the ever-present and plentiful food she came across in restaurants, and shops. They went together to the theatres and cinemas they found along the way and enjoyed the fragments of movies, and the spectacular visions and delightful music they provided.

Maricel would push back in one of the articulated chairs found in most theatres. Scout would lay at her feet, grooming or sleeping, rarely watching the movies or listening closely to the sounds from the speakers, but always aware of Maricel, happy to stay if she chose to and always ready to leave when it was her choice.

Time to Move On

Maricel was beginning to think about going even further in her explorations. The movies had informed her people are communal. Similar to her and Scout, they tended to seek out company. Despite her town having accommodations for many thousand like her, Maricel had learned she was the sole human presence. Apart from the people she met in the movies, and they were nothing more than shadows of real people playing out parts of fragmented stories.

She had searched every sector and found no one. She found no evidence anyone other than her existed. Around this time Maricel began to feel she needed to move on. It was as if something was calling to her. The sensation was faint, but she felt as if a map were forming in her head. She may have wanted to move on, but this seemed to indicate the way she should go.

As she solidified her decision to leave the town and see beyond its boundaries the direction she felt drawn to was as good as any. When Maricel first began her exploration, she had tried driving a car. Despite having a complete understanding of the process, she found the actual driving more difficult to do.

During her earlier exploration, a barely avoided accident made her decide to stick to walking. That was fine for her then. Now, however, things were changing. Maricel felt sure there were others like her and they calling to her, putting what direction to travel into her mind somehow. There may not be many others like her out there, but if there were any, she wanted to find them, just as she believed, if they knew she existed, they would want to find her.

Three days spent walking in the direction Maricel was inclined to go had not brought her closer to the edge of the town. Walking was not going to get her to where she needed to go. She had a vague direction, but no real sense of distance.

Maricel, on a subconscious level, knew she had far to go. To this end she would need a vehicle.

She found an enclosed van not too larger for her to handle but with lots of space for necessary supplies. She began practicing with it. Scout would run alongside barking joyfully. After successfully driving it around her local area numerous times, she tried an experiment. Stopping, Maricel reached over and opened the passenger door. Scout immediately jumped in, climbed on the seat beside her, and made himself comfortable. For several days after that she and Scout toured some of the places they had explored earlier.

Having achieved a level of comfort driving the van, Maricel decided not to put off the inevitable. She gathered what she thought she needed for an extended journey, although she believed she would find all of it along the road. The items she packed were things for which she had a personal affinity. Given the limitations of her experience of anything beyond the city where she awakened, it was always possible she might end up needing some of those things. She was setting out into the unknown, who knew what she would or wouldn't find.

Soon the van was fitted out to her liking and met with Scout's approval, He sat comfortably in the front passenger seat standing guard over the collection of books, DVDs, music players, spare food and other things filling the entire back of the van. Consulting with Scout who was ever ready to follow Maricel anywhere, the decision was made. They would set off the next morning.

That night, Maricel slept soundly, waking as she had every morning wanting a cup of coffee. After her now traditional drink and a shared breakfast with Scout who was less enthusiastic about the coffee, preferring cold water, they were ready to go.

It took several hours of driving before they passed through places familiar to them. Beyond that, the things they passed didn't look much different from the more familiar parts of the town.

Maricel noticed as she went there were fewer and fewer big buildings and more houses with large yards bordering her path. The streets were changing. They seemed wider. Marketing and rough looking industrial sites replaced the homes and shops.

They passed several malls Maricel noted in her memory for further theatre visits and perhaps new movies, although she knew there would be no returning to any of them. Their existence did hold out the promise of finding many more along the way to visit. This was especially important should she fail to find any fellow humans in her travels.

The kinds of buildings she encountered along the road continued to change. They appeared lower, longer and flatter. In the distance, Maricel could see an elevated roadway. As she got closer, she could see other elevated roads heading off in many directions. She encountered signs directing her to different ramps up the elevated roadway depending on where she wanted to go. One sign showed the name of a town in a westerly direction, another named a town in an easterly direction while others indicated places to the south and to the north. Several others simply read "local traffic". With all these choices, Maricel chose to stick to the largest of the local roads, the one she was already on. Following her chosen route, Maricel could see parkland increasing to dominate the view. Buildings became fewer and trees more plentiful.

She passed a sign in the three major languages saying, "You are now leaving the city. We hope you enjoyed your stay. Have a safe journey."

As she drove on, she could see the occasional house or other building standing well back from the road. The many fields and forests she passed told Maricel she was getting farther away from any large town or city. It was, she noted, countryside as bereft of humanity as her city.

While she frequently came upon gas and service stations at the side of the road, refueling was not an issue. The van, like the food supplies and anything removable Maricel had found in the city appeared to be self-replenishing. Humans and dogs, however, instinctively needed to refuel and experience the basic mammalian need to eliminate waste in comfort and with a modicum of privacy. Instinct was calling as a rest stop and service station came into view over a small hill and Maricel decided to stop. There was still some sunlight left and Maricel decided to move on after taking care of business and grabbing some food. She proceeded in the hope somewhere ahead there were other humans waiting for her.

After this brief stop, Maricel and Scout were back on the road.

As night approached, Maricel grew stiff and tired. Except for the brief pit stop, she had been driving for hours. Scout was becoming restless, moving from the floor to the passenger seat to the rear of the van and back again. Her discomfort and Scouts restlessness were enough for Maricel to decide that the next rest area or motel they came across would be their stop for the night. A place where there was something to eat and somewhere to sleep.

Minutes after making that decision, a rest area came into view. A sign informed Maricel that it had a small restaurant and sleeping booths. It seemed perfect, and she pulled in, stopping in the parking area close to the restaurant. She and Scout got out and together and headed to the restaurant. Maricel helped herself to a warm meal and dropped two burgers on the floor for Scout who attacked them voraciously. Within seconds, the floor was clear of any trace of burger and Scout was at the door. Maricel finished, tossing the remnants of her meal into a trash receptacle. She watched with scant interest as it consumed the scraps, leaving it clean and empty.

She let Scout out and followed him through the door making her way to the van to gather some personal needs for the night. Shortly after, she was back in the rest area arranging a sleeping pad in one of the small, stacked sleeping booths when she heard Scout barking. It then occurred to her that Scout had been away from her for much longer than usual when they traveled. She left her sleeping pad and went to the doorway. She opened the door to call him when she heard a deep grunting sound that could only be made by a living creature. She heard Scout's low, terrified whine in response, and this frightened her. She had to find him. Leaving the security of the rest area she ran toward where the grunting and the whine had come. This brought her into a grove of trees beside the restaurant.

Not too far off, she could see Scout cringing and backed against a tree. She quickly made her way toward him, a sense of terror growing in her as she recognized Scout's fear. Getting to him, she fell on her knees beside him. He looked at her rose to his feet and turned to face the darkness of the grove. Something moved among the trees its large form caught in the faint light from the parking lot through the trees. Bending back the smaller trees as if they were twigs there stepped into view the largest, most hideous beast that Maricel could ever have imagined. It was half again her height and much broader. A ragged and unkempt coat of fur covered its grotesque body, a parody of the human form. Large, pointed ears overshadowed the cruel shining eyes. She could sense more than see the large fangs in the open mouth below the large, projected snout. The row of huge sharp teeth underscored those hideous, hate-filled eyes. Saliva dripped from its open jaws reflecting in the faint light from the parking lot, a light that added a sickly green glow to the creature. It grunted again and Maricel could make out in that grunt the word, "food!" The creature let out a loud roar as it advanced towards them. Scout bravely bared his teeth and set himself between the advancing monster and Maricel. Scout snarled viciously. He recognized the creature that had brutally killed his family. With Maricel behind him, he had pushed down his fear ready to fight to the death to save his beloved companion. The creature roared again and shambled closer to his prey. Its snarl was interrupted by Scout's fierce barking, and it paused for a moment, then continued to approach. Scout stepped out to face it. The monster swung a cruel taloned paw at Scout who neatly ducked it. Leaping under the swinging appendage, Scout rushed in to tear a chunk from the creature's belly. It flailed at him catching him enough with his arm to knock the dog aside. It then turned towards Maricel who hunched down in her kneeling position riveted with fear. Scout struggled to his feet, breathless, and turned toward the creature. Maricel's thoughts were filled with the ironic notion she had come this far only to face a hideous death. As the monster was eyeing Maricel, she heard a crisp twang and a whirring noise. As if by magic, a shaft of tight feathers appeared behind the monster's left eye that in that moment widened into a look of sheer surprise. Its arms went up to grab at the projectile that impaled it but failed as the monster's legs seemed to buckle beneath it. As it collapsed to the ground, Maricel could see the light go out of its eyes as death embraced it. It was another first, but Maricel was in no mood to contemplate it. With Scout advancing warily towards the fallen monster, Maricel could only produce a sharp intake of breath as a second creature stepped out of the shadows, "Whew, that was a lucky shot. Everyone OK there?" Shaking in terror, Maricel attempted to rise to her feet. "Who are you?" she asked, her voice tremulous.

"I seem to have been given the name Raphael. I don't know how or by whom, but I suppose that's who I am. Who or what are you? Sorry, should ask, are you all right?" replied Raphael in a voice that expressed both a sense of wonder and of concern.

Scout had moved back to stand in front of Maricel taking a protective stance, his eyes fixed on the stranger, waiting to learn its intent. "I'm named Maricel and my companion, here, is Scout. This may sound strange, but are you human?"

"I believe so," said the stranger who had named himself Raphael.

"And that?" asked Maricel.

Stepping over to the carcass of the large creature, Raphael gave it a kick. "I certainly hope not." He replied.

When there was no response, Raphael reached for the shaft that had penetrated its head and tried to pull it free. "It's a carnivore that wouldn't hesitate to dine on humans and their dogs. It looks like a cross between a wolf, a bear, and perhaps there's a touch of human, too. Extremely vicious and very dangerous as you well know."

She watched as Raphael made several attempts to remove the arrow but was unable to do so. "Oh, well," he said, "I guess that one's gone. I still have plenty more. There are shops where I can replace them."

"It spoke." Maricel expressed her concern about her cruel and vicious attacker, "It saw me and said, "food"."

"It might have some level of intelligence to let it speak a few words, but if you're human, and I am human, you can be sure, this thing isn't," said Raphael as he kicked the carcass of the creature once again.

Raphael offered his hand to help her up. Maricel saw a hunting crossbow under his other arm. It unnerved her momentarily as she took his hand, a strange sensation for her. She let him pull her to her feet. The hand in hers was similar but larger, more rugged, and calloused. "Greetings Maricel," said Raphael as he held her hand and made a slight bow. "Will your Scout allow me to approach for a closer look?"

"Let's see," she said turning to the dog, "it's ok, Scout." The dog glanced back at her then moved from between the two to stand by her side.

"Well," said the new arrival looking Maricel up and down, "we seem to share some similarities, but humans come in different varieties."

"At least, two," responded Maricel, "although the humans I have seen in the moving pictures show only two main types, no one of them appear quite the same as another. They share many similarities: Arms, Legs, Eyes, nose, mouth, you know, the essentials."

"I what a moving picture is. Perhaps when we get a chance, you will show me," said Rafael, "but now can we move out towards the lights. This creature stinks and my eyes are watering."

"Mine, too," said Maricel and the three of them turned from the dead hulk of the monster and walked among the trees toward the lights of the parking lot. Raphael folded his crossbow and set it into a holder beside several shafts on his backpack. "Quiver," thought Maricel.

They went into the restaurant and sat at a booth. Raphael and Maricel having been alone for so long, were overwhelmed to be with another human. They stared at each other in silence. Maricel having watched the newcomer move with unexpected grace, through the door and over to the booth. The light coat of hair on his face surprised her. She could only think, "He is different, this human and myself. There will be lots to talk about."

She gave Scout a friendly scratch behind the ear while the questions gathered in her head. Raphael's thoughts were similar and after the brief pause, talk they did, long into the night. Finally, fatigue carried them off to their sleeping booths with the promise they would learn more about each other in the morning. Scout, who already had a good head start on sleep squeezed into Maricel's sleeping booth and lay in a protective posture at her feet. That night all three experienced a deep, sound sleep. Maricel and Raphael dreamed of the same highways and would awake with the feeling they should take the roads laid out in their half-forgotten dreams.

Raphael: Hunter, Weapons Expert, and Tactician

Survey

When he first awakened, Raphael sat up immediately and surveyed his surroundings. Counters and shelves containing a variety of armament and ordinance seemed to share a place in that room with the many practical household items. Raphael instantly recognized each item and knew its purpose and how to use it. Although he was hungry, his first inclination was to find out where he was and figure out what he might need to do to secure this location.

Instinct told him to dress, so he donned a soft feeling camouflage outfit, pants, pullover, thick socks and sturdy, lightweight, and comfortable boots. This done, he strapped on several belts, one through the loops in his pants and two that crossed over his shoulders. Raphael chose two weapons, a large knife, and a rifle with a telescopic sight. He filled the containers on his belt with bullets and other useful things including a compass, binoculars, and several protein bars. Raphael stepped cautiously through the door and checked the corridor. One direction led him through several rooms to what he already knew was an exit door. The other direction led to a flight of stairs that would bring him up three levels to the flat roof. This is the direction he took.

Reaching the roof through a trap door, he could see an air condition and heating unit along with several satellite dishes set back from the edge of the roof but otherwise seemed to be placed at random. A wall that was slightly less than a meter high edged the roof all the way around. Rafael made his way to the edge of the roof and looked over the wall. He turned his head to scan the landscape three floors down.

There were trees and fields in the distance, closer by there were grass-covered hillocks and copses of brush all radiant and green. Farther off through the trees he could see signs of other buildings. He could see little of these buildings except for bits of a wall through the trees and the peaks of their roofs rising above them. Two other sides of the rectangular building revealed similar scenes. On the fourth side, the view was different. Close by there were several boxy buildings of different sizes. Just beyond them, over a hill, what seemed to be various sized fingers stood silhouetted against the sky. Raphael felt they might be smokestacks or signal towers. Sooner or later, he would have to check them out.

Immediately below him, he saw a small truck and what he immediately recognized as an all-terrain vehicle, an ATV. There was no sign of life. A slight breeze moved the leaves, but other than that the surrounding view showed no signs of any significant presence Having taken time to survey his surroundings with his binoculars and with the long-range scope attached to his rifle, Raphael ascertained that there were no signs of life and therefore, there was no threat to his. He returned inside and went to the kitchen.

There he prepared a hot breakfast of oatmeal and tea. He found the refrigerator and the shelves well stocked with foodstuff and needed no directions to find and use the kettle, tea, and teapot and the microwave. It surprised him how naturally the knowledge came to him. Raphael placed his used dishes in what he recognized as a dishwasher, started it and almost instantly they were clean and dried. Later he would find them stacked and ready for the next meal.

Having eaten, Raphael decided he would take time to reconnoiter the nearer landmarks, the buildings, fenced enclosures and machines such as the truck and ATV along with some other things he had only glimpsed from the roof. Since, too, he had seen no sign of life from the roof, a closer look might reveal something. It was important to him to examine and get to know the local area better as this would likely be his home for some time to come or at least until he had time to scrutinize everything he had seen earlier from the roof lookout.

Gathering supplies, he felt he would need including a crossbow with a quiver of bolts, a knife that fit into a leather sheath on his belt, and a small pistol that fit in an ankle holster which he buckled to his leg. In a small backpack, he placed enough food and water for a long day along with a first aid kit. Raphael then made his way through the exit doors and outside for the first time to examine and explore his environs.

Raphael discovered many things to look at and, to his surprise, he knew what the various artifacts he encountered were and how they worked. He found several large vehicles, a truck with an open box and another with a closed box that could be used to carry large quantities of various items. There was a smaller truck with a crew cab, not one but two ATVs, one opened and one covered. As well, there were some tractors and plows he found in one of the nearby buildings.

Despite the variety of vehicles available, Raphael decided that his first explorations would be on foot so he could map out in detail what he encountered. On this first trip, Raphael saw abundant plant life but no other kind of life. His mind listed a larger number of living creatures of various sizes he could have and should have come across soon after leaving the house, but of these, he could see no sign. If they existed at all, they were nowhere near where he was.

Each day after that, he proceeded further and further afield in his search for some living thing other than the plant life that existed in abundance and to familiarize himself with the surrounding countryside. He came across other houses and barns and sheds, and many vehicles. All the houses, while empty of any life, were well stocked with food and supplies, each one ready for someone to take up residence. In all his travels, the only sound he heard was that of his guarded footsteps.

A more distant journey of exploration took him to a small town. Lifeless houses skirted a wide street that ran between several shops. These shops were well stocked with a broad array of products running the gamut from grocery stores filled with canned, frozen and fresh foods to farm and personal machinery all in perfect working order and ready to perform their designated tasks at a moment's notice. There were clothing stores with all sorts of odd apparel that Raphael did not bother to delve into. There were a guns and ammunition store, an automobile service station and a small restaurant with several tables and a constant smell of freshly brewed coffee. Although many of the stores looked as if they were set up that morning for the day's customers,

Raphael could still find no spoor, no evidence of any other passing mortal besides himself. While Raphael felt an anticipation for encountering living beings based on the immediacy of the stocked and ready shops, he knew, without a shadow of a doubt, he was the sole visitor to this place.

One thing that had struck him both back at his room, in and around his house and in the shops, was the wide variety of sophistication of much of the technology. He could find a simple frying pan for cooking and beside it more complex devices for doing the same thing. The most elaborate and complex was a piece of cooking technology that would instantly prepare and present any meal he might want. This variance seemed to apply to most machines and technical devices. Whenever he used one of these devices, He felt most comfortable with a device representing a middle range of sophistication.

While it was something to wonder about, he was content with his choices and that seemed to be that. His travels carried him in an ever-broadening circle around his home base, the place where he had awakened. He knew about almost everything within it. What he hadn't explored on foot, he surveyed while riding the ATV. When the snow came, it didn't surprise Raphael. He had an instinctive understanding of climate change and of the seasons.

The cooling days, he knew with certainty would lead to a period of coldness that would produce snow. He watched the trees as many of them gave up their leaves. The splendid colors of fall were short-lived and went by unnoticed by Raphael. The sudden and rapid change of seasons after a very, very long summer seemed to give Raphael a crash course in the workings of the seasons. Only the gusting wind and Raphael's footprints marked the snow that first short winter.

As the snow disappeared from the woodlands Raphael discovered unique patterns in the traces of new morning snow. They were patterns he recognized as the tracks of some tiny animal, a squirrel, or chipmunk. This was fascinating to him, and he followed the tracks until they disappeared near a small tree and could not be found again as the melting snow obscured the tracks. While notable, and exciting at the moment, what Raphael would soon come to understand was that the world around him was quickening with life. The evidence of this at first as rare as that single set of tiny tracks, soon became more and more plentiful as the time passed.

One day, Raphael spotted a tiny mouse-like creature casually walking along the trail in front of him. At first, it didn't seem aware of his approach. Then, it turned to eye this large two-legged creature with curiosity. There was no fear in its gaze, but as Raphael drew closer, instinct took over and sent it scurrying to disappear in the undergrowth. After that encounter, Raphael observed more and more wildlife. There were small birds, tiny, noisy squirrels, voles, and field mice. He also caught sight of some larger creatures, raccoons, possum, and porcupine. His response to them was as wary as was theirs to him. Spring and summer introduced him to the annoyance of insect life.

After another short winter, Raphael noticed that while earlier in his explorations, the forest and fields were devoid of wildlife, it was now plentiful. The insects were much more numerous, and their presence could be bothersome, but they did not bite him. Unknown to him, his body was producing a chemical that signaled them to take their stingers elsewhere.

He saw signs of even larger animals and noticed that a small family of what he recognized as sheep had moved in very close to his house and the larger outbuilding, the barn. They spent most of the time in a large, fenced enclosure availing themselves of food from self-replenishing bins. The rest of the time they wandered unrestricted in the nearby field. They showed no real fear of him although some were more skittish than others. The smaller ones would run to him as he approached, and he would give each a gentle scratch behind the ears, and they would be off.

When he spent overnights in the forest, he would often see among the trees, the reflections off eyes, some quite large, glowing in the light of his small fire gleaming in a device called a "Portaflame". He could cook on it and when it was cold, it gave off enough warming heat to keep him cozy, although it did send out an all call to night insects.

It seemed to have a similar effect on other denizens of the woods. They, however, unlike the pesky insects, kept their distance and in the darkness, Raphael could not identify them with any certainty. He did, however, notice one slightly larger creature that seemed to show up frequently to his campfires.

On his expeditions, both on foot and by ATV, he could sense the sound and movements of this same creature as it seemed to be following him.

Guardian

One late afternoon while on a journey that took him more than a day away from his home, Raphael stopped his ATV in a small clearing. He took out his lunch from his pack and sat down with his back against a large tree. He couldn't see it but heard familiar sounds in the nearby brush. By now Raphael was pretty well convinced that creature meant no harm to him. He believed, or perhaps at that moment, hoped that if it was malevolent, it had ample opportunity on many earlier occasions to have shown itself long since attempting an attack.

Raphael felt that the time had come to woo this beast out of hiding and see what it was. He took protein-based food from his lunch pack and tossed it out near the bushes from where the sounds were emanating. "Come on," he intoned gently, "here's food for you. Come now. Here now."

His follower would not reveal itself. However, had Raphael started away then turn back a few minutes later, he would find the foodstuff gone and signs of trampling in the grass around where the food had fallen. One time after a grueling journey to the distant village to look for some tools he might need, he stopped for lunch in a tiny park-like grove to eat lunch. Following his routine when away from home, he threw protein food to entice his follower to come out of hiding.

The surrounding trees looked as if someone had groomed them and because of that provided very little concealment close by for his follower to hide. It had been a busy day that had started very early, and Raphael felt the need to rest some before resuming his journey home. The day was warm and the grove quite cozy. The insects kept their distance, but the droning sounds they made were soothing. Raphael had meant only to rest a few minutes, but instead, he fell asleep.

He had slept for some time only to awaken with a sense of urgency. He opened eyes to find himself looking into a set of brown eyes over a tawny snout completed by a damp black nose. Fighting down a sense of panic, Raphael remained still and with a minimum of motion, took in the sight of his unexpected visitor. Fur covered, perky ears framed its wary eyes. A long red liquid tongue hung from a fang-filled mouth. The animal made a small noise and brushed its tongue across Raphael's face. It was not the most comfortable sensation, but it was much preferable to an encounter with the sharp set of fangs between which it hung. Before he could move, the dog licked his face again. Raphael laughed and sat up. The dog, for a dog it was, backed off, but not too far. "Well," said Raphael, "if it isn't my guardian. Were you tasting me to see if I was good to eat, or were you trying to make friends?"

The dog just stood there, tail wagging, but otherwise not admitting to either purpose. "OK," said Raphael, reaching for his ration bag, "If you're looking for something to eat? Then, have this."

He threw more pieces of protein towards the dog. The dog stood firm. He looked at Raphael and then down at the food. Then, never taking his eyes of Raphael he bent to snap up the offered food. The food swallowed, no time wasted chewing, the dog looked up to focus his full attention on Raphael. Raphael responded in kind and at that moment a created a bond between them. When Raphael got up to move on, the dog came with him, ranging a short distance away, but in sight. It was as if Raphael in greeting the dog as his guardian had assigned it a task it was happy to be taking on. The two very quickly became fast friends. From that moment on, Raphael would not have to explore alone.

There was no conscious naming of the dog, but its constant assumption of the guard position, whenever Raphael set off on a journey or stopped to sit and watch the world go by, over time led to Raphael referring to it as his Guardian and the label stuck. Raphael and Guardian continued to broaden their explorations. When Raphael took the ATV, something that became more frequent as they ranged farther and farther afield, Guardian would sometimes run alongside and sometimes it would climb up beside Raphael and ride. Running or riding, Guardian was ever vigilant.

To this point, Raphael had little opportunity to do much talking. He felt it was something he should be doing and so he would carry on a conversation with Guardian. As they traveled along, he would lay out his plans, identify items they came across, and explain their uses. Guardian would listen patiently, his large intelligent eyes seeming to hang on every word.

Back at the home base, Guardian would always take time performing his adopted duty, one he had taken upon himself, to watch over the sheep. If one ranged too far from the fold, he would gently steer it back. When he wasn't with Raphael, he was with them, often sitting proudly vigilant at the outer gateway of the fold. Other times he could be seen moving in their midst, licking the lambs and gently head-butting the adults, a proud master among his charges.

Guardian had eased to the domestic life as if he had always belonged. Raphael was his friend, and he treated the sheep as if they were his children. Observing Guardian, one could detect the fierce defender who would fight to the death to defend his friend Raphael and his flock. That this characteristic would be put to the ultimate test seemed remote to non-existent. How could anyone suspect that after a very long and happy time with Raphael and the sheep that with the changing of the season he would face such a test of his loyalty and courage? The time Raphael shared with Guardian was sweet for both man and dog.

Raphael had mapped the area around his home base as far as to the village to the north and to a large river some distance to the south to some kind of power plant in the west and a deserted paved highway to the east. On his mapping expeditions, Raphael had found many handiworks he identified as man-made, houses, barns, sheds, shops, tools, and vehicles, but there was no sign of a living human being, man-made with no man to make them. He also found interesting and useful natural landmarks, streams, extensive woodlands, fields, ponds, lakes, and swamps. In the beginning, he had found no life, but now the fields and forest, the streams, and ponds were teaming with life.

Except for the insects that were always checking him out, the other animals avoided him. However, with patience and time, he could discern many of them. He would sit for hours, day and night with Guardian at his side, gazing through binoculars trying to determine all the life forms that shared what he felt was his lands. With the help of some encyclopedic books he had found in his and other houses and some of the shops in town, he could identify the many individual species that lived around him.

Raphael came to believe he was the overseer of at least this part of the world. For all he knew, he might be an overseer for a much vaster area than he had yet explored. For now, he was satisfied and kept busy within the area around his home base he had explored and come to know well. Not to say that from time to time, he would explore a little further into unknown territory. There didn't seem to be a great deal of difference between the unknown and the known, so these extraterritorial trips were few.

There was plenty to do in the area he was familiar with. He occupied his time recording the plant, animal and even the insect life forms he encountered. While these were very plentiful, he would, from time to time, come across a new one. Even he was amazed at the knowledge base he had developed and could bring to his cataloging. The presence of Guardian and the sheep, the growing numbers of forest creatures he found in his own backyard, and the steady progress of his catalog of living creatures made this a happy time for Raphael.

He knew that although there were no other humans around for him to share with, he was not alone, and his catalog and research gave him a goal to move3 toward. This may have continued for a very long time and satisfying time. It should have continued, but even in this idealized existence, life could still bring unexpected and terrifying surprises. A surprise, while never expected could overwhelm the idyllic sameness and routine existence that had settled on Raphael's life and the world. An unwanted surprise could devastate in its effect.

The exploration, mapping, and cataloging had been grueling. The land that Raphael had traveled to, the land beyond the power plant that's purpose remained unclear, was rugged, rocky and filled with hidden sinkholes. Traveling through it with the ATV was so difficult to traverse that Raphael and Guardian had walked as much as they rode. It was a thankless exercise, and they found themselves impatient to return home. When they arrived back at home, they were weary and sore.

An Unexpected Terror

They were prepared to take time for rest and recreation at least for a few days. The plan was to do very little but enjoy the late spring weather. Raphael could work on refining his maps and adding some discoveries he had recently made to his catalog. Guardian could pass some happy time among his charges in the sheepfold.

Guardian found the newborns really needed watching. There were several more this year, and they seemed far more rambunctious than in the past. The day after their return passed with Raphael busy at his maps and Guardian watching over his sheep. While Guardian could sense that the sheep were more fretful than usual, he could not tell for certain why.

As the day passed into late afternoon, he smelled a noxious odor on the breeze. That might have something to do with the state of the sheep. Guardian recognized there was fear coming off the sheep. While Raphael, had he been out there with Guardian might have felt the fear coming from the sheep, the disagreeable odor that was beginning to worry the dog would be well beyond his ability to detect. This odor was unfamiliar to Guardian, but he didn't like it and suspected there was some creature out there beyond the trees.

Feeling uncertain and somewhat frightened himself, Guardian was getting restless. He began pacing the yard just outside the fold letting out an occasional worried whimper drowned out by the bleating, crowding sheep in the fold. As dusk was approaching, the odor had grown stronger and more rancorous. Now Guardian could identify it as the scent of a very dangerous, still unknown predator. He could sense that the sheep, himself and, quite likely, Raphael were in grave danger.

Raphael sensed none of this beyond the noise the sheep were making. It wasn't until the noise level of the sheep rose, and Guardian barked ferociously that he realized that something was wrong. He jumped up from the table, his notes, and maps scattering as he quickly crossed to the window. He saw nothing out there then realized the barking was coming from the sheepfold at the back of the large home.

Grabbing his crossbow and quiver he raced to a back room. Through the window he could see the sheep clustering in terror near the wall with Guardian in front of them looking out towards a small copse of bushes not far from the house. His ears lay flat, and his snout drawn back in a grimace revealing his razor-sharp teeth. While Raphael could detect fearfulness in Guardian's stance, he could also recognize the dog was displaying a sense of fierce determination. Afraid or not, Guardian was prepared to protect those sheep with his life.

Beyond the tree line towards which Guardian was issuing his challenge, Raphael could make out in the growing dusk, two figures. They were large and standing upright. At first, he felt a surge of hope, thinking they might be fellow humans, but that passed quickly. They were far too large and gave off a disgusting odor, which by now had penetrated the house.

As the first of the creatures stepped clear of the brush and into view, Raphael saw a face that was a twisted mask of horror. Large red eyes crowded down to a short muzzle. Thin lips pulled back from huge cruel fangs, a greenish saliva dripping from them. The ears were small and pointed. Dirty matted fur covered a massive body from which two long arms and two shorter legs could be seen ending in large, evil-looking claws. Like a giant version of a Hawk's talons, the creature's claws appeared very long and threateningly sharp. Raphael had no name for these beasts. They were enormous.

As he lifted the window, he saw Guardian leap at the nearest one, avoiding the sweeping claws that sought to rake him. He sank his teeth into the one monster's thick neck. The monster roared in pain and swung its talons with all its might. Guardian twisted to avoid the sweeping claws, but Raphael could see four gruesome wounds open in the dog's haunch. Guardian held on until a second swipe dislodged him and he slipped to the ground, twisting and turning to avoid the sweeping arms of the beast and the treacherous horror of the claws.

Turning away from the fallen dog, the monster began a shambling walk towards the terror-stricken sheep huddling against the wall. Guardian rose with some difficulty and attacked again, putting the beast off balance. Still trying to regain its balance, the monster lashed out with one large arm catching the dog and sending him flying. The dog's body crashed into a gatepost of the fold, and he lay there stunned.

Raphael notched his crossbow and sent a bolt into the body of the first invader. It grunted, grabbed the bolt and pulled it out, continuing towards the sheep as if immune to pain. Guardian, with great effort, rose to his feet as the second of the monsters moved quickly to confront him. Guardian leaped up to catch the beast's throat but missed and instead latched onto too loose flesh that hung from below the creature's huge arm. The dog began to rip and tear at it, bending to bring his hind legs up so his rear claws could join his teeth and front claws in a full out assault.

The beast let out a scream that expressed a blend of fear and pain and snapped and swung wildly at the dog, both bodies covered in blood. The first monster, having grabbed up one of the larger sheep was tearing it to pieces with fangs and talons, ingesting what it could and scattering the rest. Hearing its partner's tortured scream, the monster in the sheepfold stopped its ravenous assault on the sheep and turned back to see a twisting crossbow bolt catch the second monster in one of its large red eyes. The one struck forgot all about Guardian and reached up to grab the end of the bolt. It faltered, stumbled and collapsed to the ground. The other creature dropped what remained of the sheep from its mouth to let out a roar, then looked around as a stinging crossbow bolt penetrated its side.

With a prodigious leap, the creature was out of the fold and past the side of the house, heading for the tract of bush where it had first appeared. Despite its size, the creature vanished quickly among the bushes. Out of sight, but not out of hearing. Roars of pain, the crackling of underbrush and the snapping of small branches marked the creature's retreat to safety. It would save itself first and mourn its partner later. It had smelled death on its fellow monster and had known that it was pointless to stay, and risk being struck down by another of those twisting stingers.

Raphael made his way to the door and stepped outside, crossbow loaded and ready. He cautiously made his way to the sheepfold. The timid creatures were terrified, and the seemed to form one large many-headed creature as they pressed against the wall of the fold, avoiding the torn remains of their fallen brother. At the moment, the sheep were of little concern to Raphael. His focus was on his dear companion, Guardian. He rushed to kneel beside the limp and bloodied body. He reached out to tenderly touch the dog on the head. In response, the mortally injured Guardian turned its head to lick Raphael's hand. Guardian's body was badly broken and as he lay in Raphael's gentle hold, his life slipped away. He turned his eyes toward the sheep and as if satisfied that he had served his duty as protector well. He licked Raphael's hand one more time, then his eyes glazed over, and he grew still.

Raphael could not describe the feeling that engulfed him. His eyes filled with tears. A terrible sense of loss overcame him as he cradled the head of his beloved companion. Coupled with his deep and devastating sorrow came the certainty that he would track the surviving monster down and kill it. Wherever it ran to, he would find it and avenge the death of his faithful companion and gentle friend whom he had shared his life with over many seasons.

Overcome with sorrow as he was, Raphael knew he couldn't leave his friend to lie out in the elements, nor could he leave the shattered remains of Guardian's charge to draw the carrion birds. He found a large piece of plastic that had been hanging in the barn and lay Guardian's body on it. He dug a deep hole in the soft earth at the entrance to the sheepfold where Guardian had often sat to watch his flock and gently laid Guardian's body in it. "You can continue to watch over your sheep from here," he said.

Covering the body, he went to find something to mark it. He found a large flat stone and on it with the help of an etching tool, he wrote in the three languages he had awakened knowing, "Guardian. A friend," and set the stone on top of Guardian's grave. Before doing that, however, he needed to get rid of the stinking body of the monster he had killed. He would not offer it the dignity of a burial as he had given Guardian, nor even as he had treated the remains of the slain sheep.

He took a few moments to look for areas of weaknesses where a crossbow bolt or bullet might do the most effective damage. He cut off some of the claws determined to make a choker or belt to express his disregard for the cruelty and viciousness of the beast. He put them aside for a later time then dragged the body clear of the sheepfold to a distant clearing beside one of the outer sheds. The beast was huge and very heavy. It was a dead weight that Raphael had to drag and wrestle with all the way.

The day was coming to an end when he completed the pyre that contained the remains of Guardian's killer. He took a torch to it and sat back to watch it burn. The foul odor of the creatures burning fur added to the already overwhelming stench of the monster. It didn't prevent Raphael from remaining on watch over the burning body for the many hours it took to reduce it to ashes.

There were a few chores he had to do and preparations to make, then he would gather his weapons and tools and set out to track down the surviving monster and exterminate the beast that had, forever, so cruelly, changed his life. One characteristic of Raphael the hunter was his great patience. It had been built into him as a part of his particular role on this new earth. He knew that the killer was no longer close by. The monster seemed to have somehow known that the fire that was the pyre of its late partner had severed any trace of the ties that had bound them together. Likely a mate, the deceased and burned beast no longer mattered, either to the monster or to Raphael.

It might be a cruel and brutal monster, but nowhere near as vengeful as Raphael. It would not return to the sheepfold. The monster, despite his hunger, was aware at some level that it would be very dangerous to do so. The creature had faced dogs before. He knew them to be fierce, but he also knew that he was far more powerful. There was something else that frightened him. It was the stingers, the one that had dropped his mate and the two he had pulled from his side, leaving painful wounds.

Things were never very clear in his mind. His limited intelligence was pushed aside by his voracious appetite and viciousness, but he understood that the stingers could be fatal and that who or whatever shot them would not hesitate to do so again. Practical matters filled his thoughts. He was starving after the winter. He was forced to leave most of the sheep he had been trying to feed on, so his sole priority was to find food. Although the numbers of animals in the forests and fields were multiplying exponentially, the larger ones, more likely to satisfy his appetite were scarce.

This scarcity meant that the days ahead for the creature that Raphael, drawing on some innate knowledge, had decided to call a werewolf, would be long and difficult. It would take many small woodland creatures to come anywhere near satiating his enormous, carnivorous hunger and most of those would be well hidden long before he could come near. The frogs and small reptiles that he was forced to live on were unpleasant to eat and while this kept him going, it did little to improve his overpowering hunger. He would soon need to find another sheepfold, or a slow-moving deer although he knew there was little likelihood of either. So, he continued on, putting greater distance between himself, Raphael's sheepfold and his last chance at a significant feeding.

The Hunt

After completing what he needed to do around his home base and closing down the house, Raphael was ready to track and kill the werewolf. He followed the monster's path from the sheepfold and into the bushes through which it had fled. He found the second crossbow bolt, still reeking and bloody. He washed it in a nearby stream and placed it in his quiver.

By midafternoon, Raphael had a good idea of the monster's escape path. It had a good head start and there were many open trails. A few bits of broken branches at the edge of one of the trails and no other obvious reason convinced him of which trail he should follow. He had no other reason than the broken twigs for that conviction. Raphael mounted his already loaded ATV and drove to the place where the tracks of the monster became obscured. Reinforced by his conviction of which trail to take, Raphael set off with a hunter's certainty that this was the right one.

The faint stench of werewolf that came from the nearby bushes as he proceeded was enough to confirm it. While the werewolf was the vicious personification of the werebeasts of fiction and folklore, it didn't have a human form that it walked around in when the moon was not full. Full moon, quarter moon, any moon or none it remained a large vicious, shambling terror with some reasoning power and an instinct towards cruelty and mindless ferocity.

The revivers of earth, although powerful and intelligent beyond the wildest expectations of twenty-first-century man, were not omniscient. They had chosen the twenty-first century around which to base their legacy because that was the beginning of the age of space travel and a time when wide spectrum communications had begun. Much of the history of earth had been lost down the ages in that vast and incredible gap that existed between the true twenty-first century and the children of humanity as they stood on the verge of evolving into pan-dimensional beings.

The creation of Legacy Earth had been based on fragmentary information spread across thousands of settled planets; bits of DVDs, comic books and novels, newspapers, and history texts preserved in the airless wreckage of the countless centuries old immigrant spaceships. Developing continuity was a difficult task even for the vast collective intellect of these children of humanity. Hence, fact and fiction merged into a unique whole. Planetary colonies of the twenty-fourth and twenty-fifth centuries, both real and imagined, merged as did technologies developed over a time frame of 600 years from the nineteenth to the twenty-fifth centuries.

Twenty-first-century humans would recognize some aspects of Legacy Earth as familiar, but others would be for them elements of fictional speculation, sheer fantasy or horror. Legacy earth was not the twenty-first-century earth. It was expected to be, but an uncertain amalgam of five or six centuries augmented by far later constructs such as an eternal battery that would allow for any lack of real infrastructure.

This power source called the eternal battery and the computer that served it allowed for a world filled with safeguards and was built with no perceivable end date. After many centuries at an unknown time, when the safeguards began to fade, the hope was, that Legacy Earth would be ready to be a world inhabited by the self-sufficient. The unknowing on the part of these future remnants of humanity was the reason there were machines of varying sophistication and that was also why there were werewolves of a sort and as time went on legacy humans would encounter numerous other fictional, fantastical and horrific entities sharing their world.

Legacy Earth, it must be remembered, was not real earth. The original earth had been for eons, a broken ball of ash near a dead sun in a dying part of the galaxy. Its revival was a dream and a construct of entities so different from twenty-first-century humanity that any recognizable similarities had long since vanished. This new earth was a legacy of those last vestiges of humanity as they were about to sever their human connection. While none of the builders remained to observe, these were still the very early days of Legacy Earth and Raphael was one of the very few humans present at this stage of its development. He had been invested with a great deal of specialized knowledge and a particular set of skills.

He was a hunter and a soldier skilled and knowledgeable beyond any hunter or soldier who had lived on or near the original earth. Not even Raphael knew what he was capable of and, the fact was, that he might never learn or experience the full extent of his abilities. Now, he was nothing more than a capable hunter following the trail of a dangerous beast to kill it. His only purpose was to avenge the brutal and unnecessary death of his only friend and companion. As Raphael got further along the trail, the tracks of the beast became quite easy to follow.

To Raphael's mind, the monster acted as if it commanded the land. It crashed recklessly through the brush leaving a trail of damage and fed on whatever it could find. The monster's spoor showed remains of a few field mice and voles, but mostly swamp creatures, frogs and salamanders. The beast was too noisy, too rancid smelling and too slow to catch anything larger.

Sometimes along the way, Raphael saw signs that the monster had pursued something larger. There were places where it had tried to follow these animals into their hiding places, digging its way under buildings and large rocks. Few of the digs made it beneath the buildings and those that did hadn't got very far. Whatever the intended prey, it could be back out from under a building and gone before the monster could get near it.

Raphael saw numerous half-finished ditches and holes near the edge of buildings, around the base of larger trees and rocks. Broken bushes and crushed and flattened brush gave evidence of the beast's frantic effort to capture some terrified small animal. There was little evidence to suggest that these desperate hunts were successful. What Raphael did recognize was that as he moved farther down the trail, the signs of these attacks were fresher and more recent. He was gaining on the monster. Having been on the trail for several days, it felt to Raphael that catching and killing the monster was a secondary aim. There was some other reason that had set him on this path, and it was one that far exceeded the quest for vengeance.

He could hear sounds in the distance. They may be from the creature he was trailing, but although far enough off to be indistinct, they sounded more like a vehicle engine being shut down and what could have been the brief sound of a voice. The sound came from too far away for Raphael to be sure, but it was coming from the direction the monster he trailed was heading. Feeling the hunt nearing a conclusion, Raphael shut down the ATV and began to cautiously make his way on foot towards the source of the mysterious sounds.

Through the trees, he could see a large building surrounded by a flat paved surface. Angling around, he spotted a lone vehicle parked near the building. Off to his left, he heard the crashing sounds of a large creature shambling through the woods beside the building. He knew that he had found the beast he was seeking and moved quickly and quietly to intercept it. As he and the creature converged, one slipping silently through the brush, the other crashing through bush and trees with reckless abandon, the rush of heedless movement stopped, and a vicious roar replaced it. It was the sound of hunger and hatred, pain and madness. The roar he had heard was offset by the sound of fierce barking. He recognized the bark. It was a dog, and it sounded as Guardian did standing in front of the sheepfold, as if it was being protective of something.

Moving closer, Raphael pushed past a leafy bush that allowed him to see the monster. It was towering over what appeared to be a smaller version of Guardian. The dog was standing between the monster and much small creature, hidden in shadow, but standing upright.

Monster and dog moved simultaneously; the beast more interested in the creature obscured to Raphael by shadows created by spotlights on the side of the building. The dog leaped at the monster. With a short swing of its massive arm, the monster brushed away the attacking dog as if it were a piece of lint on a jacket. Realizing that the beast was about to attack the upright figure in the shadows, Raphael drew a twist bolt from his quiver and set it in the already straining crossbow. Bracing himself, he saw the dog getting to its feet and the smaller upright shape move deeper into the shadows. These registered on the periphery of his vision as his focus was on the huge werewolf.

He knew that if the dog and the shadowed figure were to survive, he must send the perfect killing shot to the most vulnerable exposed spot on the beast. He knew that there was a soft spot just back of the eyes. If he could just hit this place before the creature began its attack, its victims had a chance. He had only a split second to get a bead on the target and release the bolt. "Just stay still for a moment," he quietly whispered to the monster so as not to draw its attention.

The monster seemed to obey Raphael's silent order long enough for him to release the bolt. It penetrated the monster's head right on target, just behind the eyes. On impact, the huge head turned toward Raphael while one massive, clawed hand reached up to pull the bolt free. Its eyes grew wide as it trembled all over and slumped to the ground. Raphael set another bolt to his bow and stepped out of the bush to momentarily stand over the fallen werewolf, then he turned to face the agitated dog and the still figure in the shadows.

The creature in the shadows had crouched down in anticipation of the werewolf's attack. Now, it rose upright from the crouched position and stepped forward into the light. And in a soft, shaky voice, the first human voice other than his own that Raphael had ever heard, asked in Earth Standard, "Who are you:"

Then, without pausing, gushed out, "What was that thing? Thank you for saving us. Are you human?"

Raphael laughed, "I was about to ask you the same thing. Except for the monster...I call it a werewolf."

Later, inside the restaurant, Raphael would share food and hospitality with Maricel and Scout. For Raphael and Maricel the world had transformed. For the first time since they awakened and after a very long time, they were no longer the sole human in their world. They had little to say to each other, but that would change. They decided that if there were two humans, there could be more.

The children of humans learned a great deal about their original home in establishing Legacy Earth, but they didn't have an Adam and Eve. Instead, they had peopled the early Legacy Earth with a very small number of specialists. Their role was to join together sometime in the future into regional groups to prepare and train future generations in the lore and knowledge they would need to survive and prosper in this readymade world. The builders, however, could have no more hand in what was to happen to their legacy after they had set it in motion.

They had no idea that both Maricel and Raphael could sense a pull calling them to follow an already laid out path, the outcome of which they could neither see nor predict. This path had laid itself out as a portion of a map in both their minds, a map that would, over the many seasons to come sometimes fade completely and other times grow clear and persistent. Until they reached the as yet unknown goal, the compulsion to move towards it never left them.

Jolinda: Healer, Pharmacologist, Medical Technician, Physician

First Things

One moment it was dark and silent then lit up showing a strong respiration and heartbeat. The monitor revealed the vital signs of a healthy adult. Jolinda reached her hands to pull the thin bio-gossamer sheet that covered her away from her face and sat up.

She saw at the vital signs monitor on the stand beside her and read it. She knew it was monitoring her although there was nothing connecting her to it. This didn't trouble her. It was wireless technology, and she was familiar with it. How this could be, she had no idea, but she was.

Surveying the room, she saw most of the things on the counters and shelves served a medical purpose. To a twenty-first-century observer even one with a knowledge of medical technology, some of these would look strange and amazing and worked in ways he or she would never have dreamed possible.

The room was a small, well stocked medical center. It held an array of state-of-the-art devices that might have appeared in a twenty-first-century surgery along with numerous other devices that would be well beyond the understanding of a twenty-first-century medical practitioner. The technological devices varied in function and appearance, but Jolinda knew the moment she laid eyes on each what it was. She knew its purpose and how and when to use it. Despite the elaborate array of sophisticated medical technology, there was nothing to fulfill her current need of the moment. Jolinda was hungry.

Leaving her room Jolinda found herself in a meeting area or office. There was a desk fronting a large, comfortable chair and several others around that while functional were less cozy. Against one wall there was a counter with a sink. On the counter was a coffee maker that poured a dark substance into a cup as she stepped towards it. There was a large microwave oven beside it and a small refrigerator that on investigation she found crammed with edibles. Jolinda recognized each as she did the items on the shelves above the coffee maker and microwave.

Jolinda seated herself in the comfy chair behind the desk, sipping on a warm cup of coffee and eating a bagel with cream cheese. They brought her taste buds alive in a delightful way. Finished her bagel and coffee, she was ready to look around.

Back in her room, she opened the several doors. She found one that opened outside and one that opened into a closet containing several outfits. The material was comfortable. These one-piece outfits shared the closet with several pairs of practical shoes that were a perfect fit. There were belts and carrying packs containing a variety of medical and diagnostic tools. Two lightweight white coats hung on pegs on the closet's side wall. Beside the exit door was a large window. Through it, the world looked big.

Before braving that, Jolinda decided to clothe herself. she took an outfit and shoes to a water closet with an enclosed shower was through a third door. The mist shower was delightful. It rid her of the stickiness of the delicate material that encased her on awakening. Closing the door of the shower, a warm cloud had enveloped her. A steamy cloud pulsated against her skin. Stepping out she was dry, surrounded by a subtle and appealing fragrance.

A few minutes later; she came out dressed. She believed the clothing was a protective barrier for her against the outside world. To her amazement she sensed little difference being dressed. Everything was lightweight and comfortable.

Although the pull to head outside was strong, she first needed to take an inventory what was in her rooms. She found three examination rooms equipped with everything she would need for any medical issue. Besides the bed in which she had awakened the rest of the room was filled with all sizes and types of medical devices. The lower shelves contained a variety of medicines, and a large refrigerator contained many more. There was everything from bandages, useful for small wounds to surgery and suturing devices suitable for the most delicate surgery.

The bathroom she had changed in was also well stocked with chemical cleaners. The closets were stacked with sets of towels, a variety of powders and lotions filled the cabinet under the mirror. After her inspection, Jolinda had a mental inventory of everything in her rooms. Nothing was out of place, but something was missing. That something being someone needing medical care she could put these wonderful healing tools to work on.

Although she had yet to leave her rooms; she knew there was no one around. There was neither one needing her healing touch, nor one who didn't. She knew she was alone. Investigation outside her rooms revealed that the only living things sharing her environment were plants; small trees, fields of trimmed grass, and tiny gardens of flowers. There were no humans. The overwhelming silence made Jolinda feel she was the only person in the world. If this was the case, Jolinda felt she had arrived in it with a useless set of skills. Still, the various devices fascinated her enough that even without patients or anyone else, she wanted to learn everything about them.

She may be alone but had no time to feel lonely. There was far too much to do. She kept a careful eye on all the medical technology to make sure it remained in working order. As she expected, they all were ready for use just as food and drink and wardrobe was always present and ready for use. This didn't stop her from checking or prevent her from running regular simulations against a time when someone needed her help.

She also had lots to explore. The place where she had awakened and that rooms that made up the surgery were in a medium-sized five-story building surrounded by several larger buildings. It stood on the edge of the urban center. Not too far off, suburban areas reached out into the countryside. Her community was on the shores of a large lake. A huge river ran into the lake splitting the small city into two distinctive parts. Several ornate bridges spanned the river connecting one side of the city to the other.

As a healer, she knew how important a systematic approach was and applied it to her explorations. First, she focused on one side of the river seeking to learn what it held. The main thrust of her explorations was a search for fellow humans. In the early days investigating her small urban center, she found nothing.

After that, she searched out other surgeries, infirmaries, and hospitals. She found several in her travels and was delighted to learn they were all well- equipped. These hospitals, medical centers, and surgeries were at key points throughout the city. With no other living souls to be found Jolinda felt them strategically pointless. One of the suburban areas had a hospital, most of the other suburban areas had at least one centrally located surgery or medical center.

Besides the medical centers she had searched out, Jolinda was fascinated with the food stores. No matter how often she would visit them and take away products when she returned they were fully stocked. The items she had taken were replaced and everything was fresh and edible.

As time passed Jolinda became familiar with the vagaries of the weather. While most days were bright and sunny, clouds, rain, and chilly winds keeping her near home and limiting her exploration. Encountering winter with its first snowfall delighted Jolinda. While the air was cold, she was amazed to discover the everyday lightweight clothing she wore kept her warm. She marveled at the ice on the lake but lacked the courage to walk on it.

While the summer of her awakening lasted a long time, the seasons that followed were short. Each time they came around, she found they lasted longer. Of all the seasons, summer continued to linger much longer than the others.

As seasons passed Jolinda continued her exploration of the large community in which she lived. As she did, she noticed other living things. Birds appeared taking up residence in the neighborhood trees or on the nearby lake. She saw dark sinewy shapes moving below the lake's surface, but there was no sign of another human being. Where the water was stillest, she encountered flying insects. Crawling insects were showing up everywhere. Jolinda found the signs suggesting more and larger denizens were moving in.

Mewser

One warm, soft day in early summer, Jolinda had found her way to a park. She stopped her travel, to rest her legs and enjoy the beauty that surrounded her. She sat down on the grass and leaned back against the bole of a tree. Lost in reverie, but not asleep, something jumping on her lap with a loud, questioning "meow> brought her to alert. Looking down she met the gaze of a tiny furry creature with a longish tail and pointy ears. This was Jolinda's first introduction to the kitten about to adopt her.

The kitten was tiny, her footsteps silent, but her mewing query came across loud and clear as she walked fearlessly right up to Jolinda's face. Jolinda knew enough about animal physiology to recognize a feline, particularly the household feline termed a cat. Household cats, Jolinda knew were domestic and often lived with people. Here was a possible companion. She reached into her bag and withdrew a small piece of something cheese-like from between two pieces of bread, the handiwork of the invisible maid that restocked the food when Jolinda was out. She broke off some and offered it to the kitten, now seated high on her chest and staring straight into her eyes.

The kitten attacked the offered food ravenously. In no time at all the kitten had polished off the rest of Jolinda's offerings and a saucer of water. After that, the kitten showed no inclination to leave. It had its head around towards its tail and began a rhythmic purring. Jolinda was enchanted. She had a friend. She reached out to the tiny ball of fluff and petted it. The contented kitten stretched and continued purring. Jolinda was aware the world in which she awakened was changing.

There may be no humans yet, but she wasn't alone. The kitten looked up at her and meowed. The kitten meowed at everything, so Jolinda decided to call her Mewser. "Hi Mewser," she said softly as she stroked the kitten behind the ears.

Mewser answered with a half-yawned, "Meow,"

Jolinda took that as the sign it approved the name. They became constant companions. Mewser accompanied her on her explorations, sometimes peeking out of the pack on her back, sometimes resting on her shoulder, but, as Mewser matured, more frequently on foot. By the time Mewser reached adulthood, she and Jolinda had explored pretty well all of their small city. They had inspected the medical facilities and most of the buildings.

Their investigations brought them farther into the suburban areas and less settled countryside. Jolinda was stuck with the beauty of the country and thought about changing her base of operations. On one jaunt they passed the empty but beautiful family homes of suburbia with their perfect lawns and neatly trimmed hedges and ventured into the more rugged fields and forests beyond. There, Jolinda came across a charming medical facility attached to a lovely colonial style house.

The house was elegant and well appointed, and the resources she found in the medical facility were comparable to the surgery back home. She needed only a few medical items to bring the country facility up to her standards. Over the next ten days, with the help of a van that had been parked beside her home base, she was able to move what she considered necessities from the surgery of her awakening into the new home she and Mewser had chosen. The caution that Jolinda had shown in her systematic exploration of her city did not desert her in her new surroundings. She carefully inventoried, surveyed, and examined the area until she was satisfied that her choice was truly a good one.

With the intensity of moving and surveilling the locale finished, Jolinda was able to set up a routine that would give her more time to learn and enjoy her rustic surroundings. In one room away from the medical facilities with its small examination rooms, reception, interview areas and large storage space, Jolinda found a room with a sofa and several comfortable chairs.

On one wall was a bookshelf laden with books. Many of the books were about medicine and some were almost complete. The chairs, she noticed, were set to face a large shiny flat surface that hung on the wall causing Jolinda to think of a large table turned on its side and fastened to the wall.

A closer look revealed it to be similar to a medical device. It had buttons, dials and the sheen of polished metal. Curious, she tried a few of the buttons and waited to see what might happen. Nothing did, so she went to the connecting well-stocked kitchen.

Jolinda poured herself a drink of juice and joined Mewser already asleep on one of the chairs in the book room. She could stretch out on the large sofa and look through some of the books, or maybe read an article in the medical journal she had found earlier in one of the examination rooms.

Back in the book room, she nearly jumped out of her skin when someone spoke to her in a loud, well-modulated Earth Standard. "Good afternoon," it said.

The voice came from a table-top shape on the wall. Jolinda could see, a human, somewhat smaller than her standing in front of the wide polished surface on the wall. The speaker was looking at the chairs turned towards him. It was as if he was speaking to the chairs.

As Jolinda edged into the room to better see the stranger, he spoke again, "Today on Investigations, we will be examining the relationship between people and their pets." Instantly another human figure accompanied by a large animal somewhat similar to Mewser was standing where the speaker had been. As suddenly as they had appeared, they were torn apart by huge invisible hands. Whatever the cause, they were ripped up into tiny square shapes that filled the air around the screen with motes of light. Then, the first speaker was back. "Good afternoon," he said, "Today on Investigations we will be examining the relationship between people and their pets."

Once again, the person and the large animal appeared, and as before, they were torn into tiny square bits of light.

In reformed a third time to show original speaker back repeating the same words. As Jolinda watched in amazement, this cycle continued to repeat itself over and over again. She took little time to realize that this was a visual display not much different from a picture in a magazine except for the fact it moved and spoke. There were images, reproductions of what may have once been real. She stepped over to the screen and passed her hand through the images as they appeared. Her hand met no resistance.

She reached past the figure to press some of the buttons she had pressed when she first went through the room. The cycle of figures immediately vanished. She pressed another of the buttons. Nothing happened. Pressing the second button brought the speaker back. She went to another button and pressed it, to find herself standing close to the flames of a fiercely burning building.

As close as the flames where she didn't feel an intense heat. The burning building seemed to then shrink, but Jolinda could tell that it was the image's perspective changing, not the building. Then two human figures were framed in front of the distant backdrop of the burning building. One said to the other, "We can't stay here, it's all going to blow," and they both ran from the building and towards Jolinda.

They didn't come any closer to her. While knowing this was how she was perceiving the images, the suddenness and sense of the reality of the two figures' and their actions caused Jolinda to jump back and protectively put her hands to her ears, ready for an explosion that never came. The scene changed, and she was looking at a room with several people sitting at desks and, one pacing. While the walls were obscured, she noticed that the room contained variations of some of the medical devices she was familiar with. Those people were in a medical center.

The scene before Jolinda zoomed in on one person sitting in front of a smaller but similar screen to the one Jolinda was watching. The person watching the screen turned towards Jolinda, and expression of sadness on his face as he spoke, "The whole complex has been destroyed. There was a massive explosion, and I can't see any sign of Linda or Carl."

Jolinda pressed another of the buttons on the screen and the scene vanished leaving no images behind. She wondered if everyone else was killed in a massive fire. The sad-faced one who said, "the complex was destroyed," was still there.

"This," she thought, "is all make-believe."

Interest in the repeated images waning, Jolinda sat down on the sofa and reached for the magazine on the coffee table. She noticed a small pyramidal shaped device beside the magazine. It had a tiny symbol on it identical to the one she had seen on the bottom of the screen. There was no obvious connection between the tiny pyramid and the large screen. That it was wireless meant little to Jolinda as in her experience, everything was. "I wonder what else is on that thing?"

As the thought crossed her mind the screen on the wall lit up with a jumble of tiny screens showing a wide variety of contents in miniature 3D. That screen showed for a few seconds, then was replaced by a second set of miniature screens. While she watched, the screen continued to show these miniature screens replacing them every few seconds. There must have been hundreds of these little screens. Most showed a variety of different images while some repeated the same one.

One tiny screen filled with movement caught her attention and her gaze lingered on it. In that instant, it took over the full screen. Tiny humans were racing around the front of the screen. Some seemed to chase another one running with a ball close to his feet. Others wearing the same color shirts were spread out and running the same way as him. While this was happening, she could see a large wall that must have been tiered in levels as it was filled with tiny shouting humans waving and twirling colored pieces of cloth.

A sonorous voice was describing what was happening as the one with the ball turned and kicked it over to another who tried to dodge a third person in a different colored shirt. "What else?" thought Jolinda and as she had the thought, the multiple tiny screens re-appeared.

Over the next hour, Jolinda continued to juggle programs bouncing back and forth from the miniature multi-screens to the full screen. It didn't take her long to understand she was watching fragments of images intended to entertain. There were stories acted out, sports activities. and people talking with others or directly at the viewer. It was entertaining and Jolinda knew she would come back to it whenever she felt the need for human company.

What interested her most were the people. They looked similar in many ways, yet each one was unique. The people on the screens showed a many shades of skin color. They spoke with many accents. Some were larger, some smaller, some spoke in high-pitched voices while the voices of others were low. They wore different attire, similar to the others, but almost never the same.

Jolinda was amazed at how they could all be so similar, yet as individuals, they were each different. In contrast, Jolinda was very much the lone individual. There was no other like her.

The fragmentary bits of television shows suggested that Jolinda's solitude was unusual for humans. She saw locations like where she lived only they were mostly filled with a vast number and variety of humans. In that world, the 3D screen showed the solitude Jolinda experienced was rare to non-existent.

In watching those bits of media Jolinda felt a deeper stirring. It gave meaning to her desire to find someone else like her. This desire was galvanizing her to seeking other humans. She was considering leaving her home to search the countryside hoping to find at least one fellow human.

The media fragments had made her feel that life among others of her kind was better. It was, as she was well aware, a grand dream. Jolinda doubted that she would ever find crowds of humans as shown on the video screen but hoped she might find one. In the meantime, she enjoyed the comfort of her newfound home. She established a daily routine practicing simulations with the various medical devices. She would make sure they were prepped and ready for use each day although she expected never to use them.

She would then do some reading in the medical books. With some she was able to cover quite a lot of detail, the chapters being almost complete. She would check the grounds, making sure the grass didn't get too high and bushes didn't grow too wild obscuring her view. If there was a human in the vicinity or a threat, she didn't want to miss it. A human, she would welcome, a threat would have her place house and medical facility on lockdown. Safety was an important consideration for a solitary human female, especially as the animal population was growing.

The countryside was abounding in signs of larger creatures, although Jolinda rarely saw one of any size, except for Mewser and a few squirrels now inhabiting the nearby trees. Her workday done, she would set out a meal for herself and Mewser then together they would sit on the sofa while Jolinda read or watched 3D videos. The actual designation as Jolinda well knew was Projection Television but in her mind, the term 3D video expressed it best.

Mewser would nap beside her or climb up on her lap to be petted. Life in the country home and medical facility was a good one. Rainy days would sometimes keep Jolinda and Mewser inside.

On one such day, Jolinda had just finished reviewing a small handheld diagnostic tool. She had tested the buttons and read the readouts and was about to set it down when she heard Mewser calling. Still holding the device more like a prop for Star Trek than a bona fide medical device (perhaps Dr. McCoy's tricorder was the inspiration), she stepped into the reception area to see what was bothering Mewser.

Mewser was standing on a window ledge looking out. Jolinda Joined her feline companion there. Through the window, she saw a strangeness to the sky. An orange-grey pall seemed to envelop the world to the horizon. Huge black clouds were painting out the light into in the distance. A major storm was on the way.

Jolinda experienced thunderstorms before. Some had been fierce. The first time she had experienced the lightning and heard thunder, it was terrifying. As it had roared and flashed around her, she was convinced that it was the end of the world. Feeling there was no use hiding, she had watched the storm roll through, putting on a spectacular light and sound display. As the heavy rain obscured her surroundings, she watched in terrified wonder. As quickly as the storm came, it was over. The sun returned and the sky lightened. The whole world seemed to glow as golden beams reflected off the drying droplets hanging from the trees and covering the grass.

As the storm subsided so did her sense of terror. She left her shelter to see what had caused the glistening droplets to appear. She recognized that the droplets were water that fell from the sky. Jolinda's internal knowledge base informed her of the concept of hot and cold air masses colliding and water accumulating into dark clouds. She knew lightning came from the internal friction. That it was nothing more than bolts of static electricity passing between the earth and the clouds that caused both the brilliant white light and the enormous booming roar of thunder.

Her original fear, she understood was cautionary. A thunderstorm didn't mean the end of the world, but lightning could be harmful. The swollen streams caused by rain could also be dangerous and she recognized the need for caution. After that storms didn't trouble her.

This one, however, seemed to be different. The odd color of the sky, the intense darkness and heaviness of the clouds, and the wind that was now rocking the trees around the yard suggested that this would be a violent storm unlike any Jolinda had experienced before.

The doors had power locks, and the windows did, too. Window locks were part of an emergency lockdown system that covered them with translucent, electric shutters. Jolinda flipped the master lockdown switch on a console behind the reception desk. As the shutters closed over the windows, she went through the rooms to make sure the shutters were working properly throughout the building. They were.

She and Mewser then settled in the residence living room to sit out the storm. Transparent shutters on the main window of the living room revealed a wall of dark clouds approaching rapidly. Through the swaying trees, she could see flashes of lightning and hear the rumble of thunder. More curious than frightened, Jolinda and Mewser watched the approaching storm. Jolinda was amazed how dark the sky had become.

Although several hours of daylight remained, the clouds raced to obscure any trace of sunlight. Within minutes a false dusk overran the clinic. The lightning and thunder flashed and crashed with a wild ferocity. Heavy rain and fierce winds beat at the branches of the trees and screamed around the walls.

Hours seemed to pass with the surgery and residence battered by the storm. At times, large balls of hail fell, pounding against the roof and nearly drowning out the thunder. Trees were bending near the breaking point as branches crashed to the ground. Intense gusts of wind swept across the land in waves carrying off anything that wasn't fastened down.

Forestman and the Elvin

Windborne jetsam was carried past the window. The tattered convertible top of a small car savagely ripped from its place by a particularly ferocious gust of wind sailed past. the cacophony accompanying the storm was so complete that Jolinda momentarily could not separate it from a pounding and crashing that came from the reception room.

Fearing that the wind had blown in the door and was threatening to do some severe damage, Jolinda ran to check it out. The sheets of paper and damp clumps of leaves scattered around showed the door had been opened, but whatever else had happened, it was now shut.

A huge dark form half lay, half crouched beside it. Upon first seeing the form, Jolinda could not tell what it was. Then it donned on her, she was looking at the largest creature she had ever seen. It was huge and fur- covered. Although it didn't match up with what Jolinda knew of the human form, despite the size, the creature was humanoid. Not knowing what she confronted, Jolinda held back from the creature.

Mewser approached it fearlessly. Stopping in front of the large shaggy head, Mewser uttered several inquisitive "meows."

The creature tried to rise to a sitting position. It was having a difficult time as its arms and hands were occupied. trying to protect a tiny human–looking thing held in its huge, wooly arms. Uncertain about the invader and its intentions, Jolinda could sense no threat from the enormous creature. It was pre-occupied with trying to protect the tiny creature it held.

Seeing Jolinda, the large creature held out its arms in supplication and to present to her the tiny human-like figure. She cautiously advanced towards the creature and the tiny being it held out. Jolinda could see several tiny silver shafts impaling the huge beast. The surrounding fur was matted with blood. The wounds these shafts had made would be painful and seriously damaging. The larger creature, she could see, was weakening,

Despite its obvious suffering, the big creature was focused on Jolinda and the tiny being it held out to her. As she reached to take the tiny creature from the giant, she noticed that Mewser was licking the bloody fur of the larger beast, offering comfort. Jolinda called for light and the reception immediately brightened. The tiny thing in her arms she now saw while certainly humanoid, like the giant, was not human.

Its face was narrow, and the pointed ears were large for the size of its head. Jolinda saw the tiny body had experienced an extreme physical trauma. It must have happened recently as the little one was still alive. Jolinda carried it into the nearest examination room. Laying it gently on the examination table, she looked around for the diagnostic tool she had been working with earlier. She could see it just outside the examination room on a file cabinet where she had left it.

After getting it, she turned it on and scanned the tiny body. The scan showed evidence of severe trauma. This tiny female had either fallen from a great height or encountered some powerful destructive force. Bone density indicated that although much smaller than a human of Jolinda's size, the bones themselves were strong. There were, however, several fractures and breaks and other internal injuries.

As to healing these serious injuries, Jolinda had just the thing, a children's healing capsule. It was well beyond the technology of the twenty-first century and in it, the bones of the tiny creature would be straightened and mended, and the internal injuries stabilized and healed within hours. Had Jolinda been of the twenty-first century, she would have been amazed at the sophistication of this device and seen it as an almost magical machine. She had no awareness of the device's time frame but only knew she was grateful for it.

She carefully picked up the small, broken body and carried it to the next-door operating room where the pediatric healing capsule sat. With one finger, she raised the lid and gently set the small human-like creature inside. As she closed the cover to encase the patient in a metal and plastic cocoon, Jolinda hoped she was as human-like as she looked. Having spent considerable time trying out simulated healing with this machine, Jolinda nimbly adjusted the dial on the touchscreen, bringing the pod to life with a faint glow and gentle hum.

Returning to the reception, she was astonished to see the furry giant still lying by the door, gently caressing Mewser with a hand that was bigger than she was as the small cat continued to fuss over the enormous creature. With trepidation, Jolinda made her way to the huge creature and inspected the silver shafts extending from the bloody fur.

The giant turned its large, shaggy head to look at her, but remained docile, its large, sad eye barely able to stay open. Jolinda could see that the small silver shafts were projectiles, probably small arrows or darts. How she knew this, she wasn't sure, but she was believed that's what they were most likely tiny arrows.

She could also tell from the weakened condition of the huge creature there was more than just blood loss. Jolinda assumed that there was a poison or soporific on the business end of the arrow. Judging from the size of the arrows if that's what they were, those shooting them could not be much larger than the tiny creature the furry giant had brought in. She needed one of the arrows to determine if there was any poison on it.

Jolinda would have to remove one from the giant. She could not move the huge creature without causing it more harm. The creature's eyes were closed, and it was no longer aware of Mewser, Jolinda needed to find out what was affecting the creature soon or have a very large and heavy corpse on her hands.

She went to gather what she would need to remove one of the arrows. Jolinda needed painkiller for around the arrow and a scalpel to pull the flesh away from the arrow in case it was barbed. A basin was required to place the arrow in to avoid possible injury to herself. She would also need a diagnostic tool to determine what sort of drug was on the arrowhead. A small handheld tool she knew of could isolate a variety of poisons and some variations. It would tell her the different toxins and their antidotes on the arrowhead.

Once she learned what substance was on the arrow, she would create an antidote and get it into the creature before it died. The poison on the arrow might itself be fatal. Even if it wasn't a deadly poison shock from a muscle paralytic or knock out drug could be just as fatal. She suspected if it the wounds were made by archers and these were their arrows, then the bows would be for hunting. It would be unlikely that they would use a strong poison, one that might contaminate the prey making it dangerously inedible, or risk transference of toxin to whoever dressed or prepared it.

She moved quickly to gather what she would need and laid it out on the floor a short distance from the giant, but, she hoped, far enough away they would survive the creature's thrashing about in pain. Donning surgical gloves and a mask, she picked up a scalpel, a small retractor and a needleless jet syringe designed to inject a strong local anesthetic. She hoped it was strong enough to dull the pain as she cut into the large creature's flesh.

As she approached the creature, scalpel, retractor and syringe in a tray with towels and bandages, it lifted its head and looked questioningly at her. She saw intelligence in its look and decided to explain, "I have a syringe with a painkiller. I will use it to numb the flesh around one of the things sticking in you. I will remove it and see if it is poisoned and that is what's hurting you."

The creature seemed to understand. Jolinda was not sure how much earth standard the giant understood, but she could sense the creature knew what she needed.

Before she could proceed, the creature reached a huge hand down and grasped an arrow shaft embedded in his thigh. With a roar of pain, he pulled the shaft from his flesh and held it out to her. Fortunately, the tip was tiny and there were no barbs so removal of the others would be done in a more painless manner than the giant's method.

As she took the arrow from the enormous hand, the creature dropped its head to the ground and closed its eyes. Jolinda tested the arrowhead and her surmise about the drug was correct. It was a muscle relaxant and Jolinda with the help of the chemical discloser and the toxin-assessing device prepared the antidote.

As she removed each arrow, she injected some antidote at the site. A vector treatment device closed and cauterized each wound leaving no trace other than a nearly invisible scar. She could see as the musculature of the giant became more toned it was regaining its strength. This worried Jolinda as she had no idea how the creature would behave with her once it was back to full strength. It opened its eyes and raised its head, to look at her. To her surprise it spoke in a rough but gentle voice, "Elvin?" it asked, "Elvin?" The word was clear, but meaningless to Jolinda. "What is Elvin?"

"Elvin, I brought here. Where is Elvin?"

The creature was asking about the tiny, injured humanoid he had carried in at the height of the storm. Not knowing if the large creature would understand, she tried to explain: "I have put your little friend in a pediatric healing capsule. it isn't a human child, but its body make up is similar enough that it should mend its broken bones, realign its spine and nervous system and heal the injuries in the next hour."

"Elvin lives, then?" the creature ventured.

"Yes." said Jolinda. At that moment, a strange small shout from outside brought the giant to its feet. "Hunters! Lock door. Kill Forestman."

"What do you mean?" She asked him, "Kill Forestman?"

"Forestman," the creature pointed at his chest. "I am Sasquatch from mountains and forest. There!" It said for emphasis and made a broad sweep of its huge arm in the direction of the door. "Lock," it added.

"I did, during the storm," replied Jolinda.

"Not door. I got through."

Jolinda hadn't thought of it, but the giant had entered with the lockdown in full effect. She went to the reception desk and opened one of the drawers revealing an array of lights and switches. All but one light was on. There was a separate circuit for the main door. The surgeon's job didn't end with a lockdown. The main door to the medical facility remained open to let in the injured or frightened allowing the entrance of Forestman and the Elvin.

Through the transparent shutter on the window, Jolinda could see the storm clouds breaking up. The light, still subdued, was approaching to normal as the sun peaked through breaks in the clouds. She saw broken branches on the ground, sheets of metal lying around and a convertible top from a car and some dented bins from a distant street corner, but she could see no sign of Forestman's hunters.

"Good hide," said Forestman as he came and crouched down beside her to see through the window.

"I'll say they are good hiders," said Jolinda, who had no idea what she was looking for, "What are these hunters?"

"Elvin," said Forestman. Jolinda's tone was one of disbelief. "But you brought in an injured Elvin."

"They think I hurt, eat little Elvin. It hurt from fall. I had watched you. You only one here, but I know you a healer."

As the Forestman's story unfolded, Jolinda soon realized that the huge creature was a gentle giant. He told her that he had found the fallen Elvin, his name for the tiny human-like being on the ground. It might have fallen from a high tree branch or a large rock face, or possibly manhandled by another larger creature. Forestman knew only that the tiny being was hurt and needed medical help that lucky for the small one was not too far away.

Jolinda had no reason to doubt him. Why would he hurt the tiny creature, then bring it to the only surgery around with the only person around having the knowledge to provide medical aid? What sounded like a sharp rap on the door drew Jolinda's attention back to the present. Who else could be at the door? She stepped over and opened it. "No," shouted Forestman pulling her back from the doorway as a flash of silver streaked through the opening, barely missing her, and embedded itself in the wall behind the reception desk.

The Forestman had saved her life. With his free hand, Forestman pulled the door shut and slid a deadbolt into the locked position. There was another loud thump at the door; this time Jolinda recognized the sound. It was another silver arrow slamming into the door. It was the sound that brought Jolinda to the door earlier. For what it was worth, she now knew at least two silver arrows were stuck in the front door. She understood that if one had struck her, she would be unable to help herself and death from toxic shock would soon follow.

Despite being disconcerted by her close call, with the door shut and locked, Jolinda felt reasonably safe. She knew that the heavy stone exterior of the building with its reinforced and locked doors and thick transparent shutters presented a formidable defense against most threats. There was plenty of food and water inside and Jolinda knew they would be replicated as they were used. The entire facility was ready to handle even the longest siege. She, the elvin in the healing pod, Forestman and Mewser were secure from any number of silver arrow shooting hunters.

The issue was not about safety, but rather about why the elvin hunters were attacking the house. Did they not want their child to be healed? Jolinda knew this was not the case. She sensed they didn't understand what had happened to, mistaking Forestman for a predator. This would explain the arrows Jolinda had to remove from Forestman's arm, back, and thigh. Now they must think the surgery a hostile refuge for the giant and others of his kind. They either wanted their young one back or at least revenge. No doubt the elvin, as when hunting, were prepared to be patient and wait in hiding until they got inside. Jolinda knew nothing good would come from that.

There would be no opportunity for negotiation. Even attempting to speak through an open door would only lead to Jolinda, or Forestman being shot with deadly arrows. Their sole hope was the elvin in the healing pod.

Once the tiny patient was healed, it might explain to the other elvin what had really happened. How Forestman her carried her here to save her and how Jolinda had done that. That assumed that the elvin would be healed and understood what had happened to her. She could be confused or frightened and run out the door leaving Forestman and Jolinda still enemies.

Jolinda and her companions would have to wait for the healing pod to do its work. It was a difficult wait compounded by the jarring sight and sound of an arrow striking the transparent shutter every time they went near a window. They could now catch a glimpse of some hunters through the see-through shutters. There was at least twenty or twenty-five of them, most not much bigger than the one in the healing pod. They were all armed with small bows. Quivers hung on their shoulders containing a plentitude of silver arrows. Each hunter had arrow notched and ready to fire as they waited calmly for the opportunity.

One thing remained that concerned Jolinda. Would the little one understand when she explained their dilemma and pass the information safely on to its fellows? Jolinda would have plenty of time to worry about this, as the healing pod, while verging on miraculous, was not instantaneous. Until its work was done Jolinda, and her companions would have to sit through any assault, the elvin hunters might muster. It was not very comforting.

The elvin hunters were not prepared to make a mass assault on the building. They were smart enough and strategic enough to realize that an outright attack on such a formidable building would fail.

They had left their hiding places to stand confidently at the edge of the forest bordering the lawns and gardens of Jolinda's surgery and home. While their numbers didn't seem to change much, there was no telling how many remained in concealment. The elvin hunters on the forest edge were mainly male, the ones remaining in hiding were likely women with children. In truth, besides this group, there were no other bands of elvin within a thousand kilometers.

The well-equipped bowmen they could see were more than enough to make short work of anyone trying to leave the surgery. Their toxic arrows, one ready in each bow, stated that without question, there would be no truce and no appeal for truce from those inside the surgery. That would continue until the little one was out of the healing capsule, healthy and prepared to be their spokesman.

Jolinda took a look at Forestman and realized that she should examine him to be sure that he was free of the effects of the arrows. She helped him to an examination room. Even at full extension the examination table was dwarfed by the giant as he tried to lie down. When he rested his head on the pillow, Forestman's lower body was almost completely off the end.

Jolinda solved the problem by fastening together four examination tables brought in from other rooms. While the beds were bigger and better in the residence, they were awkward to move. The foursome of examination tables might be less comfortable, but at the moment were more practical. Forestman was a forest dweller just as his name indicated. He found the examination table more comfortable than his sleeping arrangements in the wilderness.

Jolinda removed two arrows she hadn't seen earlier and treated the last wounds with the wand and added a healing ointment. She gave him one more shot of the anti-toxin as he still seemed slightly dazed. They could do nothing now but wait. Jolinda sensed that the hunters knew they were in little danger from the forest giant or the other hiding in the building.

She could hear one or two climbing up to the roof searching for a way to get in. Jolinda, however, had the entire building in lockdown before the storm except the main entrance, and it was now locked, too. She knew the building and was confident the elvin would find no way in.

Staying away from the windows with the transparent shutters to avoid the nerve-shattering jolt as arrows struck them, Jolinda moved regularly between the elvin in the healing pod and Forestman as he lay in a semi-sleep state. Mewser, it seems, had joined him on the collection of treatment tables that was his bed and was sleeping comfortably in the crook of one huge elbow.

Time passed as the healing pod did its work. The elvin had stopped their search for any sort of entrance and left the roof. A still silence fell over the surgery. A cautious peek through shutters revealed several elvin sitting on the surgery steps while others lolled on the grass nearby. They looked relaxed, but Jolinda could see that their bows were close at hand, arrows ready. She could only see some the elvin hunters correctly assuming that the others were also keeping a relaxed but cautious watch on other entrances.

In the treatment room, a bell rang indicating the healing pod had done its work. "Like baking a cake," thought Jolinda as she made her way to the treatment room where the pediatric healing bubble encased the tiny elvin. "That's odd," she said to herself thinking of her strange comment. "I know what a cake is, and I understand the concept of baking, but from where did I get that strange analogy, "like baking a cake?" Shrugging her shoulders, she let the thought fade turning the power off on the pod and opening it.

A quick diagnostic scan showed that the physical damage was corrected and the small elvin should be as good as new. There was another analogy for Jolinda to think about, had she been aware. Jolinda saw that the tiny elvin was female and looked much younger than the hunters but appeared to be of the same species. Her only real view of the hunters was from peeking through the thick transparent window coverings more concerned about weaponry than physiology. The hunters' siege left little doubt of their kinship or why else would they be there?

A soft, feather-like downy natural coat, covered the elvin's body, but on her feet, she wore a pair of leather shoes that showed signs of skillful construction. The elvin were human-like in more than appearance.

It would be several moments before the patient would be fully awake and alert. Jolinda carried her to a small sofa in the reception area and lay her on the cushions. She then pulled up a chair to face her and observed with interest as the tiny creature made her way back to full consciousness. After a few moments, she became aware that the elvin was looking at her. There was no fear in the diminutive eyes, but some concern. Jolinda spoke gently to her, telling her that everything was all right. While the words may have held little meaning for the elvin, the tone was comforting, and the concern was replaced with a look of curiosity.

Sitting still in her chair, Jolinda watched the tiny elvin climb off the sofa to investigate the room. When the tiny girl began looking in the examination rooms, Jolinda got up and began to follow. She felt some trepidation as the elvin approached the room where Forestman was resting, Mewser still snuggled in the crook of an enormous elbow. Seeing Forestman, the elvin let out a small bird-like warble and ran to the giant. With a leap she was on the examination tables beside the giant. She began to caress the giant's forehead emitting a tiny warbling sound.

Forestman opened his huge brown eyes and looked at the tiny elvin. This brought a delighted warbling. The giant reached out a huge hand, dislodging Mewser who looked around in dismay, Mewser, seeing the elvin and meowed sleepily as Forestman touched the elvin's tiny cheek. The elvin grabbed his finger and returned the touch with her cheek. "Well," thought Jolinda, "the elvin outside may not be Forestman's friends, but this one is."

While Jolinda was charmed by the scene of affection there remained a far more serious issue to deal with. The building was surrounded by hostiles ready and willing to skewer with their toxic arrows the first person to set foot through the door. The sweet moment of interspecies affection that Jolinda was observing would be nothing more than a pathetic gesture unless the elvin outside could be encouraged to set down their bows and share in an interspecies peace.

She took a sideways glance through the window at the small but dangerous elvin. They appeared more fiercely confident and ready for action than when they first showed up.

Feeling a tug on her sleeve, Jolinda looked down into the earnest sky blue eyes of the tiny elvin. Up on a chair beside her, it twittered and warbled frantically to make itself understood. The bird-like sounds were incomprehensible to Jolinda. The elvin was trying hard to express something important. Jolinda could not grasp what it was. In frustration, the wee elvin jumped down to the floor to grab a loose fold of Jolinda's scrubs and tried to pull her. Looking down at the tiny creature, Jolinda saw only the elvin's angelic face in contrast to her dangerous-looking pointed teeth.

The elvin was trying to urge Jolinda toward the woodland giant who was now sitting up on the treatment tables. Still holding firmly to the leg of Jolinda's scrubs, the tiny elvin began to warble and twitter in the direction of Forestman. Jolinda noticed that the sounds were both calmer and far more carefully enunciated. She thought that she could almost detect words in the melodic chatter. Forestman, who had been watching and listening carefully, raised its head and looked at Jolinda. The elvin mirrored him. In the slow rasping speech that Forestman had used earlier, he said, "She wants door open. Let her out."

Jolinda was not eager to open any doors. With the door opened, the fierce little creatures could get in. Jolinda would be defenseless against them and although the giant might survive being struck with toxin-tipped arrows, she and Mewser would not. "She must speak with her clan," said Forestman, "and explain to them what has happened to her. This only hope for us as they stay, and we killed if try to leave."

Like a giant falling tree projected in reverse, Forestman rose to his feet. The elvin reached her arms up to the furry giant indicating that she wanted his hand. Bent nearly in half, Forestman put his hand down to her, and she grasped his baby finger in her hand. She waved her other hand at Jolinda showing her she wanted to do the same. Jolinda leaned over and the tiny elvin hand fitted into hers. The elvin led the two to the main door.

With trepidation, Jolinda drew back the deadbolt and switched off the electronic lock, unsealing the door. Taking the handle, she took a deep breath and pushed open the door but just a crack. Outside, beyond her seeing, the elvin bows raised and turned towards the door. At the doorway, the elvin, her voice far louder than Jolinda thought possible, began her birdsong.

When the tiny elvin finished speaking there were several moments of silence. It seemed an eternity before a response came from outside. At that, the tiny elvin, with all her strength, pushed the door wide enough to step out. Arrayed across the lawn, the elvin hunters did not lower their bows despite the entreaties of the little one at the door. A sharp, angry warble had the hunters stepping aside to open a space for an adult female to rushed past and up to the tiny refugee at the door. The adult pulled her into a relieved embrace.

After several tearful moments, the adult released her embrace, took a step back, and a musical conversation ensued. The adult turned to the hunters and spoke a sharp twittering sound. The elvin hunters hesitantly lowered their bows but did not unstring their arrows. The tiny elvin then pushed back through the door grabbed Forestman by his leg fur and urged him to join her outside. Forestman, offered no resistance. He picked her up in his giant hand and stepped out the door. The diminutive elvin had taken a relaxed pose in the arms of the giant. The hunters stepped back in surprise at the sight, raised their bows and drew back on the strings, arrows tensed and ready to fly. The young elvin warbled, stood up in Forestman's arms to offer herself as protection for the giant.

The female adult beside the young elvin, undoubtedly her mother, gave a sharp tweet, and the bows were loosened and lowered again. In a series of twitters and warbles some recognizable as earth standard, the young elvin explained what had happened. Watching the small elvin's hand gestures and the few discernable words of the bird-like speech of her recent patient's, Jolinda understood she was telling them what had brought her here.

She had been in a high tree when Forestman appeared out the woods. She changed position to watch the huge and unfamiliar creature as it passed, lost her balance and tumbled through the branches to the rugged ground below. She let out a cry of pain, and the giant turned, saw her distress, and rushed to her. She remained conscious long enough to know he examined her injuries then gently picked her up and cradled her in his huge arms.

The giant told her he would take her where they might get her some help. As the two set off for Jolinda's surgery, the injured elvin lost consciousness, With the tiny injured elvin cradled in his arms, Forestman ran toward the surgery hoping to reach it before the storm arrived.

Along the path he ran across several of the elvin hunters. They saw the elvin girl in the giant's arms and immediately assumed the worst. Not ones to wait around and analyze the situation, they turned their bows to follow the fast-moving giant, releasing their poison-tipped arrows at him.

Despite the toxin on the arrows, they didn't slow Forestman who stepped up his pace and ran with the elvin hunters in hot pursuit. The elvin in the giant's arms was unconscious and knew nothing of this. The elvin hunters followed the giant through the forest, doing their best to keep pace. Along the way, the toxins on the arrowheads began to work,

The giant, still holding tiny injured elvin began to slow. Even staggering, Forestman was moving at a speed the elvin hunters could not match. He stumbled through the fierce storm, hunched over to protect the little elvin. By the time he reached Jolinda's reception door, the toxic arrows were working on him. He grabbed the latch, opening it just as the lockdown procedure had completed. He pulled it shut behind him and slumped to the floor, still with a protective hold of the injured elvin.

Now cured. The elvin, seated proudly on the folded arms of the forest giant told what she could remember and what she could surmise. Then she proceeded to tell them how the person in the surgery had tried to save them both.

All the elvin, including the women and children came forward, joining the hunters to listen attentively to their young one's explanation. They saw she was unharmed and safe in the arms of the giant.

Her explanation complete, she jumped down from the giant's hand landing nimbly on her feet and stepped to the doorway signaling Jolinda to come out and join them. She explained in her bird-song voice that Jolinda was a healer and showed them some of the fading scars and nearly vanished bruises on her legs and arms. The signs of healing made it apparent that the injuries had been severe.

At that, the tiny one's mother stepped up to Forestman to warble her thanks and her regret at the misunderstanding. Then she turned to Jolinda and standing about waist high on Jolinda, she reached her arms as far as she could around her waist in a gesture that was a grateful hug.

One of the younger elvin hunter perhaps a little braver, or at least more curious than his fellows stepped to the door to look inside, with a squeak of fear, he tumbled backward, his bow raised, and an arrow notched as Mewser stepped out to see what was going on. The elvin girl stepped up to the hunter and put her hand on his bow arm pushing to lower it as Mewser stepped up to her and gave her a quick, rough lick that made her giggle. The friendly cat then turned to lick the curious hunter's face and he giggled too. With that, Mewser, her tail in the air, turned and went inside. This final gesture from Mewser caused all traces of tension to fade.

As the seasons passed, the elvin grew familiar with Jolinda, Forestman and particularly Mewser. Sometimes they came to get treatment for an injury and sometimes just to sit and visit, the little ones climbing all over a content Mewser. They would even bring other injured creatures, mainly birds and squirrels, for Jolinda to examine and to heal.

Some elvin liked to hang around the surgery, climb up on the desks and chairs, check out the examination rooms, chat with Forestman or play with Mewser. Forestman stayed on at the surgery proving to be a gentle and caring nurse and helper. Jolinda was no longer without company.

There was little time for loneliness as the elvin kept her busy treating them and the small animals they brought in. While the elvin were not human, their physiology was close enough that Jolinda could modify her medical devices and treatment to do the job.

Jolinda, Mewser, Forestman and the elvin became an industrious, happy community, and it wasn't long before Jolinda began to make sense of the bird-like speech of the elvin. It turned out to be an inflected Earth Standard, and she was soon able to converse fluently with them.

In spite of the pleasant life Jolinda had found with her friends, the cat, the woodland giant and the delightful and fascinating elvin, she still harbored a deep desire to meet other humans. This wouldn't change.

Had she been asked, however, Jolinda would have expressed contentment with her life. Over the seasons there were several fierce storms and a winter that was harder and longer than previous ones. During these times, Jolinda shared her surgery and home with Robin-Eyes the elvin she had first treated and her mother Moon-Feather. They became close companions and confidants. It led for a pretty satisfying existence for all.

The days moved on in succession each bringing something new or interesting for Jolinda. She began to understand the seasons, the cycle of life. She learned about the wide variety of medical technology that filled the clinic. Some of these medical tools were highly efficient and complex healing devices, and others almost useless.

The ills of the elvin although usually minor gave Jolinda plenty of opportunity to further explore and evaluate the many technical devices. While Jolinda was instantly knowledgeable about each device, they still required her delicate touch to function properly. While her inherent knowledge of devices was valuable in making correct choices for diagnostic and repair purposes, use and study served to refine her talent. She still needed to fine tune her knowledge of how best to work the devices. Just as successful chefs take recipes and adjust ingredients and measures, make it their own, Jolinda grew as a healer dealing with both illness and injury.

As a student of medical knowledge and physiology, Jolinda was intrigued by the ever-changing face of nature around her. As time passed, she noticed new and variant species and the ever-growing population of birds, animals, and insects. She encountered snakes and turtles, frogs and toads, rabbits and skunks. Many of them newly arrived in the area. She also noticed how they would disappear whenever Mewser went out.

She loved the changing seasons and what each brought, the trees and plants that graced the warm days with their greenery and floral bouquets, the crystalline scenes of winter, the changing colors of fall and the revitalization and new growth of spring. At night, she would look up at the stars, far different and far distant in many they appeared in the long past twenty-first century. She would chart the phases of the moon and wonder about the tiny bright motes of light that spread across its surface. She wondered if anyone lived on that distant globe.

She didn't know that those lights were from mining facilities, port towns and staging centers for interplanetary travel. This was the moon of the late twenty-fourth century. It was one of the countless temporal anomalies of Legacy Earth. Planets and planetary moons, even nearby solar systems had been reconstructed by the builders. This was knowledge for far off in the future. For now. Legacy Earth, virtually devoid of human life, was conundrum enough.

In her moments of relaxation, Jolinda enjoyed the ever-changing sky, the parades of clouds, the pastels hues of sunset and dawn. Her observations taught her to recognize nature's harbingers. She learned to anticipate the fierce storms that sometimes swept across the land, drenching it in rain, whipping it with destructive gale force winds, fiery lightning, and booming thunder.

An Eventful Storm

One morning with the traces of summer lingering, everyone was off pursuing their own interests. Forestman was with Robin-eyes and some of the other young elvin searching for edible berries and mushrooms. Mewser had found herself a corner to curl up in while the other elvin were either hunting, or busy mending and sewing their winter clothing. Jolinda had a few minutes to spare and sat in the garden doing what she loved, looking at the sky.

She sat there for some time before noticing a delicate shading to the sky off in the distance. It was faint as if something of enormous size had smudged crayon along the edge of the horizon darkening the sky. Jolinda knew from the prevailing wind the smudging would increase as it moved toward her, heralding a storm.

As she made her way back to the surgery, she could feel the wind pick up. She sensed that this would be more than a late summer thunderstorm. While still too early to determine the severity of the storm, it was coming fast and was bound to be rough.

It was likely to be a storm for which everyone needed to be prepared. Jolinda made her way to the elvin village in the forest near her surgery. At the village, few elvin were there to greet her. Most were off in the woods.

Jolinda was well aware that the elvin were capable of riding out a storm even as fierce as the coming one with its ferocious and dangerous winds. The best and safest shelter, however, was the stone edifice of the surgery.

Encountering Forestman on her way, she explained her concern about the storm. He hastened off to gather up Robin-eyes and her friends. At the village the elvin there were preparing for the coming storm. "Close up your homes," she told them, "and get over to the surgery."

By the time Jolinda got back and began to start the storm lockdown procedure, the elvin children and those from the village were inside, setting out baskets of food and bedrolls. Some of these violent storms lasted through the night.

Several of the hunters returning from the deep woods and finding the village deserted joined the others at the surgery. The darkened sky loomed as the wind picked up the loose leaves swirling them in eddies around the trees forcing the leaves to join in the furious dance. Most elvin were inside with Jolinda as the rain started. Forestman had yet to return. He was still out rounding up stragglers.

Jolinda shut the doors locking all but the main ones. She watched through the transparent shutters to watch for any late arrivals and Forestman. She waited, watching the storm grew in intensity. Outside, there was no one in sight. They were either already inside or hunkered down somewhere out of the storm. Since Forestman had yet to appear, she hoped that he had taken shelter to wait out the storm.

The booming thunder was near enough to shake the building, but the lightning flashes barely pierced the gloom. The rain fell in heavy sheets obscuring any hope of spotting a straggler or even one as large as Forestman through the window. The storm continued with no letup in its ferocity.

Tensions rose within the walls of the infirmary. Elvin gathered together to huddle close to the wall. Mewser meowed plaintively before jumping onto Jolinda's lap and demanding to be stroked. This was by far the worst storm Jolinda had seen, far worse than the one that first brought Forestman and Robin-eyes through her door. In no uncertain terms, the earth was proclaiming to all her vast natural power. The fury of the storm worried Jolinda. It worried her that Forestman, despite his size and strength, or anyone else was out in such dangerous conditions.

The ferocity of the storm did not let up. It seemed to increase in strength as the evening wore on. Little could be seen beyond the transparent shutter but for a few flashes of lightning that briefly penetrated the darkness and the unbroken sheets of rain. The building echoed to the sounds of the wind and the crashing of things being tossed around. The steady pounding of rain and the rumble of thunder created a nerve-wracking noise.

The storm was so intense, so filled with noise and clamber, that at first, no one could detect the pounding at the door above the battering of windborne objects. It took some time before a few elvin near the door realized it and informed Jolinda. Jolinda and some of the hunters made their way to the door. Several notched arrows. Silver arrows covering her from close behind, Jolinda, opened the door ever so slightly. She needed a firm hold on the handle as the wind fought to pull it from her grip. Looking into the seething maelstrom of wind and water, Jolinda glimpsed wet and bedraggled elvin surrounding an equally wet and bedraggled Forestman.

Forestman half carried, half dragged something larger than an elvin through the door into the interior. Jolinda shut and locked the door behind them. The limp, sodden thing Forestman had brought in, looked to a surprised Jolinda a lot like a human. This could prove to be the first human beside herself she had ever seen. She was certain enough of that to write down on the triage clipboard, "severely injured male, human."

A cursory inspection of exposed skin showed numerous tiny, festering and bloody pinholes in pairs about a centimeter apart. His body was, in fact, covered with them. It was as if someone stabbed him over and over with something sharp and two-pronged. The shallow punctures were plentiful near arteries that came close to the skin.

At first, Jolinda believed the human was beyond help, about to die from shock. His skin was cold to the touch and had a pronounced grey hue. She thought how ironic it was, her first meeting with another fellow human, would be a dead one. With the assumption he was likely dead, but hoping otherwise, Jolinda, with Forestman's help rolled him onto a stretcher and brought him to one of the treatment rooms.

The sound and fury of the storm disappeared as she focused on making a diagnosis. She searched for a pulse and found a faint one. He might still be alive. Jolinda's surgery helpers brought her the diagnostic tools she generally favored, and she scanned the body. The news the diagnostic tool gave was mixed. He was still alive, however, shock, extreme stress, and a severe blood loss suggested that without intense intervention death was imminent.

There was one device in the surgery she thought might help. It would replace his blood with a synthetic substance sustaining him until a match for his blood type could be found. Then the blood builders would kick in with gradual replacement of the synthetic with a biological copy of his original blood. With medication to reduce the effect of shock, it would still be touch and go.

The advanced technology that Jolinda needed to use would appear miraculous to a twenty-first century doctor. It still did not guarantee the survival of the patient. His own blood would need to be replenished since the only other human blood available was hers. She knew from many self-tests her blood type made her incompatible as a donor. That meant that she would be forced to use the synthetic blood during treatment. She could then try to use his own blood to generate more.

This was a huge challenge as the blood builder would be pushing its limits to replace it all of his. She was uncertain if it would produce the necessary amount of blood to support taking over his healing. It would take a great deal of time on blood treatment before the patient could handle his own life functions.

With Forestman's help Jolinda put him in adult healing pod similar to the one that cured Robin-eyes, only this one would have to include the blood treatment and blood builder functions. The devices for this were bulky enough that she could not close the pod. This would help her watch for signs of change, positive or negative. It also meant the healing pod would operate more slowly and perhaps not as well.

Jolinda knew a long wait would ensue before a visual determination of recovery could be made. Still, she would check on him frequently disappointed when she could see no change. She could only hope this wasn't a deathwatch.

Slow Recovery

The post-storm cleanup was extensive. Its rigors would provide a distraction for Jolinda and the others. Although the visits to the treatment room to check the patient's progress continued.

Cutting and piling, clearing the garden and wondering where the half canoe and other odds and ends she found might have come from did not give Jolinda much time to brood. There was little time for her to wonder about this fellow human, lying somewhere between life and death in a treatment room. Finally, a human had shown up on her doorstep after so many years of wondering if another even existed and he might well die without uttering a single word.

The cleanup finished, Jolinda could spend more time with her patient. She was disappointed to see so little progress in his condition. Synthetic blood had stabilized him, but there was still too little of patient's blood type produced to allow the healing transfusion.

Forestman or an elvin would spend some time sitting with the patient. The others would enter the room, stand around briefly and seeing no change, grow bored and leave.

Days passed with the patient clinging to life by a thread. The wounds began to heal, but the results of shock and exposure lingered on. The tiny wounds over his body suggested that whatever happened must have been horrifying.

It was well into winter when the transfusion process had begun. It proceeded slowly as it replaced the synthetic blood. Jolinda still worried about how well the healing was going. While the oxygen rich synthetic was in his system, a small respirator had worked to keep his lungs functioning smoothly. With this removed, was it even possible for the patient to resume breathing on his own? There was only one way to find out.

The transfusion complete, Jolinda removed the respirator. An audience had gathered to see what would happen. The patient began to breathe naturally causing a collective sigh of relief to pass through the observers. The patient's ability to breathe on his own meant the odds of recovery soared, He was still a long way from sitting up or even identifying himself.

Robin-eyes and her mother Moon-feather were excellent nurses. They soothed the patient with warm damp clothes, pressing them to his forehead and wiping his face when he felt cold. They changed his intravenous canisters in the drip pump and watched for any sign the patient's condition was improving. Eventually it would happen, and eventually it did. However, it was not as expected.

One moment the patient was lying near comatose. The next moment he was sitting up, a covering blanket fallen to his waist, his eyes wide with terror, shouting, "Wampyra! Wampyra!" Caregivers and curious alike raced into the treatment room. The patient, a look of sheer horror on his face tried to back away from those who coming near. The side of the healing pod prevented him from retreating too far and falling to the floor.

Jolinda tried to calm him. She reached out palms open to assure him all was well. He cringed from her touch, frantically scanning the room. Jolinda spoke in calm tones, reassuring him he was safe, and no one would hurt him. He kept muttering, first to himself, "Those terrible teeth. The teeth! They won't stop." Then in a loud voice as if issuing a warning, "Get garlic, get silver, get crossed shadows," He raised his hand placing one index finger perpendicular over the other, "They are coming. Don't let them in." He held up his fingers in a cross as if to hold the observers back. As he did this, he was looking intensely at Jolinda. "You're human!" he exclaimed, then added, "Close the doors. Do not invite them in."

The patient fell back in a faint. Jolinda could see he was still weak. His strange outburst aroused her curiosity. "What could he possibly be talking about?" she asked herself," What was the patient's frightened demands all about? Instead of asking where he was, he demanded they close doors against something they were not to invite in. And, what was that carry- on about silver, garlic and crosses?

She shooed the others from the room and went to him She lifted his head to fluff the pillow and pulled the cover back over him. The recent expression of fear and panic was replaced with a look of calm. The face was thin and tanned, with prominent cheekbones. His hair was longish and medium brown. Smile lines crinkled up from his mouth.

His features seemed pleasant despite the pallor. A permanent expression of concern hardened his otherwise soft features. Even so, the face suggested warmth and friendliness.

Later the patient again awoke but was far different from the terrified creature that surfaced earlier. He seemed sense he was safely among friends. He opened his eyes, a penetrating blue, "I'm sorry about earlier. I was confused." Before Jolinda could do anything more than smile, he continued, "What is this place? How did I get here? What are those creatures with you?"

Jolinda knew these were the initial questions. There would be many more to come. She was intent on putting him at ease and answered as honestly and concisely as she could: "This is a medical facility. I'm Jolinda and I awoke in a nearby city. Over time found my way here. I am a healer, and this is a surgery.

I've been here for many seasons living among those small creatures called elvin and my very large, gentle friend, Forestman. I chose this place because I have been gifted with considerable knowledge about medicine and medical technology. I identify myself as a medical practitioner, a healer due to the knowledge I seem to have regarding treatment of health problems. Since meeting up with the elvin I have had lots of opportunity to practice, but you are my first human patient. In fact, you are the first human I have ever seen

"Likewise," said the patient, we humans seem to be in limited supply around here. My name is Patah. You seem to have expertise on the physical side of things. I believe my knowledge focusses more on the human psyche and perhaps the soul. My only encounter with anything remotely intelligent, were the evil creatures calling themselves Wampyra.

They have followed me in large numbers for some time over a great distance and they are sure to continue to follow me. That means you are also in danger. You must beware of them, especially at night."

Patah: Psychological and spiritual analyst and counselor

A Flawed Legacy

U nlike the others, Patah didn't awake fully imbued with the knowledge needed to understand his place in the world. Like the others, he awoke with a full practical knowledge of the essentials of life, the awareness of the tools that would aid him, the names and some understanding of the creatures and the objects he would encounter. However, before he had awakened grown and resourceful as the others had, Patah had dreamed. He dreamed of the origins of Legacy Earth. He also dreamed of its source in the original earth as the evolving designers of Legacy Earth had perceived it.

Unknown to these evolved designers and builders of Legacy Earth, they had equipped Patah with a sensitivity that made him, even better than them at seeing the many flaws in their construct. Unlike them, Patah had a grasp of the reality of Legacy Earth that sensed the differences between fiction and fantasy. He awoke with a keen awareness of what was fantastical and what belonged.

In the future, He would attempt to set down a true representation of earth for himself and for its heirs. From its beginning, the reality that should belong and the fantastical that shouldn't both shared Legacy Earth. The builders hadn't seen the flaw in this, but Patah, somewhere deep in his subconscious, did. It took Patah some time to become fully conscious. The dream images still confused him.

As these faded, he became more aware of his immediate surroundings. It occurred to him that some unknown material wrapped his entire prone body. Although his breathing wasn't compromised, he felt a need to inhale a quantity of air that the gossamer biofilm that covered him would not, as it was, permit. He struggled to a sitting position tearing away the fragile material holding him down. Freeing one hand, he was able to reach up and rip the clinging material from his face.

He took a deep breath and felt energized. The memory of his dreams had slipped from his consciousness. They remained in his subconscious, and he was able to focus on his immediate surroundings and on the reality of himself. Looking around at the room in which he had awakened, Patah saw it was awash in deep rich shades of red and brown. Cherry wood bookshelves covered most of the almost maroon colored walls. Where they didn't cover the walls, classical style paintings did. A large desk and two ornate tables held an array of artifacts. They represented an eclectic interest in religious and secular themes. Along with the desk and chair, several other leather chairs and a large sofa furnished the room contrasting with the starkness of the narrow pallet on which he sat.

Among the many books and objects of art in the room, Patah recognized several technological devices with them. One tech device could contain the contents of all the books in the room along with thousands more. This was another post twenty-first-century piece of technology. The term computer was too archaic for it. It needed no screen but imparted textual content to the cerebral cortex. One could then visualize the content, or hear it or both, or just know it, depending on the wishes of the reader. Patah looked at it with suspicion as he did most of the devices he came across while surveying the room. He sensed that many of the devices would be helpful to someone suffering a kind of mental stress. To Patah's mind, they were too invasive, and the damage they wrought in a human psyche far outweighed any good they could do. Patah wasn't certain why he thought this way about them, but he was convinced some of those devices were dangerous.

At the moment, this didn't concern him much. What mattered was that after his recent awakening, he realized that he was hungry. He seemed to think bacon and eggs would fill the bill. He wasn't sure what that was, but he knew what he needed to whip it up, and he knew where he could find it. The eggs and bacon were in the fridge and the device he needed was a simple one, in fact, it was a primitive device called a skillet.

He had found another device where he could drop slices of bread into slots on the top and found a knife in drawer and butter in the fridge. With the knife, he removed the butter from its container and put some on the toasted bread. As he spread the interesting amber substance on the hot bread, he watched with curiosity as it liquefied and absorbed into the bread. The texture of the toast softened as this happened. A quick taste assured him that it was good.

As he was enjoying the tasty blend of liquefied butter and bread, the skillet beeped, telling him his bacon and eggs were ready. Patah wanted to sit at the table to eat it, but the skillet was hot and too heavy and awkward for him to bring to the table where he wished to sit. Patah found a dish and took a second knife and a fork from the utensil drawer where he also found a lifting device. With the lifter, he placed the bacon and eggs onto the plate and set it on the table.

While he was making, and buttering another two pieces of toast, he heard a different beeping from a cylindrical machine beside the toaster. At its base, he found a cup topped up with a warm, rich brownish colored liquid. Patah recognized this to be a Café au lait and as it turned out an important part of his complete breakfast. Patah delighted in the minutia his mind doled out, identifying and elaborating on what he termed, ""the breakfast ritual."

Soon enough, Patah would learn why all his wealth of knowledge, his psychological and spiritual guidance skills and his wary grasp of the technology available to him were all meaningless. The result of exploring the neighborhood where he had awakened, and its surroundings was the discovery that the human population in the entire area was him. What good was knowledge of the essence of human psychology and spirituality if there was no one with which to share it? The question was a central one and was never far from his thoughts as he explored his more distant surroundings.

Patah could see that the population of smaller creatures was increasing around him as his explorations took him farther and farther afield. He encountered many creatures but never another human. Patah learned what he could in his exploration, still feeling a deep longing to find fellow humans, Patah turned to books.

There were many books in his room and many more in the library next door. Many of the books, he discovered, much to his dismay, were fragmentary. Sometimes, he could fill in the blanks from his own knowledge. Some fictional stories were nearly complete. Except for some pleasurable moments reading parts of poems and some of the complete fiction, the books offered him little in the way of new knowledge.

Patah came across music players and video machines. The music appealed to him more than the videos, but their fragmentation and lack of continuity was disconcerting. He discovered a piano in a room and over time taught himself to play. Some of the sheet music, even the fragments inspired him, and, he found himself at the piano filling in many of the shorter gaps.

He observed the changing seasons and mostly was content with his life. His need for human fellowship overwhelmed him, and he decided he had to extend his explorations well beyond his place of awakening. He would explore his world. While his thought was to find humans like himself there, by the time he was prepared to leave his place of awakening he was willing to settle for any kind of living companion.

As he readied himself, he saw the world around him quickening with life. Animals that had been invisible to him leaving only their signs of passing, footprints in the snow, could now sometimes spot around him. He saw more and more varieties of birds and watched their population increase. Insects, rare at first, were now plentiful. Most were benign, some annoying.

None of the creatures he encountered offered companionship. When Patah was first exploring his town, he had come upon numerous vehicles and was able to operate every one of them. After much experimentation, he found that a bicycle offered him the best solution for traveling. With it he would cover much more ground than on foot. It could take him in and out of tight places, and he could stop a near to anything he might want to investigate close up.

Beginning the Quest

When he decided to be on his way in his quest for fellow humans, he started out with a bicycle, but that soon proved inadequate for the distances and terrain he hoped to travel. Despite the protection one would provide him from the ravages of inclement weather, he was uncomfortable with cars or trucks. He settled on a motorized vehicle that was bicycle-like. Futuristic for a twenty-first-century vehicle, it had handlebars and pedals and a wide enclosed box behind the seat for storage. The saddle was broader and more comfortable than a bike's.

The futuristic aspect was it had no wheels. Instead, it rode over rough or smooth terrain using anti-gravity propulsion. The storage area behind the operator had a large enough cargo space for Patah to pack those items that he was fond of and other things he might need including flashlights, several handguns and the fragmentary multi-faith Bible with its beautiful illustrations and elaborate typeface print. To these he added some useful tools and several sizes of knives Patah was finished packing and ready to leave.

He boarded the Anti-Grav bike and set off through the town to one road that he was certain would take him outside the city and into the unknown. He wasn't sure why he chose this route. It was a way that he had explored the least, yet it, above all the others, beckoned to him. This was, he believed, the way he should take to search for other humans.

As he went, he couldn't help marveling at the farms and country estates. They seemed so well kept but going up to them he could see that despite their readiness for human residents, they were uninhabited. That didn't surprise him. He had a good understanding of how things worked on Legacy Earth. There appeared to be a balance that something unknown to him maintained. If he used something, food, a log for the fireplace, he would find it replaced next time he looked, in the refrigerator or on the woodpile. Patah knew this served the equilibrium of the new world. He also knew that this was not a natural aspect of earth. He knew that this was a new earth, legacy earth a re-creation of something long gone. While he suspected that in the distant future, this all might change, it would not likely happen until a there was a large human population.

That was for Patah the big if, the 'if' that there was human population. He had his doubts this would happen because he had yet to encounter another living human. Patah felt a crushing fear that despite his intense desire for human company and his drive to find it that he might well remain alone his entire life.

The only encouragement that might mitigate this was Patah's observations of the growing populations among the various wildlife. They had been virtually non-existent when he first awoke, but over the many seasons he had spent in the same location, and now on his journey, he was encountering more varieties of creatures and greater numbers.

Most were tiny, but there were growing signs of larger animals. The horse and cattle appeared on the farms he now passed, their increasing population a vast change from his first encounter with farms and their empty fields. The population of the domestic creatures grew, but their numbers were nowhere near the animals in the wild. It suggested to Patah that domestic space was not to be used up by animal culture under whatever plan the earth constructors had.

Whoever they were and whatever amazing and godlike powers they had; the builders were clearly not gods. Their grasp of the planet earth in the early second millennium was far from perfect. Patah saw this in the fragmentary and incomplete books and videos. He also saw that there was a significant range of sophistication in the mechanical and technical devices he had encountered. They ran the gamut from simple and primitive to extremely sophisticated and complex high-tech.

In his mind, the builders were not quite clear on the time frame they were trying to recreate. He could see that what they lacked in knowledge of the specifics, they made up for in their grasp of the creative process, which is why they were constructors, not creators. His awareness of this and his place as a human within such a framework augmented his belief that at some point he would, at some point, encounter other humans.

This belief also caused him to become aware of the incongruities in this world. Little did he know, that soon enough, he would encounter the incongruous, something that would confirm for him that there was considerable incongruity and that it was a significant part of this newly constructed world, this legacy earth.

He had set out with a sense of hopefulness and nothing he had yet encountered changed that. That and the beauty and variety of his surroundings as he made his way down the road buoyed him. On his journey, he followed a multitude of roads, trails and paved highway that carried him through lovely little towns, larger communities and tiny remote settlements, all of which, while teaming with life, was devoid of any trace of a living human being.

As he went, he made himself at home in any number of residences. Depending what he found he would stay a day or spend a season. He read every book he could get his hands on and found some that seemed complete. He would add the best of these to his small but growing collection kept in the storage space of his Anti-Grav bike. Most, he left behind. He sampled television programs and computer websites that provided him with momentary glances at what the original twenty-first-century earth was like countless centuries past.

The novelty of the journey was wearing thin as he proceeded along the roads that called him. Passing uninhabited towns and villages, and the beautiful and varied landscapes along the way without having anyone to share it with subdued any charm it might have offered him. He had covered considerable distance since leaving the place of his first awakening. He doubted he could ever find his way back. It didn't much matter; he had no intention of turning back.

His route, it seemed, was laid out for him and there was only one direction to go. It helped him to decide which way to go at intersections and forks in the road. He sometimes wondered as he turned onto a different road if his decisions were random. While on one level that seemed to be the case, on another level, he wasn't quite sure given the certainty that seemed to accompany his decisions.

Throughout the long journey, he had seen very few living creatures other than birds. On rare occasions, a deer might cross his path. He caught sight of a couple of porcupines and a skunk, but nothing significant. From time to time he might hear something or catch a glimpse of something moving among the distant trees of a forest encroaching on the road he had taken.

These sightings were so few and scattered, he was uncertain if they were real or only imagined. Deep down, he suspected that larger creatures lived in the woodland and forest that he passed. Some of these were large, bigger than a porcupine or skunk and more lumbering than the fleet and graceful deer. He had decided that these creatures, whatever they might be, were neither human nor approachable. He made no attempt to investigate further but continued on his travels.

After countless days, his Anti-Grav bike began to slow, losing maneuverability and dragging along the ground forcing him to exchange it for another one he found in a shop on the edge of a small city. The shop was unlike any Patah had seen before. It was more a museum than store. The sales floor was huge and stocked full with a wide and impressive variety of two-wheel and two-wheel type transport.

He was especially intrigued by a distinctly unwieldy and hard to mount Penny Farthing bicycle that was lined up along with all the others. There were standard pedal-powered bicycles, bicycles with small gasoline and electric motors and several neurostatic electric powered bikes that stored and recycled their own energy. There were enormous three wheel bikes with gasoline engines, others with neurostatic electric motors powering those bikes to run forever. Finally, there were a series of Anti-Grav bikes, the largest of which, had a huge storage space and an automatic weather protection cap.

The roads Patah took were sometimes quite rough, and he knew that the Anti-Grav bike handled the bumpiest trail smoothly and quietly. What's more, the larger storage compartment could easily handle Patah's growing collection of books and other items and still having enough room to house many more future finds.

He switched on the glide control and walked his chosen bike out of the store and parked it beside his old one. He then began the slow and surprisingly lengthy process of transferring his collection into the new bike's large storage compartment. While it took far longer than Patah expected, his collection being much larger than he realized, there was still enough daylight left for Patah to decide to move on.

Leaving the store parking area, Patah began to weave his way through the city streets. In his mind, the journey had one purpose and one purpose only, and that was to continue the pursuit of any sign of living humanity. The route he took brought him to roads and highways that skirted the city. His justification for having followed that route was that he would find no humans in the middle of the city. Had he analyzed this thought carefully he might have questioned its credibility, but he didn't and cheerfully continued along the path he believed he had chosen.

Malls and shopping centers of various sizes and purposes, apartment type buildings, and what Patah recognized as private residences flanked the highways along the urban fringe. Turning onto a beltway that claimed to bypass the city, he could see that the buildings off to the sides were usually lower, more sprawling and the chain link fences that surrounded many of the held a variety of large trucks. It all had an industrial feel to it. After passing a number of such sites, he found himself back in the countryside, the city in his rearview mirror. The large suburban estates soon gave way to farms and forest.

Illusory Human

As the city fell farther behind leaving no trace, the shadows grew longer. The night was coming. He would need a place to stop soon and the paved two-lane highway he drove along had signs beside it promising a small community ahead where he would find a comfortable and interesting place to stay.

As he approached, he could see through the trees structures that had a gothic appearance. That appealed to Patah. Coming through a last small grove of trees, Patah came upon a small square with a large, steepled church that dominated its surrounds. Patah had stayed in church residences before and found them to be peaceful places. The Manse with its comfortable furniture and collection of books promised a few days of relaxation and intellectual stimulation.

The last traces of daylight were fading as he pulled into the square where the church stood. It was there that he saw a strange sight that excited and exhilarated him, but that also carried with it a curious sense of foreboding.

Ahead, on the edge of the square, a small, naked human looking creature appeared entangled with a much larger, furred animal. They together on the side of the road as Patah approached. At first, he thought the larger creature was attacking the human-like one. As he came closer, he could see that the larger creature was not moving while the human-like entity was, its face down against the large animal's neck. As Patah got near, the small one jumped up to look towards the oncoming vehicle, hissed loudly, turned and ran off at an incredible rate of speed.

Although the smaller, human-like creature had left at a speed that Patah could only call amazing, he was excited. The runner appeared more human than anything Patah had yet seen. The hasty departure had prevented him from being able to make a precise determination.

Climbing down from his bike, Patah could see that the still, dark figure of the larger beast with its dark matted fur was most likely a young bear. Although Patah had never seen a bear, it was included in that innate set of knowledge he had regarding so many things, including wild animals. Examining the body in the rapidly failing light, Patah could see a dark viscous substance near the neck where the smaller human-like being had buried its face. While that fluid was likely blood, it didn't concern Patah. It was that other creature that he was most interested in, the little runner.

Daylight was little more than a fading pink remnant of sunlight in the western sky, so Patah had no opportunity for an extensive search. And since the human-like creature had vanished without a trace, it was with some disappointment that he turned his thoughts towards getting somewhere to stay for the night. Being in front of a gothic looking church, Patah brought his bike to one of the two garages that connected to the Manse.

He opened the first door by putting in four zeros on a keypad beside it. Patah had learned much earlier that all keypads were set to 0000. He guided the bike inside and parked it. He entered the door into the Manse, his travel bag in hand. Upon entering, Patah could see that this Manse was particularly elegant and well appointed. He was, however, still far too excited about his brief sighting of what could very well be a fellow human to take in the splendor of his surroundings immediately.

It had taken several moments before he registered the elegance of the room, the velvet curtains on the windows and the dark, cherry wood sideboards and bookcases, the plush chairs and large, mahogany desk, the fireplace edged in rich flecked stone; the sofa facing it and the fur-like softness of the carpet, the soft enveloping shades of wood browns and deep maroons, so much like where he had first awakened, eventually soothed him, taking his mind off the small human-like being that he had seen earlier. He began doubt himself. Perhaps what he thought he had seen was an illusion, some other animal that momentarily seemed human. Still, he suspected it was more than that.

The day had been arduous, and he needed to rest. Checking the refrigerator in the kitchen a room away from the beautiful office sitting room, he found a bottle of claret. Corkscrew and glass in hand, he went to the sofa facing the fireplace. He found a book that looked interesting. He turned up the gas fireplace, sat down and poured himself a glass of claret. He began to read the book while the fire in the fireplace crackled and flickered. Patah began to shed the effects of the long and busy day finally come to an end.

Still ensconced on the sofa, Patah awoke to see morning light streaming in around the edge of the window curtains. Sitting on the end table near his head was the still nearly full bottle of claret, a half glass of the wine beside it. The book lay open on the floor. All evidence sleep had come quickly for Patah.

The sofa had proven as comfortable or more so than most of the beds he had slept in along the path of his journey. Well rested, he got up, stretched and proceeded with the morning routine that he had developed back in the place of his first awakening and had continued to follow as much as possible on his journey.

He did his morning ablutions, found a clean outfit in his bag and put it on. He then looked around for a washing machine and dryer to restore the clothing he had slept in. In his natural wariness, Patah preferred to sleep in his clothes to be prepared if there ever was a need for a hurried exit.

He went to the kitchen and prepared a breakfast that would restore him.

As he sat at breakfast, his thoughts turned to the human-like creature he had encountered the evening before. Last night's doubts were quickly discarded. The creature was real; its size suggesting that it might have been a human a human child. What it was doing on top of that bear-like animal puzzled Patah. Finding the child might answer that question, too. He knew it was out there somewhere. He would have to search.

Patah knew that a random search was not the route to take, so for the next number of days, he explored the town mapping and gaining insight into its layout. A careful review of the map helped Patah to determine the most likely places to search.

Despite the obvious speed of the small being as it ran from him, Patah felt that it would be relatively close to the church where he now was. He would plan out his search coordinates based on the types of buildings in the neighborhood and their level of accessibility. Each day he would go a bit farther searching each house and building for any sign of recent habitation. A considerable number of days passed without Patah finding any sign of any inhabitant from attic to cellar.

As his search narrowed down to the last few buildings, Patah began to feel that his sighting must have been nothing more than hallucination brought on by fatigue and wishful thinking. The bear-like animal had long past been buried leaving no real sign that either creature existed. Patah began to think that he might have dreamed it all especially after all this time when his memory of the incident had lost most of its clarity.

It would soon be time to continue his journey. He felt some disappointment as he prepared for his leaving. The Manse had been a comfortable home, and he would miss it, but there would be more such buildings as he made his way onward. While his certainty that he may have seen a human was now shrouded in doubt, his instinctive need to search out and find fellow humans was now stronger than ever.

In spite of his lack of success so far, Patah was even more convinced that a careful search procedure was more likely to have success than a random one. He decided the next sizeable town he got to would be the site to put his developing search theories to the test.

Less than a day separated him from the nearest significantly- sized town on his chosen path. Even more so than the previous town, the buildings in this one seemed older with a strong gothic feel. Seeking out a good place to live while he carried on his detailed investigation of the town, Patah came across the largest church that he had ever seen. It was even larger than those he had seen in the sizeable city where he had first awakened, ones he had thoroughly searched before setting out on his journey.

The residence, or manse, if it could be called that, was not attached to the church building. It was a small apartment complex separate but close beside it. Patah made a quick walk through and found several smaller, well-appointed apartments. Each contained bookcases flush with leather-covered books, plush furniture, with the wood brown and rich maroon and red colors that he especially liked. The books and other media were the same in every apartment.

There was a larger two-story apartment with bedrooms on the second floor. Down the wide circular stairway was a good-sized living room much like the previous house Patah had stayed in. Another room connected to it by a set of double doors. In that chamber, a massive bare-topped and dust free desk was placed in such a way that the person sitting in the luxurious chair behind it could view outside through the lead trimmed windows or into an attached sitting room with the slightest of head movement. Two well-appointed armchairs stood before the desk while a large bookcase and wet bar filled the wall behind it, well within reach of the chair. A beautiful dark wood door, leading into a small reception area held a smaller desk and an entranceway from the outside. The door stood open welcoming any visitor into its cozy environs.

The total effect appealed to Patah even the bathrooms and the functional stainless steel and marble of the kitchen. It would be an excellent place to serve as a home base from which he could conduct a thorough search of the town. It would be a lengthy trip from the churchyard as he could see from the upper story windows of the residence that the town was nearly big enough to qualify as a city. However long the search, the comfortable two- level apartment would suit him well. He brought his Anti-Grav bike around to one of the large garages at the back of the building and began to unpack the things he would need for an extended stay.

Systematic Search

Having learned some valuable and useful things in his systematic search through the previous town, Patah first sought out a municipal building like a city hall. There he would locate a map of the town that he hoped would itemize all the various buildings and even state their current purpose. The one he found in the city hall of this town was fairly complete. Patah could see that it would be very helpful to his search and brought it back to where he was staying. There, he could spread it out on the large desk and work on it at his leisure.

With the help of a pen and straight edge, he began to draw lines of division through it. Eventually, he had divided the map of the town up into quadrants. His plan was to take one quadrant at a time and study it thoroughly before moving on. After carefully surveying the first quadrant, he felt he would be able to establish enough of a timeline to judge approximately how long it would take him to intensely explore every place on the map.

He expected that it would take him a great deal of time to cover the entire town unless he was lucky and encountered humans, or some intelligent beings early on. An encouraging thought that Patah needed to put aside based on previous searches. It seemed unlikely he would find humans, or for that matter, any sapient being. Still, the search process alone would provide Patah with the opportunity to gain knowledge of this world as it was slowly being revealed to him. Each encounter, every novel object or experience, every object, as he saw it for the very first time, informed him of its function and processes.

Although Patah was aware that each bit of knowledge his search revealed was a first encounter for him, he couldn't help feeling that he was remembering. It was as if he had these encounters and made these discoveries at some time in the past. Despite the feelings of déjà vu each new discovery caused, he knew with certainty that each was for him, a first-time encounter.

Of one thing, he was certain, the more he knew about the world, the more he would know where to look for fellow humans. That was assuming there were any to find.

Patah could not shake the conviction that there were other human beings, and a large part of his destiny was to find them.

The first quadrant to investigate according to Patah's plan included his apartment, the neighboring cathedral, and the surrounding buildings. Most of the buildings in this quadrant shared similar architecture. This meant the search would be difficult. Like the residence, the cathedral contained an inordinate number of storerooms, confessional booths, alcoves and small chambers some holding shrines to particular saintly beings and some relatively empty except for a few chairs. Some smaller rooms could be found throughout the building from cellar to bell tower. Each had to be searched for hidden passages or any sign of human presence, past or current.

The neighboring buildings were as difficult to search as they all contained numerous closets, storage areas and other tiny rooms of vague purpose leading off from the main chambers.

Patah spent a great many days carefully searching every building within the initial quadrant. Having spent so much time, he was disappointed almost bordering on despair as he realized just how vast an amount of time, his search was going to take. Be that as it may, he knew that he could not give up and, happily, as he extended his search into other quadrants he became more efficient in his search technique. Not every house or every room required an intense level of search.

Seasons changed as the search stretched on. Patah was becoming disillusioned. He found no trace of a human or any creature larger than a rat, and there were precious few.

The building-to-building search continued and despite Patah's growing efficiency at it, the possibilities for concealment inside and out were plentiful. Patah returned to his apartment at the end of each long day, exhausted. His plans to spend his evenings embracing the warmth of human contact via books and fragments of video were all but forgotten in his fatigue.

He could barely finish eating before falling into bed. As his head hit the pillow, he was asleep remaining so until morning light awakened him to another day. His morning routines had shrunk to a few minutes' preparation, a cup of coffee and some small item of food taken from a refrigerator or pantry, and he was out the door on another endless quest to find any trace of humanity.

Within the boundaries of the quadrant, he was currently searching was a large mausoleum surrounded by well-groomed, but empty green space.

He began his search of the mausoleum with the clear understanding it would be a particularly long and arduous job. Looking through the chambers would take time not to mention the time spent opening the crypts. He was not terribly concerned about that. He expected to find them empty. They were certainly not appropriate for concealment, and no humanity, alive or dead had turned up at any time during his search. The likelihood this would change was slim to none.

The search plan, however, called for him to investigate the crypts. It was his plan, and he was determined to follow it faithfully.

Since the day was coming to an end, Patah decided that the crypts would wait until tomorrow and he made his way back to his residence, now some distance away through the empty streets.

That night he found himself aroused from a deep sleep by the sounds of giggling, a child-like laughter. Although he had never heard the sound of laughter adult or child other than on the occasional video, he still knew it to be childish laughter. At first, he thought the sound was a video player, but they had not been touched in a long time.

The sound was not coming from inside the apartment complex. It was coming from outside. looking toward the source of the noise, the window beside his bed, Patah saw children's faces, several of them, smiling at him through the window. Those faces looked almost human although two of them were upside down.

This was too bizarre, and he thought he was dreaming. Those grinning faces had a narrow, almost feral look. They were virtually identical to the face of the tiny naked creature he saw with the bear that and hissed at him before running away. Although a long time had passed, the faces in the window brought the distant memory back into sharp focus. Patah could not quite grasp what he was seeing. He wondered if he was dreaming he was awake and fantasizing about what obsessed him for so long?

The faces continued to linger at his window. Some he noticed moved away, and some changed places, but they grinned and giggled and looked straight at him. It was dawning on him that this was no dream. There were grinning giggling children at his bedroom window. Making this seem more peculiar the bedroom was on the second floor. The window was high above the ground, yet these grinning children seemed secure and able to move around with ease.

Patah went to the window. He wanted to speak to them. but before he could, his visitors disappeared. Opening the window, he saw no sign of them. "Come back, come back," he called.

A distant giggle was all he heard. He waited at the window until the first light of dawn began to edge its way up the sky. His visitors did not return.

Patah was too energized to return to sleep. He went to the kitchen and made a hearty breakfast. He hadn't done for a long time. He readied himself for a day of searching, now knowing there was something that looked human out there. He wanted to find them as quickly as possible. With this goal in mind, he set off much earlier than usual to begin his searching. By the time he reached the mausoleum, the sun had cleared the horizon.

Patah's renewed confidence didn't make his search of the mausoleum any less time consuming and tedious. Exploring the upper levels, including the crypts took most of the day. He was barely halfway through his search of the upper levels as the daylight began to fade. The upbeat feeling he had brought to his search that morning, had faded to disappointment as the day was ending. He had found nothing. It was especially upsetting that he had failed to find even the smallest sign of his visitors from the previous night.

Tired and disillusioned after his sleepless night and early morning, Patah made his way back home where he ate a quick supper. Pouring himself a drink from a bottle labeled 'single malt scotch,' he selected a book from among the few he had opened earlier. It was one that seemed nearly complete. a novel by a Stephen King called Salem's Lot. He doubted from the cover that it was a political treatise of some long-ago monarch; he began to read. Although there were some gaps, the story flowed quite well. The idea of soulless beings that survived by drinking the blood of humans fascinated and terrified him. He brought the book to his bedroom and set it on the night table. His plan to read some more while lying in bed ended the moment his head touched the pillow.

He slept for some time, only to be awakened once again by the giggling and the child-like faces gathered outside his bedroom window. Perhaps it was falling asleep to the imagery of Stephen King, or perhaps he was just more perceptive, but he saw something different. He saw that their grins did not necessarily indicate pleasure. It was now obvious to Patah the grins were propped up by the presence of two very large canine teeth. In fact, the two long sharp looking teeth, one on each side of the mouth, clearly dominated each of the grinning faces.

This troubled Patah. He was beginning to doubt that his visitors were human at all. Humans he had seen in pictures and videos didn't have the narrow faces with the huge sharp teeth poking out of their mouths. He had seen nothing quite like these creatures in any of the film segments or books and magazines he had looked through. The grinning faces seemed to him more dangerous, making him think of the blood-sucking creatures from Salem's Lot. He also knew from experience that humans could not cling to stone walls, balancing and moving around like a predatory insect.

This time, he did not venture to open the windows, but rather, pulled the curtains and somewhat nervously returned to his bed. He felt little inclined to sleep and for a while lay still, listening to the giggles and hissing from outside the window. Eventually, the sound stopped. The visitors must have gotten bored with no large human to contemplate and left. Welcoming the silence, Patah fell into a deep sleep.

The visitations continued for several nights. Patah was certainly curious about these nightly visitors but was uncertain about opening the windows to them. His innate knowledge provided enough information to make him wary and uncomfortable when they appeared. He now kept the curtains closed at night,

As a rule, Patah felt an aversion to weaponry but found himself a rifle and some ammunition for it in a nearby gun shop. He also picked up a few other items from a service station, a large wrench, a screwdriver, and some chains. He kept them beside his bed, close at hand to the window where the visitors seemed to exclusively gather.

Shortly after midnight, he heard a sharp knock coming from the outside of the reception area door. Throwing on a robe, he headed downstairs to see what was there. He quickly turned back into his bedroom and picked up the screwdriver and slipped it into a pocket of his robe.

The knock came again as Patah came down the stairs, through the office and over to the door. Looking out the small window beside the door, Patah was amazed to behold a small, nattily attired man. He was no more than one and a half meters tall. On his head, he had a black homburg causally canted against his right ear. Beneath his feral eyes and neatly trimmed Van Dyke, he displayed a colorful ascot on a white collared shirt over which he wore a flared Waistcoat. He had gray tweed slacks and very shiny black, high top boots. In his left hand, he held a silver walking stick with a pearl tip. Touching the tip of his hat with his right index finger, he smiled, revealing two long sharp teeth.

Patah sensed no warmth in that smile, but apart from the two sharp teeth like those of his nightly visitors, he sensed no threat from the diminutive and elegantly dressed creature on the doorstep. Patah pulled the doorway open enough to peer at his midnight visitor. "Good evening, good sir," the little man smiled a disturbing, but apparently sincere smile. "I am called the Count, and I have come to apologize for my children. It is my understanding that they have been disturbing your sleep. My children and I, you see, sir, are nocturnal. My children are drawn to you because they have never before encountered anyone like you, and they are enthralled by the sensation they get from your warm sweet blood.

I have ordered them to stay away, and, in exchange, I would ask you not to return to the mausoleum as it is in that building that we make our home. As I told you, we are nocturnal, and if in your rummaging around, you should expose one of my children to daylight, the consequences for the little one would be quite devastating. Now I must bid you good night." And he turned away.

"No, please," said Patah, "come in. You're the first human I have met. I have been looking for a very long time. Please come in."

The visitor turned back, a large smile on his face. Then, his eyes glanced past Patah and through the door to the large crucifix and Star of David hanging side by side on the wall. His eyes narrowed, and the smile vanished from his face, "Oh no, I cannot come in. In fact, I must leave this moment, but please no more in the mausoleum in the daylight hours. For my children's sake, I beg you."

Then he was gone. Patah stood at the doorway peering into the darkness unable to determine where the little man might have gone. It had happened so quickly. I was as if he had vanished before his eyes. Shutting the door Patah went to the office. He poured himself a drink, tossed it down and headed back to bed. He was bemused by the visit of the strange little man and wanted to immediately rush off and find him. Patah wished to continue the chat and ask the questions that filled his mind. As he lay on the bed, Patah was aware that like the small naked child in the last town, he would never find him.

The Wampyra was true to his word. There was no sign of grinning, giggling faces at the window that night. A little later, Patah fell asleep. He thought he was unable to sleep, but, was startled to find the sunlight coming through the window.

His sense of tossing and turning reflected his state of mind. He understood that some part of him was restless and disturbed and the strange little man was a big part of it.

Honoring the request of the little man, Patah decided to stop his search of the mausoleum, at least for now. Instead, he went to a large library that he had been through earlier. This time his search would be an intellectual one, a search for information and knowledge.

Patah had an innate grasp of how the library card catalog system worked, but the printed instructions above the electronic card catalog helped hasten the process. He began to look for anything he could find on nocturnal humans, "what did the Count call them, creatures of the night?"

The catalog was fairly complete, but the books he found were not very useful. Most had large gaps of information while others spoke of bats and toads and small furry creatures. Several days' search yielded nothing that explained the Count and his children. On the verge of despairing that he would ever find any usable information, he came across a book entitled, The Encyclopedia of Popular Culture, circa 2000, whatever that meant.

According to the Encyclopedia, the term 'creatures of the night' was often used in reference to fictional creatures called vampires, beings that had originally been human until bitten by a senior vampire or sire. Vampires were believed to be soulless and, for the most part, pure evil. They lived on the blood of humans, A few of their victims they turned into vampires like themselves, but most they drained their blood killing them.

These creatures were averse to sunlight. It could burn them to ash. A similar result could be achieved by driving a wooden stake through their heart. They were repelled by garlic and by religious icons and symbols such as a crucifix or holy water, a Star of David and others. Contact with such items could severely harm or outright kill vampires.

Vampires were also believed to have preternatural powers that allowed them to do things beyond the scope of mortals. They could run very fast, in some cases become bats and fly or climb up walls. Despite these powers, they could not enter a home unless invited in by someone with some authority within the house, a resident, family member or servant. Even when invited, the presence of religious symbols or exposed garlic would prevent them from gaining access.

The vampires of fiction were often shown as elegant and cultured beings the result of a long life span, and while generally portrayed as vicious and evil, fiction did indicate some exceptions. References to vampire or vampire-like creatures could be found in ancient folklore and numerous works of fiction.

Having read the novel Salem's Lot, Patah had some knowledge of these fictional beasts. The last thing the Encyclopedia pointed out was that vampires were fictional.

The Encyclopedia had illustrations showing images of fictional vampires. Some appeared quite human while others were more sinister with misshapen faces and fingers, large, pointed ears and huge, sharply pointed teeth. Most were pictured with large canine teeth used to puncture the skin over an artery, usually the jugular vein in the neck. Those razor sharp fangs would let them draw out and consume the blood.

Except for a small section on vampire bats, there was nothing else about vampires or sharp teethed small human-like beings. Patah knew for sure that these creatures, including the little man called the Count, were neither small, winged rodents nor fictional. As to their being evil and destructive Patah, as yet, was unable to draw any conclusions.

He did remember the Count telling him that his children were attracted to him because of his warm, sweet blood. On the other hand, the strange little man seemed quite pleasant and amenable, but his grinning, so-called children, looking at him through the window had made Patah uncomfortable.

Stephen King's chilling tale of vampires, Salem's Lot had intrigued him and in its own way, explained more to Patah than the Encyclopedia had. Most of Ann Rice's books were quite fragmentary although he saw glimpses of the richness of her imagery and description. Those books, along with most of the others were difficult to follow. Spared from his frenzied pattern search for a few days, Patah was able to relax and spend some time reading and checking out video versions of the stories he had selected.

Just as the Count had promised, Patah was no longer disturbed by grinning faces at his window or the sound of giggling in the night. As grateful as he was for the undisturbed sleep, he was concerned that these extraordinary beings might have utterly vanished from his life. Even if they were not human, they were similar enough to provide companionship. What was more, he might be able to learn from them about true fellow humans.

Despite what he had been able to learn about the children of the night, the vampires, Patah only knew two things for certain. Just as the little man had told him, they were creatures of the night and daylight was devastating to them. The other thing he felt sure of was that the naked ones, the ones the Count had called his children, could apparently scamper around on walls as easily as they could run along the ground. He understood nothing more about them.

Patah had seen no sign of the little beings during the day and was pretty certain that the Count was truthful in saying that they hid from the sun in the darkest reaches of the mausoleum. Relieved as he was that they were not gathered around his window giggling and hissing, he still wanted to see and learn more about them, to spend time with them. If they would no longer come to him, he would go to them.

Patah's plan was simple. He would return to the mausoleum after sunset, then wait to see if they appeared. Over the next few days, he planned out his nighttime journey. He walked the route a number of times committing it to heart. He wanted to be sure he could get there and back without the risk of getting injured or losing his way in the dark if he needed to move fast.

When the day came that he would put his plan into action, he gathered some useful supplies, several flashlights, a walking stick and a backpack to carry some foods and other offerings. With evening fading to darkness, he put his pack on his shoulders, gathered up what he needed. He picked up both a small crucifix and a Star of David as an afterthought, shoved them into his pocket and set out.

Initially, he had considered taking his Anti-Grav bike or another vehicle but decided it would be safer and less threatening for him to walk. Enough daylight remained to let him see his route quite well. The air was clear and warm enough for a comfortable walk

As he arrived at the mausoleum, traces of sunlight lingered, casting a scarlet and gold sheen. The entrance to the mausoleum glowed brilliantly in the fading colors of the sun as it slipped slowly below the horizon. Enveloped in this splendor, Patah entered the main gathering point of the gigantic building.

He set his backpack on a writing table, dragged it to the center of the room and pulled up a chair. He put out a bowl of chocolate covered nuts and mints, turned on a small lantern he had brought along and pulled a book from an inside pocket. While he waited, he read his book in the lamplight.

Feeling relaxed and engrossed in his reading, Patah didn't notice when the last vestiges of sunlight were extinguished. The change was a subtle one in the area where he was seated. The room did not go dark as the sunlight faded, but dozens of lamps around the walls and high above began to compensate, holding back the encroaching darkness.

What Sort of Creature?

"We are creatures of the night, but as you can see, not necessarily of the dark."

The voice came from right beside Patah giving him a start. Looking up from his book, he could see the strange little man standing at his side, "This may not be safe for you; my children will be awake soon and hungering for blood. They are numerous, and not always easily controlled."

"What sort of creature are you?" asked Patah

"We are called Wampyra. That is the name I have always known.

"You have many children?"

"Ah, you ask personal questions. No matter, I will answer. It will make little difference for you when my children arrive and be certain, they will. Your warm, sweet blood attracts them. My Fem is in the darkest, deepest part of the building. There she remains, and with me, we create our children. She will grow them in her womb as many as ten a day.

As they come into the world, I need to bite each one and share blood with them. If I don't, they quickly starve and die. They will then need fresh blood regularly to survive. Their nights are about hunting for blood. Some will become like

173

me. Some Fems may be born, too, but that is rare. Sires are as I am, and fems are special. The fems allow us to breed. We the Sires understand speech. We can read and speak Assianangle, a natural language of this world. We track the knowledge of who we are and how we survive and prosper."

As the Count finished his explanation, Patah felt a weight on his shoulder as a tiny Wampyra drove its large teeth into his jugular. Feeling his blood being drawn in by the creature, he tried to grab it and pull it off him. He was met momentarily with resistance then the Wampyra fell away from him and landed unmoving on the ground. The Wampyra sire bent down to pick it up as he did it shriveled into dust. "My child is dead. What horror is this!"

He reached out a sharp nailed finger and wiped it across the wound in Patah's neck, dabbing at the blood. He brought the droplet of Patah's blood to his mouth. His immediate reaction was a grimace, and he began to spit violently. "Your blood is poisonous!" he exclaimed.

"You must leave here now," his tone bitterly angry.

"I need to know more, "cried Patah.

"Leave," said the Count, "Get back to your home. Be gone from here by tomorrow if you value your life."

Patah persisted, "But the children, can I help?"

The Count raised his walking stick and pointed it at Patah, a sharp blade protruding from its end, "You are death to them, death to us. Go now before others come or I will kill you."

The Count jabbed his walking stick blade at Patah who had already grabbed his lantern and backpack, ducked away from the attack, got to his feet and ran. He made it to his home just as a horde of Wampyra converged on him.

Swinging his lantern wildly with one hand, he threw open the door and was inside. Before he could close the door, he could see a number of small naked creatures with wide toothy grins, pushing at the open doorway but unable to get any closer. He shut the door in their faces and went into the office area closing that door behind him as well.

The tiny Wampyra had been unable to enter despite the open door. There was another useful bit of knowledge he had gleaned supporting his reading. The Wampyra could not enter his home without an invitation.

In his bedroom, the window framed numerous grinning faces. To Patah, the term leering faces described them better. While Patah didn't think they would or even could break the window and force themselves inside, he wasn't certain.

He closed the curtains tight, but the rustling and hissing and the giggling that now sounded quite malevolent to him remained loud and disturbing. Remembering what he had read in the encyclopedia, he thought he might try something to send them off. Reaching into his jacket pocket, Patah pulled out the two religious icons that he had taken with him earlier. He opened the curtains and held out the crucifix and the Star of David towards the window, one in each hand. The Wampyra's reaction was remarkable. At the sight of the religious icons, they screeched, almost as if they were in pain, covered their eyes. Their fear was almost palpable as they disappeared from view.

Another piece of the lore he had read held true. Perhaps some others would as well. He set the two icons on the window ledge leaning against the window and closed the curtains again.

He sat on the edge of the bed, head in hand and reviewed the evening. His blood was fatal to the Wampyra. They would die from just the slightest taste. They could not enter a home without an invitation from someone who lived there. He thought, too, about the spiritual aspect of the lore he had read. Vampires were soulless creatures and without compunction were capable of great evil.

One of the avenues of knowledge that was inherent to Patah as he awoke was an understanding of the concepts related to human spirituality. It was not a path he spent much time pursuing except for some readings and one or two videos. It was very little for the vast amount of time passed since he first awoke. Now he was wondering about the soul. Did those creatures have souls or not? In fact, he wondered whether he had a soul. He didn't know how he got into this world, but it wasn't the way the human writers' books and makers of videos did.

With greater insight into his makers, he recognized that as powerful as they were, they were not creators. Rather, they were reconstructors. They lacked the infinite creative power required and could neither instill nor prevent the instilling of a soul.

Patah, in the study of his own mind, had recognized a deep longing that was more than a desire for human companionship. He felt more than that, the desire to do good for this world. Despite his weaknesses and failings, he wanted to make things better, truer. Perhaps that was proof of the existence of a soul. Patah was not sure.

All this introspection didn't answer the question about the Wampyras' soul. although, as far as he could tell, he was the only actual human, and it limited his basis for comparison to zero. How could he make any judgment regarding souls, or any other aspect of humanity, psychically or spiritually?

The knowledge Patah awoke with was heavily weighted toward fundamental humanity, its spirituality, and its psychology. He would have to assume that any humans he might encounter would fit under that umbrella. If not, his knowledge was superfluous and that would make no sense at all. He had to consider his innate knowledge to be genuine.

In that case, he could posit a soul for humans. As to the Wampyra, if they were soulless then they were in fact quite dangerous, something he had already learned. Even if only the rare sires had the intellectual capacity for thought and for speech, the others were under their complete direction. Unlike animals, then, they could not be seen as innocents. The response of the children to the religious icons could not be entirely instinctive. Without a soul, they could not be motivated in any way towards good, never rising beyond neutrality and likely directed towards evil. This would make Wampyra inimical towards humans.

While Patah was aware that he had no evidential proof, all the evidence he could muster suggested that the Wampyra, were, in many ways, very like the Vampires of fiction and legend and therefore, evil. Perhaps they weren't intrinsically evil but were so in support of their self-interest. It didn't matter why and so the Count had given him useful advice. Patah should leave as quickly as possible.

Patah realized that the Count's warning was nothing so altruistic as to protect Patah, but rather to protect his children from the fatal toxicity of Patah's blood. Any Wampyra sire would be prepared to kill Patah without hesitation to protect his offspring. Patah knew them to be dangerous creatures. His blood might kill them, but there were many ways that they could kill him, too, not the least being the blade in the Count's walking stick.

He was torn. Should he move on and never look back or stay to destroy as many of these dangerous creatures as possible before leaving? The Count, thinking that his children were about to drain Patah's blood and kill him, had told him that about ten offspring a day were being produced. This meant a dramatic increase in the Wampyra population over a very short time as new sires and fems would soon be adding even more to the total. Any human community that might exist would certainly be small and easily overcome by the vast numbers of Wampyra this particular hive alone could produce. His choice was clear, the Wampyra needed to be stopped, and he would have to do it.

Ending Evil

That morning, ax in hand, Patah made his way to the mausoleum. He opened all the curtains and all the doors. Sunlight filled every part of the mausoleum as he opened up skylights. He then searched the lower levels but turned up nothing. They were too well hidden. In anger, he drove his ax into the wall. As the crack in the wall that his ax had made opened the space behind it to daylight, he heard a terrified screech. One of the Count's children was hiding back there, could there be more?

Patah began hammering away at the wall with his ax opening the space behind it to daylight. He could see dozens of small Wampyra through the breaks he had made in the wall and watched as the sunlight touched their small naked bodies. Where the sunlight touched them, smoke began to rise. They began rapidly to shrivel. Within moments, nothing remained but a fine ash where the Wampyra had been. He opened a number of walls and destroyed some more Wampyra, but the space behind most of the walls was empty. Patah knew if he wished to destroy all the Wampyra, this was not the way. It was time to move on.

Going back to his apartment, Patah quickly packed his accumulated belongings into the Anti-Grav bike. He gathered up as many religious icons he could find and attached them various places around the vehicle. By late afternoon he was ready to move on.

He boarded the bike and followed a route through the town that would bring him near the mausoleum. As he passed by it, he noticed some heavy machinery in a service area across the road. He parked his bike and climbed aboard a bulldozer. It took a few minutes, but he figured out how to operate it.

He drove it into the central reception area of the mausoleum and began to smash the walls with its large plow blade. Having opened up most of the walls, killing a few more Wampyra, he could see that the room was filled with debris. Using the bulldozer, he pushed it all against one wall. Leaving the machine against the pile of rubble, he made his way back to the service center. He had noticed a large tanker truck parked beside the gas pumps.

He took a moment to climb up and open one of the vents. The tank was filled with gasoline. He knew what he had to do. He started the truck and drove it over to the mausoleum, following the route he had taken with the bulldozer. He ran it up against the pile of rubble he had set up earlier, then got out and opened all the covers. Gas began to leak onto the floor spreading towards the pile of rubble and the bulldozer. Patah went to the cab of the truck and looked behind the driver's seat for an emergency kit. He opened it and took out a flare.

Walking back to the rear of the truck where gasoline was spilling to the floor, he ignited the flare, threw it into the puddle, then ran as quickly as he could away from the gas bursting into flame. He made it out the door just as a loud whoosh came from inside.

Never looking back, he ran to the anti-grav bike and was back into the street and accelerated out of there as fast as he could. He was a long distance away when he heard a loud rumble and the sound of an explosion. Still not looking back, he passed the edge of the town and continued into the countryside.

By then it was growing dark. The sun was about to set, so Patah pulled into one of the larger houses along the road, put the bike into an attached garage and entered the house. He climbed to the second story and looked out the window back toward the town. As the sky darkened, he could see through the trees a flickering glow. Fire was consuming the mausoleum and most likely some of the surrounding buildings. Knowing what he had done did not sit well with Patah. He could not clear his head of doubt. Everything he had done flew in the face of what he wanted to believe. He lamented the destruction and surprisingly, felt bad for the Wampyra, but he had made what he believed was the right decision.

Before going to bed, he surrounded himself with religious icons to keep the Wampyra at bay, but he neither saw nor heard any sign of the diminutive monsters. He slept with a sense of safety for the first time in days comforted by the belief that vengeful Wampyra had no idea where he was.

Patah, however, was an innocent regarding evil.

The Chase

A very limited number of Wampyra had escaped the fiery destruction of the mausoleum. The old Count and his fem were dead, but among the survivors, there was a new Count and fem. The new Count, sharing the knowledge of the old one determined that the human perpetrator of the destruction of so many of the children must pay. The new Count, despite the toxicity of Patah's blood, had made an extreme but true generalization about human blood. Any humans, should he encounter any other than the one who had destroyed so many of his brothers and sisters, would likely share his toxic blood. This made humans the enemy. Patah would have to die.

To this end, after relocating and beginning to rebuild the hive, the new Count sent out several groups of his children to find Patah. Should any one of the groups find even faint traces of the odor of Patah's blood, they were to track him down and kill him. The Count did not tell them that in carrying out this order, they too would die.

It took a considerable length of time for one of the groups to find Patah, but it did. While it was long enough that Patah lost some of his wariness, it was not long enough for him to totally forget. The Wampyra, for their part, were hindered by the daylight and the fact that Patah usually found a place to stay before nightfall. They were also held back by the religious icons he kept with him, the ones on his bike, the ones he set in the windows of whatever room he slept in and the Star of David that he kept on a chain around his neck. The Wampyra waited until one evening when Patah was a little late in finding a place to spend the night. On the road, some distance from any secure housing, Patah stopped briefly, dismounted the bike and moved off to relieve himself. The chain around his neck that held the Star of David got tangled in a branch, and instead of untangling it as he would have earlier along his journey, he removed it from his neck. He would retrieve it on his way back to the bike.

This is exactly what the Wampyra were waiting for. Having seen that he had removed the repellant icon from his neck, they could see that where he was, he had no icons to hold them back. They scrambled down from the trees where they were hiding and leaped on Patah.

Patah cried out in pain as he felt numerous teeth biting into his flesh. The first arrivals bit at his exposed flesh; some arriving moments later proceeded to bite right through the clothing. The frenzy was so intense that the other attackers failed to see the first of their kind dropping off to the ground. They did not see their fellows' bodies shriveling into ash even as it happened to them.

Bleeding from hundreds of tiny wounds, Patah began to run. He headed into the bush in hopes that the branches would prevent the Wampyra from getting to him. They scrambled through the branches of the trees, close above, but unable to get to him in mass. Those that in pairs or individually were able to get to him and bite quickly fell away and crumbled to dust. If the others noticed what was happening to their fellows, they were too intent on catching up to Patah, to react.

As he ran, Patah grabbed at and struck and tried to pull off his assailants. Pain and the loss of blood began to slow him. He tripped over a fallen log and dropped in a heap to the ground. The few remaining Wampyra climbed over his body biting to draw his warm sweet but unbeknownst to them instantly fatal blood into their rudimentary bloodstream and enormous single vaulted heart. Their moment of triumph was fleeting as the instant the blood touched their teeth and lips, they began to shrivel up, and their drying bodies turn to a fine powder that the gentle breeze carried off leaving no sign that they had ever been.

With all his assailants gone without the slightest trace beyond leaving multiple blood tinged wounds covering most of his body, Patah staggered to his feet and tried to run. All he could muster was a slow trot, and that quite quickly deteriorated into a staggering walk. Overwhelmed by the pain of a thousand tiny wounds Patah pressed on as droplets of blood mixed with the anticoagulant in the Wampyras' saliva continued to flow. He had no idea how far he had gone into the bush when overcome with the loss of blood; he fell into a swoon after which, he neither saw, nor heard, nor indeed, remembered anything.

He didn't hear the laughter of the elvin and their giant companion as they made their way past with the baskets of berries they had picked from the grove beside the nearby stream. Some were still gathered there, not far from where Patah lay unmoving and unfeeling.

He didn't hear the young elvin screaming in mock terror as they raced to Jolinda's surgery before the storm struck. He didn't hear the storm or feel the rain, neither did he feel the screeching gusts of wind nor the things that ran before it, hurtling against his body. As the storm raged around him, he lay on the verge of death impervious to the roiling tempest. He didn't feel himself being picked up by the giant creature and carried gently along the path towards the medical center just beyond the trees. He didn't feel himself being examined or being put into the healing module and being attached to the blood exchanger where he would remain for a considerable time as the machine tried to regenerate his blood supply and heal the thousands of minuscule bites that covered his body.

As he hung on the edge of death's abyss, feeling nothing. Deep in his mind, where conscious thought could not penetrate, he kept repeating to himself, "What a waste. What a waste. I am dying without ever serving, or even knowing the purpose I was put here."

What that purpose might be, Patah's tiny spark of mind could not imagine.

As his consciousness slowly began to return, he was back in the terror of the Wampyra attack. Poorly focused grinning faces surrounded him and made him believe that he was in some kind of hell, a hell framed in abject horror. Then came the clearer images of the Wampyra. He could see those ghastly mouths with their razor-sharp teeth rushing towards him. They were so totally present for him that he had to warn everyone.

He did not know who they were, but he yelled at them, trying to warn them about the Wampyra, to tell them that those killers were everywhere. Then his fear seemed to fade as he returned to full consciousness and saw a face that he immediately recognized as human. Beyond that face, he could see several more faces, diminutive like the Wampyra children, but without the horrific grin. In their eyes, he could see concern. It took him a moment to realize that those to faces belonged to small creatures that appeared to be seated comfortably on the folded arms of a gigantic furry creature that shared their look of concern on its massive visage. Momentarily, he felt that he had fallen back into an unconscious fantasy, but he held his eyes open, and the creatures did not waver or change or disappear. It slowly dawned on him that he really saw what he thought he saw. He had found another human and those others who, unlike the Wampyra showed no malevolence towards him. Still weak, but more content than he ever remembered feeling, he fell back to sleep.

As Patah's health improved and strength returned, he participated more in his newfound community, built around the health facility and the human physician who ran it. His fears about the Wampyra began to fade over time.

He knew that his attackers were now nothing but dust blowing in the wind and the Count confident that his children had carried out his orders would expect none to return. While the numbers of the Count's children were again swelling, it would be a very long time before they would make their way to where Patah, Jolinda, and their little community lived, and by then, there would be no one there.

Having found Jolinda, Patah quickly realized that his quest for fellow humans was not finished. Although no words were ever spoken between Patah and Jolinda, they both felt the need to seek out more humans. They knew for certain that they would not find them where they were. As had happened to Patah earlier on, they began to sense the call of the journey ahead of them.

Only Patah's gratefulness and Jolinda's obligation to the community held them there, but they both knew that in a not so far off future, they would have to take up the quest again.

Shanira: Architect, Engineer, Builder and Artist

The first thing Shanira was aware of, was brilliant light. The second thing she became aware of was she was completely covered and held down by something. After a moment of panic, she realized that as she moved, the covering was tearing. She pushed herself to a sitting position, pulling the delicate clinging biofabric away from her face and opened her eyes.

She immediately saw the light she had first noticed was coming through two large sheets of glass that from her perspective, were the windows to the outside. She sensed it was natural light meaning it was daytime.

She pushed and shifted around, ripping much of the biofabric away until she was able to twist her body to the side until she was sitting on the edge of the pallet she had been lying on when she first awoke. Her feet were touching the floor, so she instinctively stood up and surveyed the room. She really didn't take in much on her first look around, focusing, instead on a closed door close by. Stepping over, she opened the door and looked in. She saw a small room with several cubicles and a large, body length mirror confronting her. She stepped up to the mirror and scanned the image before her. She right away recognized the image looking back at her was the reflection of herself. She could see she was human female, and everything was where it belonged on a healthy, young adult of that gender.

Leaving the mirror, she turned to one of the cubicles and stepped into it. She was immediately enveloped by a fragrant, soothing moist cloud. Slow and undulating, it caressed her from head to toe. The enveloping cloud lingered beyond that for a moment then thinned and vanished leaving her feeling clean and energized.

Quitting the cubicle and looking around the small room, she could see, hanging from a peg on the wall what she recognized as a one piece uniform. She knew it was the uniform of something called the Builders' Guild and it was there for her. "must be a member," she thought, taking it from the peg and putting it on. She stretched her arms through the sleeves and her feet through the leggings and into soft comfortable boots. She felt comfortably embraced by the uniform as her fingers examined the belt hanging around her hips and the strangely familiar items attached to it.

It struck her it was not only the tools seeming oddly paradoxical, but also everything in her surroundings. She knew with absolute certainty she was seeing all this for the very first time, yet it all seemed so familiar.

She tried to make sense of it but couldn't, so she let it go and took another look at her image in the mirror. She liked what she saw, a fit young woman in her prime. The only age she could attach to the image was her conviction it was 0 years and a very few minutes. This did not quite jibe with the level of maturation and development of her reflected self, but there you had it. It was the way she had arrived in this world and as far as she could tell, everything was as it should be. She had taken all this in with just a brief glance.

Stepping back into the larger room, Shanira went over to the expanse of window and looked out. A floor below she could see a quite massive, cobbled courtyard that dominated the scene close to the building she was in. It had fountains and gardens, tables with seats for chess and checkers, park benches, a magazine kiosk, and a snack bar with a number of chairs and tables around it. Beyond she could see walls, windows and entrances and further beyond, distant towers. They all indicated buildings very similar to the one from which she was making her observations. This view was the herald of a very large metropolis.

With a short time spent at the window and a scan around the room, Shanira realized that she knew this building better than she knew her own hand. It was as if she had designed and built these buildings herself. This was especially good at this moment as she experienced the pangs of hunger. Without knowing how, she knew right below her room on the ground level, there was a first class Deli where she could get a good meal. Without hesitation, Shanira headed down to it. She was sure the elevators were working just fine, which they were, but she had decided she would rather take the stairs. The sense of movement was exhilarating and taking the stairs was a pleasure.

When she got to the main floor and saw the Deli, she congratulated herself on her perspicacity. The Deli doors were open, but the Deli, itself was deserted. There were no customers and no staff, but the air was filled with delicious scents, fresh coffee, bacon, and toast, to mention the most prominent. Shanira knew exactly what to do. She got herself a cup and filled it with warm brown brew from a coffee dispenser. She helped herself to a muffin and a plate of bacon and eggs that offered themselves to her coming out of something called a Bakenator as she passed it.

There was everything she needed for a very pleasant meal except company for her to share it with. Although she felt deeply she would like human company and, at some point, seek it out, she was too excited by her surroundings. She wanted to explore.

Her breakfast complete, she returned to her room. Searching through the shelves of tools, she found several portable devices no twenty-first century construction boss or engineer would recognize. One she could hold in the palm of her hand measured the strength and density of stone or metal, or even a combination of both. Another measured height and depth of any standing structure, man-made or natural just by pointing at it. A third gauged the flexibility of construction materials such as steel, concrete and super plastics. These were the favorite materials of the builders of this city. They were Shanira's favorite building materials, too, but she had a soft spot for natural wood. At that particular moment, she wasn't sure what wood actually was and what she like about it was something of a mystery to her.

The bulk of her questions and her curiosity would, to a large extent, be satisfied during her many exploratory journeys within the city boundaries. At this point, however, she was about to embark on her very first exploration of the part of the world in which she had awakened.

Setting out for her first investigations proved an interesting dichotomy for her. On the one hand, she was familiar with the style, design and materials in the buildings, sidewalks and streets at which she looked. On the other hand, everything was new to her, beyond novelty because it was, in fact, the very first time she had laid eyes on any of it. She might have intimate knowledge of the construction materials and techniques used, but she also knew with certainty she had never seen or worked using these materials and techniques ever. Despite all that, she knew and understood anything constructed of brick and mortar, concrete, steel, superplastic and every kind of building material. She knew how to construct buildings, bridges even the boats lined the nearby river were as familiar to Shanira as if she personally had built them. Yet, from the moment she had left her room, every vista she encountered, every sight she beheld on turning a corner was new to her. Many seasons would pass before these disparate sensations would begin to resolve themselves.

She delighted in exploring the city checking out the internal and external structures of the various buildings. She read blueprints and sketches comparing them to the finished products. She enjoyed the courtyards and the city squares and was enthralled by the architecturally diverse buildings she came across. Her favorite places, however, were the large steel, superplastic and concrete bridges and she especially loved the boats in all their various sizes and compositions lining the river's banks from where it began to widen to where it opened out onto the vast body of water edging one side of the city.

Shanira was completely satisfied she could design the bridges and even build some like the smaller ones with her own hands using the construction equipment she had discovered among the warehouses lining the wharfs and piers along the water's edge. She had disassembled and re assembled many of the cars and trucks but found them less interesting than the boats.

The seasons passed and she came to know every girder, every slab, every door and window and the surface and deep structures of the buildings in the city. She constructed a few small bridges spanning the narrower parts of the river with bits and pieces of building material she had found. While she did this, she would take breaks to walk the decks of the boats and ships moored along the riverbank. An idea began to germinate in the back of her mind. She would build a boat, a fast, high-powered machine with lots of cozy living space. Eventually she realized this was exactly what she wanted to do. Thus, began the long and arduous task of gathering the materials and finding the appropriate dry dock on which to build it. With block and tackle, mobile cranes and flatbed trucks, Shanira was able to find and accumulate the materials she would need to build her boat, one to outshine any found along the river or moored at docks and the pleasure craft marina.

The completed boat could have been called a speedboat or a cruiser, or even a luxury yacht, because it was something of each. I was beautiful and tantalizingly comfortable, far nicer than the building in which she had awakened. Mooring it just were the river began to broaden into the city harbor, Shanira gathered her things from her first home and brought everything there and the boat became her new residence. Using it as her base, she continued to explore the city until the day she realized that the city as a source for her explorations was pretty well exhausted. She had learned everything the city had to offer about architecture and construction. Shanira began to feel restless. She had grown more conscious of the fact she was alone. The feelings of loneliness informed her she needed companionship, someone, perhaps some other humans with which she could share her interests and experiences.

It occurred to her she had the means to pursue such a search, was in fact, living on it. As she thought about it, the course she should take became clearer.

She began to gather the things she would need for a long nautical journey into the unknown. She was well aware this journey would carry her far from the city of her awakening and perhaps for a time far from land. She became quite excited about the possibility somewhere out there she might find companions, or at least find other cities where she might discover new and different building designs and materials.

They morning of her planned departure was bright, the sun rising leisurely into a cloudless sky. Anxious to be on her way, she started up the cosmic ion generators, a power source far more sophisticated than anything to be found in the twenty-first century and cast off from shore. Except for the complaints of some startled gulls and the soft churning sound of the twin propellers, in nautical terms, screws, there was nothing to break the near silence of the morning. As she left the river behind, she added throttle until the boat was quickly enroute, leaving the land, and the city behind.

With the prow sliced through the water with a liquid slapping sound, Shanira turned and took one long look back at the city, her home for all of her life. It rapidly began to shrink and fade in the mist thrown up from the water by the powerful cosmic ion engines. She didn't linger in her backward gaze. Shanira knew where she had been and now it was time to see where she was going.

With the wide-open throttle pressing her forward, the shoreline began to shrink and vanish into the mist as evening approached. With darkness on its way, Shanira turned on the radar and sonar that would warn her as they approached a landmass or island or came near shoals or shallows. She engaged auto cruise and slid the pilot's chair back into a more restful position. The motion over the water and the gentle hum of the cosmic ion engines were relaxing and very shortly Shanira fell asleep.

While Shanira slept, the radar and sonar searched for obstacles on the waterway that might affect the cruiser's path and the auto-cruise was prepared to steer it clear of them. As it was, there was no need, the body of water, whether lake or sea, was wide and clear of islands and shoals.

When Shanira finally awoke, the morning sun was rising, and clouds of mist hung over the water. She could see no sign of land in any direction. A look at the radar screen confirmed she was far from any shore.

As the day brightened, the mist burned off leaving an unobstructed view of open water on every horizon. Shanira reveled in the warmth of the sunshine and in the incredible sense of freedom she had with just her boat and the wide expanse of water. She enjoyed this for several hours, moving with no apparent destination in mind. Then, as the day wore on, she began to think about what she should do. The subconscious mandate to seek out fellow humans surfaced and sent her to the auto-cruise to insert a set of co-ordinates. For some mysterious reason, she felt certain it was the direction she should take, although she had no idea where it would lead her.

For much of the remaining day, there was no sign of change in her solitude. She continued on, just her in her boat and the endless sky and water. As the afternoon stretched on, she thought she could see a dark line on the horizon ahead of her. By early evening the dark line had thickened. Eventually it began to resolve itself into a rocky wall of dark forested terrain, rising higher and more distinct as she approached.

With the last of the light from the setting sun, Shanira was able to find a sheltered inlet. Surrounded by the silence of the dark woods, she could hear the wavelets from her wake slapping against the shore a short distance away. She shut down the cosmic ion engines and dropped anchor.

Down in the sleeping compartment, she was rocked to sleep to the roll of the waves and their tap, tap, tapping against the hull.

She slept without fear or worry just as she had back in the city. While here there was nothing to threaten here, there would soon come a time when she would not be able to sleep so confidently without setting a boarding alarm and having a weapon close at hand. Although she didn't yet know it, her calm and peaceful world was about to change. For now, however, she was able to sleep unconcerned and undisturbed.

Morning brought a heavy overcast and a fine, misty rain. Shanira opened the canopy over the bridge. Looking out at her surroundings, she found the visibility so poor she could hardly make out the shoreline despite the fact she wasn't anchored very far off. It made sense for her to stay where she was until the visibility improved enough so she could see where she was going, especially so close to land.

Shanira and her boat were encased in a pea soup fog for three long days. The first day passed reasonably quickly, but the second day seemed to crawl. The contentment she first felt tinkering around the stranded boat was she found, by the second day, tinged with a feeling of restlessness. Something, whatever it was had her input the coordinates she did into the auto-cruise seemed to be urging her to be on her way. There was no doubt she would have been off if the fog or rain lifted for even a few moments, and as the boat rolled over some substantial swells she knew outside the small bay, the waves could prove to be quite dangerous so close to land. Anxious to be underway, Shanira still realized she needed to wait until the fog cleared and the waves died down for her to proceed. She remained at anchor for the rest of the day and all of the next.

Shanira used the time to scan the paper copies onboard maps which were produced and printed out from the time she had set out. Unfortunately, they stopped generating when the boat stopped at anchor. They were quite limited in scope as most of them reflected nothing but the wide expanse of open water she had travelled. That part of the map made it look as if she had dropped right off the face of the world. The most recent edge of the print out revealed nothing more than the dark and rugged shoreline where the forest bordered it. There was little to be learned from it.

On the fourth day, the fog began to lift. The rain stopped and the rolling swells in the inlet where the boat was anchored began to subside suggesting the onshore wind had dropped and the waters beyond the protective inlet had calmed.

Shanira folded the canopy and put it away. She sat down in the pilot's chair and fired up the cosmic ion generators. She pressed the button to automatically raise the anchor. There was a brief struggle as the anchor fought to free itself from the jagged rocks flooring the bottom of the inlet. The boat under Shanira's hand began to slowly ease its way out towards open water.

Despite the clearing fog with the sun threatening to breakthrough, the forest girdling the inlet continued to look dark, deep and ominous. Shanira didn't look back as she steered toward open water.

Once past the rocky shoreline at the mouth of the inlet and into open water, Shanira reengaged to auto-cruise. She soon found herself running toward the rising sun just far enough from shore to avoid the huge blocks of rock breaking the surface. For much of the day, she headed in the same direction, open water to her left, rocky, forested shore to her right.

Around midafternoon, Shanira began to detect a change in her surroundings. The shore was less rocky, and water bound weeds peaked through the shallows. They became more numerous until Shanira found herself travelling along a weed-lined stream. Soundings informed her that although the bottom had risen significantly, the stream was more than deep enough to allow her boat safe passage.

Shanira began to worry she might run out of navigable water. She could see no break in the shore far off to her right or to the abundance of seaweed rising above the water level to her left and in front. As she proceeded, her surrounds took on the appearance of swamp, with clumps of earth covered in wild masses of greenery beginning to encroach. The stream she was following through all this remained a constant depth. By evening, the surroundings were quite marshy. Shanira decided while she still had some room beneath, she would drop anchor and wait for daylight to continue.

As she drifted off to sleep enveloped in the dark silence of the night, at the limits of her hearing she thought she had sensed screaming. The sound was so faint as to barely be audible. Shanira thought she must have been hearing the faint buzz of insects or other small creatures among the weeds calling softly to each other. As she surrendered to sleep, her thoughts were not of tiny creatures but of something larger, more human, screaming in terror and pain. Before these thoughts could really resolve themselves, Shanira was asleep.

With dawn and the light of a new day, the clear air revealed a swampy islet filled area almost as far as the eye could see. Forested strands of larger landmasses were tiny dark strokes on the far edge of the swamps in both directions. A clear, deep stream ran like a shining silver snake between the encroaching weeds and hummocks. In this stream about four of Shanira's boat spans across, Shanira's cruiser, still resting at anchor had stretched the anchor line as far as it could as if eager to set off up the stream on which she rode. Since there was no telling where the current pulling at the boat would lead it, Shanira raised anchor and set the controls to low, just enough to maintain rudder control if needed and let the current carry her forward. Used to racing across open water, this process was painfully slow, Shanira could sense she was headed in what felt to be the right direction.

Shanira kept a close watch on the boat's progress. She could certainly not afford to run aground as she was alone and without the assistance she would need to get free. Her careful focus on the depth of the stream so held her attention, she nearly missed the dark shape drifting in the water some distance ahead of her. When she did spot it, she thought it might be a rock. As she approached, however, the stream depth remained constant, and the bottom remained flat and smooth.

The closer she got to it, she was able to see whatever it was, was drifting. It was clear it wasn't a rock, but it might be a log. She wasn't close enough as yet to make out any details.

Eventually she could see it was not a log or part of a tree. She wondered if it might be some large, drowned animal. When she finally came up beside it, she could see it was quite large, at least as long as she was tall. When she reached out with a gaff to turn it, she was amazed to see a human looking upper body attached to a fishlike flank and tail. Leaning over the side to get a better look, she could see an oddly human looking head and face. She had to get this thing aboard for a closer look.

With the help of a pair of motorized pulleys, a lanyard and the lid from one of the storage bins, she was able to bring the body alongside and lift it aboard. There could be no doubt, it was not human, but the upper body and head were human enough. The eyes were wide, the nose flat and the teeth small and pointed. The cheeks and neck on each side, just below the small, human like ears, were wide to allow for a set of gill slits. The skin was not skin but made up of small pinkish scales leading down to the transition where they began to enlarge and darken. The lower body was very similar to a fish. Human arms with sharp fins along their sides reached down to large hands with webbed fingers.

Shanira could see deep gashes on its shoulder and neck. The external breathing organ on its left side was quite seriously injured. She gently rolled it over to examine it further and saw on its back five deep gashes in the flesh as if five sharp, rough blades had been dragged across it. Whatever had made these injuries had considerable strength.

Rolling it over further, she could see the breathing organ on the right side seemed intact. Right then, the fishman's eyes began to flutter and there was a sharp intake of breath through its nose. The creature began to thrash around trying to get its arms under its body and use them to pick himself off the deck.

It was trying to sit up on its own, so Shanira helped it to a sitting position. It stared at her with terror filled eyes as it raised its good arm in a protective gesture. It was as if the creature was defending itself against an expected blow. As Shanira watched, his large eyes glaze over with a transparent layer and begin to close and the large head slumped forward.

Shanira held it so it would not fall back against the gunwale and add more injury. The huge eyes opened slowly to gaze at her. There was a look of surprise on the face and the creature seemed confused. Clearly, Shanira's gentle support was something far different than what the fishman expected. The broad wide-eyed face continued to hold it gaze until it began to cough. It's back and shoulders continued to bleed. Using some boxes and life jackets within reach, Shanira was able to support the creature in a partial sitting position. She slipped over to the pilot's chair and began rummaging underneath the seat for the first aid kit fastened in place there. Releasing it, she carried it over to the wounded fishman. She was hoping the medications within the kit, while made for humans would work on a fishman.

She liberally spread the pain killing and healing ointments over the wounds on the creature's back and shoulder. She applied poultices to the wounds and taped them down.

As the blood staunched, the painkiller in the ointment took effect and the fishman visibly relaxed. It began to lift itself up but was far too weak to do so. Shanira put her hand on the unwounded shoulder to stop his efforts. He didn't resist.

Shanira had not had a lot of opportunity to talk in her solitary state, but now there was someone to talk to. Not certain if the creature would understand her, she spoke with carefully enunciated clarity; "Don't move too much. Give the medication time to work."

She had no idea what had prompted her to say this in Assianangle, but it was apparently the right choice. The fishman visibly became calmer. Quiet except for the occasional snort of breath through its nose, the fishman, sat braced against the inner hull as the medications begun their work. As the pain became more bearable, its eyes grew clearer and more focused. He made no sound as he watched intently as Shanira travelled the deck, checking the radar and sonar output screens and examining the surroundings with a pair of binoculars. Every few minutes she would come back to look at the fishman, checking his bandages. No word was passed between them at these times.

As the day stretched into afternoon and the heat of the day, on one of Shanira's inspection of the wound coverings, the fishman spoke. Its voice was soft and strained. It was a small voice for such a large creature. All it said in clear Assianangle was, "I need water."

Shanira went down to the galley and brought up a large glass of water. He reached out and took it carefully, but instead of drinking it, he poured it on his lower body.

Looking up at her, his eyes now much brighter showed clear intelligence." I need much more water," he said in a soft clear voice, "My skin will dry and crack."

Shanira understood. She opened one of the deck holds and took out a bailing pump. Tossing the end of the draw hose over the side into the water, she began pumping a fine spray over the fishman's body. After a few minutes of being wet down, the fishman raised his hand to signal her to stop, which she did.

The fishman looked up at her and nodded his head slightly to express his thanks. He spoke again, his tone crisper and stronger," What manner of being are you. You have appendages to move on land as do the Hoblins, ye you have shown yourself not to be as cruel as they are."

He gasped for breath. Being a mainly aquatic creature, and being out of water, he was relying on limited lung capacity to both draw breath and speak.

"I am a human being," said Shanira, "and perhaps the only one. I have come from my place of awakening in search of others like myself. I am following a route which seems as if it was laid out for me, and it has brought me here. Who or what are you?"

Over the next few hours with several waterings and many pauses to draw breath, Shanira learned a great deal about this strange creature and his people. They called themselves the Marefolk and they had lived in the shallows of the nearby islands since time began. Although the water was their home and they were capable of travelling great distances in its depths, they preferred the shallows where they could hold their upper bodies above the water communicating verbally with their fellows and breathing through their human like lungs. They had lived peacefully this way for many generations until disruptions in the earth lifted some parts of the bottom close to and some above the surface of the water. Land and plant islands replaced the shallows in some places. This swampy land extended for a great distance. No one knew how far. It was some time later the first Hoblins appeared. A few of these creatures had wandered out onto the marshy surface where the shallows had been.

The Marefolk welcomed them, offering foods they had gathered from the depths. At first there were only a few of these skeletally thin, fuzzy grey creatures with their long clawed hands and feet designed to dig into the marshy terrain to gather food. They were peaceful enough, rarely interacting with the Marefolk until large numbers of them began to gather on the marshes near the Marefolk's homes. Then, with no apparent provocation, they began to attack the Marefolk, killing them and dragging their bodies deep into the marshland to be consumed.

The Marefolk tried to fight back, but their natural gentle nature prevented them from matching the brutality of their enemy. The Marefolk had moved deeper into the shallows away from the marshes, but sometimes families of Marefolk forgot, came to near the marshes and were attacked and killed. Sometimes groups of Hoblins on rough rafts would invade the shallows brutally attacking the Marefolk clawing and beating them with cudgels and carrying off whatever they could. In many cases the victims carried off were the Marefolk young.

One of these attacks by raft born Hoblins had happened the previous night. The Mareman Shanira had pulled from the water had been fighting to protect his family. He had pulled a Hoblin into the water, which apparently was one of their greatest fears and was holding it down when another Hoblin slashed him with his claws while clubbing him with the cudgel it used to pole its raft.

Trying to escape with his life. The Mareman, who called himself Thunder-fin had dove down, striking his head quite badly on the pebbled bottom. In a daze, he kept swimming unaware he was moving away from the conflict. Weakened from loss of blood and other injuries, he passed out and rose to the surface where he floated, unconscious until Shanira found him.

Shanira told him she would return him to his people. After Shanira reviewed with him the seriousness of his injuries, he reluctantly agreed it should be after sunrise when the threat of the Hoblins had passed. This would be the time to find his fellow survivors. Thunder-fin would approach first in case the others perceived Shanira as an enemy and either attacked or ran away. He could then explain to them Shanira was a friend and no danger to them.

Concerned Thunder-fin would have difficulty on the boat overnight, Shanira asked if he would be able to survive without going back into the water. He responded by asking her to show him how the water spray worked. She showed him and left it with him. He told her now, he would be fine on the boat. Satisfied, Shanira went off to sleep.

The sounds of night were peaceful. The humming of insects, the soft cries of small nocturnal animals, and the rustle of the wind through the reeds merged with the distant sound of waves slapping against a far off shore. Sleep came quickly.

The sun came up a blur of brightness cutting through the mist. Only a small part of the stream and the weeds and marshy hummocks marking its edge could be seen from the cruiser's main deck. Beyond, everything was obscured within a veil of grey. It was an inauspicious morning to go searching for the battle scarred remains of a Marefolk community. Perhaps if the sun's struggle to break through and cast off the fog succeeded, they could set out then.

On inspection, Thunder-fin's wounds were healing rapidly. He had stopped needing the bailing pump due to the fine mist beginning shortly after midnight and slept well. This allowed his remarkable natural capacity for healing to kick in.

When Shanira expressed her concern about moving forward through the still thick fog, Thunder-fin explained the deep stream was the one constant among the islands, shallows and marsh. It extended, a virtually straight path, a long distance before reaching open waters several days away. Although he had travelled much of the stream, he had only made his way to those open waters once, many years before. He did remember seeing some manmade structures where the stream widened, but he could not remember seeing anyone or anything living there.

Judging from what little he recognized from Shanira's cruiser, he had, apparently swam a long way from his Marefolk communal area before passing out and drifting towards where Shanira found him. Having been wounded and delirious, he had no idea how far he had gone since leaving the battle.

Since it was still quite foggy and the visibility significantly limited, Shanira would have to proceed slowly and cautiously. It might take a considerable amount of time to reach the site of Thunder-fin's home.

While Shanira had breakfast, Thunder-fin nibbled at some dried fish and a few pieces of prepared meats. Shanira could not be sure if was the strangeness of the food or his discomfort and anxiety curtailing his appetite. When she asked him, Thunder-fin told her the dried fish tasted quite good, and the prepared meats although having and odd taste, were fine. He just wasn't very hungry. Shanira immediately realized Thunder-fin was very anxious to get home and see who had survived the encounter with the Hoblins.

Shanira redressed his wounds and they set off under minimum power. The cosmic engines as content to go at a snail's pace as they were to jet across the water, purred softly as they went. Between the slowness and the limited visibility, the trip was frustratingly uncomfortable. As the time passed, Thunder-fin grew more agitated. Shanira could see despite the speed at which his wounds were healing, they were still bothering him. Despite an earlier application of pain killing lotion, Shanira could see his anxiety was as much a part of his discomfort as was his concern over what he would find as they got near his home.

Thunder-fin's worry was almost palpable and Shanira was acutely aware of the thoughts dogging him. Had the

Hoblins killed or carried off all of his fellows? If there were survivors would any of his family members be among them?

The mist began to clear as the made their way down stream. With the improving visibility, Shanira who had been focusing intently on the stream just beyond the bow, could now relax as the vista began to open up.

A short distance ahead, Shanira could see a dark shape drifting in the water among the nearby weeds. Had the visibility not improved, it was likely she would have gone past, never seeing it. She brought the boat closer to the edge of the weeds for a better look. She helped Thunder-fin change position so he could see as well. It wasn't enough for him. He insisted he had to go into the water to learn exactly what the dark shape floating among the weeds actually was.

Realizing there would be no talking the Mareman out of this, Shanira dropped anchor and covered the worst of his wounds with waterproof dressings and helped ease him over the side. She watched him slip through the water with a wonderful grace and ease despite his injuries, He went around the shape several times then began to tow it back to the boat by a tiny belt of shells fastened around her waist.

From her perspective at the rear of the boat, she could see it was indeed one of the Marefolk and a female. When Thunder-fin brought the body up against the transom she could see wounds around the gills were quite severe and blood discolored her light hair. If the Maremaid was not already dead, rolling her aboard over the back of the transom with Thunder-fin pushing and Shanira pulling could very well kill her. There really was no choice. She would certainly die if left in the water.

Shanira was very grateful for the fact when she opened the first aid kit, every time, the medications and bandages were replenished. She medicated and dressed the wounds to the gill and the blood seeping swelling on her head. She lay her down on her back on the deck then reached to help Thunder-fin make his slow and painful climb back on board. The female was much smaller then Thunder-fin and he explained to Shanira she was an adolescent and a long way from full maturity.

Thunder-fin did not recognize her indicating to Shanira the Marefolk colony in the area might be significantly larger than she expected. Thunder-fin explained how recently some families from distant communities downstream had fled to the Hoblins and sought refuge with his community She might belong to one of those groups, but he couldn't be sure. He had spent most of his time recently away from the community watching out for Hoblins and had just been relieved and returned home the day of the Hoblin attacked.

The Maremaid was comatose, but breathing weakly, with her lungs. As the fog and mist withdrew, Shanira set up the bailing pump, so it sprayed a continuous fine spray on both the female and on Thunder-fin.

As they continued along the stream they began to hear in the distance a soft keening. "This is my community." Thunder-fin whispered, "They are mourning the lost and the dead."

Shanira had seen no sign of any Marefolk when Thunder-fin told her to stop. "They are close by," he explained," but are probably hiding from your boat. I will find them and tell them you are our friend. Perhaps I can find someone who knows the girl, too."

Shanira dropped anchor, shut down the engines, and helped Thunder-Fin over the transom and watched him slip down into the water. She was still quite concerned for him. Although his wounds seemed to be healing quickly, he had other injuries and would certainly need more time to mend. She could see Thunder-fin as he slipped his head under water, her eyes following him as he became an undulating blur headed off into the weeds. The youthful female on the deck groaned but did not open her eyes.

After an excruciating wait seeming much longer than it was, Shanira saw several dark shapes moving through the water among the weeds. They were coming in her direction. She took one of the flare guns from an emergency storage hold. While she knew when putting it there, it would be of little use in bringing assistance in a world without any humans should something happen to the boat. It could serve as a useful weapon should she have a need.

She hoped one of those dark shapes would be Thunder-fin. The moment the thought crossed her mind, Thunder-fin's head broke water. Three others followed. "I have told the community about you, but they are afraid. I returned with those who were willing to trust me. I've have brought my father and my brother and a recent arrival to our community, a father whose daughter has been missing since the conflict. He had chosen to come, despite his fear when Thunder-fin described the injured female. His daughter who seemed to fit the description, had disappeared sometime during the Hoblin attack. His mission was one of hope. As they pulled themselves aboard with the help of a rope ladder, Shanira had connected to the transom and the rear portion of the right the gunwale, she could see they all bore evidence of battle, though none not as extensive as Thunder-fin or the unconscious female.

The father of the missing daughter immediately recognized the comatose female was the one he sought. He saw her injuries and began to keen, "Oh my lovely. Oh, lost to me."

Shanira stopped him right away. "She still lives," she told him.

Still, they both knew the wounds were severe. If they could only find a medical clinic soon.

She expressed her concerns to Thunder-fin, mentioning the medical clinic. On hearing this, the father of the injured Maremaid spoke up. He told her of a number of buildings on what he termed the hard land near the streams distant end. It would take a journey of several days, but if among those buildings there was a medical clinic, Shanira felt she knew enough about the technology she might find there she had a chance to restore Thunder-fin and the girl to near perfect health.

Perhaps then others who had been injured would trust her enough they would come to let her heal them so they would be able to fight the Hoblins the next time they came.

She explained this to the Marefolk on board who agreed it was the only way they could prove to the rest of the Marefolk Shanira wanted to help them. Shanira hauled up the anchor, fired up the cosmic ion engines applied the throttle. The cruiser was soon racing along the clear stream between the weedy shallows and the marsh. Several times Shanira thought she caught a glimpse of a face rising from the water, but the high speed craft shot forward so fast it kept her from confirming she had made some sightings of less frightened Marefolk.

With the spray rising over the canopy, there was no risk of her guests' skin drying out. In fact, she could see Thunder-fin and his father and brother were quite enjoying the ride. The young Maremaid's father stayed close to his daughter. Occasionally he touched the bandages covering her shoulders and gills or gently caressed her hair at the edge of the bandage on her head wound.

The guidance system allowed them to maintain a good speed through the night. They were making much better time than the Marefolk had made on their way to find refuge with Thunder-fin's community. By midafternoon of the second day, the steam was visibly widening and pushed the marshland and the shallows farther and farther to the side.

Breaking out into open water, Shanira could see off to starboard a small town with several piers stretching out into the water. Several sailing craft rocked gently against their tethers. Shanira could see the town and it harbor were protected by a high rocky arm stretching out into the water serving as a shield against the vast open water beyond. With consummate skill, Shanira guided the boat to the nearest dock.

Tying up, she went to find a vehicle with which she could carry the water bound Maremaid to a clinic, assuming she found one. If one did exist, it would likely be fairly close to where she had docked her boat.

She hadn't gone too far when she found a flatbed truck and moments later had backed it onto the dock. The wounded Maremaid, still unconscious was strapped to the same large bin cover Shanira had used to bring Thunder-fin aboard when she first found him.

The Marefolk were able to use their powerful arms and strong lower body to climb onto the dock then pass the unconscious Marefolk girl hand to hand and place her aboard the flat bed. Before the rest of the Marefolk climbed up with her, Thunder-fin and his brother used bailing pumps to spray water over her and soak the flatbed. There was enough moisture there to keep them comfortable for some time.

As Shanira pulled slowly off the dock, Thunder-fin informed her through the open rear window there was a heavy disgusting odor of Hoblin present. Shanira could smell a fetid odor pervading the surroundings. Even as she drove away from the dock, the odor persisted. The disgusting odor was everywhere.

It was still daylight and according to the Marefolk, the Hoblins preferred the darkness of night to be about, but still Shanira and the Marefolk would have to be careful in case any were around.

Fortunately, the truck had a quiet engine and assumed a slow and steady pace allowing it to navigate the streets without attracting Hoblins if any were there. Rounding a corner about halfway into town, Shanira saw a building with a large caduceus engraved in the stone above the main doors. In her city, this had been the sign for a medical clinic or hospital. She pulled up close as she could to those main doors.

A ramp extending from the doors allowed the Marefolk to make their way up to the entrance carrying the injured Maremaid on the stretcher, actually a superplastic bin cover from Shanira's boat. It was amazingly strong and light and worked perfectly to transport the young female.

The smell of Hoblin and the added stench of their droppings filled the air outside the center. Through the doors, the air was fresh and clean, a sure sign the Hoblins had yet to solve the workings of a door.

Inside, Shanira searched the rooms for the various medical devices until she found several large pods designed for healing. Shanira was relieved, having speculated, without prior knowledge a coastal town on a forested island might see more than its share of wounded and there was more there than only a healing pod. Of course, there was no one to confirm her speculation just as there was no one with medical qualifications to operate the devices. She couldn't waste time worrying about it. As a designer and builder, she had the blueprints and specs for these medical devices in her head. Her knowledge of them entailed the feeling of certainty she may have constructed such devices herself, although she knew she never had. Being a solitary human in a minimally populated world, the knowledge was part of her mental programming. This knowledge she had of how the devices functioned was clear in her mind, allowing her to set up and calibrate the needed energy for healing.

Since Shanira's medical skills were limited to the design, purpose, and function of the machines, she didn't have the diagnostic skills to know the settings the Marefolk would require for optimum healing. With some effort, the two wounded creatures were maneuvered into separate pods and Shanira adjusted the controls to what she hoped were conservative, but effective settings.

As the pods pulsed to life, Shanira was able to find some nearby showers which would allow Thunder-fin's brother and father to keep their skin wetted down. The Maremaid's father was reluctant to leave his daughter's side, but with some coaxing and explaining it was out of his hands, she got him to take some time in the shower. He returned frequently to check on his daughter.

Gauging the progress of the healing, Shanira felt confident enough to increase the power settings and within the hour she could see Thunder-fin's wounds were nearly healed. And his gill restored. The Maremaid's injuries were quite severe, and she remained unconscious in her pod as Thunder-fin climbed from his, able to use his powerful arms with no discomfort to make his way to the shower.

It was some time later Shanira saw indications of movement through the viewing window of the Maremaid's pod. Between the power of the pod and her own natural healing capability, her wounds were pale scar lines now where not much earlier there had been deep wounds. From the looks of things, the young Maremaid's body was fully healed, but she was still comatose.

Shanira and the others had no idea why this was the case. They could only hope the psychological shock of the Hoblin attack and the severity of the wounds they inflicted on the young Maremaid would begin to fade just as the physiological symptoms had. They carried her to the shower in the hope the life-giving water might help. The other four Marefolk spent the night in the showers on each side of the one holding the young female. Sleeping very little, they were able to relax under an alternating fine spray of water and a soft, cleansing mist. Shanira found a cot in one of the examination rooms. She didn't worry about her boat, its built in protections would keep any unwanted visitors away. The Hoblins, if any were around, would likely avoid the docks as they feared deep water. According to the Marefolk, they would rather walk the shores to reach the shallows where the stream narrowed and from there pole across to the marsh rather than cross at the more open water. That night, however, there were no Hoblins.

Morning found the Marefolk feeling better than they had in many days. Thunder-fin showed no outward evidence he had ever been wounded The Maremaid, too, was physically healed and to the relief of all, over the night her coma turned into genuine sleep. As they prepared to leave, she was still not awake. She was carried out by her father and the others to the flatbed truck and placed on it with the help of the Maremen. Refreshed and restored all four of them were able to hold the sleeping Maremaid, passing her back and forth without disturbing her, their muscular lower bodies allowing them to move with surprising ease and agility over the ground. The fetid odor of Hoblin, while still strong, was far from fresh. It had been some time since the Hoblins were last in the town.

On the voyage upstream the Maremen, joined with Thunder-fin and met with a number of different Marefolk communities. They had all suffered great losses and there were many wounded. They were told to gather their wounded but stay in hiding until Shanira and her boat returned back downstream. Then they would closely follow the boat bringing along the injured to the town and the medical clinic.

By the time they reached the last community of Marefolk, the Maremaid was awake. Although still dazed, she recognized her father and clung to him. Headed back downstream towards the open water and the town, the boat was leading an ever growing procession of Marefolk. Some of the worst injured had been brought on board. Everyone constantly scanned the marshes for signs of Hoblins. Thunder-fin and his father and brother went overboard from time to time to organize and marshal a defense perimeter around the growing numbers. At the town, the Marefolk amassed around the piers and docks while the injured were trucked to the medical facility for treatment. The healing pods did their work and soon most of the newly healed were back to join their families and the collective of their fellows.

Some of the more seriously wounded took longer to heal and in a few cases the injuries were so severe the pods were unable to return them to full health, but all were better.

That evening, the Hoblins began to gather on the marshy shore across from the town. Shanira could see they were ugly creatures covered in light grey wool. Their arms were long and gangly ending in huge hands bearing long razor sharp talons. Their feet, too, were huge heavily taloned with long toes splayed out like snowshoes to walk the marshes. Their sharp curved noses almost touched their mouths with their long, treacherous looking fangs. They had misshapen red eyes exuding looks of pure hatred.

They howled and postured and waved their poling cudgels around. Shanira noted while they had enough rafts and logs to mount an armada they did not attempt to cross the deep open water to get to the Marefolk. She could also see some Hoblins farther upstream who were crossing. She knew what had to be done. Explaining to the fittest and strongest of the Marefolk what they needed to do, she set off with some of them to break into the buildings near the docks looking for gaffs, hammers and especially knives, screwdrivers and even broomsticks to attach them to and make deadly spears.

They gathered anything to serve as a weapon and Shanira quickly demonstrated some thrusting techniques. The Marefolk caught on immediately and shortly thereafter a group of Marefolk guardians with these weapons in hand swam up the shallows to meet the Hoblins as they crossed.

The Marefolk attack was swift and effective. Still swimming they left the deep water and took up positions among the weeds. They had arrived at the place where the Hoblins were crossing just as their first rafts were reaching the shallows. The Marefolk began to attack the Hoblins with their jury-rigged spears, jabbing and slashing., driving the Hoblins back out into deep water. The Marefolk then began to attack the rafts, tipping the Hoblins into the water. The Hoblins proved to be poor swimmers justifying their fear of the deep water and many were unable to make it back to the marshy shore. The stream current was pulling them helplessly toward the open water. Terrified and disoriented, some splashed and kicked carrying them further out into the deadly deeps. Others wallowed toward the docks where they were met by the now armed Marefolk who did their best to dispatch them or drive them out into the deeps to drown.

The ones succeeded in making it to the marshy land were in no condition to continue the raid. The remaining Hoblins withdrew, disappearing into the twilight. The Marefolk, having experienced their first real success against the vicious Hoblins, cheered and leapt from the water like dolphins. They had learned some effective defensive techniques and had discovered they could stand up to the Hoblins. They, of course, also knew the Hoblins were persistent and stealthy, and they would always have to be on the lookout for them.

Shanira found a channel dredger at one of the docks. She showed some of the elders how to operate it, reminding them of the Hoblins' legitimate fear of open water. She advised them to use the dredger to keep back the marsh from encroaching on the stream. A wide deep stream gave the Marefolk's a real advantage over Hoblin raiders.

In the future, there would still be skirmishes, but they would be few as the advantage the brutal Hoblins had was now lost.

Shanira spent some time among the Marefolk and found them to be gentle and kind and delightful companions for a solitary human female. Eventually Shanira felt compelled to carry on her journey. Thunder-fin and his brother, Flashing-fin shared a sense of adventure most Marefolk did not. They asked to join Shanira on her ongoing travels as did the now healthy young Maremaid, River-Jewel, and her father Sandy-hue. They had no family left and really had not become a part of the local Marefolk community. They spent much of their time close to Shanira, aboard the boat or in the nearby shallows. Shanira was delighted with the companionship something only dreamed of as she left the city of her awakening.

As Shanira's cruiser made its way through the open water beyond the island and the marshes, she would reduce throttle on her boat allowing her Marefolk friends to sometimes swim joyfully beside it. Other times they would join Shanira on board relaxing in the spray from the bailer and watching the watery world go by. Shanira truly enjoyed the shared moments and with her four Marefolk travel companions, she felt very happy. However, deep down inside, she still continued to feel a need to find some of her own kind.

BRUNELL: BIOLOGIST, Geologist and Agriculturalist

A heavy rain was falling with the sound of thousands of tap dancers rehearsing on the rooftop. The air was thick with moisture. The first thought Brunell had on hearing it was, "Rain! This is good."

His next thought was, "Where and I and why can't I move?"

He pushed up with his body against the material pinning him down. Hus push was so intense the delicate fabric tore easily almost causing him to fall from the cushioned pallet on which he had been lying.

Pulling the stray pieces of fabric from his face, Brunell sat up and looked around. At first glance he thought he was in a bedroom of some kind, but the number of items, tools, books, and electronic devices made him hen think he was in a workroom or office.

His ability to recognize all those things on the shelves around him was comforting to Brunell and he stood, removing the stray remaining bits of the fabric continuing to cling to him. He walked over to the window to watch the rain teaming down. "This could be good, "he thought as he looked out on the flat farmland stretching into the distance away from him.

It disappeared into the curtain of rain, preventing Brunell from seeing just how spacious it was. He wasn't sure what exactly was happening out there, but he wasn't as sure he had been, "or perhaps this is bad."

He recognized everything around him and would be able to explain to anyone their uses and how they worked, but prior to hearing the pounding of the rain, he could remember nothing. He had no idea how long or how hard it had been raining.

While all the things around him were familiar, they also seemed strange. It was as if he were looking at them for the first time but had used them all before. He felt he couldn't trust his memory and decided he would just go with what he believed he knew, asking no questions about how he knew it. What he knew for certain he needed to get rid of the sticky remnants of the biofabric and then find something to wear. He also knew he needed breakfast which a very interesting idea was causing him to ask himself a mysterious question," How long have I been fasting?"

He enjoyed a warm mist shower leaving him feeling soothed and dry. He found some clothing in a closet, dressed and went to look for something he knew as the kitchen. There he would find something to eat.

Once in the kitchen, Brunell found a very interesting device. It was called a "cooker" and its purpose was to prepare meals.

Brunell knew exactly how the cooker worked and keyed in breakfast. He gave no thought to the magical technology behind it as he keyed in bacon, crispy; eggs, sunny side up; toast with butter and jam; coffee, mildly sweet and white. He touched the button marked "start" and within seconds, the buzzer went off and there it was, everything just as he had ordered. He went to grab the plate with the bacon and eggs, but it was painfully hot. He searched the cupboards and shelves for oven mitts and immediately knew what they were when he saw them. He carried the plate to the table, went back and got the plate with toast and the cup of coffee. The toast was buttered and covered with raspberry jam. He felt comfortable and happy as he ate the first of many similar breakfasts. It was a good many mornings before he tried some other menus. After eating, he put the plates and cups into a slot where they went to be cleaned. Brunell had no idea where they went and what was done to them. Whatever happened they or the perfect match for them was there and ready for the next meal.

Checking out the house he could see it was designed for more than one person. The thought struck him as a momentary ache, a feeling of sadness and then it passed.

The place he liked best was the room holding all the books about agriculture and the machines of farming. There were many books less clear as to their subject. Some seemed to be stories. Others seemed to be treatises on animal and plant biology. He tried them all. As he read through them he found gaps and omissions. In some cases, key parts of a story or treatise was missing.

He came across a computer connected to the internet in one of the rooms, but quickly learned there was not very much out there to find. His farm data was filed and cross-referenced on it. A large TV on one of the walls showed more of the broken-up stories fragmented in a way similar to what he had found with the books. In the case of the TV, the characters were able to move of their own free will but were often interrupted and sometimes completely vanished, only to be replaced by another set of characters. He could see these characters despite differences in clothing, and for him, more importantly, body kind and facial differences looked very much like him. They had to be images of humans. These images, however, might appear human, but Brunell knew none of them really existed in this world other than on a video screen. He thought of these moving pictures as half-formed memories of something no longer existing.

His jaunts around the neighborhood brought Brunell to the conclusion that he was the only real living human among those shadows on the TV screen. Still, something deep inside him told him that there were real humans out there somewhere, and eventually he would find them.

For now, he believed his responsibility was to care for his farm and learn all he could about it and the crops he grew. As a significant amount of time passed, animals began to show up. He discovered many small species in the surrounding woods, and streams. Eventually larger animals domesticated for farm life would appear the farm from somewhere.

A long driveway led from the house to a paved road. He had driven it a short distance a few times, but eventually he would follow the paved road a fairly long distance each way, checking out the empty villages it ran through. For the most part, especially early on, the farm was enough for Brunell. He read the books, walked the land plowed and watered and even planted. He felt a joy in the growing plants, the greenness and the many changes, the reaping, the wonder of new growth and the dying as the seasons passed.

As time went by, Brunell began to notice changes some of which were not so pleasant. The numbers of insects destructive to plant life increased steadily. There were blights affecting his crops at different times. Protecting the seeding and growing plants became more critical. He used sprays he found in one of the storage sheds near the barn. He was beginning to find himself in a battle with nature. Eventually he began to realize a balance was developing between the destructive side of nature and its positive aspects. Although he found the actual farming was no longer as simple as in the first days, it had become more routine and straightforward. Having discovered the workable crop treatments to protect his farm from any kind of predator. The insecticides and herbicides Brunell used to treat his crops were non-toxic and safe for all except the targeted pests. Using drones to spread the treatments, and re dust the trouble spots, proved especially helpful for Brunell given the vast size of the farm.

One day as Brunell was out in one of the more distant parts of the farm, he was surprised to find a large number of tiny creatures lying unmoving and likely dead under a bushy tree at the edge of the field. Driving close, he got off his tractor to take a closer look at what these unidentified pests might be. He picked one up and was astonished to see it was very much like a tiny human except it had a double pair of wings like a dragon fly and along its spine between the wing roots, a needlelike projection. Walking carefully among these tiny fallen creatures, he saw one still showing signs of life. As he reached down to pick it up, the tiny creature opened its eyes. They were multifaceted and a beautiful golden color. As he took it into his hands, he felt a tiny sting. The needle on the creature's back had extended and pierced his finger.

He shook the hand to release the needle and felt numbness around the wound. The tiny being fell to the ground and his needle retracted revealing a tiny droplet of fluid at its tip. He didn't have to wonder it was about as the needle wound as the numbness in his fingertip gave way to an itch and a small red blister encasing the puncture. Brunell didn't know that the tiny creature had lacked the strength to inject the wound with all the poison the needle carried, saving the farmer from a great deal of pain. These creatures might look like cute tiny flying humans, but they had a nasty sting.

Brunell knew that whatever they were, he would have to careful. If one touch of the needle from a creature on the verge of death could cause such pain and the itching. He felt around the wound, the bite of several could be far more serious and possibly fatal. What Brunell would eventually learn the poison was deadly to most small animals, while larger ones were more likely to feel distress and painful discomfort especially if stung more than once.

In the case of humans, it would take far more than the combined stings of every member of the doomed colony, perhaps even more, to do any real serious damage. The antitoxins in the blood of legacy humans were powerful and protective. It was, however, something that Brunell really didn't want to test. The itching from the sting irritated Brunell's finger for most of the day.

Although Brunell felt bad about the deaths of these tine human appearing beings, he did understand in killing the tiny creatures, he had prevented himself and his animals from the stings of these creatures for a while, anyway. Much later, he would learn just how malevolent these tiny beings were.

He would learn these beings were not satisfied with filling their needs and would go out of their way to torment any innocent animals they might come across. Because the needle attached to their spine and the poison it could injected took time to replenish after being used, they also attacked with hand weapons, bits of sharp stone or hawthorns. Many small animals would be brutalized with toxin and puncture wounds and left to die. Larger creatures would often be in serious distress after encountering a group of these Faye folk.

The insecticide dusting of Brunell's drones had most likely destroyed the first Faye colony. It would be considerable time before another colony would arrive on the scene. In the meantime, Brunell began to encounter more and more animals. Some were curious and came to find out what they could about being part of Brunell's farm, outbuildings, and fields and to learn what they could about the creature who might accept them or send them off with noise or flame or toxic dust. Others approached seeking a safe haven from the wilds.

Two large dogs began to warily observe Brunell as he went about his business. As time passed they grew bolder. They were young dogs more curious than careful as they instinctively craved the friendship of the human. From his reading, he knew what dogs were and how helpful they could be on a farm.

When they would come near, Brunell began to throw them bits of food to entice them to come closer. Over time, their instinctive desire for the friendship of Brunell overcame their instinctive wariness. After several close and friendly encounters with the kind and generous Brunell, they became his constant companions accompanying him on his farm rounds and even sharing the house with him.

On one round, they had, together, found the mother pig with her two piglets. There was no sign of a boar, and the mother was clearly frightened, but less frightened of Brunell and the two dogs than of the forest beyond the farms edge. Eventually, Brunell was able to introduce her to what he had known all along as a pigsty. When the mother and her piglets decided, they would enter and investigate the sty, Brunell chose to leave the gate open. When the pigs had clearly decided this was home, Brunell still left the gate open. As the piglets grew older, he would close the gate but never lock it so by bunting with their heads, they could open it, something they rarely did.

Over the seasons Brunell and his two companions whom he called Ranger and Tess, found and brought in a number of wandering animals. They found some sheep and a couple of cows as well as a bull. While tame enough, they kept a distance from the house. One morning he found several brooding hens and a rooster had arrived to take over the previously empty chicken coop.

Brunell and the dogs had driven out to a distant field near the edge of a deep forest. There, they came across two small colts, little more than foals, To Brunell, they seemed very young to be on their own. Ranger was more curious than usual and followed the aimless path they had left back into the woods. He barked to call Brunell who came to join him. Ranger had found the colts' mother, or at least what was left of her. Some creature, certainly not a small one, had attacked and killed the it. Whatever the creature was the attack had been vicious. With teeth and claws the mare had been nearly torn apart, yet there was no sign the killer had stayed around, as most wild animals Brunell had encountered did, to gorge itself on the fresh meat of the kill.

The absolute brutality of the killer so close to the farm fields was enough to let Brunell know he and the dogs would have to be careful and assiduously watchful as it was clear the forest now harbored some truly terrifying beasts presenting a significant danger to the farm animals and even Brunell.

Brunell brought the two colts to the stables beside the barn. This, like all the other buildings had been designed and built ready for habitation since Brunell had first awakened.

The farm with its fields and gardens and now its collection of domestic animals inspired Brunell and for a good, long time he was very happy in his self-contained little world.

THE FAYE PLAGUE

Over time, several colonies of Faye folk settled in the forest edging the farm. At first, they presented no problem, keeping to the forest and focusing their cruelty on the more helpless of the woodland creatures. For several seasons an uncertain truce between the farm and the Faye seemed to have been achieved.

From time to time, however, small groups of Faye would come near the house. On rare occasions they would raid the barn, stealing grain and stinging some of the more curious animals.

A couple of times the dogs were stung while they were sleeping. After that Brunell encouraged the dogs to stay inside especially in the early mornings and early evening when the Faye seemed to be most active

The uneasy truce between the Faye and the farm came crashing down one late spring day when a computer glitch sent one of Brunell's crop dusting drones slightly off course.

The computer error sent the drone close to a community of Faye folk encroaching on the farmland. While the drone did not come close enough to the community to do much direct harm, some residue of the insecticide dust did find its way to some of the Faye. It caused some tiny burns on a few of the Faye's skin and caused others some difficulty with their breathing. The computer quickly corrected the drone's flight path taking and keeping it far from the Faye community. The damage, however, had been done. The malevolence of the Faye, until then directed at the woodland animals and on rare occasions against some of the animals on the farm, was now turned against Brunell. Their reluctance to do this initially was not due to a live and let live philosophy on the part of the Faye but was based on fear. The giant and the dogs, if they wished, could easily destroy any Faye community. With the community rapidly expanding and being joined by other communities, the farm and its busy routines became more of an annoyance than a worry to them.

While they remained relentless in in their torment of the woodland creatures, they now brought their cruelty into the fields and gardens. While the dogs and Brunell were their ultimate targets as they routinely terrorized the farm animals. The easiest targets were the smaller farm animals. Brunell often found the chickens, rabbits and the like covered with painful wounds. Many died as a result of early morning or evening raids by the Faye folk.

Brunell did everything he could short of poisoning the communities with the crop dusting drones, to keep these tiny cruel beasts away from his animals. No matter what he tried, the Faye proved clever enough and evil enough to circumvent them. They broke windows in the outbuildings, found their way through vents and chimneys and even the tiniest of openings. They found out how to cut screens and dug under doorways and even found ways to disconnect electrical barriers. Only the main house was safe from intrusion by the Faye, and Brunell was beginning to wonder how long it would last.

It became difficult to work the farm as the creatures would swarm the enclosed cab of the tractor screaming at him, trying to get in, and throwing particles of dirt at his eyes.

Many of Brunell's food plants were decimated as Faye poison got into the stalks and stems, killing roots and leaves. Brunell began to fight back using his drones along with some very powerful pesticides. Through this, a balance was achieved. Decimated colonies meant fewer attackers. When the population grew too large, the drones would find them again.

Brunell found it a costly battle just keeping the balance. The pesticide was difficult to handle; small birds and animals were often in the targeted area. Between the dusting and the Faye attacks, things got quite bad. Breeding dropped off. Most of the animals feared to leave the barns and outhouses. Grazing animals could not last a full day in the fields and even on the hottest of days, Brunell dare not have a window or a door left open.

There were small and not so small tragedies. When Tess gave birth to puppies, the Faye found them and killed them. Tess, attempting to protect her babies was hurt badly by the toxic stingers of the Faye. She was never the same afterwards. Pining for her pups and suffering from the ongoing torment of the Faye toxins in her system, Tess wasted away and eventually died. She was a sweet natured dog and both Ranger and Brunell felt her loss deeply.

It became too much for Brunell who began to think he needed another human around to help him carry on the fight with the Faye. His only served to add to the growing need to find some fellow humans to have some human companionship and human support. It was taking everything Brunell had physically and mentally to keep up the farm and battle the Faye.

He began to think there might be other farms and perhaps farms with humans around where there were no Faye folk. He knew if he let up for a moment, all would be doomed, but even trying his best to carry on the struggle began to seem a waste of time. The farm was decimated, animals were dead or dying, Crops were destroyed from over dusting and the intentional and systematic destruction by the Faye.

When the morning came, Brunell woke up to the horrible realization only he and Ranger remained. He knew he needed to make a critical decision about the future. He could remain to be the prime target of the surrounding Faye colonies and the likely outcome or take Ranger and some of his most valuable possessions and move on.

Getting away from the Faye folk and seeking out fellow humans made more sense than staying. He sent the drones out one more time dropping vast amounts of pesticide and herbicide over the Faye colonies. This provided Brunell with some time to pack up one of the trucks and set off down the long driveway to the highway beyond. As he and Ranger came to the end of the driveway, Brunell felt there was no question as to the way he would go. He wasn't quite sure why, but it was as if a GPS switched on in his head and revealed to him, "Other humans are in this direction."

Since the choice would otherwise be random and there were only two directions to take, it made little difference to him, which way he would go. He may as well listen to the internal guide and go the way it suggested. Since his only intention for the moment was to get as far away from the Faye as possible, he was on the highway and off. The first part of the journey was familiar because he had taken the highway to the nearby deserted villages lining it. He and Ranger were soon well beyond the familiar, driving into the night until finally stopping to rest at highway gas bar as the morning sun peaked over his shoulder.

After a brief respite, Brunell and Ranger drove on for several long hours until they came across the welcoming sign of a roadside motel. There was no one there to greet them so Brunell helped himself to a key, found the room it opened and settled in for a long sleep.

Ranger had gotten lots of sleep back in the truck and so, he stood guard, but was not called on to defend his sleeping master.

Waking up early after a long and worry free sleep, Brunell led Ranger to the attached restaurant. It was, of course deserted, but there was breakfast there, ready for both of them. Will sipping on his second coffee, Brunell began to wonder if the food preparation went on every day, all day, or did it only happen when he was around. Did his presence in the motel somehow inform the restaurant there would be a guest for breakfast or did it all kick into gear, prepared itself, cleaned itself, and began to prepare for the next meal. Since there was no way he could ever find the answer to this puzzle by hanging around, he decided to press on. Perhaps he would find an answer somewhere farther along the road. In the meantime, he would continue his journey accepting directions from the vague map in his mind. As far as Brunell could tell, the map was barely there. It never really showed itself, but whenever he came to a fork in the road or an intersection, he would somehow sense the preferred route. What really mattered to Brunell was there had been no sign of the Faye since leaving the farm. The journey he had set out on to escape those tiny evil creatures, now become one of pleasure.

Brunell and Ranger would find interesting places to stay along the way. Some they abandoned after a day and some they stayed in longer. Brunell could spend days examining the flora and fauna, discovering he was far more than a farmer. He was a highly knowledgeable botanist and zoologist. His knowledge base included an understanding of the naturopathic usage of different plants. He knew a great deal about the body structures of the animals he encountered. The adventure of the journey, as slow as it was, was as much about Brunell's growing practical knowledge and kindred skills as it was about the sheer joy of the open road.

He and Ranger stopped frequently, stayed as long as they wanted enjoying the luxury of fully fitted households, food, drink and recreation. There was always a TV, sometimes holographic and sometimes not. There were videos for TV, lots of books, and a wide variety of games, computer based and otherwise, always readily available. Few of them were even near complete, but they did provide Brunell with some insight into the human community.

Brunell would spend hours in the fields and forests with Ranger by his side looking for new and unique plant and animal life. Wherever he looked, he found no other humans to share his interests and discoveries.

Still, this was a happy time for Brunell. His life was rich with new learning experiences, the freedom he felt, stopping where he wanted and discovering the interesting and novel as the environment around him continued to change. From the lowlands of his awakening, through prairie like terrain, rolling hills and craggy rock faces suggesting ancient mountains that may or may not have existed on the original earth, Brunell's journey was never dull. It was never dull, especially for Brunell who found himself steeped in the subjects he loved, biology and geology.

Moving onwards, always with the hope of finding humans, as Brunell and Ranger usually did, they seemed to be following a fixed and preplanned route, the direction to go or the road to take. It was usually so subtle decisions on when to turn onto a new road, how far to take it and the like, seemed to Brunell to be spontaneous and random. Yet when acting on what appeared to be a random choice, Brunell always had a feeling of rightness about the choice he made. The route and time-line remained vague in Brunell's mind, but in those moments when he thought about these things, he couldn't help but feel, somewhere in the back of his mind, a real, solid plan was in place.

If there was such a plan, and it seemed quite possible to Brunell there was, then it was a very open ended one. Brunell could sense no time-line. He often wondered what exactly the final goal would be. Turning some corner out there, wherever and whenever, would he find himself in a large human habitation. Of course, there could always be the case as the plan felt so open ended there was no final goal, but Brunell hoped it wasn't so. It might also be the plan was so open-ended because it was leading to a convergence coming from different places. This was what he hoped this vague and open-ended plan was all about. He believed there could be others like him on a journey making time, as they headed toward some distant meeting place, to gather information, refine their skills, and consolidate their learning. He and they could even be being tested by some unknown power. It was variations on this theme Brunell found himself coming back to when he took the time to think about it.

He was pretty sure if somewhere down the road there was a large human community, he would probably already have encountered a few of them. Whatever the truth might end up to be, it was pretty fruitless to spend much time thinking about it. All he knew is he felt no great need to hurry.

Seasons passed as Brunell, and Ranger made their way down the road to some possible destination. Brunell's thoughts were rarely on this. Generally, he was more interested in cataloguing, testing and cultivating any new or different kind of plant-life he found along the way. His wealth of zoological knowledge extended to include some veterinary skills. He tried his hand at surgery on the few injured animals he came across with some success.

Brunell remained very aware the creatures most closely reflecting human features he had encountered were the tiny Faye folk, and they were far less friendly than the animals he cared for.

After a very long stay in a park featuring a botanical garden, Brunell had begun to feel extraordinary pressure to move on. He had barely completed his research on the exotic plants he had discovered and would usually spend a few days after to compile his notes and recordings. Not this time. The need to move on was irresistible. He quickly loaded up the truck, never a simple task under any conditions, but especially when feeling such urgency. Over the course of time at each longer stop, much of the things already in the truck found their way into the residence while additional items, plants, clippings and other findings would be added to them. They all needed to be carefully packed and tightly secured before the truck was ready to move.

Since the feeling to get moving had intensified early in the morning, Brunell, didn't fight it but proceeded to pack the truck. All was ready as mid-day approached when the truck pulled out the park and back on the two-lane hard top highway.

CONVERGENCE

Despite the pressure Brunell had felt to be on the road, the rest of the day was uneventful. Towards evening He found himself driving beside a large body of water. The far shore, across the water, drew closer as he progressed. It looked to Brunell as if he had come upon a very wide river or a channel of sorts between the mainland and an island. In either case, he felt he might find some variant or novel plant and animal life along its bank. It certainly seemed to him like a different biosphere than any he had come across earlier on his journey. "This looks interesting, "he said to Ranger who seemed to agree.

While Brunell knew Ranger would agree with whatever decisions he made, he still felt the need to add, "Let's find a nice house, grab some dinner and hit the sack and we can get up early and do some exploring. What do you say, Ranger?"

Ranger, happily barking in response to his human companion's upbeat tone, appeared to be in agreement. Ranger was quite agreeable to Brunell's decisions, especially the eating part.

There were some very interesting looking homes some distance off the road, overlooking the water. Brunell spotted one appearing especially welcoming one close to a large bridge, spanning the water. He turned the truck into the driveway and up to the back door.

The house proved to be very satisfying. The kitchen was well stocked, and the beds were comfortable. Brunell chose a large room on the main floor giving him an excellent view of the water and the far shore. He put his gear in the room then returned to the kitchen to gather up dinner for Ranger and him.

Between the early rise to pack and the long time spent driving, Brunell was exhausted. If he harbored any plans to read or take a walk, they vanished the moment he laid back on the bed. He was out without switching off the lights, something they would do themselves as the evening dissolved into night and the system sensed Brunell on the bed and Ranger on the carpeted floor beside it were well asleep.

The sun was well above the horizon when the two travelers awoke. It was a beautifully clear, warm day. Brunell could barely contain his excitement at the opportunity to study the transitional flora and fauna at the water's edge.

After a quick breakfast, Brunell, sample bag and necessary tools in hand, was quickly off down the hill to the shoreline. Ranger was doing some exploring of his own.

Juggling his digging and clipping tools, and a basket of small plastic containers, a microscope and a magnifying glass in his shirt pocket, Brunell had found a nice marshy spot where the water and the land environment seemed to blend. Setting his equipment aside, Brunell knelt down in the thin marshy layer at the water's edge and was quickly examining every piece of greenery, every moving creature on land and in the water with a joyful focus.

As the morning gave way to noon, Brunell continued his examinations. He was delighted to have found some species he hadn't seen before as well as some extraordinary variations on some familiar ones.

Brunell was so engrossed in his discoveries and didn't immediately notice Ranger's excited barking. It was only when it became persistent did he leave off what he was doing and make his way along the shore and around a small brush covered finger of land jutting out into the water. There, almost hidden in the reeds was Ranger looking out towards the deep water and insistently barking. Brunell had never heard such an excited bark out of Ranger. As he rushed to the almost hysterical dog's side, Brunell thought he heard a raspy voice ask the question, "human?"

He could see Ranger's sight was fixed on something a short distance out in the deeper water. He Followed Ranger's gaze out toward the deeper water and for less than a second, he thought he saw movement in the water and a large greyish shadow beneath the water moving quickly off into the deeper water.

He wasn't sure if he had really heard a voice over Ranger's barking. Given the ruckus Ranger was raising, it might have been an auditory illusion. While it was easy enough for Brunell to put it off to the dog's unusual behavior, he had, indeed, heard one word spoken in Assianangle, the word "human."

After a very few more minutes, Ranger stopped running back and forth along the beach, and walked over to Brunell and returned to usual calmness. Lowering his hand to scratch Ranger behind the ear, Brunell looked off across the water. He had seen movement and a large greyish shape in the water. Although it was a fleeting thing for him, there was certainly something out of the ordinary there to set off the usually serene and dignified dog in such a way.

Distracted now from his earlier scrutiny of the shoreline plants and animals, Brunell decided to make his way to the house for lunch.

After a lunch of sandwiches and a large glass of ice-cold flavored tea, Brunell and Ranger set out on a long walk. Brunell found himself wondering about what he might have seen or heard back at the shore earlier. While Brunell was lost in his thoughts, Ranger was checking out everything he could as he went along. He left countless messages and mysteriously seemed to find a few to read. Their walk carried them onto the bridge spanning a very large body of water Brunell would eventually find out was the moth of a river. Although the water seemed to be barely moving, he could see along the edge of deep water, steady motion. He knew it was deep as he couldn't see through to the bottom except near the shore. Those shadows he had seen in the water earlier in the day, as large as they seemed to be, could easily disappear into the depths and remain unseen.

At about the middle of the bridge, Brunell crossed to the other side. He could see a large body of water off in the distance. It could be a lake or a landlocked sea. Along the far shore he noticed an exceptionally lovely cruiser, quite large, but wonderfully sleek, tied up to the shore. The engine mounts suggested cosmic ion generators meaning she was likely even faster than she looked. After taking in the beauty of the cruiser, Brunell saw it was tied up very close to a large grocery outlet. The back door nearest to the cruiser was slightly ajar. This aroused Brunell's curiosity, but he was not quite prepared to investigate.

The morning had been quite productive up until the odd events surrounding Ranger's uncharacteristic outburst, Brunell found himself wondering if he should go back to his examination along the shore or just relax for the rest of the day and set off to wherever early in the morning.

Not yet having made up his mind, Brunell went back to the house and set out his morning collection of shoreline plants and tiny creatures and within moments was engrossed in study.

Before he knew it, evening was approaching. He got himself a bottle of beer from the fridge and went out onto the deck overlooking the river to sit and enjoy his drink.

The lazy motion of the river, the setting sun and his third beer relaxed him into an almost hypnotic state. He seemed to see movement just below the surface of the water. He thought he heard sounds, but when he tried to focus on them, they were gone. He put this all down to his state of mind and his unfamiliarity with large bodies of water. He decided Ranger had been barking at a shore bird or a turtle or something similar. There was no voice to ask the question, "human," just the natural sounds and undulations of a large and stately stream. Brunell felt this place had put him on edge and so he made the decision. He and Ranger would be off first thing in the morning.

Because the stay was so short, pre-departure was a busy time. Brunell had to catalogue his findings and place his samples into the coolers along the inside panels of the truck. Soon enough he was ready. He called Ranger who jumped into the passenger side of the cab, ready as always for the next adventure.

Brunell pulled out of the tree-shaded drive and onto the highway. Moments later he was crossing over the bridge he had walked on the night before. Nearing the middle of the long bridge, Brunell slowed to look up and down what he had decided was a river. He glanced over to where he had seen the beautiful cruiser, but there was no sign of it and the doors at the back of the supermarket seemed to be closed. It seemed strange to him, and he wondered if someone had been there and had driven off with the boat. It was an intriguing idea, but Brunell chose to take what he believed was the realistic conclusion. Where he had walked, close to the railing of the bridge had allowed him a view of the cruiser. He had to believe his position in the truck, now over half way across the bridge with the intervening railings was hiding the boat, still there, from his sight.

Brunell had been alone except for Ranger and much earlier, Tess, for a very long time. He had never seen or met another human except in videos and on TV and those were really only fleeting glances. He felt it was unlikely he had found another human or any creature remotely like a human. Little did he know how wrong he was. He had no idea of the incredible life changes the next few days would bring.

Driving along the riverside highway was a novel experience for Brunell and he found he enjoyed the contrast between river and countryside. He drove slowly to take in the full experience. He knew somewhere ahead was a place he and Ranger could stay, a place where he could once again explore the transition point between land and water. He would spend more time analyzing and cataloguing. He wanted to know about everything living and growing in this inestimable world and the environmental varieties at its foundation. He wanted to know this, not based on inherent knowledge, or words in a book, but through personal experience.

Coming into an exquisite little riverside town, Brunell decided to leave the highway and check out some of the side streets. As he ambled through the town from the countrified edge to the buildings along the riverbank, he couldn't help but relish the different aspects of this town from off the beaten path, so to speak. Leaving the highway to check out the byways of this lovely little town was, to Brunell's mind, and excellent decision.

The town and its buildings seemed to have an older, more traditional feeling. It was dotted with small elegant looking parks. The town was to all appearances, a blend of old and new. It was, of course, an illusion as every place or building Brunell had encountered were, on close inspection, relatively the same in age. The buildings had a gothic look giving the town a settled look while celebrating its modernity with small outdoor malls fronted by a wide sidewalks and random seating. Brunell could almost visualize people sitting, or walking, shopping or just letting the world pass by, but of course the parks, the malls and the sidewalk seating were all empty. The world passed by unwatched.

Rounding the corner onto a street running along the river's edge, Brunell could swear he was seeing the same cruiser he had admired yesterday from the bridge so far behind, tied up beside a Marina some distance ahead.

He was disturbed by a sense of incongruity. He had thought the design was unique the previous day, but perhaps what he thought unique back then wasn't original at all.

He didn't like this conclusion. He had a feeling it was the same boat. He tried to get to the marina but found himself working his way through a maze of streets. The twists and turns seemed to be taking him farther away from the river before bringing him back toward it.

When he pulled into the marina he could see no sign of the cruiser. Brunell felt the route through all the side streets it took to get there had confused him, and he had somehow arrived at a similar but different marina.

Leaving the truck, Brunell made his way to the end of the marina dock and looked each way along the river. He could see no sign of the cruiser in either direction. The riverbank ran straight along the edge of the town. There were no curves to obscure the view. Brunell was sure he would be able to see the cruiser if it was tied up along the shore.

Brunell felt certain this was the right marina. This is where he saw the boat tied up and now it was gone. If it was more than just a figment of his imagination, which he was quite sure it was, then who was driving it? Where was it going?

Brunell called Ranger, who had been sniffing out the ground around the marina tuck shop, and the two of them climbed back into the truck. He made his way back to the highway and headed off in the direction he had been going, convinced the cruiser was heading in the same direction he was. It was the way the prow was pointing both times he had seen it. He was now determined to find out if it was the same cruiser as he had seen earlier from the bridge. If it was the same boat, he was determined he would find it again.

The search for the cruiser became an immediate priority for Brunell. His botanical and zoological research and cataloguing was forgotten. Brunell would continue his way along the riverside highway searching for this mysterious cruiser. If it were real, he would find it.

The search proved time consuming and arduous. It took him deep into the night as he checked every possible mooring place he came across, while always keeping a lookout for some form of running lights mid river.

By midnight he felt as if he was chasing a ghost. He began to look for a decent place to spend the rest of the night. He found one near the water and set himself up so they would not miss anything passing by on the river. Sleep did not come easily for Brunell. He found himself waking up to scan the river at any real or imagined sound no matter how faint or how familiar. He could not really decide if what he was doing served any purpose or was simply foolish. It was, indeed, quite possible he was pursuing the fantasy of his own wishful thinking.

Brunell maintained this level of quasi-wakefulness for several hours expecting, he would hear the engine and wake up should a boat pass his location. His knowledge of the cosmic ion generator was limited and at a practical level, his experience was non-existent.

While he slept, the cruiser crawled past. The speed was just enough to progress against the current. Its cosmic ion engines made no sound at all. Any noise the boat might have made in passing blended with the other nighttime sounds.

Around a bend in the river not far from where Brunell slept, the cruiser pulled in near the far shore and dropped anchor.

Brunell was not very happy when the morning sun awakened him. He felt too well rested despite the amount of time he had forced himself to stay awake and his intention to sleep lightly. He was disappointed in himself, feeling he could have slept through the sound of an un-mufflered truck pulling up the drive behind his. Of course, there was no such truck, but the cruiser could be either down river or upriver from him. He didn't even think it unlikely it was tied up beside the grocery outlet near the bridge. Brunell still had his doubts about the cruiser. There may possibly be a cruiser with humans on board, or one with human-like creatures on board, or there might be thousands of similar looking cruisers moored along the river and as empty of life as the houses he had stopped at along the way.

The irresistible possibility there may be more to this cruiser prevented him from any idea of zoological and botanical research at the shore or anywhere. It wasn't too much longer before he and Ranger were back on the road mirroring the path of the river. Driving slowly, he kept his eyes peeled along the riverbank in search of a familiar boat.

He hadn't gotten very far before catching sight of what he was looking for. He saw a cruiser lying at anchor near the far shore. He couldn't be certain, but he was pretty sure if it wasn't the same cruiser he had seen near the bridge back at the river mouth, it was an exact match. Was this the proof he would see many more versions of the same vessel, or was it unique and therefore the same one he had seen at the bridge and later spotted at the marina the day before in the riverside town?

He had to stop. He pulled off the road where a copse of trees would conceal his presence. Opening the window to look out towards the river, he picked up binoculars he had left on the console between the two seats. "Guard the truck, Ranger." He instructed the dog as he left the truck and proceeded down the slope and to the trees near the water's edge. From this vantage point where he could see the cruiser without anyone on the cruiser seeing him, he sat down on a fallen log resting his back against the still standing stump. He settled in to watch for life aboard the distant cruiser.

It didn't take long. Within minutes of settling, Brunell was rewarded with the view of an odd humanlike creature reaching to pull itself aboard the boat. Watching with amazement, Brunell was about to shout out to it when he was startled to discover as the lower part of its body cleared the water, the human like aspect stopped at the waist becoming a large fishlike body with fins and a tail. He quickly changed his mind about shouting. Brunell wasn't quite sure of what he was seeing as three more similar creatures, one distinctly female, joined the first arrival on the deck. They pulled themselves out of Brunell's view behind the gunwale of the boat.

The Faye folk, although quite tiny, looked very much like a small human. Despite their size and their human-like appearance, they were vicious, cruel and very dangerous. Those creatures climbing on board the boat were large, larger in size than Brunell. They looked like they could do a lot of damage, especially to a lone human with only a dog, brave as Ranger was, to help him. Until he knew a lot more about them, he would watch them from hiding. When they moved on, he would follow them with his truck, staying as close as he could without being detected.

Until now the road had followed close to the river, but from time to time a copse of trees or cluster of buildings would block the view of the river. More of concern to Brunell was the possibility the road could head off away from the river, perhaps turning inland to avoid marshy land. Even if the road did follow the river with a minimum amount of diversion, the cruiser might just keep to the far shore giving Brunell little chance to make close observation of the creatures and be able to form any useful opinions about their nature. Oddly enough, as with the Faye, nowhere in his innate zoological knowledge was there even a suggestion of creatures such as these.

Although for the moment the river seemed to be narrowing, it was only the slightest of change and there was nothing guaranteeing it wouldn't broaden again farther upstream.

Brunell was well aware chasing the boat upriver in hopes of learning more about those on board was not a sure thing. Still, the only hope he had of finding out who or what these fish people were and what their disposition might be was to attempt to follow them. He was not yet prepared to take to the river and was well aware no other boat he could find could catch up to the cruiser if it throttled up. The truck was his best chance so long as the road kept close to the river, and he could keep far enough out of sight along the way. While driving the truck, he would have to be instantly ready to stop quickly and pull off the road either into the bushes on the river's edge or into a driveway across the highway from the river, Brunell would do whatever it would take to keep the boat insight and him out of it.

Right then, the cruiser began to move. The pace it set was not exactly a crawl, but for Brunell, it was providential. It was moving slowly enough to allow him to get back in the truck and begin his pursuit. As the day passed, Brunell found he was able to drive at a reasonably steady speed and still keep the cruiser in sight. Luckily for him, the road continued to faithfully follow the river.

As he drove, he explained his plans to Ranger who listened patiently despite wishing the communication were done in the form of food. Brunell found the best tactic when the river and highway parted from each other was to speed up in hopes the river and highway would come back together, which they generally did after a fairly short distance. He would then wait in cover until he could see the boat again. This continued throughout the day. Just before dark, the cruiser stopped again and dropped anchor. It looked to Brunell as if it was planning to stay the night. Brunell stopped too.

The road was a good height above the level of the river. If he drove any further, they would likely see him and either take off quickly, or perhaps do something possibly putting him at some risk. There were a couple of smaller cabins close to the shore where Brunell was stopped. He quietly made his way down to the one nearest where the boat was moored. With Ranger at his heels, he entered the cabin making as little noise as possible. A quick scan of the interior revealed a doorway leading out to a small, screened in porch overlooking the water.

Brunell found a reclining chair and brought it into the porch. It would allow him to remain low and out of sight while providing him with a good view of the cruiser. From his prospect, he could see the part fish, part human-like creatures coming and going over the back of the boat. This time, he could also see the head and upper body of a fifth member of the boat crew. This one, unlike the others, appeared to be dressed and was moving upright, very differently than the four he had watched getting on and off the boat. Brunell couldn't help but wonder if he was truly looking at a fellow human.

He wasn't certain what he should do. It was entirely possible this apparent human was either a prisoner of the others or as much a threat as they might be.

The fifth creature looked to Brunell to be a female with a very good possibility of being human. She didn't appear to be in any sort of distress seemingly moving freely among the fish men although the side of the boat kept him from seeing exactly what was transpiring. While they may be comfortable among themselves, he had no idea what the consequences of introducing he and Ranger into the picture might be. Brunell didn't feel he was ready yet to show himself. He decided he would keep watch and continue to follow them clandestinely and see what he could learn about how they might react if he showed up.

For the first time, he could see lights from some small windows below deck. When the lights went out and the cruiser didn't cast off from its moorings, Brunell felt certain they were spending the night right there.

Closing doors and drawing curtains, then searching for food with a shaded flashlight, Brunell was careful no one on the boat would see any evidence of life in this cabin despite its closeness to the riverbank. He didn't want to spook them or draw any untoward attention to himself. He found some food and made a meal for Ranger and himself.

Meal complete, he shut off the flashlight and made his way out onto the porch again. It was quite dark, but he found a comfortable sofa and lay down. As he drifted off he reminded himself Cosmic Ion Generators were silent. He felt he would hear something if the boat decided to head off during the night, the sound of water pushing off the prow, the anchor being hauled up and the slap of waves against the shore from the running boat's wake.

It seemed those aboard the boat were as much in need of sleep as Brunell. When he awoke in the early hours of the morning, the boat was still there.

He had decided he should be in the truck and ready to roll when the vessel weighed anchor. He rousted Ranger and ransacked the fridge and cupboards for the kind of food needed to sustain Ranger and him on a day confined to the limited space of the truck cab.

With one eye looking out for activity aboard the cruiser, Brunell made sandwiches, gathered some drinks and other things he felt he might need, and made his way as quickly and obtrusively back to the truck. Brunell aware there may be very little time for them to stop as they followed the boat made sure all morning business especially Ranger's had been taken care of.

Seated in the truck, engines off, Brunell focused on the distant boat. It was some time before he saw activity aboard and considerably more before they weighed anchor and got underway.

During the wait, there was no chance for Brunell to grab even a short nap. This would not be an easy day for him. The boaters with their number, might alternate driving and being lookouts while he was alone. Ranger's interest in the boat was slight to none. He couldn't be much help as a relief, but at least he was a good companion.

The day was bright and clear. The boat seemed to the meandering, moving slowly upriver.

On several occasions Brunell had to remind himself to follow slowly and cautiously, staying a good way back of the boat. A few times he found himself losing focus and speeding up and then he would have to make a conscious effort not to bring attention to the truck by stopping and giving the boat more lead time. At the moment, there didn't seem to be a sign a crewmember on the boat had yet spotted him.

Towards noon, Brunell noticed the cruiser was moving off its midstream track and began to move closer to the highway side just as he entered a small town. Likely the boat crew was looking for something in the town, perhaps a place where they could tie up and gather supplies.

Buildings separated the road from the river, so he had to be especially cautious. He could easily drive past the boat, or the sound of the truck might send them into hiding.

He decided the best option for him was to stop and check around the side of the buildings to catch a glimpse of the river and hopefully, the vessel he was tracking.

Carefully making his way as close to the river as he could, Brunell was able to see the vessel he was following some distance upriver tied up to the shore. He returned to his truck and drove it as close as he felt he could without drawing attention to him or it. He got out of the truck and this time; Ranger joined him.

Ranger didn't really know what game Brunell was playing, but it seemed like fun to him to creep cautiously among the bushes beside the buildings.

Brunell reached a small wooden fence behind a small warehouse next to where the cruiser was tied up. He crouched down to conceal himself and watch the cruiser from a much closer view than he had ever before had.

Ranger, however, failed to notice the game had changed and stepped out onto the wide grass and concrete riverside walkway. At the same moment as one of the fish people was climbing over the gunwale. Half way over the edge of the boat, it stopped and looked straight at Ranger. The fishman was frozen in place as he and Ranger stared at each other.

Brunell could see the fishman was uncertain about the dog, but Ranger appeared delighted to encounter someone new. Wagging his tail, he ambled towards the fishman. As Ranger approached, the fishman slowly slid back onto the deck. He made some comment to someone hidden to Brunell's sight by the side of the cruiser. A second head appeared beside the fishman. This one Brunell could see, was the one who appeared to be bipedal.

He could see their concern regarding the dog, and he hissed quietly hoping to get Ranger's attention. But Ranger either didn't hear him or his attention was otherwise occupied by the interesting creatures he could see at the back of the cruiser. He walked up to the boat and gave it a sniff. The two heads, fishman and possibly human, were visible aboard the cruiser warily watched the movement of the dog. Then Ranger turned back a short distance and sat down as if inviting them to join him,

Brunell was terrified. Ranger was a dear and loyal companion, and he didn't want anything to happen to him. The two watchers appeared concerned enough they might feel endangered by Ranger and do something to hurt him. Brunell felt he had no choice but to join Ranger. He took a deep breath then stood up and whistled for Ranger to come to him. Two faces aboard the cruiser turned to look at him and he could see the surprise on their faces, "Sorry," he called to them in Assianangle, "Ranger won't hurt you. He's very friendly."

Ranger, responding to the whistle reluctantly walked back to his friend. Brunell scratched him behind the ears then held his arms out towards the startled eyes on the boat, showing he wasn't armed. Tail still wagging, Ranger took his place beside him. "He is friendly," Brunell said again, then added, sounding a little foolish to himself, "we're both friendly."

The one Brunell thought of as the female biped, spoke, "You look human. Are you a human?"

"Yes, I am human," responded Brunell, "Yes, indeed, I am human. Any humans there?"

The bipedal female pulled herself up onto the gunwale. "Yes."

Brunell had been correct. Clearly, she was not half fish half human. She had two legs, no fish tail. She jumped from the gunwale of the boat, landed on the grass, and began to walk toward Brunell. He felt strangely shy as she approached but refused to take a step backward. She looked him over, "I don't know what to say," She said softly, "I've waited for this moment for so very long."

"As have I," Brunell raised his glance towards the now four on deck.

Indicating the cruiser with her hand, "The ones on the boat are called Mare folk. The joined me on my journey, leaving their homes a long way back on the larger water. They are a little shy of strangers with legs. They have a deadly enemy who walks on legs."

"Well believe me, I am no one's enemy. There is just Ranger and me. My name is Brunell."

"I'm Shanira," she said and immediately the tension slipped away.

Brunell quickly discovered Shanira was the boat master, the human designer and builder of the graceful vessel. She invited Brunell aboard to meet her Marefolk friends. They told him about the Hoblins and how Shanira helped them. Brunell recounted his encounter with the Faye folk. Silver-flash, the Maremaid explained how back by the long bridge she had swam close to the shore curious about Ranger. When Ranger began to bark, and jump about, she moved back from him in fear and tried to make herself invisible among the shore weeds. When she thought she saw something standing on two legs, but looking more like Shanira than any Hoblin, she had, in her shock, accidently spoken her thought aloud, "human." before slipping back into the deeps to make her way back to the boat.

Frightened and confused about what she may have seen, she chose to say nothing to Shanira and the others. This confirmed for Brunell he had heard a voice and someone capable of speech had been there. He had truly heard and seen what he had begun to seriously doubt. It was a relief.

Shanira then spoke of the compulsion or need to make her way to some unspecified destination along the river. Brunell told of a similar compulsion. They both wondered if it was intended to bring about this very meeting. If it was the case, the compulsion should have disappeared, but it was still there, urging both of them onward.

Brunell went back to get his truck and brought it close to the cruiser.

They remained there for a considerable amount of time getting to know each other, sharing knowledge and for the humans, just to enjoy the presence of another human.

Eventually the call to proceed with their journey became difficult to resist. They decided for the time being, at least, they would continue their journey as they had started it, Shanira on the boat, Brunell in his truck. They would keep track of each other and meet frequently to compare notes.

RENDEZVOUS
On the Road

The first goal of the awakened had been achieved. They had each found another human to join up with and support. Like soldiers in battle, the relationships were strong and defensive. The original desire to seek out other humans had not been resolved, the intensity felt regarding finding fellow humans did not stop at the pairings, but had, in fact, caused them to grow more intense.

Shortly after their encounter with the werewolf, Maricel and Raphael had shared the intense feeling that it was important to continue the quest to find more humans. Together they set off on a journey following coinciding maps in each of their minds that seemed to unfold as the journey proceeded.

Brunel and Shanira felt a similar increase in their need to find more humans. They, too, shared the same somewhat vague directions of where something or someone wanted them to go.

Once Patah had regained his strength the call to he and Jolinda to journey on was strong enough to cause them to leave the idyllic and protective home where Jolinda had lived for so long with the Elvin and Forestman. Robin-eyes, Soft feather and of course Forestman along with Jolinda's first companion, Mewser accompanied the two humans on a vague but insistent set of mental instructions laying out the route they were to take to find more humans.

The mind maps shared by the pairs, although separated by great distances and directions unfolded slowly towards a convergence. There was no destination set out for them and apparently, no timeline. The directions, too, were fluid. At times, they were barely discernible and at other times clear and compulsively insistent.

After spending untold seasons without the presence of fellow humans, the urgency the pairs felt was complex. The clarity of the mind map was not consistent, sometimes driving them on and sometimes leaving them be, yet in the back of their minds they could sense it was always there.

There were times along the way when the pairs would stop spending as much as a dozen seasons, although usually considerably less, in one place or another. It was during these stopovers knowledge and understandings of this unique new world were learned. A crucial knowledge was imparted to them as they went along, a knowledge they could not find within the inherent knowledge with which they had awakened. Many of the more disconcerting evils of this world somehow seemed to exist out of phase with the natural flow of life. The evils they had encountered; the werewolves, Wampyra, Faye and Hoblins were an introduction to a level of evil presently sharing this world but was somehow not a natural part of it.

Each pair and their companions would eventually encounter more aspects of this evil as they made their journey of convergence. The call to move on as the mind map waxed clearer came packed with a sense of adventure and a promise of discovery. It was as if the journey was laid out for them in such a way as they proceeded, the stopovers they made provided essential refinements to their knowledge base and skills as well as an opportunity to build their understanding of how Legacy Earth met with or deviated from the foundational knowledge to which they had awakened. It was a long staircase with many landings. Each landing was different from the previous in the skills it sharpened and knowledge it set out.

Even to the most capable observer, it would be difficult to tell if the ebb and flow of the convergent journey was part of a prearranged program or simply a natural adaptation to circumstances as they arose. Whether it was in response to a fixed plan or a natural evolution, however, made little difference to the ultimate purpose of the journey.

For the most part, the journey of each of the three sets of paired humans was a pleasant one for all concerned, especially the early part. Friendship shared between humans was an exciting concept. Life stories were told. The results of research and innate knowledge were shared.

MARICEL AND RAPHAEL

For Maricel and Raphael, the thoughts about werewolves faded from the conscious mind and were confined to their vast and growing reservoirs of knowledge.

Together they explored and inventoried and grew their knowledge. Shops and malls, museums and libraries and all the other buildings in the towns and in the countryside along their route were all sources of knowledge and places to practice and refine intellectual and physical skills and understanding.

On route, they had passed through several cities and larger town but had lately begun to notice the communities, especially the larger ones were further apart and smaller in size. The last place they had spent some time in what could be termed a city was remarkable. It had several museums, one of which was a sizeable armed forces museum beside a small military base containing a substantial armory.

There were artifacts galore for Maricel to investigate and the fact most were military in function, investigation of the armory and museum held as much interest in Raphael.

For some time, the concentrated their attention on the device of warfare, a variety weapons and vehicles, armament and every related object they could find. From the armory and the base, they moved on to the museum. After spending a great deal of time reviewing the history of warfare as the builders of legacy earth saw it, Maricel moved on to the other museums to see what they had to offer.

The town seemed to be built around the base and the three museums. The architecture was very different to the other towns and cities they had visited. To an original twenty-first century resident's eye, it had the appearance of a medieval European city. Arches and buttresses where everywhere. Some of the central bridges crossing a moderately sized river were towered and covered with apartments and small retail outlets.

While Raphael and Maricel marveled at the beauty of the architecture, Maricel continued investigate the other museums and art galleries, discovering many fascinating things among their plentiful, but incomplete collections. Considerable research and speculation was needed to fill in the many gaps. While their growing knowledge base helped many gaps in the presentations remained.

While Maricel spent more time examining the artifacts she found in the museums, art galleries and other homes and businesses, Raphael would spend some time in the Base library reading any documents he could find on tactics and strategy and military history.

Sometimes he would join Maricel when she began looking into a site for the first time. While their interests were similar in many areas and their research often blended, the focus for each was fixed primarily on their individual specialties.

This small city proved a treasure trove for both of them and held their interest for several seasons. By the time the call to move on came, they had moved from sharing one vehicle to two. The vehicles were larger and by the time they were ready to carry on, the two large vans were loaded down with artifacts, books and documents. Among them were many interesting devices spanning five centuries including a variety of weapons to be found in Raphael's truck.

The call of the road reached a level of intensity they hadn't felt before. It was indeed time to leave. Despite the insistence to set off, the map in their minds was less certain. The route they were to join was somewhere across the river and well beyond town. There were a number of routes to bring them across one or other of the bridges to meet up with the highway they needed to follow. As they began making their way to the nearest bridge, they would soon learn why the most efficient path was not presented as the exclusive one in their minds' eye map.

TROLLS

AS the bridge came into sight, it seemed to them more a small community with its high walls built up and over the roar and containing shops and apartments. In their separate vehicles, Raphael in the lead, he and Maricel could see something was occupying, or at least at one time occupied many of these units. Waste was haphazardly spread across the roadway and sidewalks. While everything appeared intact, huge piles of glass fragments could be seen below the windows as if those windows had been shattered and repaired many times.

More likely the windows were shattered many times and the global replenishment program replaced any items taken from shops, kitchens, restaurants and the like had replenished them. Neither could sense a human presence in the wanton destruction this represented.

Stopping their vans, they both got out to survey the scene. They had a question about whether or not the bridge was safe to cross with all the debris and shattered glass filling the roadway. The question was answered the moment they set foot on the edge of the bridge for a closer look. A horrible howl went up the moment they touched the bridge. It was loud and strange and clearly not human. They began backing up slowly as they saw creatures, clearly not human, coming from the shops and apartments onto the street. They were large and very pale, grayish white in color. Loincloths of filthy animal skins were all they wore. Their heads were hairless, their facial features were grotesque, pointed ears stood out on the sides of their heads. Their eyes were huge with large yellow pupils appearing to be hooded by prominent, jutting eyebrows and loose folds of skin just below and above the eyebrow ridge. The nose was pushed back and flattened against the face, with flaring nostrils. The most fearsome part was the huge mouth spreading almost ear to ear and showing four, very large and pointed tusks, two from each corner framing an upper and lower row of sharp fangs. The torsos were short and stocky with large arms nearly reaching to the ground and thick bandied legs. Hands and feet ended in long taloned fingers and toes.

Raphael and Maricel had neither time nor desire to linger and watch these oncoming monsters, nor any wish to speak to them as the quickly turned and raced back to their trucks. Jumping into the already running trucks, they reversed simultaneously, tires screeching. With a single motion, they both twisted the wheel rolling up onto the sidewalk almost to the wall of a large building, slammed the gears into forward and were off back down the road. They were so close together they would seem like one articulated vehicle to any bystander watching.

After ten or so minutes winding through the various city streets, weaving a path taking them well away from those horrors on the bridge, they stopped. They each checked their mirrors and let the engines idle and waited until they were sure they had not been followed. Raphael pulled his van up close beside Maricel's and lowered his window. The passenger side window on Maricel's vehicle lowered as well. Raphael shouted, "What the hell were those things?"

"No idea," replied Maricel, "but I got the clear impression we should stay away from them."

"Did you, now," said Raphael and they both exploded into relieved laughter.

Maricel was still finding it hard to keep a straight face as she asked, "How do we get out of here and onto the road we need to take. We have to get across the river somehow.

"Well," Raphael paused briefly to review the map like images in his mind, "we'll have to cross somewhere, but wherever it is, I'd rather not have to run through another group like them. I think there is a back road about a half day's drive along the river with a small bridge. We can try and cross there."

"Worth a try," Maricel shrugged, "if they live on bridges and do most of their hunting there, a back road bridge will likely have only a few of those things. If we can hit the bridge at the right speed, we might get across safely."

"We'll have to try," said Raphael, "I don't think we can turn back at this point and following this side of the river may take us far out of our way. Let's do it."

Taking some time to prepare themselves for both the out of the way journey and the possibility of trouble crossing the bridge, they set out. Maricel would lead and Raphael would follow close behind. Since the creatures at the last bridge like the werewolves, seemed to have no interest in negotiation, both Raphael and Maricel would carry high caliber handguns. The both fervently hoped they would never have to use them.

They set off, making their way to the edge of the town and along the twisting country road eventually bringing them to the one lane bridge they hoped would allow them to cross the river. If they could cross successfully, then they could get themselves on track for the next part of their journey.

After most of the day spent on the rough and twisting country road, the rounded a corner to see in front of them a long straight stretch of road. In the distance, they could just barely make out the bridge. Although they couldn't see very well from so far away, the river had narrowed, and the bridge didn't appear so long, and the side rails were low.

They stopped almost immediately and got out of their vans keeping their guns close to hand. Using high-powered binoculars, they took turns checking the bridge and its surroundings for any sign of one of those bridge trolls they had encountered earlier. These creatures, ugly and threatening were, indeed a variation of the bridge trolls of ancient earthly folklore.

There was no sign of any life to be seen near the bridge and while it did offer hope the crossing would be uneventful, the stillness around the bridge was in itself ominous. At the last bridge, the trolls didn't appear until the two humans crossed the threshold of the bridge.

The lack of an obvious presence near the bridge offered the possibility that if they approached the bridge at a high speed, they might be across and down the road having avoided any serious encounter.

Using the binoculars again, the picked out a landmark to be the acceleration point. The twisted roots of a giant tree having fallen near the edge of the road was neither too close, nor too far from the bridge. The gigantic root standing like some gigantic many-armed alien was something they would not miss as an acceleration point. Upon reaching it, they would then accelerate to bring them to the bridge at a very high speed. They would cross the bridge at full speed and maintain it for as long as they could beyond the bridge. They would go in tandem with Maricel in the front. "Have your gun ready so you can grab it and shoot one handed," Raphael reminded her, "Use your other to hold the steering wheel in line and you won't have to take your eyes of the road for a second."

THE LAST LAUGH

Maricel climbed into the van, shut the door and for the first time, fastened her seatbelt. She lay the gun on her lap holding it in place with the lap strap, tightly enough to keep it in place and lightly enough to be quickly freed and brought to bear on any threat.

Raphael had followed suit and was in place in his van. Maricel waved at him through the open window as the van began to roll forward. As the rolled up the window, she could see Raphael responding in kind. "Get on the floor," Maricel urged Scout.

She gave him a push and he seemed to take the hint and lay down on the floor curled in a tight ball. It was as if he had understood the undertone of anxiety in Maricel's voice.

The vans began moving forward, one behind the other, picking up speed as they proceeded, until reaching the acceleration point. Then, they would push the accelerator pedal to the floor and hold on tight.

They reached the gnarled tree root within half a second of each other. As they almost simultaneously floored the accelerator, the wheels squealed and the vans shuddered slightly then began racing toward the bridge, one just behind the other riding the center of the road to avoid any loose gravel to deflect their course. The bridge loomed and it looked narrow. It would require a straight and steady course right down the middle line of the bridge to avoid any contact with the railings. The vans shot toward the bridge at incredible speed. As soon as Maricel's front wheels touched the edge of the bridge where it met the road, she saw a greyish white form climbing its way over the railing from beneath the bridge. It leaped onto the road to face her. She could see the monstrous head with the huge fans and the cruel eyes. For a brief moment, she thought it was about to leap straight at her, then the van struck it. The van shuddered but didn't slow tossing the body aside like a rag doll. There was an awful crunching and bumping as the wheels passed over the body, then Maricel was off the bridge. She shivered, feeling sick and shaky, but the feeling passed quickly as she looked in the rearview mirror. There were two of the monstrosities, one at each front door of the Raphael's van. She caught a quick glance or the passenger window of Raphael's van shattering and the. The troll flew back from the window but continued to hold on to the rearview mirror with one huge, clawed hand, its feet dragging on the road. It tried vainly to climb back up to the window. Raphael's van began to weave as the monster on the driver's side was hammering at the window. As Raphael turned the barrel of his pistol toward its hideous face and fired, the van wobbled and left the road running down into a shallow ditch. The troll at the driver's window fell off, its head pulverized by the impact of the high caliber bullet. Raphael had shot it at point blank range. With the van tilting as it slid into the ditch still carrying a lot of speed, the troll on the passenger side was able to get a hold on the window edge. Raphael, slightly off balance, was trying to bring the pistol to bear on it.

At the sight of Raphael's truck leaving the rood and careening along the ditch, Maricel jammed on the breaks and slammed he vehicle into reverse. As she did, she caught sight of a third troll making its way across the van roof toward the cab

Approaching Raphael's van, she braked sharply, threw open her door and stepped out. As a shot rang out from Raphael's car sending the second troll back out the window to sprawl unmoving on the road, Maricel took aim at the troll on the roof of Raphael's van with her hand gun and pulled the trigger. A sharp pain ran up her wrist as the third troll stopped its forward motion and fell off the side of the van and onto the ground. Despite the pain, Maricel was not quite ready to drop her gun. She transferred the gun to her left hand as she slowly approached Raphael's tilting van. Her wrist throbbed as she rubbed it against her leg. Raphael pushed open the door of his van and half jumped, half stepped, shaking, onto the road. "You all right?" he shouted.

Maricel could just nod. The throbbing in her wrist was beginning to fade as normal feeling was returning to it. Raphael and Scout who had followed Maricel out of the car walked over to the inert form on the road. A quick sniff told Scout this was one odor he did not enjoy.

The troll Maricel had shot was groaning but couldn't get up. It was snapping what remained of its jaw and mouth. Its hate filled eyes stared menacingly at the two. The third troll lay crushed under the rear wheel of the van. As they watched, horror struck, the two trolls, clearly dead, began to disintegrate into shapeless piles of ash. The third one lingered a few moments longer then followed suit. A brief blustery wind and it would be as if they had never existed.

Looking back toward the bridge, they could see no sign of movement. They felt a sense of relief, but still needed to take a few moments without talking while staring blankly at nothing in particular as they tried to calm themselves.

Raphael came out of it first. "We need the van," he said looking at his van tilted half off the road, the wheels in the ditch buried up to the axle in dry soft sand.

He walked to the back doors and flung them open. "Let's try to lighten the load and see if we can get this thing back on the road."

"I don't want to stay around here too long," he added.

Maricel, her wrist nearly back to normal, stuck her gun in her belt. "Do we have anything to tow it out with?"

"Yes, I brought some cord with a high tensile rating. It should hold."

Wishing to be well away before sundown, they lightened the load as much as they could and tied Raphael's cord to the frames of both trucks.

Maricel climbed into her van and with Raphael's direction moved forward until she could feel the cord tighten.

Raphael jumped into his van and started the engine. He signaled Maricel to start pulling. She could feel the tension on the cord connecting the two large vehicles. As she pulled forward she could hear the engine straining, the back wheels scattering gravel as they sought purchase to pull the weight in back of them free.

Raphael tried to line up the wheels as best he could to reduce resistance. At first, he used the engine to try and move the vehicle forward, but the driving wheel began to spin uselessly. He shifted the van into neutral and slowly, painfully, the van began to inch forward.

It proved a long and difficult operation but eventually they got the van back on the road.

By the time they had reloaded Raphael's van and were ready to move on the sun was moving towards the distant horizon. With one last look at the three dead trolls, now nothing more than three shapeless piles of ash already being dispersed by the light afternoon breeze., then set off. As Raphael drove along behind Maricel, the windows of his van, broken by the defensive gunshots brought in the cooling evening air.

The new rattles and squeaks in both machines made it clear they would have to find replacements before they went much further.

As the last tendrils of day pulled back slowly releasing its grip on the trees framing the road, they came upon a roadhouse and motor inn.

Beside the Inn a variety of sizes of vehicles were parked near several sets of gas pumps. "We can check those out in the morning," Raphael turned from the collection of vehicles and began walking towards the Roadhouse, "but right now I'm cold and famished, and, to tell the truth, I'm still feeling a bit shaky after meeting those monsters at the bridge,"

Maricel agreed and joined him.

Inside the roadhouse, the grills were ready, the freezers and refrigerators well stocked. They polished off a hearty meal leaving plenty for Scout. Well fed, they went into the Inn lounge with several beers in hand. While it was neither too cold or too hot inside, a fire blazed in the fireplace and although it gave off no heat, they both sat down in the deep leather chairs in front of it and opened their first bottles of beer for the evening. Each took a nice long swig and melted into the relaxing comfort of their chairs.

Scout finished a lengthy exploration of the Inn's main floor lay down at Maricel's feet. "Well," said Maricel, "I guess we crossed that bridge when we came to it."

There was a brief pause then both Maricel and Raphael broke out laughing. The sheer unexpectedness caused beer to shoot out Raphael's nose and he laughed even harder. Scout gave a consternated look toward Raphael causing him to laugh even harder.

The intensity of the day, something relatively rare for them, especially since the incident with the werewolf was in the distant past, had built up a lot of tension. When they were finally able to control their laughter, they began to recognize just how much tension they had been under. The laughter had begun to break the tension and for the first time since the day began, they were both able to relax. Within moments, Raphael had dropped his half empty bottle onto a side table and was softly snoring.

Maricel got up and walked down the hall with scout at her heels. She opened the first door she came to and saw a bed. Within seconds of her head touching the pillow, she was fast asleep with Scout curled up beside her.

Maricel awoke refreshed and energized from a long sleep and made her way with Scout to the Roadhouse to have breakfast. Raphael joined her shortly after. They decided the first order of business was to check out replacement vehicles.

Out by the gas pumps they kicked the tires on a number of vehicles of various sizes. They came across several trucks able to hold their collections with room for more but after the previous day's incident, the felt that it might be a better idea to travel together in one of the larger trucks. Choosing one that combined some of the best features of twenty-first and twenty-second century truck design. The 'aerograv' shocks that could handle the roughest road as if it were a smooth super highway, and the early pre-cosmic generator powering it, would let them travel in comfort and with far fewer refueling stops.

The rest of the day was spent transferring their collections to the chosen truck. When it was loaded and ready to roll, they decided to spend a few days relaxing and rehashing their encounter with the trolls. They would now have to be careful at every bridge they came to. Yet they also were aware from the time before leaving the museum town, they had crossed many bridges without incident. Raphael spoke for both when he said, "Let's hope these monsters have not gotten too far from the museum town and are confined to the one river."

"I hope you're right, Raphael, but we really can't take the chance."

"For sure," replied Raphael, "Before we leave here, we should have one or two bridge crossing plans in place."

Shortly later with some ideas in place for getting across bridges, they again felt the call of the road. Raphael took the wheel first while Maricel sat in the passenger seat, Scout beside her.

JOLINDA AND PATAH

Jolinda and Patah's journey took them through a landscape of gentle forest covered hills, farms and quaint little villages, towns and one or two cities. Each of these, Jolinda and her friends the elvin and the Forestman were eager to explore. For Jolinda who had seen very few larger towns and cities, each one they came upon was an adventure. Patah didn't feel secure out in the open. He would join them in their explorations during the day but made sure he was back at the bus they travelled in, or the hotel or home in which they were staying, by sundown.

Like Mewser, Patah tended to confine his evening hunting close to the protective walls of where he, Jolinda and the others were staying or in the curtained sleeping areas inside the huge bus serving as their home on the road.

True to her primary interest, Jolinda spent a great deal of time visiting clinics and hospitals looking out for novel or interesting medical equipment, books and journals. She would also join Forestman checking out the libraries, museums and art galleries. On these particular expeditions, Patah would happily join them, his caveat being, "Back before dark."

Forestman and the Elvin were especially interested in sculpture and painting and with the help of Jolinda and Patah were able to bring paints and canvas, easels, modeling clay and essentially all the artist's tools they could carry back to the bus where they would try their hand at creating their own works of art.

After reading up on techniques and practicing, Robin-Eyes proved to be particularly adept at sculpting. Forestman, despite his huge hands was soon able to produce some very interesting picture and paintings. Moon-Feather used tiny delicate lines to sketch the machines Jolinda found most interesting.

Patah was content spending most of his spare time and evenings reading or watching the artists at work. While as humans, he and Jolinda shared a special bond, they spent most of their time, when not on the road, pursuing their specialties, Jolinda, physical medicine and Patah, the mysteries of the human mind and the complexities of the human soul.

The unexpected evil nature of the Wampyra troubled him. They were not part of the innate knowledge identifying most other living creatures for him. Whenever the opportunity, either with Jolinda or Forestman, Patah would discuss the Wampyra, discuss evil, wondering about the nature of a soul belonging to a creature living to kill. Unlike predatory animals they had many human traits. Did they even have a soul? While Patah knew it was beyond understanding, it perplexed him, and he found it very hard to shake.

Jolinda often tried to play the Devil's Advocate, but she had no first-hand experience with the Wampyra. She had seen the wounds from their assault on Patah but didn't feel those scars as deeply as he did.

For Jolinda, the healer, all life was precious. For Patah the healer of mind and soul, he began to suspect there were creatures out there, like the Wampyra who did not wish to have their souls healed. Equally possible, and even more frightening to Patah was the thought these beings had no soul to heal. Their souls were nothing more than life force. These thoughts troubled Patah deeply but until he could look upon intrinsic evil with manifest understanding, he was uncertain he would be able to grow into his role as psychological guide and spiritual counselor.

While Jolinda and the others sensed Patah's inner battle, they were unable to help him. Still, Patah never lost his warmth, his happy demeanor and his deep sense of caring for Jolinda and his friends.

While the others pondered the world as it was, Patah was the only one who wondered what reason awakened him and the others to this brand new world. What was this world meant to be? Who were the imperfect creators who seemed to have gotten so much wrong? Their ignorance of many things was clear in the incomplete and gap-ridden books and movies. Were these creatures, such as the Wampyra, who didn't seem to fit in with the world, further evidence of the builders' not getting it exactly right?

As the time passed and the journey followed its course in bits and starts, Patah found some resolution. The builders didn't quite get it right, but eventually it would be dealt with. He was convinced of this just as he and Jolinda were convinced there were more humans, perhaps many more, to be encountered and their journey was drawing them toward an ultimate meeting.

In Patah's mind the Wampyra whether intrinsically evil, or without souls. were urban creatures for the most part. It would be a group of country-based creatures finally bringing his ideas on good and evil into clear view. He would ultimately come to terms with the world as it currently was and grow into the leader he was destined to be.

Seated beside the driver, Jolinda, who was taking her turn behind the wheel, Patah watched the city seemingly diminish as the made their way toward the outskirts. Almost organically, to Patah's mind, the buildings grew smaller and grew farther apart.

After several days of driving through verdant forest and farms set out against the rolling hills, the land began to change. It was more rugged. There were far more fir trees. The forest appeared wilder and looked less well kept. The rolling hills had given way to rocky outcroppings. As if the undulating walls of granite beyond the forest edge were producing interference, their mind map began to fade. As they came to a major crossroad, they discovered they weren't sure which direction they needed to take.

Pausing at the intersection for some direction, they spotted a large and elegant building just off the road. Deciding to take a look at it closer up the turned into the drive. Huge gates opened as they approached, and a long circular drive brought them to the front doors of a large, beautiful structure. It had the appearance of a very wealthy private college or a specialized research facility. There was no name to be seen on the outside and, of course, no sign of anyone to greet them as they entered to find themselves in a huge reception area with numerous extremely comfortable chairs and sofas, reading desks and coffee tables scattered among them.

At one end a large window and counter revealed a server its, cupboards and fridges loaded with a variety of snacks, small meals, sandwiches and many different desserts. There were large coffee makers, and hot water containers for tea with a variety of different packaged teas beside them. Cold drinks including juices, beer, wine and soda drinks were lined up behind glass-doored coolers.

Further inspection of the main floor of the building revealed stately bedrooms, a variety of different sized meeting rooms, a spacious book filled library and an indoor saltwater swimming pool with hot tub and sauna.

While this place resembled some of the better hotels and motels they had looked through and sometimes stayed in the past, there was something uniquely different about this place. It contained, multi-faith chapel, laboratories, a variety of meeting rooms, classrooms, and seminar rooms.

All of these and the huge library, cafeteria area, bedrooms and lounge suggested a place for study and meditation, a place where scholars came to read, study, research and gather the knowledge and the understanding they needed to bring back to their home communities. Patah and Jolinda speculated it might be a kind of post-graduate institution.

There seemed to be some evidence in the presence of the chapel and the layout it was likely supervised and serviced by a community devoted to sharing knowledge. They could find no sign anyone had ever actually been there. It was just another one of the countless living spaces Patah and Jolinda had encountered on their journey remarkable by their lack of human inhabitants.

They were both in awe of this building, however. The library was filled with books and documents, tracts and magazine covering every possible subject of study. Most, of course, were truncated by gaps, and incompletions. Despite those, the library offered them enough information to last a lifetime. Not far from this magnificent library, there was an infirmary boasting all the medical equipment Jolinda had accumulated in her travels and much more.

With their mind maps temporarily in recession or at least so they hoped, there was much to examine and learn right where they were.

When their route called to them once more, they would be ready to move on.

While the building was certainly intriguing to the elvin and Forestman what appealed to them the most was the enormous and carefully cultivated parkland surrounding it. The yard with its park like gardens and trees and neatly laid out paths excited them. Most days would find Forestman and the elvin enjoying the many features of the large, neatly groomed area surrounded the building. They explored every aspect of the spacious outdoor property including the nooks and crannies on the exterior of the huge building itself.

Jolinda moved from the infirmary to the library and back to learn more about the medical equipment she found. For physicians living in the late twenty-fourth century of the original earth, some of these pieces of almost miraculous equipment would be considered state of the art or even leading edge.

Patah would take piles of books and magazines out to the reception area, find a comfortable chair of which there were many and settle in to read, stopping only for an occasional coffee or sandwich from the server.

Their stay was a very contented one. Seasons passed with little thought given to mind maps or moving on. Mewser learned every inch of the large estate, the elvin and Forestman became familiar with the flora and fauna of the park. They were all well documented on stone markers, voice and video recordings they had learned to use. This place was unlike any they had visited before, even Jolinda's original clinic where they all met. Living here was like being on a permanent vacation for all of them. For Forestman and the elvin, the park features, the pools, secret hiding places, the many grottos and the huge maze kept them intrigued and busy. It provided them with endless relaxation and joy.

For Jolinda and Patah, the stay was more like a working holiday. They were as relaxed as the others, enjoying the good life as if it would go on forever. If the mind map never resurfaced, they could be satisfied here. There was enough for them to take in to last several lifetimes.

STONE DWARVES

It was amazing how quickly this new world could change from idyllic to terrifying, as it eventually did for them. Robin-Eyes was the first to encounter the Stone Dwarves marking the beginning of a dangerous and threatening time forced to live secured inside the building they had come to call the college.

Robin-Eyes has been sitting on the grass near the front doors playing with Mewser when suddenly, Mewser hissed and turned from her crouching in attack posture. At the same moment, Robin-Eyes saw the Dwarve. She could see it was a small, stocky humanoid and she might have attempted to run to run over to it if it wasn't for the way Mewser had responded. Only then did Robin-Eyes see the short thick well-muscled arm of the Stone Dwarve holding an axe.

It showed no sign of interest in either cat or small elvin apparently not noticing them until Robin-Eyes stood up and called a friendly greeting. The Dwarve immediately raised the axe and sent it twirling toward the tiny elvin girl. If Forestman hadn't come around the corner of the building right then to see what was happening the axe would have surely cloven the wee elvin in two. Forestman did not hesitate but sped to his elvin friend and lifted her away from the tossed axe. As he lifted her to safety the corner edge of the axe nicked his calf. The pain from the touch of the

axe was excruciating, but still made the effort to sweep up
Mewser in his free hand and half ran, half staggered to the
doorway.

As he stepped through the doorway, slamming the door
behind him, the Dwarve had recovered its axe and tossed it
again. It hit the door with a loud thump. Setting Robin-Eyes
and Mewser down quite gently, Forestman looked back at
the door. Thick as it was, the axe had crimped it. He
slammed the lock on and then took a moment to look at
his injured calf. All he could see was a tiny cut and a
considerable amount of blood. For the small size of the
wound, the pain was extreme. He knew right away just like
the elvin hunting arrows the axe blade must have carried
some toxic substance. So far, the only reaction he felt from
the wound was pain. He knew he had to find Jolinda quickly,
before any other bad effects from the axe wound showed
up. Checking the infirmary first to find it empty, Forestman
hurried into the reception hall and found Jolinda talking
with Patah. As he came in, they both turned to see what was
agitating the usually placid giant.

Jolinda saw the blood flowing down his calf and pooling
on his large hairy foot immediately. She then saw the look
of agony in his eyes and quickly got up to rush to his side,
Patah following close behind. As Jolinda led Forestman back
to the infirmary, the gentle giant, in a calm and even tone
told Patah to hurry and lock the doors. Patah didn't hesitate
to ask why.

In the infirmary, Jolinda had Forestman sit on a large
treatment chair while she had a close look at his wound. The
cut was clean enough and relatively small, but the flesh at the

edges of the injury was purple and puckered. She could tell a toxin had been on whatever made the cut. She wasn't sure what it was would irritate the flesh at the wound, but this reaction was similar to the effect of the poison on the elvin hunting arrows.

She went to her bag sitting on a desk by the door and reached into it to take out a vial of antidote she had made and a syringe. She filled the syringe from the vial and injected it into Forestman's leg near the site of the wound. Forestman relaxed almost instantly. The edges of the cut smoothed, and the giant's natural color returned. She then squirted some anti-toxin onto a plaster and placed it on the wound.

"Ok," she said to no one in particular, "let's watch it for a while."

"How did this happen?" asked Patah.

Forestman told them of the axe wielding elvin-like creature, no taller, but much broader of body. He explained what had nearly happened to Robin-Eyes and Mewser's response to the diminutive creature. "Is everybody inside?" a tone of concern in Jolinda's voice.

Forestman nodded.

"Then we best make sure all the doors are locked before we find an unwanted axe wielding visitor,"

Patah came into the room to tell them he had taken care of the doors and locks. He nodded his head as Jolinda reiterated Forestman's story as he had seen the little axe man too.

"Isn't there a master lock switch overriding all the individual locks." asked Jolinda. "There is, "said, Patah. "Let me get to it."

He rushed off to the service room near the front desk. Modeled on plans for a University, meditation and learning center, the building had been designed and built with the utmost security in mind. Patah decided right then the builders may have been less than perfect about many things, but their constructions were quite efficient and easily secured. Whether this place's origins were based on something that once existed, or designed from fiction, it really didn't matter, because it had been made real on this regenerated earth.

The college was well stocked and impenetrable. Even if supplies didn't regenerate the way they did on Legacy Earth, it could survive a siege for a very long time. How it would fare in modern warfare with state of the art weapons was one question, but for what Jolinda, Patah and friends were up against it was an ideal refuge.

Security cameras showed the Stone Dwarve releasing his axe from the door. He was about to take a swing at it but stopped and looked around. He trotted back into the parkland where he was met by a large number of his fellows. They were unaware of security cameras and door handles as well. They were content to hammer at the one door until they either broke through or their axes fell to pieces. As the number of Stone Dwarves increased, it became obvious to those on the inside that these small powerful creatures wanted in. Given the original attack on Robin-Eyes if they were to get in, the deadly consequences for the friends inside was certain. They dare not let one in.

The Stone Dwarves had no use for a building such as the college. They didn't want anyone or anything else to control it. It angered them. They felt everything in their path was theirs and the only life permitted to exist there were fellow Stone Dwarves. The plant life only remained to serve them although they had no compunctions about destroying that too. They would not stop attacking the college until they controlled the building and those now inside were eliminated. They would do their best to make it uninhabitable, then move on. Of course, their cause was lost one because of regeneration. They would be barely out the door when everything inside the college except for Jolinda, Patah and the others would be back as it was.

At first the hammering focused on the one door. The sound was loud enough to remind the current residents it would be wise not to attempt to leave the safety of the building be. Because the door was the one used by the giant carrying the elvin and the cat to escape the deadly axe. They saw it as the only entrance to the building. After further exploring the exterior, they found several more similar doors. Uncertain in their basic ignorance of human habitation, the Stone Dwarves suspected that they might also prove to be ways in, and they began to pound on them with their axes. By nightfall there was pounding on every one of the doors and there were a good number of them. The damage the axe blades caused the doors was minimal and would stay so no matter how long they chopped and hammered at them.

The constant din from the axes hammering at the doors became annoying very rapidly. The only escape, and not a complete one, was to move to the suites on the fourth floor. This was only partly satisfactory as Jolinda and Patah didn't really know just how strong the building security might be under the ongoing pressure on the doors.

They were worried the Stone Dwarves might figure out the windows were a way in as well and try their axes on them. The worry was unnecessary as the windows were explosion proof and could withstand the Dwarves' axes just as well as the doors could. That and the fact The Stone Dwarves could not differentiate between wall and window meant the windows would never become targets of the Dwarves axes.

While the doors seemed vulnerable as they crimped and dented under the blows of the Stone Dwarves' axes, this was a part of the security design. The flexibility of the doors only served to fix them into the strong solid frames more tightly. The damage, no matter how bad it might look was only superficial.

Those inside the college were completely safe as long as they stayed inside.

After many days, had passed with the hammering at the doors unabated, and it was clear they would persist until they got in. What this meant for those inside apart from the constant annoyance of the noise from the axes striking the doors, was they were virtual prisoners. While they could reduce the noise to the background by shutting all the fire doors and staying on the fourth floor, they would remain prisoners until they found a way to get past or get rid of the Stone Dwarves.

Any effort to communicate with these intense and single-minded creatures was useless. Just the sight of a face at a window, as those inside discovered in very short order, would enflame the Dwarves. They would swarm toward it, hurling their axes, their broad, bearded visages radiating hate. When they moved away from the windows, the Dwarves would all go back to hammering on the door.

Jolinda and Patah were able to continue their reading and research for some time after the attack started, the others worked on their art, but sorely missed the opportunity to be outside. They had learned all they could about these Dwarves, which was precious little. The few fragments they could find in the literature suggested they lived underground in communal areas dug out of sheer rock. The quality of this information, while not necessarily factual or even relevant to the crowd of tiny creatures surrounding the college and continuously pounding on the doors, did raise some concern. If it was true the Dwarves were skilled miners, then the walls of the college would be no protection for the occupants of the college should the Stone Dwarves bring such a skill to bear against the brick walls of the building.

So far, the Stone Dwarves had not proved very inventive in their attack. Their modus operandi remained limited to swarming the doors and hitting it with everything they had which amounted to nothing more than their individual axes and the strength in their arms to swing them. The windows only drew their attention when they could see somebody inside through them.

The Stone Dwarves did not appear to like open heights so the third and fourth levels of the college provided some reprieve from the loud pounding on the doors and the unsettling sight of twelve or fifteen dwarves rushing at a window with axes raised.

Jolinda, Patah and the others found their exile lasting a disturbingly long time. The need to move on. hadn't troubled them since they arrived at the college, but now it began to build. The next step on the journey began to form within the humans' minds and while it had not quite reached a level of urgency, it was becoming something of a problem.

Until they could get to the bus, life and limb intact, they could make no attempt to follow their psychically projected directions. They had to find some way to escape the Stone Dwarves' siege and get back on the road.

They had lived long enough with the disconcerting hammering and the lack of certainty about their safety if they remained there. The time had come to devise a plan of escape allowing them to get back on the bus and far away from these threatening creatures. Then they could worry about the next leg of their journey.

Escaping the Dwarves would be no easy task as there was no longer any doubt that Should any of them fall into the hands of the Dwarves, they would be treated without mercy. They may not be the Wampyra, which still haunted Patah, but they were just as demonic, single-minded, and dangerous.

With the urge to move on growing more insistent by the day, Jolinda, Patah and their companions needed a strong plan if they were to get to the bus and make their escape from the vicious Dwarves and their terrible axes.

They began to inventory any items useful to them in their defense and in what they hoped could be used to expedite their escape. Whatever they found even possibly useful, they brought to the reception hall and with under the incentive of the constant hammering, research began. They had found everything from high-powered music players, loudspeakers, a wide variety of chemicals, canisters, sheets of aluminum, steel pipes and several boxes of emergency flares among others. The question was what to do with it.

At first, they thought they would make bombs and along with the hand guns they had found in a locker in the basement, battle the Stone Dwarves, reduce their numbers and create enough fear among them to drive the remaining Stone Dwarves off.

The idea didn't sit very well with any of them. They were not killers even in self-defense. There was also the concern the Dwarves were much too persistent and would likely increase their aggressive assault on the college, climb to the roof or forget the doors and go after the stone walls a bomb blast might weaken. Damaging the outer walls might do nothing more than reduce the strength of the barrier between them and the Dwarves. It might also serve to draw the attention of the Dwarves to the walls and inspire them to work stone of the walls. They might find this more to their favor than blunting their axes on high strength steel doors.

Any kind of firefight was out of the question. It might even prevent them from getting to the bus and force them into a far more dangerous state of siege.

They would have to find a means to draw the Dwarves away from the bus and the front doors of the college long enough for them to get to the bus and be gone before they returned. They needed to create a distraction and not just a small one.

Whatever it would be, it would have to be very persuasive to catch the Dwarves' attention and hold it long enough for an escape to be made.

"How about we give them a sound and light show," suggested Patah.

"It will have to be sudden and loud and shocking to get their attention and send any at the front or around the bus to the back of the building." Added Jolinda.

The others enthusiastically joined in, "Turn on the sprinklers, too."

"Those music players are very loud at full volume. We could turn those on and play different pieces of music from each.

"We can use the canisters and chemicals to make loud and colorful explosions."

"If its set up to start suddenly and all at once, they should come to see what it is."

The full effect won't be sustained for long, but if we can get to the bus fast with as much as we can carry, we might be down the driveway to the highway at least before they notice we're gone."

Everyone was in full agreement this was the plan giving them the best possible opportunity to escape.

ESCAPE

They spent the next few days setting up the speakers along the third floor windows at the back end of the building, creating chemical fireworks and setting up launchers to vault them into the back yard. They adjusted the spotlights so they would strobe and set the parkland sprinkler system to maximum. Once it was done, they gathered what they decided was important for them to bring along. They placed everything from books to medical devises, food and drink and beloved pieces of art onto wheeled desks and infirmary gurneys. Once the spectacle was started and the Stone Dwarves gone from the front of the building, they would have to move quickly. Each would have a job to do. Forestman would push the desk and a gurney to the front doors of the bus. Moon-Feather would unlock the storage doors for him to open and he would quickly load it. Jolinda would push a gurney down for Forestman to load, then climb aboard with Mewser get to the driver's seat and fire up the engine. The elvin would bring the food they could carry on board. Patah, after starting the back of the building show would transport whatever he could, gurney, wheel chair and pull them to the storage area and toss whatever they carried in. Together he and Forestman would make sure the storage bays were closed and climb aboard.

This should all be accomplished in the shortest time possible while the Dwarves were still fascinated and consternated by the activity at the back of the college.

For the lights and fireworks to be effective it had to be dark but with enough daylight left to find and load the bus so they wouldn't need to use lanterns attracting the attention of some of the Dwarves.

Everything had been loaded onto a variety of gurneys, wheeled carts and wheeled desks. Robin-Eyes and Moon-Feather placed bags of food on two office chairs they knew they could handle despite their small size. The food was important because they did not really know how far they would have to go before they could safely stop.

The rag tag rolling stock was prioritized. Their goal was to take whatever they could get on the bus before the Stone Dwarves noticed them. If the Dwarves spotted them before they were fully loaded, they would just leave what was left and board.

Everything was lined up at the large front doors of the building in its assigned order. As soon as the Dwarves were out of sight, rushing to see what the commotion was, Jolinda, Forestman and the elvin would push everything through the doors to the outside. Patah would catch up as they finished. Once the doors closed, the college and whatever it contained would be sealed to them as well as to the Dwarves.

The behavior of the Stone Dwarves over the course of their siege showed wanton disregard for the parkland, smashing the concrete and steel benches and the information displays. They pulled down trees and trampled the gardens. Knowing full well this wanton destruction would be carried indoors by the Dwarves, Jolinda and the others were determined not to let it happen. From this came the decision to seal the building when they left. This, of course, made it even more imperative they were on the bus and underway before any Dwarves wandered back to the front of the building and saw them.

They had connected everything for the spectacle by long wires so they could set them off remotely from near the main doors and no one would have to run back taking the stairs, risking injury, and losing valuable time.

They gathered with the gurneys, wheeled carts, and chairs at the main doors while Patah, in the center of the reception lounge prepared to set their diversionary spectacle in motion.

The sun had dropped beyond the distant hills, and it began to grow dark. As the daylight faded toward twilight, Patah called out, "Everybody ready?"

The response was a resounding yes.

"Ok, here we go."

Patah pushed the lever setting off the commotion at the back of the building to the on position. The noise was instantly deafening as a number of music players roared to life. Even in the reception area at the front of the building, bright flashes from the strobing spotlights could be seen. Despite all this, the major aspect of the spectacle, the primary diversion from the fireworks did not seem to be engaging.

While the others waited at the door watching to see if the Dwarves from the front were on their way to see what was happening, Patah raced down the hallway and up the stairs to where the explosive rockets were set he saw immediately a wire had come disconnected. He grabbed the loose wire and connected it to the igniter. His hands were inside his sleeves to reduce the burning pain of the electrical discharge. The pain was extreme, although mercifully brief as the first of the rockets shot through the open window and into the air beyond, exploding in a massive shower of multicolored sparks. As the second rocket launched, he raced back, reaching the reception as the doors were being flung open and the gurneys and carts and chairs were being pushed out. He raced to join them pushing one of the last gurneys down the ramp to the bus just behind Forestman who was making his second trip. The storage bays were open and beginning to fill as Jolinda opened the bus doors, picked up Mewser and clambered aboard, the elvin in close pursuit. She dropped quickly into the driver's seat and turned the ignition. Despite the amount of time the bus had sat idle, it started right away, its quiet rumble almost indiscernible over the pounding cacophony of music and exploding rockets.

Slamming the baggage bay hatches shut, Forestman and Patah ran to the door. Forestman was carefully squeezing his ponderous frame through the door of the bus with Patah just behind him. Looking around as he waited to get on board behind the giant, Patah noticed movement of in the distance near the far end of the building. "Dwarve," he shouted pushing against Forestman.

It was amazing how fast those stocky little characters could run given the shortness of their legs. Patah had barely got onto the bus when there came the thump of an axe blade striking the closing door where he had been less than a moment ago. "Get moving," He cried out to Jolinda, and the bus was underway.

The Stone Dwarve who had thrown the axe at Patah tried to grab at the door but was brushed off. He was able to grab the rear bumper as a second Dwarve jumped up on the back of the bus. Turning off the lights, Jolinda called to the others, "Darken the windows."

Those in the bus, except for the driver could see the one Stone Dwarve with the axe as he grabbed on to the ladder running up the rear of the bus to the roof. Although those inside could see out, it couldn't see in and began to climb the ladder. The other Dwarve, the one without the axe, they couldn't see, edged its way along the bumper to the ladder. It saw the other Dwarve already up the ladder, go over onto the top of the bus and so it too began to climb the ladder to join his fellow on the roof. It was not an easy climb given the wind, the speed of the bus and the ground racing beneath. Moon-Feather called out to Jolinda in her high, sweet musical voice telling her a second Stone Dwarve was trying to get to the roof.

Those who didn't know Moon-Feather might find the sound of her voice soothing, but Jolinda was familiar with it. She heard the words, not the tone.

"Tell me when it gets to the top," she called back.

A second later she heard Moon-Feather's melodic voice, "I think it's there, now."

Jolinda began swerving the huge vehicle from one side of the road to the other with apparently no obvious effect on the Dwarves on the bus roof. Their progress was slow across the top as they fought against the wind and the swaying from the snaking motion of the bus over the road.

The Dwarf with the axe began to hammer on the roof. They could see from below it was denting the roof and would soon open a hole in it.

From her place behind the wheel, Jolinda shouted, "everyone hold on tight."

She waited to see through the rear view mirror they all had braced themselves. Then she slammed on the brakes. The bus shuddered, losing speed instantly. The one Stone Dwarve, axe in hand flew past the front window. Wide, startled eyes stared at Jolinda as it fell from the roof and struck the pavement just ahead of the bus. It didn't move as the bus passed over its diminutive body.

The other Stone Dwarve in desperation had been able to grab on to a windshield wiper as it slid off the roof and was holding on for dear life.

Jolinda switched on the wipers resulting in a scene that would have been grotesquely comic if it were not so horrifying. The Dwarve slid back and forth, its nose and mouth rubbing against the glass of the windshield. The Dwarve's eyes flicked around as if looking for an escape. When, for a brief moment the sliding face made momentary eye contact with Jolinda, the Stone Dwarve's eyes projected a look radiating absolute hatred. The scene played out for several seconds before the Dwarve tried to reach out for Jolinda's throat not realizing a layer of thick glass was between them. This caused the Dwarve to lose its grip on the wiper blade and slip off the front of the bus and down the slippery, unadorned side of the vehicle to the ground. There was a slight bump as the wheels rode over something. Despite the obviously evil nature of the Dwarves, Jolinda hoped the bump they felt was caused from running over a pothole. With the growing darkness, there was no way of ever knowing. All any aboard the bus could see was a small dark shadow on the road rapidly shrinking into the distance.

Relieved, but feeling no particular sense of cheer, they drove through the night, Jolinda and Patah taking turns at the wheel. They continued driving through the next day until the fuel gauge was approaching zero. Rather than wait for it to regenerate over night, they stopped at a large roadside fueling area and rest stop. Before exiting the bus, they carefully searched the area through the windows, but could see no sign of Dwarve like or other creatures. Patah stayed behind the wheel ready for a quick exit as the others got out and did an exterior check. The check revealed nothing more in the way of creatures except for the reminders of their existence. They had left behind a dent near the bottom of the door made by a Dwarve axe as well as some slight denting on the roof and a bent windshield wiper.

The damage was slight and would not affect the bus, so they filled the fuel tank and were back on the road following the route laid out as the map was unfolding in Jolinda and Patah's minds.

SHANIRA AND BRUNELL

Shanira and Brunell were continuing to travel separately. They would meet each night to discuss their understanding of the psychic map waxed and waned as they went along. Over time, they like the others had experienced the fading or complete disappearance of the map in their minds and had found themselves staying for large amounts of time in one or another riverside community. In these cases, they usually found plenty to occupy themselves with, whether reading, exploring and in Shanira's case disassembling and reassembling various machines.

The past few days had revealed some disconcerting information. The land route Brunell would take in his truck was moving steadily away from the river some distance ahead. As far as they could tell from their own understanding and maps they found in a book store, this was a significant diversion. It would ultimately find them travelling very far apart. They had no idea, the maps being more local than general, if river and road would ever join up again.

Brunell had a truck full of unique implements and agricultural research while Shanira's cruiser was becoming quite loaded down with her own collection of books, maps and blueprints as well as many other devices in various states of disassembly. Neither Brunell, nor Shanira would leave their accumulated items behind. Yet, neither had any intention of deserting their accompanying human and other friends. The river was a lifeline for the Marefolk, and they could not leave it behind. The vistas of land, field, farm, and forest were comforting to Brunell and Shanira loved her cruiser the product of her own design and construction.

A map on the wall inside a restaurant they visited together provided some useful information for them. Not too far ahead was a small city where the river widened into a fairly large lake. Beyond the city, the road began its drift away from the river. Since they could sense very little beyond, they decided to stay there for a while and see if some compromise could be found letting them all travel together.

Arriving at the city lakefront, Shanira was able to find a large industrial area with a Marina standing next to a large hotel. Brunell was able to make his way through the city streets and met up with them shortly after they had arrived.

The Marefolk explored the lake, its harbor facilities and the small islands dotting it. Brunell took the time to inventory the contents of his truck and visit some of the local museums and libraries and to do some reading, a somewhat disconcerting activity given the many gaps and missing material in most of them. He found little in the way of novel agricultural technology except for a few things generally related to local agricultural industries.

Meanwhile, Shanira had been experimenting with miniature tow barges, testing the action of the currents on them and what could safely be designed to be towed behind her cruiser and hold the contents of Brunell's truck as well as the larger, more cumbersome items she had collected and placed on board the cruiser over the course of her travels. With the help of the Mare folk and the machinery and tools in the marina dry dock and several of the small river barges moored along the bank, Shanira was able to build in fairly short order, a singular barge able to carry a large load. Best of all, it would interfere very little with the speed and maneuverability of the cruiser.

The barge would hold Brunell's truck and a great deal of Maricel's collection with plenty of expansion space should they find more. It also provided the Marefolk with more comfortable access and a built in sprinkler system allowing them to spend more time aboard while travelling.

The day the barge was finished and rolled out to be connected to the tie bars and tow rigging Shanira had added to the rear of her cruiser, Brunell had taken a couple of bottles of champagne from the hotel bar. One was to be used to christen the new barge. The second bottle was for the cruiser itself, but Brunell chose to hold this one back until the time was right.

They christened the barge "the Follower" and had a spontaneous celebration to welcome this new addition to the convoy.

Loading Brunell's truck aboard the barge was a slow procedure, but the design was superb, and all the loading went smoothly. Soon they again ready to set off on their mysterious ongoing journey.

As they pushed off from the marina slip, Brunell surveyed the cruiser. He was amazed to find the sleek and efficient craft had plenty of space below deck, a well-stocked cooking area and several cozy sleeping quarters. They could stay aboard for many days, anchoring off shore at night when they didn't find worthy accommodations on shore, or to visit less habited places they were interested in exploring as they went along.

The following few days were uneventful. The lake began to narrow, and they discovered three various sized rivers fed into it. There was, however, in their minds, no doubt regarding which one to take.

The river they were directed to, they discovered as they moved away from the lake, was deep and the current middling strong against them. To the naked eye, the river in its widest expanses appeared to amble along and was ultimately no challenge to Shanira's well-designed and sleek cruiser or to the streamlined barge trailing behind it.

The weight of the barge was so buoyant and well balanced it barely added any significant drag. The cruiser lost little speed potential, although on this part of the river, at least, speed was not essential to their steady progress.

No one aboard had any idea how important this factor would become not too far ahead.

Sitting on the foredeck one warm lazy evening, Shanira, Brunell and the Marefolk were enjoying each other's company. Ranger who apparently had assigned himself night watch slept near Brunell. Shanira had just finished letting the cruiser drift in toward the right hand shore and dropped anchor.

"This is such a wonderful boat you have built, Shanira," said Brunell, "What do you call it?"

"Call it!" exclaimed Shanira.

"Well," continued Brunell, "We named the barge The Follower, but we have no name for what it is following. You know most boats this size and ships have names. You must have one for this."

"Well," Shanira spoke casually, "actually, to me it has just been, the boat."

"It's more than just a boat, Shanira. It is sleek and elegant and has certainly served you well."

"Yes, it has, and it will continue to do so. You'll find it will serve you well, too."

"I haven't the slightest doubt. In fact, Ranger and I have never felt more at home than on this beautiful vessel."

River-Jewel agreed, "She is a graceful as any of the Marefolk the way she slices so cleanly and powerfully through the water,"

"Interesting you called the boat she, River-Jewel. Is it because of our friend the builder, here, or do you have another reason?" asked Brunell.

"Partly," returned River-Jewel, "She is strong and resilient, and a great protector as is Shanira, but it is her soft beautiful lines and her gracefulness and gentle she feels as we speed through the water. That is why, to me, this boat is a she."

Brunell nodded and turned to Shanira, "We must come up with a name suiting this vessel."

Shanira smiled. She did love her cruiser and she had to admit it had in her mind taken on a personality of its own. She remembered how she had shared her life with it before meeting the Marefolk, and how it continued to present itself as a unique member of this little company, "She is a special vessel and does deserve a special name. One identifying her in a way we can all relate to."

"Yes," Brunell was adamant, "we must think this over carefully and find a name we can all agree on. We all have our ideas and so, let's put them together and see what we can come up with."

For the rest of the evening and the next day, they stayed at anchor discussing possible names. Many were suggested, but none were settled on. They came up with a lot of names, Dancer, strider, glider and rider. They thought about waves and light, streams and grace and fleetness. They called out to each other, "Foam Rider," or "Sparkle strider."

The others would stop, think it over then nod of shake their heads depending on how the particular name struck them. Finally, it was River Jewel who said, "all of this over a name. The cruiser is as quick and ineffable as sunlight as it glides across the reflection in the water scattering it into shimmering droplets. Why not call it Sunbeam Glider?"

River Jewel hadn't actually said ineffable, but she did bring the discussion to an end as she tried to express in her own words the idea of ineffability. It was enough for the rest of them to try and grasp her elusive thought process to cause them to agree. The cruiser would be called "Sunbeam Glider" and at the next marina they found, the name would be proudly emblazoned on the prow.

"And," exclaimed Shanira proudly, "she will be my "Sunny". The newly declared "Sunbeam Glider", or "Sunny" for short, said nothing. Once the name had been stenciled to both her sides, near the prow, one could almost sense in her bearing, satisfaction and more than a little pride at her new name.

So it was, that Shanira and Brunell along with the Marefolk and Ranger continued their journey aboard the ever cooperative Sunbeam Glider and The Follower. As they progressed upstream, almost imperceptibly, the on shore surrounding began to change.

Thick stretches of verdant forest had given way to sparsely scattered, almost skeletal trees and scrub. The river rounded a bend to flow through a wide high walled ravine. It seemed to those aboard the boat that in turning that corner they had fallen off the earth onto a desert world. As the walls pulled back from the riverbank, they could see that the land was painted in a variety of shades of brown and tan. Plant-life was sparse and almost nonexistent and what there was reflected the multiple shades of brown of the surrounding desert and distant rocky hills.

The river no longer reflected the greens and blues of earlier on. Now in the distance it seemed to be a smoggy teal while close to the cruiser, it appeared to hold shades of brown and dark, lichen green and the depths were a murky blackness. The river seemed to snake its way through desert into badlands of high cliffs and mesas.

As they wended their way up the winding river, they were surprised from time to time to see buildings overlooking the edge of the water. Eventually they came to an unconventionally large Marina and Inn sprawling along the riverbank. Even close to the shore the buildings were surrounded by the dry rocks and sand of the desert and backed by distant hills that appeared more gravel than granite. From what they could tell from the deck, the décor of the sprawling building seemed to be at one with the rest of its surroundings.

Although the call of the river was reasonably strong and ultimately, they would continue to follow it, there was something about this odd place that invited them to stay a while. Jolinda guided Sunny and The Follower to the large jetty that reached out to where the river widened. There they could tie up the cruiser and accompanying barge and walk or swim right up to the Inn doors.

As Shanira, Brunell and Ranger walked up to the main doors, they found the still air to be intensely hot and so dry it almost pinched their nostrils. The Marefolk took some time to explore the slow moving waters, finding shelter from the intense sun under the jetty or further out in the murky darkness of the deep.

In sharp contrast to the outside, the air inside the Inn was cool and fresh,

To our journeyers, the surroundings looked so strange and out of place with all they had passed before that it seemed the legacy builders had accidently dropped a piece of alien landscape intended for some far off desert planet onto the otherwise rich and fertile earth.

The soil close to the shore seemed to be completely devoid of life. Around the side and back of the buildings and stretching off to the stark hills in the distance, they could see on closer inspection brown moss and tan grasses and a few widely dispersed scrub bushes. From where they were looking, inside the front hall of the Inn, they couldn't tell if the scrub was dead, or was blending into the background. The heat of the day seemed intensified by the sunlight gleaming off the particles of silica that appeared to dominate the landscape.

The Marefolk found the surface of the river too warm and uncomfortable for them except for the deep dark current that seemed to flow with a life of its own far below the surface. The murkiness of the deep current, the soup-like warmth of the surface and the dusty, dry air sent the Marefolk inside to spend the night in the large swimming pool, with the heat turned off. The high ratio of plain fresh water to the purifying solvents meant that they could stay there with little discomfort.

Despite the alien and bizarre landscape, they could not turn back. The route that called to them continued upriver. They knew that several smaller streams that were somewhere up ahead of them fed the large river, but they did not yet know which branch they needed to take. They could not go forward.

The waters from these feeder rivers seemed to shun the shallows and the strange land that bordered it, feeding instead the deep mid river current.

At night, a hot wind blew incessantly through the distant hills, and around the buttes and mesas, moaning and sighing. They quickly discovered that despite the creature comforts of the Inn, this was not a place any of them wished to remain for very long. Until the route ahead became clearer, however, the Inn, at least was cool and well supplied.

There was a quality to the land that disturbed them. It seemed as if it was a giant monster, half buried that was about to spring up and pounce on them. That and the heat and dryness kept the journeyers inside most of the time. When they did go out, the Marefolk stayed in the river while Shanira, Brunell and Ranger stayed close to it as well. The dry back acres held little interest for them although Brunell did some cataloguing of the scrub and the tiny biting insects that lived on them.

HARPIES

From a distance, they looked like dirty angels as if they had lay in the dirt making images of themselves. As they came closer, their avian heritage, such as it was, became clearer. Their faces were a cruel cross between a human and a bird of prey. Their noses were hooked and chitinous, their eyes were round, large beads. Long lobed pointy ears and small sharp teeth in a small slash of a mouth below the beak-like nose completed the facial features. The legs and feet were thin and bird-like with long taloned toes that helped them cling to the rocky Cliffside, or branches. Boney sharp nailed fingers merged into a forearm of corded muscle. From the elbow up, the arms were connected to large leathery scale covered wings. Their lanky bodies made them look like tall, winged skeletons. Only when they first launched into flight did they reveal their full length. On the ground and in the air, their bodies were hunched, and their heads seemed to hang down from long scaly necks.

The most chilling aspect of these creatures was in the words they spoke and the sound they made speaking them. The sounds emitted from their mouths were high pitched, gravelly and incredibly loud. Utterances came out as horrendous screeches. Carefully listening to these utterances, an almost impossible thing to do, they would prove to be in Assianangle and those who heard them could not miss the threats the bore.

The first to sight them was Shanira. She was aboard Sunbeam Glider doing her daily inspection of the engine and drive mechanisms. Although it was morning, the heat was stifling forcing her to come out from below deck to get a breath of less cloying air. While the air on deck provided little in the way of relief from the stagnant heat below decks, the openness of the deck was welcomed after spending time below.

Sitting on one of the padded benches against the cruisers deck side, Shanira stretched and began to close her eyes. As she did, she thought she had detected some movement from across the river. She may have noticed, but at first, took little note. She Then slowly it began to dawn on her that all the time at the desert inn they had seen no movement beyond a few flying insects and minuscule lizards. She quickly opened her eyes and began to scan the horizon in the direction she had seen the movement. Against the background of the distant cliffs beyond the far side of the river, she could see nothing. Nothing seemed to be moving out there and for a moment she considered that she had seen nothing, that it was a trick of the eye. Then, downstream and across the river she though she saw something on a ledge high above the water. Despite the distance, she was sure she saw something that didn't belong, that hadn't been there before. It looked like something sitting there, perhaps a large bird or another desert animal.

Beside the step up to the captain's chair were her binoculars. She shifted carefully to reach for them while trying not to take her eyes off the distant form. Taking hold of the binoculars, she could not have taken her eyes off the distant form for more than a split second, but when she looked through them she could see nothing there. Scanning the horizon with the binoculars she could detect no sign of anything unusual. While that might have ended it Shanira was not prepared to doubt herself. She was fully convinced that something had been there looking back at her from the distance cliff top. She was not seeing things.

She stayed aboard Sunny for a while, scanning the surroundings for anything out of the ordinary but could find nothing. Putting down the binoculars, she headed back below decks to finish her maintenance project.

Later, returning to the cool of the inn, she told Brunell of what she termed an "odd occurrence."

Brunell, like Shanira was not one to easily dismiss anything out of the ordinary, "Perhaps it was a shadow or a strange play of light that was responsible, but because we have seen very little life here doesn't mean that there isn't any. I think we should all make a point of keeping a lookout," suggested Brunell. Shanira and the others having heard her story agreed.

From then on, they each regularly took some time scanning the horizon for movement or anything that looked out of place. For all their careful scanning, there saw nothing.

Significant time had passed with no sign of anything untoward. Shanira was back on Sunbeam Glider in the stifling heat below decks doing her regular maintenance. She had just shut down the engine after running a test of the starter, when she heard a distant screeching sound that seemed to be saying "leave here" in mangled Assianangle. The voice was not clear, but the screech was. Shanira was certain something was out there. She quickly finished off what she was doing and went up on deck. She took her binoculars and began to scan the horizon. At first, she could see nothing out of the ordinary, then, on distant cliff overlooking the water, she saw it again. At first it didn't move, and she kept her eye on it. There would be no turning away to grab binoculars. She had them and through their lenses she was able to get a closer look. She could see its shape and color not quite blending in with drab browns and washed out greys of the terrain. It seemed more off-white against the blue of the sky. Just as Shanira's watchfulness began to take its toll and force her to blink, the form seemed to elongate upward, two wings spreading out behind it. Although she was not quite certain of what she was seeing, she could hear a screeching sound coming from the direction was looking. Enunciated within that screech were the words, spoken in Assianangle, "Leave here."

In spite of the cruel heat, Shanira felt a chill at the sound. It was not just the screeching, or the words, but the overall sense of a terrible threat that came with them.

She made her way quickly along the dock to the inn and as she passed through the door, a glance back revealed that it was still there, standing erect, its bat like wings spread. She called out to Brunell who came running. He had never heard such fear and anxiety in her voice since they had met. As he approached where she was standing near the main doors, Shanira pointed towards the far off, bird like creature, "What is that?" she asked in an agitated voice.

"I don't know," said Brunell.

Not having heard the screeching of the creature, he was quite calm. "It could be a bird of some sort."

"Or some kind of person with wings," interjected Shanira, clearly still upset by what she had heard, "Its call is dreadful, an irritating and threatening screech. It was clearly telling us to leave here. Whatever it is, I have a bad feeling about it. Where are the others?"

"Thunder-Fin and Flash-Fin are in the pool. I don't know where the others are. Ranger just came in. River-Jewel had brought him out to play in the water," replied Brunell.

"Yes," Shanira spoke much more calmly as the impact of the screeching had faded, "Ranger can't handle the water here for very long. It's too warm to be very refreshing for him." River-Jewel and Sandy-Hue must still be in the river."

Thunder-Fin, who had heard the anxious tone in Shanira's voice had made his way to the door. They pointed the mysterious creature out to him. "Sandy-Hue has probably taken River-Jewel down to the deep current to cool off. They've been out for a while. They may have come up down river and be on their way back now," explained Thunder-Fin, adding, "I hope it isn't dangerous."

"Well," said Brunell, "Those two might be out of our reach, but that thing, whatever it is, up on that cliff has yet to move. So far, it's staying up there on the ledge, spreading its wings, but not flying."

"Let's hope it stays that way," said Shanira, "and that they get back safely."

As each of those inside the inn returned to the main entrance from time to time to check the mysterious creature on the distant cliff, they could see that it remained there. It was there for the longest time and Shanira and the others began to consider it a new permanent fixture, then, as suddenly as it had appeared, it was gone.

Of more concern to them, it was growing late, sunset was at hand, but River-Jewel and Sandy-Hue had not yet returned. They had never before stayed away so late.

The Maremen and Shanira were about to do a search of the river and Brunell was going to take Ranger and check along the riverbank for any sign of them when a pounding came at the door. The two of them were there, pressed as close to the door as they could get as Brunell let them in. Both were shaking and their relief at being inside was almost palpable. These were creatures that loved the outdoors. They had lived most of their lives between the water and the open air. Indoors, especially in the smaller places they had stayed, the Marefolk would grow agitated if they had to stay inside for too long. Showers and pools were usually short-term stopgaps for them. They preferred to relax and even sleep in the shallows along the river's edge or near Sunbeam Glider and The Follower. Their best times were when Shanira weighed anchor and they could race alongside the cruiser. Never before had Shanira or Brunell seen River-Jewel and Sandy-Hue so happy to be inside.

Shanira could see some of her earlier fear in their eyes, "What happened to you two. We were really starting to worry."

They were all dismayed by what River-Jewel and Sandy-Hue told them. As Thunder-Fin had suggested earlier, the two had gone to the cool deep currents and were letting it carry them down stream, then they swam back for a second run. They surfaced and saw that the sun was low in the horizon and decided to get back. Although the water was warm and soupy, River-Jewel decided to swim the river shallows back so that she could enjoy the play of the sunlight on the underwater flora. River-Jewel, ever the artist, liked to gather inspiration for her sculpture and painting from this, and Sandy-Hue was generous with his daughter's wishes as she was the only remaining member of his family. He might have preferred the cooler depths for the return journey, but for her sake, he agreed to swim the shallows with her. They were casually swimming just below the surface when a large dark shadow blocked out the sun. Whatever the shadow was, it seemed to hover over them just above the water. Curious, they lifted their heads out of the water to see what this shadow that seemed to be tracking them might be. As they broke the surface they could see three shadowy flying creatures above them. "At first," said Sandy-Hue," they looked like three dirty sheets with wings. They were indistinct with the sun behind them."

At the moment, they broke water, the three creatures began to scream and screech at them. It was a terrifying sound. They first thought it was just hideous noise coming from the three creatures then they realized that they were screeching words, "Leave here! Leave here."

They began to dart down towards them on their massive wings, then dart away, then back again. As they did that, they continued to screech their warning. Saliva droplets fell from their mouths as the screamed at them. The strange flying creatures' tiny sharp teeth gleamed with the saliva. Saliva, or whatever it was, it stung where it touched their exposed skin.

Sandy-Hue grabbed the terrified River-Jewel's arm and dragged her down toward the deeps and away from those horrid, terrifying creatures.

Sandy-Hue came to the surface several times only to find those three terrible creatures coming close to screech their message and spray their toxic saliva, circle away and return again.

Swimming hard against the current, they finally came to the surface under the dock close to the inn. There was no screeching, no poisonous dark shadows diving at them.

Hoping this reprieve would allow them to get to the inn, they climbed on to the dock knowing that they would be quite vulnerable should these creatures reappear, so the move as quickly as they could to get to the Inn doors hoping that there would be someone there to let them in. They saw no sign of the airborne monsters as they scrambled along the dock to the Inn doors. Nearly overcome with fear they had pressed against them pounding for someone to come and let them in.

Brunell could tell from the two Marefolk that they shared the same overwhelming fear that Shanira had first shown at having seen the creature and heard its screeched warning.

Since it had grown dark, Brunell offered to go out first thing in the morning with Ranger and take a look around for whatever these assailants were. River-Jewel and Sandy-Hue both tried to dissuade him. Shanira, who was over her fear of the creatures, was ultimately able to convince them. They agreed to let him go out, but only for a short while and then only if he was armed.

Even though it was quite late, no one wanted to leave the security of the group to go to their sleeping area. Eventually, fatigue overruled anxiety and the longer they were away from the creatures, the calmer they felt, and they went off to try and sleep. It was, however, a fitful night for River-Jewel and her dad and for Shanira. The others including Brunell who had not yet encountered these mystifying screechers were able to get some rest.

Brunell found the others at breakfast just after sun up. He joined them, then prepared to go out to look for these things that had so terrified some of his companions. Despite the heat he put on two heavy shirts and thick denim jeans. The work boots he had brought from his farm would provide excellent protection. He had brought up three rifles from his section in The Follower because originally, he had wanted to study them. He only had a few shells for each but carefully loaded two of them. One was a shotgun, the other a smaller, lighter form of rifle called a carbine. They were both clip fed, the shotgun carried eight shells and the carbine fifteen. Brunell was as ready to face the screechers as he ever would be.

They gathered at the main doors that looked out on the marina, dock, and river and attempted to encourage Brunell as he and Ranger stepped through the door. Feeling more foolish than concerned, Brunell found himself wrapped in a cocoon of heat. Even at that very early part of the day the air was close and muggy. He immediately began to perspire. He looked out across the river but could see nothing. No screeching shattered the still air as he walked out onto the dock from where he could better survey the surrounding distant hills. He could see nothing out there, so he decided to go around to the back of the five-story building that was the Inn. He could see nothing there either, then Ranger who had come around the corner of the building a few paces behind him began to bark and ran back toward the front of the building. At that moment, a dark shape came off the roof and dove toward Ranger, it hideously taloned toes stretched and ready to grab him. As it went for the dog, it screeched. It was the most horrible sound Brunell had ever heard. Even the stifling heat could not prevent the chills from running down his spine.

The screeching beast approached Ranger; its scaled leathery wings outstretched held still in its gliding tilt. As it reached to sink its talons into Ranger, he turned quickly, avoiding the deadly claws except for the end of one sharp talon that scraped across his back. Ranger let out a squeal of pain before moving of from the creature as it tried to change direction and continue the pursuit.

Brunell knew he had to stop the attack, but the target was a difficult one. The body was hidden by what looked like a loose shroud that encircled it. The body, what there was of it could not be seen clearly. In a split second Brunell decided the shotgun was likely to be more effective in this instance because of the pellet scatter. It was more likely to have more effect on the creature than a single lead projectile. He raised the shotgun and tried to aim.

Ranger was leading the creature on a zigzag course and while it got close, was unable to catch the dog. It decided its best chance was to gain some altitude and anticipate the dog's movement before dropping back to the attack. It was so focused on its pursuit it had failed to notice Brunell. When it began to rise, then dive toward the ground. the creature passed before Brunell's sight; he squeezed the trigger. The sound of the gun was deafening. It sounded more like a bomb exploding than a gunshot. As the sound echoed back from the far off hills, the creature froze in place like a rag blowing in the wind. It pounded its wings on the ground, but couldn't move, but it continued to screech, "Leave here. Leave here, stay away or die."

At that particular moment, Brunell had no interest in what the fallen monster had to say. He called to Ranger and they both ran as fast as they could toward the front doors of the Inn. As they did, two more winged creatures leaped off the roof, adding their shrieks to those of their fallen comrade. They forgot about Brunell and Ranger, speeding to their fallen sister. As Brunell and the dog reached the door, one of the shrieking horrors turned and began to wing its way toward them. The second followed immediately, but by the time they could catch up, Brunell and Ranger were inside with the doors closed. The two stopped, landing on the canopy above the door and bent themselves down past the canopy to try to look inside. Brunell held the shotgun ready should they try to open the door or break a window to get in He held off firing because he sensed that shooting through the glass might help them to get in. rather than stopping them. Although he pointed the shotgun at the two figures looking in the door, and held his finger firmly on the trigger, he made no move to shoot. He had no idea of how important the wisdom of his decision was. The windows and doors were made of a ballistic glass that was far more advanced than anything found in the original twenty-first century. Had Brunell shot at the glass doors, ricocheting shotgun pellets would have caused more harm between

Brunell and his companions while leaving the doors unblemished and the creatures looking in completely unharmed.

Doors and windows meant nothing to these creatures. Nothing beyond the exterior registered in their tiny minds and shortly they left, likely to attend to their downed comrade. He turned to see Shanira, and Thunder-Fin had joined him. "What the hell are those things?" he asked, trembling uncontrollably now that he had lowered the gun.

"Harpies," said Shanira. "I read somewhere about creatures similar to these. They were monsters that had the head of a woman and a bird's body, but they were creatures of fiction and mythology. They weren't real."

"Well, I'd be hard pressed to call those women's heads," replied, Brunell, "and their wings are more like a bat's than any bird I've seen, but the biggest difference is these harpies are very real."

From then on, the harpies always seemed to be around. Sometimes they were far enough off for Shanira to run to Sunbeam Glider, then race back to the Inn when someone would call to let her know that they had moved off again.

The Marefolk could sometimes attempt to get to the river, but a few times they had to stay in the deeper water until after dark before being able to get back to the Inn safely.

Ranger had lost all interest in going out after the talon strike on his back had healed. The small wound, although not serious, had proven quite painful for a considerable length of time suggesting that the talons, like the saliva had toxic properties.

Brunell's few trips outside were to take up a position behind a couple of chaise lounges with his shotgun in hand to provide cover for Shanira returning from the cruiser or the Marefolk from the river.

Even when the harpies were out of sight, there was no escaping their hideous shrieks. They endured this for a good number of days before Brunell, trying to concentrate on the book he was reading, was distracted by a distant harpy shriek telling him he would die if he didn't leave. In uncharacteristic frustration, he stood up and tossed the book at one of the unused fireplaces, shattering several small vases on the mantelpiece.

"That's it," he shouted," I can't stand it. We have to get away from those loathsome creatures before they drive us all mad."

The others, as rattled as Brunell was, agreed.

There was a period of time around midnight when the harpies fell silent or moved out of range. While it was the darkest time of night, it was a relief to those in the Inn. They would sit and talk during this time, usually about moving on. Lately, these shared thoughts became more intense. They had come to the conclusion that they would have to escape the nerve-wracking presence of these dangerous harpy monsters. The darkest time, from a little before midnight to about 2:30 or 2:00 in the morning would be the time to load what they needed aboard and prepare the cruiser and barge for a quick getaway. The next two nights they spent getting ready to leave. Sunbeam Glider and The Follower were loaded with supplies, the cherished possessions brought into the Inn, and any research and materials they had encountered in this dry desert world, which wasn't very much.

They brought extra foodstuff and other necessities from the Inn, feeling no guilt about taking what they felt they needed, because they would barely be through the doors on the way to the cruiser when everything missing from inside the Inn would be replaced in that magical, mystical way everything was constantly being reset.

Neither Brunell nor Shanira had any idea of what was ahead of them or where they were to go, but they knew all too well that they could no longer stay.

With Shanira's Sunny and The Follower loaded, the next step was to get everyone on board and out of sight.

The river was too treacherous in its winding path among the cliffs and hills to be risked in the dark, even with the Sunbeam Glider's powerful lights. They would have to wait until there was enough light.

With Brunell providing cover under the deck roof by the pier and behind the chaise lounge, they made their way to the cruiser and barge as the first pink show of light rose over the hilltops. The Marefolk took their places inside the barge, and Ranger went below as Shanira fired up the cosmic ion generators. Then Brunell broke for the boat accompanied by the distant shriek of a harpy. He cast off as the shrieks and screeches grew louder. Scrambling aboard, he made his way to the bridge area. Two seats faced the console. Shanira sat in the pilot's chair and Brunell, shotgun in hand, took the seat beside her. Above their heads, a polymer covering more than a finger width thick protected the two seats from an attack from above. Shanira, working the throttle, had the cruiser pointing upstream and moving with precision toward the very middle of the river. Brunell then swung the chair he was sitting in around so that he was facing the back of the boat and its trailer, The Follower.

Beside him was a small arsenal of shotguns, handguns, a semi-automatic carbine and boxes of ammunition most open and ready for immediate use. If there was to be a war, Brunell and Shanira were well prepared to contribute their share.

As Brunell took his place, Shanira advanced the throttle, and the Sunbeam Glider was underway. She slowly eased the throttle forward as the cruiser turned upstream having left the shallows behind. By mid-river, the cruiser and its trailer were moving quite fast.

As the cliff walls began to encroach on the river looming large and threatening, dark shapes began to appear overhead. The shrieks and screeches, almost unbearable in their volume and intensity, identified those shapes as harpies. It made Shanira almost wish that she had installed a loud motor to drown out some of the hideous screeching from overhead, but she knew that her silent cosmic ion driven engines could far out run any other engine, noisy or not.

Brunell parted the plastic curtains to clear his view into the sky, a shotgun ready to shoot any harpy that might get too close. He was still uncertain about the harpy body concealed by the shroud like coverings that even in flight seemed to hang loosely on them.

As the number of harpies just above the rear transom of the cruiser was growing, Brunell was preparing to shoot. If he couldn't see the harpy's body clearly through the shroud, he could at least scatter them and make them think twice about getting too close. The harpies seemed wary of the gun and kept their distance. Clearly, they had been informed about what a gun could do.

Just as Brunell began to think that only a few warning shots might be all that would be needed to hold the harpies off, Shanira shouted," One's coming over the top from the front. It's low, look out!"

Brunell turned to see it stretch out its talons to grab the plastic curtain that limited the other harpies' view of the humans. He was ready and fired off a shot. At that close range, the harpy's head seemed to vaporize. Its body tumbled lifeless to the deck. Others had come too close for comfort to Brunell and Shanira and Brunell began to fire repeatedly, momentarily knocked off balance by the painful pellets, they quickly returned to their attack.

Brunell became more careful with the shot placement aiming for the harpies' heads, which had become easy targets at that range. Headshots seemed to work as several harpies fell. He dropped the shotgun and picked up the semi-automatic. He watched as several more crashed to the water to rock in Sunny's wake like empty sheets.

With several of their fellows down, the harpies began to pull back from the speeding boat, but continued to follow at a safe distance, talons extended and continue to shriek, "Go," and "Leave," and "You will die today!"

What else they were saying was unintelligible to Shanira, Brunell and the others. It just sounded like meaningless screeching that set their teeth on edge. They didn't really need to know what the harpies were shrieking at them, the intent was clear, drive them off or destroy them. The guns made the a little less anxious about the second outcome.

The harpies had backed away and disappeared beyond the cliff tops. Those on board the cruiser suspected that it was only a momentary reprieve. They could still clearly hear the shrieking and screeching.

Brunell took a moment of reprieve to look for the first harpy he had shot, the one that fell on the deck. To his surprise, there was nothing there but a small pile of dirty grey ash, being carried off behind The Follower in the draft caused by the speeding cruiser. The only other creature he knew of that shared a similar fate were the Faye. He would find their bodies scattered across a field after a dusting by the drones and by the next day, they would all be completely gone except for a layer of grey ash discoloring the naturally dark soil of the farm.

He had little time to contemplate this as the river was carrying them to where lofty cliff faces overlooked the river. As they approached, he could see the harpies dropping down from the heights directly above. They were hoping to surprise the gunman, but as they came over the edge of the cliff, Shanira caught sight of some movement in the upper part of Sunbeam Glider's wide windshield. She called a warning to Brunell who immediately who stepped out from under the polymer cover onto the open deck and began shooting. He was able to get the closer ones with headshots. Their bodies fell against the gunwale and the forward deck then slipped off to land in the river, drifting away on the current like forgotten remnants from a carpet clearance store. The other harpies, some clearly wounded, did their best to bank away from the shooter below and return to the heights and safety. Some couldn't make the steep climb, but found footholds on the cliff face, their hunt ended.

Just beyond the sandy cliff walled canyon, the land around them began to level out. As they moved farther away from the cliffs, the bits of greenery that at first dotted the small hills, began to spread and merge creating lushness that Brunell, Shanira and the others had not seen for quite a long time. The air was cooler, and no harpies followed, making it significantly quieter. The green hatch that could be seen along the riverbank held the promise of bushes, and perhaps even trees farther up the river.

With one worry behind them another came to replace it. In the distance ahead, the look of the river changed, sandy deltas heralded merging streams and at the moment they had no clue which branch of the dividing river they should take.

Shanira slowed the cruiser down. It would take some time to solve this puzzle. Brunell went to the stern slipping on the few bits of ash remaining from the downed harpy. He reached down to touch the grey, dusty substance and immediately felt a stinging in his hand. Ranger had come above deck but wouldn't get too close to the small remaining layer of ashes on the rear deck. Brunell reached over the side near one of the two cosmic ion generators at the rear of the boat and extended his stinging fingers to let the now cooler water from off the river wash over them. Within seconds, the stinging stopped completely. The acidity washed away.

Looking back at the bits of ash remaining, Brunell could see the paint on the deck was where the ash touched was bubbled and peeling. Looking around for places the harpies had come in contact with the boat, he found several places paint was peeling. Brunell took the bailing pump hose Shanira used to keep the bodies of the then injured Thunder-Fin and the other Marefolk from drying out. He sprayed down those spots until all the ash has been washed off into the river.

Thunder-Fin came aboard just as he was finishing the job. He took a cautious path around the damaged places on the deck and gunwales. Even in death, the harpies could be dangerous.

They reached the first of the smaller rivers feeding the one they were on, Shanira brought the cruiser to a halt and dropped in three anchors to hold Sunbeam Glider and The Follower against the stronger current. She signaled for Brunell and Thunder–Fin to come over. Since their route still remained unclear and several rivers met up with this one not far ahead, it seemed a good idea to have the Marefolk check out the feeder rivers, go up them a short distance and find which would offer the clearest, safest passage.

Thunder-Fin was about to lower himself into the river to get the others when Shanira stopped him. It had been made clear to her and Brunell the route they had to take. The vision had come with unexpected clarity to both, but it was Shanira who knew immediately which way to go. She had Brunell and Thunder-Fin raise the anchors and engaged the engines, moving slowly towards the mouth of the nearest merging river. "This is the one," she shouted as she turned Sunny on to it.

Everything seemed to improve all around. The land grew lusher, the air was comfortable and the river although less wide that the one they had been on, was clear and deep and slow moving. The sense of clarity regarding their route remained strong. With confidence, they proceeded up stream. The companions on the journey were quite content. They enjoyed the nights at anchor and others spent in some of the few buildings the came across along the way.

When they went ashore, they found the landscape to be far more inviting. Eventually they stopped the incessant scanning of the sky for signs of the harpies. It seemed pretty certain that they were creatures of the badlands, but every time a bird or other animal made a loud call, all eyes turned quickly toward the sky.

The Road to Union

Maricel and Raphael, Jolinda and Patah, Shanira and Brunell, the first awakened, made their way to where ever they were going following the maps laid out in their minds. They felt a growing sense that they nearing the end of their journey. They had no idea where or what their destination was but could feel it fast approaching. The sensation was different than it had been earlier on. Back then, they had felt they were moving toward some unknown place. Now it almost felt as if the destination was rushing to meet them.

They felt a giddiness that stayed with them even as they carefully surveyed their surroundings for enemies. They watched for old enemies that they had faced before and new ones that they had yet to meet. Although they knew these hostile creatures were out there, they also sensed that the route ahead of them was clear and free of evil.

They had a firm belief that something enormous was about to occur, something beautiful and good. They also sensed a darkness there, small and vague, but like the positive aspects, slowly growing as they approached. This contained their enthusiasm and slowed down what had become a relentless pace. Their non-human companions seemed to share this contradictory sense as well, the desire to make haste that was matched by an equally persuasive feeling that they should be cautious and not rush.

The destination toward which they were being led was a huge valley surrounded by mountains allowing only one way in, a break in the protective hills through which flowed a river beside which, ran a wide paved road.

The huge rock faces off in the distance on each side of the entrance seemed to create a funnel effect through the break in the mountains. On passing the narrowest point, the funnel spout, a broad and verdant valley spread out to the horizon below the high mountain walls that surrounded it. Those mountains at the farthest point from the entrance were purplish and indistinct showing that the valley was of astonishing size.

The road and its companion river passed through alternating grasslands and forests. A huge lake centered the valley. On a narrow bay that reached out from the larger lake near the far shore, a gigantic building, larger than any other to be seen on legacy earth stood among the trees near the water's edge.

From above, the building as if in imitation of the valley revealed itself to be a vast wall enclosing a large space containing a number of various sized buildings, each looking somewhat different from the others. There were farms and vehicle storage places, a heliport and a landing strip.

A docking slip cut its way from the lake under an archway leading to the interior. Several roads diverged from the main one making their way to similar arches protected by series of secure doorways that when open would allow large vehicles to make their way into the gigantic enclosure beyond. The main road came to an end under a large, canopied roof in front of huge glass doorways into a large lobby. Through tinted windows, almost indistinguishable, mysterious shapes floated through the gigantic room and visible hallways. Some of these holographic shapes looked like local animals while others looked like humans engaged in a variety of recreational activities. If they hadn't formed a panoramic scene, well above even someone like Forestman's reach, they might well be mistaken for living beings so realistic were these three dimensional images.

ARRIVALS

The first to make their way down the funneling entrance to the interior valley were Maricel and Raphael and, of course, Scout. Maricel and Raphael were immediately struck by the beauty and novelty of their surroundings. On either side of the road and across the expanse of the accompanying river and as far ahead as they could see were the most intriguing of multi-hued plants in a variety of species surrounding them in a harmony of color.

The river, calm and stately reflected back the azure of the sky. Shade of gold and green peeked from beneath the folds of the riverbank out of the sun. The hills rising up to the mountainsides were tree lined and bright green against the dark earth tones and the grey of granite. The distant mountains were shrouded in a purplish hue. It all spoke to them of a quiet restfulness and to a sense of completion. They felt that they had found something extraordinary. They had no idea the truth of this would be borne out in short order.

Most of the day had passed before they had any thought of stopping. Looking around they could see that they were virtually surrounded by mountains that seemed to hold them and the valley in a warm embrace. The air was fresh, a light breeze played over they many-hued fields filling the air with a sweet, natural perfume. They sensed that they were extremely close to the destination they had been making their way to for so very long.

They could see the river widening out into a crystalline lake ahead and followed the curving road as it followed close to the shore.

As if to guide their way, sunlight seemed to linger in the valley although the sun itself had set beyond the furthest mountains. They could see far ahead in the distance a large grove of trees. As the got nearer, they caught glimpses of something through the trees. Although it appeared to be something like a wall of a building, the extent of the bits they did see, suggested something far larger than any building they had ever come across before.

While there was a pressing desire to find out what this place was, there was also a sense of caution. Their encounters with the werewolves and the bridge trolls were enough warning to them to proceed to any landmark carefully and to be fully alert for possible danger. They decided to pull off the road near a small group of trees and wait until morning to proceed.

Despite the sense of calmness and contentment that the valley imparted on them, they decided that someone should be on watch while the other one slept.

Maricel took the first. Raphael crawled into the bunk area of the cab and took his place in the upper level. He didn't feel the slightest tension and before he knew it his alarm was going off telling him it was his term to take the watch.

He exchanged places with Maricel who fell into a relaxed sleep almost immediately.

The sun dawned on an extraordinarily gorgeous morning. If the positive reality was enhanced by the valley itself or existed in the minds of the Maricel and Brunell was not clear to them. It was likely some of both as the valley did seem to enhance the senses and instill an extraordinary feeling of wonder and joy in Maricel, Raphael, and from his eager bounciness to be out of the cab and running, Scout as well.

Without further delay, Maricel started the truck and began to proceed cautiously along the road toward the large grove of trees and the still partly seen building beyond.

As the road swung around the trees and headed toward the lake, they could finally see the building the trees had concealed from them. It was, indeed, a gigantic building with walls of indeterminable length spreading off in both directions and they approached the front. The front of the building was built right up to the edge of the lake. Driving up to the glass encased front of the building with its huge doors, and the strange floating figures that could barely be seen though the tint of the windows, Maricel and Raphael could see that the driveway would either let them circle back or take them up to a doorway in the wall. There was a boat slip beside it. As they approached the end of the driveway, huge doors opened to let them into and through the building to the space behind.

They could see that the boat slip and the road continued beyond the walls.

Massive as the building was, it enclosed a huge amount of space filled with roadways, canals and other huge buildings. A single engine plane and a twin-engine jet sat on a runway tarmac. A second single engine plane on pontoons floated in a straight long part of a canal that paralleled the runway.

They could see that the main building was, in fact the outer edge of a gigantic enclosure. From the outside, it had looked like a large resort or spa. Inside the enclosure, it looked more like a large, walled fortress.

Having passed through the doorway into the building and is massive enclosure, Maricel needed to find out just how free they were in there. She stopped the truck and began backing toward the doors. As they began to open, Maricel, her concern now satisfied, drove up to park beside a large patio with a pool and beautifully tended gardens. A large door beside where they parked close to the Outer building bore the sign "Lobby Entrance" Maricel, Raphael and Scout exited the truck and made their way past the tables and chairs, past the patio and through the doors into the lobby.

They passed an elegantly furnished indoor lounge and two restaurants before entering the enormous, yet oddly cozy looking front lobby and reception area.

They marveled at the 3D images moving casually around above their heads. An image of a dog swung into view and Scout began to bark. Maricel and Raphael both began to laugh.

They were the only ones there to greet them. As they stood there, looking around watching the holographs circling the room, they knew that they a successfully reached the destination that had been drawing them since shortly after they first awakened. They had reached their goal, but they had no idea why. It was if they were plunked there without a purpose.

Yes, the building and its surroundings were spectacular. No doubt there were few places that compared with this one. There was a graciousness that matched the spaciousness, and it was probably a decent place to stop and end their ceaseless journeying. So, they decided that for the time being they would find some rooms and make it their home. While there was very little that they felt they had to do, there was plenty for them to do. They decided that for the next while at least, they would explore what Raphael had named Fort Spa at a leisurely pace. Before that, they would relax and enjoy the resort aspect of their new home. "I don't know about you," Maricel said as she entered the suite she had chosen, "but I have absolutely no intention of cleaning this place."

"You would have a lifetime's worth of work. Plenty to keep you busy, but I'm with you. If it stops cleaning itself, there is way too much of it for you and me," laughed Raphael and they went off for their first night's sleep in their apparently permanent home. Raphael read for a while and Maricel, with Scout at her feet drifted quickly off to the most peaceful and restful of sleep.

The next morning found them beginning their explorations after a wonderful breakfast in one of the smaller restaurants that seemed to be everywhere. Raphael had named it well. It was both a fortress and a spa. The walls were thicker than any found in an ordinary resort or spa. The windows were made of a hard, impervious glass and the doors while looking elegant and fragile, decorated things were in fact impenetrable.

The main entrance doors were not only able to sustain incredibly high impact, but individually, and from a master control, they could be sealed and covered by a shield of hard metal hat dropped down to close off the outer world.

Although Maricel and Raphael seemed to know this in the same way that they knew the way to get here, they had found manuals behind the registration desk that confirmed this. Even so, in their lack of clear purpose Raphael and Maricel put these amazing defenses to the test, bullets, swinging iron, hit by a truck nothing the threw at the doors and walls left no sign of damage, not even a tiny dent of scratch. Against the walls there might be a few small cracks or a bit of crumbling that would reset itself before a second attempt could be made to expand the damage. Having proved the virtual impregnability of the defenses to themselves, for whatever reason, they began to enjoy the recreational resources, the lake, the games rooms, the gyms and pools, the two theatres boasting a large collection of nearly complete movies from the twentieth through to the twenty second century. They especially liked the 3D ones with their realistic hologram casts. Scout, on the other hand wasn't so sure. He would make a point of sniffing every holograph of a human or animal and was always surprised that not only did they give off no sent, they could move right through him, and he could move right through them.

There was even a casino that paid out quite generously from time to time. Yet, like the stores, the restaurants, the café's and bars, everything was quickly regenerated back to the way it was when they first arrived.

Life was pretty comfortable, the relaxed, the explored at leisure, checked the inventories of the many storage rooms and enclosed places inside the main building. Although their inspections had barely covered one or two percent of what was stored in all the different areas, they did notice a wide variety of weaponry. Some of the armaments they found were to the eyes of a military Specialist and an Artifacts specialist were very heavy duty.

Having done a preliminary inventory and knowing that there were still lots to discover, Maricel and Raphael decided that since there were only the two of them, they couldn't do much with the ordinance and other materials beside stare in awe at them, that they may as well spend some quality time enjoying the resort and spa features while waiting to see, having made the journey and achieved their destination, what would happen next.

In the meantime, there were lots of nearly complete books to read, tracts to listen to, and movies to watch and wonder at. Indoors there were pools and saunas, workout rooms, games rooms, intimate cafes and fine bars and restaurants. Outdoors, the lake was fresh and inviting. There were walking trails through the forest and on to the foothills. There was plenty for them to do while they waited for whatever was to come next.

IS THIS HOME?

Somewhere not too far down the road, Jolinda, Patah and company were making their way along. They were so overwhelmed by a growing recognition of the beauty and the sense of peacefulness of the valley as they made their way towards the distant mountains that they had to stop so the elvin and Forestman could bask in the joy of where they found themselves. Out of the bus, the elvin would run. dance around, and sing, all thoughts of Stone Dwarves and Wampyra forgotten in their contentedness. Mewser would find a warm cozy spot nearby and sleep while basking in the sunlight. Forestman would move among the trees talking to them and patting their bark as if they were old friends. He would then find his way back to Jolinda and Patah standing in front of the bus, gazing at the distant mountains in silence. None of them had felt so carefree. They may not have been sure about what their arrival at the final destination, not so far ahead, would bring, but the awareness that they were heading towards the conclusion of their long journey left them sleeping more peacefully.

They took the time to enjoy their surroundings. The scenery was spectacular, the sunsets, gorgeous and meditative. Whether it was truly more special than any place they had yet been was open for speculation, but the buoyancy it brought to their spirits certainly made it seem so.

As they approached the mountains and began to sense the sides closing in, they remained relaxed.

The serenity of the scenery and the warm hazy days made this part of the journey a happy one. It was as if they were going on vacation with regular stops for picnics and taking the time to enjoy their surroundings.

Had they known that not far behind them on the clear calm river that paralleled the road a cruiser towing a barge was making its way toward them, they would have been more than content to wait there for them.

The road, however, continued to beckon them on toward the fast approaching end point. The long and sometimes harrowing journey would soon be over.

They rolled down the funneling mountain walls that marked the entrance to a spectacular valley encircled by purple mountains, fields of multi-colored wild flowers and inviting greenery of rich forest strands. There was something there to make them all feel at home, especially the huge building hidden by the trees as the swing around the edge of the crystal clear lake.

While the impulse was to get to that enormous building slowly revealing itself through the trees as quickly as possible, it was mitigated by a wariness instilled by experience. Approaching slowly and carefully they were relieved to see no sign of the Stone Dwarves. Perhaps one more night in the bus, in full site of the building was in order.

"Is that a bus?" exclaimed Raphael as he passed beside one of the security monitors. Whatever it was, it hadn't been there earlier. He ran to find Maricel.

SHIP TO SHORE

The river had lost any trace of silt. It was pure and crystalline with a slight amber tint. Even at the deepest place, the bottom was clear to see. For the Marefolk this was so incredibly inviting, they slipped into it, diving deeply, racing in circles playing underwater tag.

Shanira pulled her Sunny near the bank and dropped anchor. Soon she and the rest of the crew, Brunell and Ranger were enjoying the refreshing pristine waters. Swimming to the nearest bank, Brunell looked out in delight at the wide variety and color of the flora that grew along the edge of the river and back to the distant forest stands. The plants, especially the flowers were so diverse that Brunell could hardly believe that the multihued display and the fragrance of the flowers was a natural phenomenon. It was as if someone had gathered the most beautiful plants and the most fragrant and placed them here creating an unnaturally radiant wild garden.

Brunell understood that the rules of this amazing world in which he had awakened were not that exacting. He, like the others recognized that the realities of this world often denied their innate understandings of what life in this world should be like. He had seen the unexplained badlands and the curious harpies. He had battled with the Faye. He knew whatever he ate or had taken to add to his collection were quickly regenerated. Food and drink were almost always prepared and ready for consumption. Sometimes one might have to push a button or two, but that was all. In supermarkets and grocery stores foods were always fresh and ready with no sign of anyone to tend them, or prepare the foods, or keep everything clean.

All the first awakened knew instinctively that while this was clearly the case in this world, it didn't ring true to their inherent knowledge of how such a world should work.

They knew how the world should work. Someone would plant the food, or gather it, someone needed to harvest it, or butcher it and it had to be prepared by someone. Stores needed to be stocked by someone and if something was damaged or broken, an exact replica replacement should not be found at the site where it originated, instead, someone would have to rebuild or repair it. Of course, there should be far more than two humans in the world, but at this moment, as far as Brunell and Shanira could tell, there wasn't.

The garden-like quality of the surroundings while outside the innate expectations of the awakened, was not really a surprise for them.

They had journeyed long and far to this place. It had called them and therefore held some important meaning for them. They just couldn't figure out what it was.

The almost artificial strangeness of the beautiful area they found themselves in seemed to inform them that there was something more they needed to do. Whatever that might be, they knew that they would eventually come to know it when they needed to.

STAND OFF

It wasn't until morning that Jolinda and Patah noticed that the building's lower windows were covered with what appeared to be heavy steel shutters. They had not heard them being put on suggesting a very high-end silent technological process, electrical or mechanical. What the shuttered windows did tell them was that someone or something was inside.

While Jolinda went into the bus where they stored the few weapons they had, Patah and Forestman used binoculars to look for any sign of movement from the buildings.

Robin-Eyes and her mother had used their stealth and ability to climb up into the trees closest to the windows and keep themselves concealed while they looked out for any threat. They saw no sign of life.

When Jolinda came up beside Patah, she held a semi-automatic rifle and two pistols, the sum total of their available weapons. Patah, who was reluctant to handle weapons at the best of times, found the feeling of revulsion towards the gun Jolinda offered him was stronger than ever. Jolinda, too, felt uncomfortable. As a physician and healer, she had a distaste for any sort of weapon that's main intent was to do harm. Today, her level of discomfort with the rifle and the pistols was far beyond what she had ever felt before.

Quietly, they decided to lay the guns down on a fallen tree trunk and stay down low, close enough to grab one if they needed to.

Inside the building, Maricel and Raphael had gone to one of the armament cabinets. Maricel found herself feeling a strong sense of revulsion as she picked up a small pistol. Raphael the hunter, for the first time since his awakening did not feel comfortable with the rifle he had chosen. Both inside and outside Fort Spa, the feeling of reluctance to take up arms was the same.

Patah had a sense that this excessive reluctance to even touch a weapon was much like the mind maps that had eventually led them here. He chose to change the situation by walking up to the cleared space between the trees and the wall. He raised his empty hands above his head.

"My name is Patah and I'm a human," he shouted, "those in our company have been summoned here. We have no idea why, but here we are. We know someone is in there. We are carrying no weapons. Show yourselves. Let's talk."

The shutter on the window began to rise up and roll out of sight. He could see two humans standing just inside the window. They were looking intensely at him.

A loud voice issued from some place above the window as one of the figures behind it could be seen to speak. "Bring your bus and your company as you call it, around to the front of the building near the lake shore. We can meet there and talk."

Patah nodded his acceptance and returned with the others to the bus.

"He looked human to me," said Raphael, "I believe they mean no harm."

In the bus, Patah was expressing the very same sentiments. At the front of the building, they saw an open gate and drove through it into the inner yard and parked their bus beside the large truck already there.

As they came out of the bus, Raphael and Maricel were there to greet them. They were quite taken aback by the diminutive elvin and especially the large and imposing figure of Forestman. They watched Mewser and Scout check each other out then go their separate ways. That was a sign for all of them. There was no hostility here.

The next few days were a whirlwind of getting to know each other and exploratory activity. Raphael and Maricel showed them what they had discovered about Fort Spa in the days they had already spent there.

Then there was new ground to cover. While the humans checked out the building, the elvin and Forestman surveyed the area inside the enclosure. They marveled at what they saw and although they didn't understand most of it, quickly felt at home.

Eventually they would look at everything including the airplanes and the airstrip and all the heavy weaponry and ordinance. What most excited them was the sense that they were home. There was nothing drawing them on, no dormant itch suggesting that there was any more to their journey.

One afternoon, only days after Patah and Jolinda had arrived, they were seated for a communal meal, four humans, two elvin and Forestman. The conversation was pleasant, the meal delicious and they could not have felt more relaxed and united as a group when an alarm went off. They froze for a beat then as one were up and running to the nearest window.

AT THE WATER'S EDGE

The Marefolk surfaced not far from Shanira who was relaxing on the soft grass. Brunell was farther away examining a bright red flower. Calling the two to the riverbank, the told them that the river widened not too far ahead and became a large crystal clear lake. A strange sensation swept over the two humans. The suddenly needed to see that lake. Within minutes everyone was back on board and while the sun still remained a leisurely lowering ball of fire high in the sky, rest and recreation was over.

Shanira and Brunell couldn't help but feel there was something important about that lake and they had to see it. Sunbeam Glider, with The Follower right behind turned upriver.

In a very short time, the golden amber tint of the river was being replaced before their eyes by a vista of shimmering blue. Ahead of them the shore fell further away. The lake was huge and as they entered, the mountains closing in on either side it appeared from what they could see to be almost circular. They travelled across the gently undulating surface for some time before the far shore came into view beneath the distant mountains.

They were still a good way from that distant shore when Brunell, looking through his binoculars, saw what seemed to be a wall of red stones partly concealed by trees far ahead of them. The lake was large and even at high speed, it would take some time before they reached the far shore and that mysterious red wall.

As the distant wall came more into focus, those aboard the cruiser felt a sense of wariness. While this wariness was more a product of their past when their peace was shattered by the shrieking harpies, Shanira slowed the cruiser down despite there being no sign of threat and the sonar showed deep clear water all around them.

While the others scanned the horizon for any movement, Brunell, watching through his powerful binoculars, could see the large reddish wall begin to resolve itself into a small portion of a very large building.

Despite some misgivings and knowing that the peace they now enjoyed could be quickly broken, Shanira persisted on heading towards the far shore and the curious building it held.

"Do you not think we should get out some of the guns we used against the harpies? In case these are other enemies." asked Thunder-Fin

"We probably should," replied Shanira, "but I feel reluctant to do so."

"I feel the same way, responded Brunell, as he raised the seat of the bench where he had put away the guns and ammunition after the harpy attacks had been over for a while., "Whatever it is out there, it has rendered us pretty much helpless as far as self-defense is concerned. We can only hope that it's for the right reason."

Two flare guns sat on the dashboard close to Shanira's hand. She was aware that they were there but could not bear the thought that they could be used as weapons, and dangerous ones at that.

AND THEN THERE WERE Six

The first look out the window, toward the road revealed nothing. The alarm, however, was issuing from down the hall in the direction of the lobby. They all headed off toward the lobby in search of the source of the alarm. They found it in a security room.

Red lights were flashing on the top of the central and largest monitor. Across its screen in flashing letters it read, "unidentified object found, approaching lakeside."

Above the letters, the video screen showed the lake vista and centered on the screen, a large, dark object could be seen approaching. Several minutes passed before the object began to resolve itself into a speedboat with something large in tow.

"That is a pretty nice looking boat," said Patah.

"Who or what do you think is on board?" asked Maricel.

Raphael pointed out, "From the way it's coming straight towards us, I doubt its doing it on its own."

Back on the sunbeam Glider, Brunell stood up to look over the front deck with his binoculars. Although highly magnified, Brunell's upper body could be seen fairly clearly on the large monitor. "That looks like a human to me," said Jolinda, "He has binoculars. Perhaps one of us could go out and signal him. If he is hostile, we should know fairly quickly.

"I'll do it," said Patah, "Get me a table cloth or towel. I'll wave it to get his attention."

Towel in hand, Patah stepped out the main doors and made his way to the nearest small dock jutting out into the lake. Standing at the end, Patah began to wave the large white towel back and forth. "There's a human ahead waving a large piece of cloth of some sort at us. I don't see any weapons. Can you see him?" shouted Brunell.

"Yes," replied Shanira, 'In fact, I'm heading towards the dock he's standing on."

Inside the building the others watched as Patah continues to wave the towel, and the boat continued to make its way toward him. As the boat got within shouting distance of the dock, a pair of doors opened inwards revealing a channel extending from the lake and into the interior of the enclosure. "Is it safe?" shouted Brunell.

"Should be," returned Patah, "we've already parked a truck and a bus in there."

As Shanira lowered her speed to a slow crawl, Brunell grabbed the top of the windscreen and leaned toward the man on the dock. "Any humans beside yourself here?"

"So far, four including me along with some other friends. You?"

"There's two of us and we are bringing some other friends too."

"Pull into that slip and go through that will take you inside. We'll be out to greet you as soon as I tell them things are good," Patah paused a beat, "They are good, right?"

"Absolutely," said Brunell, "this is the place we've been trying to get to for a very long time."

Shanira guided Sunny through the doorway and under the lift bridge that rose up above and into the interior of Fort Spa in a docking spit near a large truck and even larger bus. Brunell jumped ashore and tied Sunny up, giving her an affectionate pat on the gunwale. "Well," he said to no one in particular, "here we are."

Pulling himself onto the wall surrounding the large, multicraft slip, Thunder-Fin spoke, "I feel that this is good!"

Jolinda, Maricel and Raphael followed by Forestman and the elvin came out to greet them. "Welcome to Fort Spa." Grinned Maricel as Patah came through the doors to join them. Introductions made, they went inside to find places where they might start to put down roots.

The Marefolk found a spacious indoor pool and as if it was made just for them, it was divided into several divisions where they could individually set up their watery living quarters. From there, they had easy access to everything especially the lake that connected to the pool by an underwater passage.

Earlier on Forestman and the elvin had found an enclosed and covered place that contained a lovely spacious garden and many small but numerous trees. The elvin had chosen a cozy well-treed corner of the room, leaving the rest to Forestman. This place and the pool made such perfect homes for the non-human friends that it might well have been made especially with them in mind.

The humans had travelled a long way to be with other humans, so the rooms they chose were not far from the lobby and each other, opening out onto a comfortable lounge and fully stocked, as always, restaurant.

HAVEN

As the days passed, the first awakened, now together, were able to share their stories and tell about the dangers they had encountered along the way. It was chilling to realize that there was so much palpable evil in such a beautiful world.

Somehow, they felt free of the evil here in what had become Fort Spa and surrounding valley.

Together and separately the explored the main buildings. In the below ground levels of they discovered passages through which they could get to every building and main room in the gigantic complex. There were numerous electric and antigravity vehicles to take them to any location they wished to get to, quickly and efficiently. They took the time to make their way around the huge interior square using both above ground roads and paths and the underground passages and checked out the variety of buildings and other things of interest it contained. The aircraft, especially the floatplane and the helicopter, intrigued Shanira and Raphael. Of special interest to Shanira was the single engine, high wing four seaters, sitting on the tarmac. She was certain that given time, she could learn to fly it

While the twin-engine jet with its spacious luxurious cabin was fascinating, no one was anxious to handle the controls or go for a ride.

They were interested to discover that the smaller aircraft and the helicopter were powered by fuel cells. Eventually they would learn the limitations of those fuel cells. They could fly the planes, but if they went too far beyond their peaceful valley, there would not be enough fuel to make it safely back to Fort Spa. Still, both Shanira and Raphael felt the desire to learn to fly and justified that desire by telling themselves that regular reconnaissance flights could help them quickly learn if something or someone undesirable had found its way into the valley.

In very short order, Shanira had picked up the knowledge that let her take the fixed wing aircraft into the air and safely land it. Before too long she was a very competent pilot taking off, flying, and setting down the land plane and the floatplane with ease.

Raphael liked the helicopter and spent a long time reading about the specifics of helicopter flight. It was difficult to learn, and his first few attempts barely got him off the ground. Eventually with care and caution and a few near mishaps, he began to develop a feel for the controls.

Meanwhile Maricel with the help of Moon-Feather began to inventory the artifacts that filled the buildings. There was so much that she felt it would take her and Moon-Feather many seasons to identify and catalogue it all.

Jolinda found a very well supplied clinic with several lesser infirmaries throughout the main buildings. Together, she and Patah and sometimes, Maricel studied the technological wonders of the healing devices and set them up in the clinic's hospital ward. They distributed some others among the infirmaries.

Time passed with no end of things to do. Apart from the superb recreational facilities, they found manuals, simulators and instructional videos some nearly complete, for every technological, mechanical, or manual contraption the place had to offer.

It was an interesting place but well deserved of the paradoxical title Fort Spa. It was, in fact, a military complex disguised as a resort, or perhaps it was a resort disguised as a military complex.

The rest and recreation opportunities were endless. Weapons were numerous and powerful and clearly of the highest order ready for any kind of conflict. There were vast numbers of medical devices.

The military feel clashed with the surrounding beauty while the R and R blended to perfection with the scenery.

For the six humans, the sasquatch, two elvin, four Marefolk, two dogs and a cat, it was so gigantic that they could move locations everyday as at a Mad Hatters tea party and they would still need a great many seasons to use them all. Brunell estimated that the outer building alone could handle forty or fifty thousand humans with plenty of room to spare.

Having only seen five other humans beside themselves, the first awakened could not fathom the need for such a huge complex with its fortress-like capabilities and massive recreational facilities. They wondered if there were to be more humans to come and if this was the case, why was it that they had come across no evidence of more humans on their journey here, not a group and except for themselves, not another one.

What they did know was that they had been drawn together to this place. Grateful as they were for each other, they couldn't help but wonder if there were others and hoping that they would soon join them. Hope and expectation remained that. No other humans came, and their idyllic life went unmarred by Stone Dwarves, harpies, Wampyra, Faye, Trolls or Hoblins. The peace and camaraderie made life delightful. The forest and water folk reveled in their surroundings, the forest stands, the lake, and the flower-covered fields. For them, every day was an adventure with nothing but happy endings along with a few scrapes and bruises. Evening would generally find all the company gathered for a meal. They were able to share their many stories from the moment of their awakening to their arrival at this place. There was much speculation regarding what it all meant.

While time passed, it didn't seem to touch the first awakened. The pets seemed to age, but very slowly, only the sentient non-humans whose normal life span was far beyond that of the humans of origin earth. True, after the twenty-third century most humans lived several hundred earth years. Before that, of course, the human life span was much shorter.

In many ways, Legacy Earth, was not original earth, especially among the first six awakened. They did not seem to age at all and would not, barring serious accident, for much longer that even the twenty-fourth century humans. They knew that serious accidents could happen. Patah was, for example, near death when found, yet he survived and perhaps the six awakened were destined to survive for a long, long time. This was something they spent very little time contemplating and no time discussing. Whatever the case, they lived with the understanding that it could all end tomorrow, or even sooner.

The first awakened were indeed marvelous beings, but they were in every way, human. What made their world really different from origin earth was the presence of the mythological and fictional denizens of origin earth who were represented here on Legacy Earth. Not exact matches for the creatures of fiction, they were altered to fit the strictures reality imposed.

Some were allies like the Elvin, the Marefolk and Forestman and some represented an evil unique to this incarnation: Wampyra, Faye, Hoblins, Harpies and Trolls, the Stone Dwarves and the Werewolves.

For the first awakened these creatures were a part of their reality.

THE SECOND AWAKENING

The first awakened and their friends explored Fort Spa and the surrounding valley. They mapped it from the air, hiked its trails, drove its roads, and boated its lake and rivers. They became intimately familiar with it. Eventually they came to know every corner of the valley, every square millimeter of their Fort Spa and were aware of and at one time or another utilized almost all it had to offer.

Their life in this little corner of the world was close to complete. It got to the point that they thought little about the world beyond. Whatever fate had brought them there they trusted it.

Unbeknown to them, in the cities and towns and the countryside beyond, even in some they might have passed through early on, a second and much larger wave of human awakenings were happening. Like the first six, they found themselves waking up to a world they seemed to know quite well, while fully aware of the fact, they were completely unfamiliar with it.

Not all awakenings were the same. Some awoke alone, others woke in pairs or even small groups. They were given nowhere near the time to examine their surroundings as the first six had. Before too long, their compulsion to journey formed a clear map in all their minds. While the route they needed to take might be different from others, the destination was set out, and it was the same for all of them.

The compulsion while not striking them until they had some time to orient themselves in their particular area of knowledge and in their particular home, came shortly after the last of those to awaken were able to acclimatize themselves to the world in which they lived.

Their journeys began. For some it would be a short one because they awoke not too far away. For others, it would be long and arduous journey, sometimes costly as the encountered some aspect of the overt evil with which they shared their world.

As they went, they met up met up with other groups of humans on the journey until an armada of human journeyers filled roads, rivers and highways. Still a large amount of time had passed before the first trickle of journeyers approached the funnel road and were about to enter the valley. Despite the fact that some of the journeyers, perhaps even half of them at one time or another had encountered cruel and vicious monsters along the way, the world remained generous providing them with food, transportation and shelter as they went.

Despite natural immunity, a number of second awakeners were lost to the Wampyra on their journey, while others fell to the poisonous stingers of the Faye, or brutal encounters with trolls and werewolves, Stone Dwarves, harpies and other monstrous creatures.

Some came across companion animals that joined them on their trek and a few had made alliances with creatures of the light, forest elvin, Marefolk, a smaller kind of centaur, and one or two sasquatches.

While still many days away from the valley and Fort Spa, the first awakened, secure in their valley haven sensed them coming. It felt to them as if they could hear thousands of feet pounding the ground as they came nearer. They weren't exactly sure what it was that was coming, but they could sense that many were approaching. In fact, of the 6000 second awakening, over 5000 were steadily converging on haven valley. Despite the sensation of feet pounding the roads, few were coming on foot.

It was a rag tag collection of humanity that came. This human armada stretched out for great distances and from every direction, all sharing the same goal.

They had no idea who or what was summoning them only that it was somewhere they all needed to be. They hung out of buses, rode on the backs and tops of trucks and vans, crammed into cars and cycled. Some boated and some even walked.

While the first awakened humans could sense the coming masses, Forestman was the first of the non-human companions to actually feel the approaching throng.

Forestman had grown close with Patah. They would spend hours together discussing origins and what the purpose of this world might be. They read books on subjects of shared interest and spoke of psychology and spirituality including the natures of humans, Forestman, of Elvin and Marefolk. Together they sought to understand the creatures that seemed intent on harming them. They talked about what might be motivating them. Where they intrinsically evil or so different from the humans and their allies, due to the very construct of their natures? The wondered if they would ever be able to negotiate with them and asked themselves, "how?" They couldn't be certain if their minds were even capable of any sort of ethical or moral understanding.

At one of these sessions, Forestman suddenly stopped the conversation with Patah, sat up and looked at the human across the table, then looked around, his eyes nearly as large as saucers. "Something is coming," he said, "I can feel thousands of beings getting nearer but I can't tell what they are."

"Yes," replied Patah, I and the other humans have been feeling this for some time now. Raphael took the helicopter up this morning to see if he could find anyone or anything approaching the valley. He could see nothing to corroborate this feeling."

"You are right, Forestman," continued Patah, "whatever it is, whatever they are, there is something coming. And it will be arriving soon."

Both Patah and Forestman suddenly felt restless. Rising from their chairs the set off feeling the deep need to find the others. Now that Forestman could sense it, there could be little doubt that something was, indeed, closing in on them.

"Well," thought Patah," If they mean no harm, let them come.," adding aloud, "We have lots of room."

As if reading his mind, Forestman asked, "You think something is coming, people, perhaps, to join us?"

Patah shook his head, "I just don't know. I just don't know."

They found the others outside at the edge of the lake, The Marefolk were frolicking in the shallows while Robin-Eyes and Moon-Feather were building sandcastles under the watchful eyes of Ranger and Scout, both having made themselves comfortable on the warm sand. Mewser watched from a relaxed position on a deck chair a safe distance from the water. Maricel, Shanira, Jolinda and Brunell were watching silently from beach chairs, their thoughts far away.

"Where's Raphael?" Patah asked pulling up a chair beside Maricel while

Forestman took a seat on some breakwater pilings. Mewser came down from the chair to jump up on Forestman's huge lap.

"He's taken the copter up again. You can see him, that tiny dot in the sky near the far end of the lake. He's checking the roadway coming in to see if he can see anything," said Maricel.

"His fuel charge is low," added Shanira, "he should be on his way back soon."

When the helicopter roared overhead, the humans and Forestman left the others to their play. Mewser, who had found a comfortable spot on Forestman's shoulder chose not to move and came with them. They went to a coffee shop near the entrance that looked out on the heliport and waited for Raphael to come inside and report what he had seen. Then, and for several days after, Raphael returned from his copter survey of the entrance with nothing to report. Meanwhile, the humans and Forestman sensed that whatever was coming was close at hand.

On the fifth day, Raphael finally saw several vehicles some distance away along the road, heading for the valley entrance. Beyond that he could see nothing else. It wouldn't be until late the next day he would see a huge armada of vehicles approaching.

As the vehicles came closer, the first ones already being funneled into the valley, Fort Spa was put in a very practical defense mode. The first floor windows and doors and the second floor windows were shuttered. They took up positions around the part of the wall that faced the entrance and the only road in.

Maricel stayed in the Security room just off the main lobby watching the various monitors that surveyed the exterior of the building and out along the road. The main entrance to the building was the only unbarricaded doorway, but the glass in the main doors and window was as impervious to any kind of assault as any of the metal shutters.

Several vehicles began to approach around the lakeside road. They moved slowly and cautiously. These were the first to come and no one in Fort Spa had any idea what to expect. Interestingly enough, they shared a sense of optimism that had guided them when they first met each other so long ago.

Those first vehicles, a large bus and two big vans pulled around to the front of the building and stopped near the main doors. A number of unarmed humans emerged from the vehicles. Several walked boldly toward the main doors while the others stayed close to their vehicles.

One of those at the door tried to open it. When she couldn't, she knocked on the glass door very hard.

Maricel picked up a microphone beside her, her words coming through a speaker just above the main doors. Allow though the cameras allowed her to seem them quite clearly, the first thing she said was, "Please take a few steps backward so the cameras can see you clearly."

They responded, immediately stepping back from the door.

"You are mostly human, am I correct?" she asked.

The same one who had knocked, spoke in response, "We want to know if it was you who awakened us and made us come here?"

By then, the others inside Fort Spa were making their way to the front lobby.

"If you have any weapons, please leave them on the ground," Maricel made it a request, not a command.

They shook their heads, "We don't have any weapons," and showed their hands palms up, the same one spoke and then repeated her earlier question, "Are you the ones that called us here?"

Maricel, calm but authoritative, addressed the speaker "Choose two others to join you. The doors will be open to let the three of you in."

The doors opened a crack and for a moment it looked as if the group was going to surge toward them. "Just three of you, please," said Maricel in a soft voice.

Resisting the obvious desire to go inside, the crowd held back while three, two females and a male approached the door. The first pulled it completely open and one after another they stepped inside. There was wariness in their expressions and cautiousness to their movement.

Just inside the door, Patah, Shanira and Brunell could be seen. The stepped forward, hands raised in greeting. The woman who had spoken earlier asked again, "Are you the ones who awakened us and brought us here?"

"No," said Patah, "like yourselves, we were compelled to come here. We have no idea who or what woke us, only that we are here."

Patah and Shanira ushered the three into to the lounge beside the lobby and had them sit. Through the conversation that ensued, the first awakened learned that unlike themselves who had awakened quite a while ago and spent a great amount of time to get to this place, the new arrivals had awakened not so very long ago and around the same time. They had been compelled to make the journey in very short order. Most had not been around more than fifteen seasons.

They had little opportunity to grow their knowledge. Despite those limitations on this group, numbering close to one hundred humans, the first awakened discovered that among the new arrivals most, perhaps all, seemed to reflect the individuals of the first six in their innate knowledge.

Welcomed to Fort Spa, the three were told to have their vehicles brought in to the interior parking. They would meet them at the doors near the parking area and boat slip.

An entirely human group of ninety-seven joined the family of the first awakened. They were introduced to the others and to Fort Spa. They familiarized themselves with the surroundings and chose their living quarters.

Despite the numbers, this remained a communal group. They took meals together in one of the larger restaurants just off a lounge sizeable enough to take up the overflow. After a few days to build familiarity with the Fort, they too began to sense the approaching numbers.

As the days passed several other small parties appeared at the doors. They were mostly human, but there were among them, some elvin and other non-human species as well as another relative of Forestman.

Those who shared Maricel's particular gifts were teamed up with her. Those with medical knowledge and the elvin went with Jolinda. Those gifted with the knowledge of the earth sciences joined with Brunell. The architects, designers and builders teamed up with Shanira. While those of a psychological and spiritual bent, the healers of the inner self, including the Forestman and the other sasquatch, Woodsprowler, joined Patah with the intent of learning from each as much as possible about their particular field.

The hunter soldiers joined Raphael, inventorying and studying weapons technology and learning to fly the small planes and helicopter.

There was just enough time for them to develop their competencies to the point where they could assist in training and leading others. In fact, on the very last training session in the helicopter, while Raphael was assisting the last of the recent hunter, soldier arrivals on the on the subtle efficiencies of the controls, they flew close to the entrance. They were about to practice some routine maneuvers when they were astonished to see down the road and along the river a huge armada of vehicles and boats crowding towards them. Those in the helicopter could not miss the fact that there were many humans in those vehicles. There could be no doubt that there were thousands of them, and they were on their way into the valley and Fort Spa.

Back at Fort Spa a short time later, Raphael and the helicopter trainee recounted what they had seen. Raphael called it a swarm of humanity.

As they arrived, the first thing they wanted to know was who or what had called them to this place and for what purpose. They were all disappointed to learn from those who were there before them, that they had no answers for them.

A vast number of humans were welcomed into Fort Spa along with more than a few non-human allies. Amazingly, the Fort was able to accommodate everyone and all the vehicles without any need to crowd.

Many of the most recent arrivals, had combined skills and knowledge but in most cases, they were more limited when compared to the first six and the earlier arrivals. Many were primarily hunter, soldiers or potential healers, but many more had some knowledge and a preference for other fields including farming, earth sciences, psychology, artifact study, design and construction, and areas of spirituality.

This variety and melding of interests and skills interested the first six and the early arrivals. They speculated why so many had strong hunter and soldiering traits. It might prove to be meaningless, but as a group they suspected that it did not bode well.

Eventually their suspicions would be confirmed one way or the other. In the meantime, there was plenty of space, more than enough supplies and lots of things for everyone to do. What was used, of course, was quickly replaced. They had little concern regarding this, as that was how it had always been for them. A perfect replica of everything that was used was, with hardly any noticeable delay, put back in the original location.

The first six had thought about this from time to time. They were not absolutely certain but agreed that sometime in the near or distant future, replication and replacement would end and the populace of Legacy earth, especially the humans would have to provide for themselves. No evidence currently existed even to suggest that this might happen. In the meantime, larders were always well stocked and remained so despite the fact that 5000 and more were being fed daily. Everything they took was replaced. Even the helicopter after a fortunately non-fatal crash, had been replaced.

Despite the fact that there were more than enough living quarters for everyone in Fort Spa and if one so chose, one could easily avoid any of his or her fellows for a good long time. Most didn't do that, mini communities formed but all shared the one main concern. Why were they here? They had left cities and towns and rich farmlands and although they all agreed that the valley was particularly beautiful, and restful and Forṭ Spa and its surroundings comfortable and homey, it wasn't enough. They hated the fact that they had no answers to the critical question of why they were obliged to come here. They wanted to know why they were here in a beautiful valley surrounded by rugged mountains, living in a place that was either a huge fortress or a gigantic resort?

They were not being held prisoner. They could enjoy the facilities of the resort areas, move freely through the interior, or open doors if they wished. They were free to go outside either within the enclosure or outside and explore the valley. They could even leave the valley, but the compulsion always brought them back. Those who preferred a more rural life built small communities in the countryside. Many of these began to spring up in the foothills and near the mountains.

The Spectras of Bradley Station

One larger group under the leadership of a second awakened who identified himself as Bradley started a small community in a fertile area near the mountains. Bradley who was among the first of the second awakening to come to the valley while a Brunell-like biologist and geologist had an abiding interest in agriculture. He had researched and trained with Brunell and wanted very much to try an experiment in self-sustaining agriculture. The first six felt his idea was a positive one and encouraged him to pursue it.

While the experiment was showing signs of success, the community members were not isolated. Bradley with some of his fellow community members returned regularly to Fort Spa. There were some supplies that only Fort Spa could provide. While there, they would meet with a committee of mostly agriculturalist and builders under the guidance of Brunell. They would discuss the progress of the experiment, pointing to the successes, and work together around problem solving the stumbling blocks they encountered from time to time with their experimentation.

Over time, the committee began to notice that the people from the Bradley experimental agriculture station were showing up less frequently and had become quite taciturn. The seemed less interested in sharing information with the committee, in fact, less interested in speaking with anyone except to order their supplies and direct the loading. What used to make for a pleasant day was now over in short order and the truck on its way back to Bradley station.

It had been a happy group that set out with Bradley to become partners in his experiment. In the early days, they seemed open and ready to talk with the others. They laughed and joked with each other as the loaded the trucks then returned to join either the agricultural committee or just visit in one of the coffee shops or small restaurants.

This all seemed to change, and eventually those who used to spend time with them at Fort Spa were concerned. They looked glum, said little, came and left quickly. They began to come for supplies much less frequently and it was doubtful that they had yet reached a stage of self-sufficiency were that would make any sense. The same was true for those from some of the other outlying communities, especially the ones close to the distant mountains beyond Fort Spa.

Curious as to why this was happening, why these communities were neglecting to report in or even come to pick up supplies, Brunell and Raphael to go out and check on these communities. Hoping to find some answers they, along with two others, took the helicopter to Bradley station.

From some distance away, they could see the signs of neglect. What had been well-tended community had changed. The gardens were being overgrown with weeds. Windows were broken. Vehicles stood at the side of the road, their doors open, seemingly left behind and forgotten. Buildings had not been cared for. Few people could be seen and those they did see appeared to moving about aimlessly, heads down, shoulders slumped. No one came to greet them as they touched down.

The town of Bradley station was built around a large supply center and research offices. That's where Raphael, Brunell and the crew headed on landing. They found themselves walking along deserted streets, grass and weeds growing through the gravel. No one could be seen at the usually busy supply center and offices. Brunell was wondering if this was a sign that the land was reclaiming itself just as the many things they used over time that were replicated. This seemed different. Replication was generally very quick and there was never a diminishment of quality. This place was going to seed. The plants, not even the native ones, looked very healthy. This was not the land replicating itself, it was land growing over because no one bothered to stop it. This was very disturbing.

Brunell entered the research office to find Bradley slouched at one of the desks. He was alone, staring off into space. Seeing him here looking so despondent reminded Brunell of himself when the Faye had destroyed his plants and livestock. Approaching him, Brunell asked, "Bradley, are you all right? What's happening here?"

Bradley looked up slowly. His voice was low as if it was a chore to speak, "Oh, hello Brunell, Raphael, what brings you here?"

Raphael was incredulous, "Bradley, this place is a mess. Where is everyone?"

Bradley sighed, "Don't know. Haven't seen many around lately."

"Yeah," there was an edge to Raphael's voice, "What's up with that?"

"Don't know," Bradley said, slowly rising to his feet, "Folks just stopped working. It's as if nothing mattered anymore. Some people are getting sick, and no one seems to be bothered to help them."

Brunell shook his head, "Last time I was here, everything was so upbeat. What has happened since then?"

"Guess it's the nightmares, Brunell, "Bradley lifted his hat and scratched his disheveled hair, "They seem to suck out any kind of good feeling."

"Nightmares?" snapped Raphael.

"Yeah, they started near the beginning of the season. Began with those who lived farther from the center here, those living closer to the mountains. It moved from there to the center of town. People were complaining of nightmares." Bradley's voice began to face as he spoke, "They began to say that what we were doing here was futile. It all was meaningless, and they just didn't

want to be bothered anymore."

Brunell and the others were beginning to sense the depression and disillusionment. They headed back toward the helicopter bringing Bradley with them.

Raphael had a feeling that they needed to get out of there fast, and Brunell agreed. If they didn't leave soon, they felt that they would be overcome with sadness just as Bradley was. Bradley didn't board the helicopter with them, he just stood there staring blankly in their direction.

In the helicopter, returning to Fort Sap, they four in the helicopter could not shake the negative feelings they seemed to have picked up at Bradley station.

Even as Raphael guided the chopper over the outer wall of Fort Spa, he found himself beginning to feel that everything was useless.

As the helicopter crossed the threshold of Fort Spa, there was a sudden crackling sound accompanied by several flashes of light inside the cockpit. The negative sensations vanished immediately. "What just happened?" asked a surprised Brunell

They had no answer for him but everyone aboard the helicopter had recognized that there had been a change that came over them as they crossed into Fort Spa. Those feelings of despondency disappeared with the flashes of light.

"What in the hell is this thing? "came a voice from the back.

As Raphael guided the helicopter onto its pad and switched off the power, Brunell looked back. One of the crew was holding up what looked like a small burnt handkerchief.

With the helicopter shut down, a quick examination on the interior revealed several more of the small burnt handkerchiefs. On closer inspection, they turned out to be skinny rat like creatures with wings like dirty dishcloths.

"These the harpies you told us about, Brunell?" asked Raphael.

"No, way too small, but they do have some similarity."

As Brunell said this, the creatures began to crumble into ash. "Well, now, that's the same," he added.

"Same thing with the trolls," pointed out Raphael, adding what everyone there already knew, "These are bad news."

Several other expeditions returned with similar stories. There were stories of nightmares and despondency and incredible neglect. The expedition members also felt these some feelings of despondency as they made their way back to Fort Spa. As the passed into the fortress, either, boat, car, or aircraft, there was a crackling and flashes of light and several similar rat-like creatures looking like dirty handkerchiefs where found inside the cab, or cockpit. The feeling of depression left instantly with those tiny flashes as they crossed into Fort Spa. What was worrisome to them all was that until the flashes as they crossed the threshold of Fort Spa, they could see not sign of the creatures.

"They can't be invisible!" Brunell was examining one of the carcasses. It was tiny and fragile, but all too real. Maricel joined the Brunell and the team of biologists examining them. They were trying to speculate on why they hadn't been seen until they were dead, killed by some kind of screening shield that apparently enveloped Fort Spa. "Perhaps they can distort light some of the anti-radar drones," speculated Maricel.

"What are they?" asked Brunell.

Maricel bent close to one of the little creatures to study it, "I know about anti-radar drones, but I am not sure, technically, how they the work. They are military aircraft flown from the ground. They are designed with reflective material that scatters radar, along with a design that seems to distort light making them virtually invisible to radar and the naked eye. That's as much as I know, but I think I have an idea of what's going on. These creatures fool they eyes because there is something in their shape and something on their surfaces that deflects light around them. Whatever it is, it seems to burn off when they die, but while they are alive..."

"So, when you are looking at one of these creatures, even directly, they are very hard, nearly impossible to see," concluded Brunell.

There was real concern not only about the invisibility of these creatures, but also about the psychological effects that they produce. Evidence from the cockpits and cabs certainly pointed to these little rat-type beings as the sources of the depression, despondency and neglect in the outlying communities.

Patah had entered the room. Leaning on the doorjamb, he spoke casually, "Why don't we feed what we know and what we suspect into one of the computers? Some of my team has been checking them out and there seems to be a very extensive database. May be something there."

The others were surprised; they didn't know the computer team had got that far with those mysterious and almost incomprehensible devices. It was almost as if their functioning had been deliberately obscured, but for Patah and his computer team, it seemed that information regarding them were being slowly unraveled for them just as the mind maps of the first six had unfolded slowly over time.

The fact that the computers were becoming available delighted the biology researchers, "Where can we do this?" asked Brunell.

"Probably at any computer, but I'll show you the best place," Patah turned and headed down the hall. The others following right behind, Brunell with specimen in hand.

Patah brought them to one of the larger computer sites in the building. A wall of monitors flashed iconic messages. "These," said Patah, pointing at an array of devices on one table. "are 3D printers. On the next table, those are 3D scanners. Put the little monster on one of those scanners and ask the question."

Brunell dropped the creature on one of the scanners. "What do we ask?"

"If this is what I think it is," said Maricel, quickly surveying the array of computers, 3D devices and monitors, "then we just ask the room."

"Clearly we still have lots to learn about this place," said Brunell as he turned toward the monitor. "What is that thing, computer?"

There was a moment of quiet in the room, then a soft spoken, pedantic voice seemingly emanating from every part of the room began speaking. "This creature is terminated and is only moments from collapsing into ashes as have most of the others brought into the building. I have preserved this one as long as I could to make sure you were able to bring it here before it corrupts to ashes. It is a member of a group of different creatures unique to this re-creation of the planet earth and its environs. It is a member of a species called spectras. In its living state, it is very difficult to see as its living outer skin bends light obscuring it to near invisibility. Octogel goggles that can be found in storerooms c302 and x67 will render living Spectras visible.

Be warned, the spectra are a neurofeeder. It draws feelings of happiness, contentment and joy to itself. Those spending significant time in the presence will find themselves feeling depressed and despondent. An early sign of the presence is unexplained nightmares. As the time others, especially humans remain in the presence of spectras, they will lose interest in day-to-day activities. Prolonged exposure to spectras can lead to suicide either through an active process of self-destruction, or, as is more frequently the case through self-neglect. Spectras are quite fragile and can be easily destroyed when seen. Neutrino rays in the facility's protective shield will terminate them and burn off the light distorting outer skin, instantly restoring normal thought processes and render them visible. Any sort of physical blow will disable and ultimately terminate spectras. Pellets, knives and small caliber weapons are also quite effective. Spectras are identified by this database to be considered dangerous. End. This creature is terminated and is collapsing into ashes... "

The computer voice was beginning to repeat the information when Patah spoke up, "Thank you, that's enough."

The voice immediately stopped and the monitors that had been showing images of spectras as the computer spoke returned to their previous screens.

Taking a few minutes to absorb the information the computer provided, Raphael then sent men off immediately to search the named storage rooms for Octogel goggles.

"Well," said Maricel, "apparently, they aren't hard to kill, just hard to find."

Almost immediately after gathering several hundred Octogel goggles, preparations were being made to send anti-spectra teams out to the outlying communities and experimental stations. The intention was to eliminate the spectra that were haunting the residents and restore the communities.

About Wampyra

One team returned from several communities near the entrance to the valley. The team had discovered problems similar to the spectra related ones near the mountains, but in two communities the residents complained of symptoms that were more that of fatigue, and frustrated anger. They told the team that in their community people were having difficulty sleeping. Although they could see nothing, they all reported childish laughter that seemed to last all night. Several who had been out at night reported being attacked and stung by some moderately sized creature. The attack was short lived as they recipients of the stinging made it inside as quickly as they could. In one community, a night watchman was missing. Except for those few minor attacks, they had seen nothing more than a few piles of ash near where the attacks had occurred.

Patah immediately recognized what this was. It was Wampyra. The outlying communities were under attack by creatures hostile to humanity. There were now at least two known species doing this, Spectras and Wampyra.

The computer's database confirmed Patah's conclusion. It explained that although human blood was toxic to the Wampyra and even a drop or two could cause their rapid death and subsequent disintegration leaving nothing but a trace of ash.

Despite that, the Wampyra with their blood-sucking fangs could be persistent. The Sire would gladly sacrifice large numbers of his children to exact revenge. He might also send his children to torment people with their childlike laughter and a neurostimulant that exuded from their bodies could, with the slightest touch, generate feelings of panic in humans, keep them worried and exhausted, and interfere with normal, healthy sleep patterns.

The Wampyra along with the fems and sires needed a location free from light and a bit of soil from their birthplace where they could pass the daylight hours in a semi-comatose sleep. Their size and quickness made them difficult to see in the dark. The fem, in concert with the sire could produce as many as 60 offspring each night. While the sire could live freely in the open from dusk to dawn, the fem, once a mother, was relatively immobile and remained in the dark carrying out its primary function of breeding new Wampyra. All Wampyra hated the ability of humans and other creatures to be active both during the day and at night.

Their hatred of humans was extreme, and they sought to eradicate all of humanity and their non-human allies. Although Wampyra were resistant to weapons, a wooden stake through the central plane of their bodies, burning, beheading, and exposure to any form of sunlight along with drawing blood from a human were all fatal to them.

They avoided water and could only enter a home if invited by any of the persons living there. Once welcomed in, they would return again and again with their giggles and their hypnotic exudence, driving any humans spending any time in the house mad. If they could get back into the house, they might come in enough numbers to attack the humans inside, possibly causing them to bleed to or leaving them comatose to die from shock, exposure or starvation. Many Wampyra would die to do this.

Natural light, spotlights and flashes with high lumens and the repeater crossbows with their wooden bolts were the best weapons against the Wampyra. All of which were found in various storage rooms throughout Fort Spa.

These items, spotlights and flares could keep the Wampyra at bay as they could not tell if the light they gave off might be synthesized natural light. Direct contact with synthesized natural light could begin the disintegration process. Any kind of light would reveal them and hold them long enough for a wooden bolt from a crossbow to kill them with a direct hit to their central core.

Shattered Peace

Squads were sent to the outlying communities with the weapons to eradicate either spectra or Wampyra. This was barely underway when reports came in telling of swarms of Faye killing livestock and threatening humans. Raphael began to think that they would have to patrol all parts of the valley for hostiles. Given the large number of second awakening who shared Raphael's inherent skill as the hunters and soldiers and who had worked with him and his leadership team, regular full-scale sweeps of the valley were possible.

Raphael presented this to the others who agreed that the safety of the valley was of prime importance. Shortly after, survey and reconnaissance teams went out on regular patrols throughout the valley to search out unknown or hostile presence. Beside the spectras, the Wampyra, and the Faye, there were now reports of other threatening creatures that sounded very much like the Hoblins and the Stone Dwarves. One patrol, while checking a forest stand between Fort Spa and the entrance to the valley were set upon by a group of Stone Dwarves rushed out from between the trees swing their axes. The attack, while without evidence of any tactical plan, was deadly. Several of the patrol had been wounded and two killed by the attacking Dwarves before they could react.

Once the randomness of the attack had been determined, the patrol drew around their wounded, some facing out others facing in and began to systematically repel the attackers. Dwarves within the circle were met with pistols and large bush knives. While the Dwarves either continued to swing their axes, or throw them, they were less effective than at first. The humans were able to dodge and deflect the axes while, firing their pistols at the fierce, but clearly undirected Stone Dwarves. The Dwarves made themselves excellent targets and soon the inside of the circle was clear of living Dwarves. Those on the circle facing out were sweeping the forest with light caliber machine guns aimed low for best effect.

Some elvin hunters had gone to the trees and were picking out targets among the Dwarves for their toxin tipped arrows. The battle was over in a matter of minutes although it seemed much longer for the patrol members. They watched incredulously as the Stone Dwarves crumbled into ashes around them. Spreading out from their location, the patrol found a number of piles of ash, but no Stone Dwarves were encountered. The attack was devastating. Of the few that were wounded, most had superficial injuries, but the toxins on the axes caused extreme pain.

The patrol leader called Fort Spa requesting ambulances for the three most seriously wounded and anti-toxins for the other four. They would also need to retrieve the two dead, one human and one elvin hunter. For the humans and their allies, this made it very clear. The peace of the valley was being shattered in a very big way.

The first human and allied losses while only two were huge. Everyone in Fort Spa, including the growing numbers of refugees from the outlying communities who were returning to the fort attended. Many were in shock. Fort Spa was now just the Fort.

For the humans and their allies, this made it very clear. The peace of the valley was being shattered in a very big way.

Super Computer

It was Patah and his team working on communications and their ongoing attempt to understand the gigantic computer that finally asked the right question and got the answer. That answer might not have been as comforting as they had hoped, but it did explain a great deal to them including the why, when and how of their being called to the valley.

The computer gave the history of legacy earth. The sun of the original earth had long ago gone super nova and for eons beyond counting it had been a dark cinder in space. The earth was a tiny cinder trying to hold on to a wobbly orbit around the solar waste. The last gesture of a transcendent humanity was to restore the earth and its surroundings out into the Milky Way galaxy. In a time when computers had long ceased to exist, the greatest, most powerful computer ever built was installed on this new earth. Its reach circumvented the globe and was responsible for restoring and replicating anything that was taken, eaten, or in any way used.

The commands the computer was given were specific and would be carried out until it could no longer do so due to lack of materials or computer failure, "neither of which," the computer itself made clear, "would occur for a very long time," as in eons.

The computer also informed them that its own evolving intellect, while continuing to serve its function to protect the legacy could allow it to act in ways not necessarily a part of its original programming. It could at some point when it calculated that the population was large enough and ready, that it could remove some of its replication service to make mankind more self-sustaining. This, it clearly pointed out, would be a long time in the future.

The computer continued to explain that the humans who created it and legacy earth chose to begin with the era when the people of earth first began the exploration of space. However, historical documentation was rare, most lost over the countless centuries as human habitation spread through much of this part of the universe and beyond.

Between the highly evolved humanity and the technology they used, the reality of the period they had chosen was virtually unknown. They were certain only of humans and a few limited species co-existing at that time, but the fragments of earth history they had discovered in their search of wherever they had known humanity to have even momentarily been, were included in the in the environmental design of legacy earth. When they laid out the framework for this, they created the computer to protect and support the humanity that they would place there.

The computer's programming was sophisticated beyond understanding and very open ended, it had done a very thorough evaluation of legacy earth and everything and everyone on it since just prior to the first awakening when it came on line.

It had learned that there are a great number of beings inamicable with humans. While some may be native to a reconstructed earth, most are not. They have an alien chemistry that makes them very different from humans, and even their non-human allies. Their hostility to humans is so extreme that they represent a threatening presence and are likely capable of destroying the human species.

This, of course, ran counter to the computer's programming. The computer admitted that despite its great power, it did not have the capability to choose those who are the enemy of man and destroy them. It was the humans of legacy earth who were the ones needed to overcome these enemies. Their non-human allies were, for the computer, an unexpected bonus.

The computer informed them that it had called them all here for the purpose of defending legacy earth. The computer had determined that this valley was to be the site of the battle for earth and designed and built Fort Spa. It had also designed the plan that allowed the first six a great deal of time to internalize their learning, knowledge base, and understanding of their unique version of earth.

Each had a set of skills that required refining. This would allow them to serve as teachers and resources for the second awakened. The first six had enough experience to share with the second group meaning they would not need nearly so much time before getting to Fort Spa. When they had awakened, it called them to come quickly. It drew the enemies of mankind to come to the valley as well.

The computer promised as much assistance as it was capable of giving; replication, strategy and tactics, Information about individual hostiles, enemy movement and maintain the invisible perimeter shields. The humans would be required to physically overcome the hostile forces and drive them from this earth or be destroyed ending the legacy.

The computer continued to explain that the basis of victory was found in the will. The group that most wanted to claim earth and persisted with their will to succeed would ultimately be the ones to achieve victory. It was not just a matter of military success, but also strength of purpose. It further warned them that they had yet to encounter the serious anti-human hostiles, the most ferocious and purposeful of the enemy, but they soon would.

After that, the computer began to profile the hostiles gathering against them near the valley entrance. Some of the humans were aware of some of these having already come across them before deciding to evacuate and return to the Fort. Some humans and their allies had already given their lives in defense of their villages and stations and providing rear guard for evacuation. Fortunately, if that is the right term to use when the lives of valuable companions had been lost, the numbers of fallen were few.

There were still others that the humans and their allies had yet to meet. Some that encompassed a level of hatred for humans and their allies that they could only be termed evil. These malevolent creatures were a far more serious threat than any they had yet met. The very worst of these, the computer explained, were the Diamonics.

Unlike many of the other dangerous creatures they had come upon, most of which were single-minded in their hostility, the Diamonics were not. As a species, they were intelligent and crafty. They were psychically powerful, able to create illusions that bordered on reality and could use illusory visions to draw their enemy into close quarters where they could kill them with tridents, spears and large battle axes. Some of the lesser Diamonics also used bows and arrows.

One difference between the allies and the hostiles that favored the humans, and their allies was the firepower they could bring to bear. The allied weaponry was far more sophisticated and able to find enemy targets at a great distance and destroy them.

The Diamonics and their supporters were limited in their weaponry. Some, because of the neurological nature of their form of attack or the toxicity they exuded rarely carried weapons, while the others seemed to be limited to primitive weapons, the bow and arrow being the most sophisticated.

The computer advised them not to take the hostiles lightly. They were persistent and unfeeling in their animosity and their numbers were large as they bred quickly.

The leader of the hostiles and the most dangerous of the diamonics was the Ramshorn. It stood over two meters tall on cloven hooves. It had golden yellow skin, a prehensile tail and high rams' horns framing a wide mouth with sharp teeth, a flat nose and huge red eyes. Ramshorn were very strong with sharp and probably toxic nails on their hands.

The Lesser Diamonics may not have been as impressive as the Ramshorn but were just as dangerous. Smaller in size, the Lesser Diamonics included several variations, The Tricorns had three sharp horns Two on the side of the head and one centered on the forehead. The Monocorns had the central horn and were slightly smaller than the Tricorns. The Imps were quite a bit smaller and hornless. Their claws were very toxic as was their bite. The most common of these seemed to be the Tricorns and the Monocorns, the Imps were more elusive. If there were Duocorns, they were yet to be found. They all shared the psychic powers that enabled them to create very realistic illusions. Their weapons of choice tended towards those used in brutal close quarter fighting.

The entire Diamonic species was the driving force behind a plan to displace humans on earth from the tiny imp to the large Ramshorn, the diamonics represented the closest thing to pure evil that could be found on legacy earth.

The prototype of the diamonics like the other hostile beings originated in myth and fiction. In the case of the Diamonics, they most closely identified with beings known as devils or demons. In the mythology of original earth, the devil and the demons were considered to be evil incarnate. In that sense the Diamonics were as close a copy as possible, not evil incarnate but the paramount of evil. The only significant difference was that the Diamonics were mortal.

The Diamonics were neither mythic nor fictional. They were very real, intelligent, canny and had found a way to take control of the other evil and hostile beings, directing them to the valley. This was the Diamonics opening gambit in the battle for earth. The creatures that they had sent ahead, monsters in their own right, were intended to sow fear and create discord among the humans, but the humans were not as quick to give in as the Diamonics had hoped.

According to the computer and its vast database, it was unlikely that the human inhabitants or the allies would encounter any of these Diamonics, unless they sensed approaching victory or if the likelihood of overthrow by the humans was close at hand.

The computer revealed that each of the hostile creatures the humans and allies would face in the early stages of this monumental war to the finish were all difficult to kill. No surprise to those who had at some time encountered them during their journey.

Innate aspects of their physical structure assured this. Spectras deflected light making them virtually impossible to see, Wampyra were immune to projectiles of metal or lead, succumbing only to wooden shafts, beheading if one could get close enough, burning and exposing them to natural light. High explosives, too, but that seemed like overkill. The Stone Dwarves had their axes and their hard skin and musculature and squat physiques making them difficult targets. Direct contact with hard steel in the form of a sword or axe or a well-placed bullet could kill them if it struck them in a vital area, but the dwarves never stopped moving. They were not easy targets.

Hoblins and trolls were fast and flexible. Their strength and speed made them difficult to catch. They had no other defensive capabilities. Their size and number and ability to fly provided protection for the Faye as a community, but not for the individual. Werewolves with their razor sharp claws and teeth, had size, and mobility in forested areas along with their ferocious nature. The harpies were moving targets, much of their body concealed behind a shroud of skin.

Most were fairly low on the intelligence scale, although they could articulate their thoughts in Assianangle. They were persistent and could demonstrate intense focus especially when in pursuit of victims. The Wampyra sire was human-like in its understanding and ability to think clearly and express its thoughts in very sophisticated Assianangle. Each sire controlled many Wampyra who would unfalteringly obey his will.

The Diamonics had very high intelligence and inordinate strength no matter the class designation or size. They had some form of parapsychological ability that could project false images into the minds of the humans and their allies causing mass illusions or inspire dread, and misdirection among their enemies. They could also briefly take control of some lower animals and reptiles.

Overture

The computer couldn't or wouldn't make any predictions as to the result of conflict with the forces of evil. The humans and their allies vacillated between feelings of confidence, they knew a lot about their enemy, and anxiety regarding the enemy's strength and power and particularly, its absolute ruthlessness. While the humans and their allies waited, the hostile forces gathered near the entrance of the valley or skulked in the far reaches of the valley near the furthest mountains. The threat of the battle for earth loomed closer and closer.

The computer made it very cleared to those at Fort Spa that there could be no peaceful cohabitation with these creatures. There could be no middle ground.

The search and destroy teams sent out to deal with the spectra and the Wampyra seemed to be having some success only to discover signs of other predators.

In one community situated at the foot of the mountain beside the valley entrance they had lost several of their human and elvin members to axe wounds. Another group on the far shore of the lake complained that some of the number had encountered some ugly, foul smelling creatures covered in a light grey wool with hands and feet bearing long razor sharp claws and fangs. They had attacked the villagers with claws and clubs. While they had been able to drive them off with no losses, but several wounded, they were horrified by the ferocity of the attack.

Swarms of faye were seen clustering near where the river joined the lake. Similar reports poured in from search and destroy teams throughout the valley. The reports were serious enough to call in the teams after having them spread the word that all humans and their non-human associates should immediately withdraw from their communities and return to Fort Spa. To assure that the message got to everyone, Patah had the computer send out a compulsion to return to the fort, just as it had sent out the original compulsion that first brought them there.

Within days, nearly all the humans and the others from the outlying experimental communities were back inside home base and getting ready for a siege.

SIEGE AND SALLY

Preparation for a siege was going well. Small weapons and larger ordnance were set up to be easily accessible anywhere in the building. Food and water were laid out in close proximity to each ordnance cache and locations on the roof and in the upper windows where heavy arms were set. Besides the regular medical clinics throughout the building, make shift hospital areas were set up close to areas were injured defenders within the building or wounded coming hastily from outside could be initially treated.

Withdrawal maps were available should they have to draw back to a large internal keep near the landing strip. Pathways were cleared and small mobile carts were set out ready to carry defenders from one hot spot to another should attacks come from different areas.

The computer continued to assure the humans and their allies that the fort was unbreachable and the already present defenses would prevent any hostiles from getting in no matter how long the attack. Rocks, spears, axes, arrows and other projectiles could find their way inside and do some harm. Despite this, the computers were set to identify where a large buildup of enemy forces might occur. Maricel and Raphael were doing this while Brunell and his teams were clearing back the forest to avoid being surprised. The clearing they made left a large open space between forest and wall so any movement large or small within the space could be clearly seen and any attack cut short.

Jolinda's team prepared the medical technology, setting up well equipped recovery units in the various health centers and make shift hospitals throughout the Fort and inner area.

Access ways were bolstered and ready to be defended. Underground passages leading out of the fort set with mechanisms and explosives intended to close them down should hostile forces attempt to enter the fort through them. Shanira's teams were responsible for these.

Patah and his team kept in constant communication with the master computer. Its vast data banks and sub processers were encased in huge, shielded caverns that stretched around the globe. In the case of disaster, the computer had backup programming in a number of

locations ready to kick in meaning it was unlikely to fall
into the hands of the enemy or serve them in any way. The
communications team reviewed the strengths and weakness
of the various hostiles again and again. Each time they
reviewed, the got to know their enemy a little better.

Despite all the preparation, there was no sign of any
of the hostile creatures near the fort. Day to day routines
continued. The resort aspects continued to be enjoyed full.
The lake was, as ever, cool and refreshing and the air was mild
and pleasant and many continued to seek recreation outside
the fort. To this end those who continued to choose the
loveliness of the outdoors away from the fort regularly went
over routes and defensive procedures to ensure their efficient
withdrawal back into the fort at the first sign of hostiles.
Most of these groups were accompanied by armed guards
while other guards stood by near entrances ready to provide
directions and cover for withdrawal from the exterior
recreation areas if needed.

Throughout the valley, the villages and experimental
stations stood empty. Everyone had returned to Fort Spa,
where they once again made their home just as they had
when they first arrived.

The force field that had first come in to play when
Spectras were accidently brought back to the fort in cabs or
cockpits offered those within the fort complete protection
from the hostile beings. The force field extended to great
depth into the ground and great height into the air. No
would be invader could fly high enough or dig deep enough
to bypass it.

Despite all the preparation and the awareness that the hostiles were amassing in huge numbers in the far corners of the valley and could at any time, it still came as a surprise to many when the outright attack began.

The first wave of hostiles came as a massive frontal attack. Huge numbers of stone dwarves, their axes brandished were interspersed with hideous grey-skinned Hoblins, clubs held high. The faye came in clouds, werewolves and trolls could be seen among the vanguard of the attack, while the devastating shrieks of the harpies shattered the silence putting the defenders on edge.

Some humans and allies, despite the practice were caught so completely by surprise that they were overcome and cut down by the advancing hordes.

Guards did their best to hold the way for a full-fledged retreat and thanks to them the majority were able to reach the gates and get inside safely. Many came to the gates slapping at the faye and their stingers.

The force field stopped the onrush as faye, Dwarves and Hoblins with a burst of light died and began crumbling to ash, just like the spectras earlier, their lives sucked out of them as they tried to penetrate the fort. Above the wall, harpy shrieks were cut short as the impacted the field above the building.

Inside the fort, treatment was already underway for those stung by faye, or bearing the breaks and bruises from the hoblin clubs. Those suffering the extreme pain of gashes from the toxic blades of the Stone Dwarves axes were being led to the healing pods or their miniature versions and being injected with anti-toxin.

The healing underway, many gathered at various observation points to watch the steady press of attackers while others raced to man their weapons at the upper windows and on the roof. Many hostiles fell to their firepower, but even more contributed to the growing piles of ash in their relentless press to get to the force field protected walls and the hated humans beyond.

The hostiles perished against the force field and from weapons fire in astronomical numbers. This senseless slaughter seemed to go on for hours. Then, as quickly as they had appeared, the hostiles withdrew leaving vast piles of dirty grey ash to blow in the breeze while partly ravaged bodies of dying dwarves and Hoblins lay scattered about.

The ensuing silence lasted for a few minutes, then was broken by a loud voice that seemed to emanate from everywhere but was also inside the humans' and their allies' heads. The tone was arrogant and commanding. "I am the Ramshorn, emperor of this world, my domain. My world is home only for mine and for my thralls and servants. There is no place for humanity here. I offer you one chance. Leave this place and proceed to the dark entranceway at the foot of the distant mountains and pass through it to wherever it will bring you.

If this does not happen this very day, I will send my minions against you until every stone of your great walls has crumbled to dust and every life within destroyed. I await your compliance."

Back in the main computer room Patah looked up at the central holographic dais where a human like form stood and returned his look. "computer, did you hear that?" asked Patah.

"If you mean the Ramshorn message, I copy it."

"What does it mean?"

"It means that this particular Ramshorn diamonic has claimed dominion over the earth and has demanded that all humans leave through the interdimensional transit space that is found at the foot of the high mountains at the most distant part of the valley."

"I understand that he has claimed to have dominion over all the earth, "said Patah, "but what does he mean that we are to leave through, what did you call it, an interdimensional transit space?"

"The only right Ramshorn has is to call himself what he chooses," explained the computer, "he has no power over the earth, nor the ability to force you humans to exit the earth. If you leave the fortress, he will do his best to have you all killed long before you would reach the interdimensional transit space."

"We understand that the Ramshorn is merciless, but what is the transit space?" asked a somewhat piqued Patah.

"These were entrance ways through which those who were building the new earth could enter without disrupting the world building process. Remnants of the old earth and all you see, including me were brought here through these gaps. In fact, you and all the beings on this earth, including the ramshorn and his cohort were brought in seed form from wherever the builders where. Most of these gaps have closed. A few remain, shrinking steadily. At this point, these interdimensional transit points are thought to be unstable wormholes that lead to various other worlds. Beyond that my programming provides nothing more."

"Thought by who?" Patah looked searchingly at the holographic speaker.

"My data fields were instilled by the builders. I can't tell you anything more about these transit points." Said the computer in a tone that sounded almost disdainful."

"Do we leave," Patah wanted to know.

"While that is solely a decision left up to you and your fellows, I must tell you that this world was designed and constructed for humanity. Even if you were successful in reaching the transit point, which is highly unlikely, there is no telling where you would end up, but it is likely a far less habitable place than this one.

Ramshorn has far less claim to this world than you and the other humans do. However, it has gathered a prodigious force of followers to itself. Establishing your claim to this world will not be easy.

I cannot direct you; I can only advise. The Ramshorn has absolute antipathy towards your species and those others with native ties to origin earth. Its goal is to eradicate humanity not send you into exile."

The decision was put to the humans and their allies along with the computer's warning that the diamonics wished to eradicate them and the promise to let them leave through an interdimensional door was insincere.

There was no question, no debate, the decision was that this was their world and the humans, and their allies would stay and defend it against the Ramshorn and its minions.

The computer had assured them of the strength and permanence of the fort's defenses, that the fortress was capable of withstanding any attack. The siege could go on endlessly.

Those inside the fort felt that they would allow the siege to play out in the hope that eventually enough of the hostile, Ramshorn's minions, would succumb to the force field that the others would withdraw.

They had no idea of the hostile persistence of the Ramshorn and their power over their minions nor did they have any idea of the huge numbers that could be called upon to attack the fort.

When the day ended with no sign of the humans and their allies leaving Fort Spa, the siege began in earnest. As dusk fell, Wampyra and other night creatures joined the other attackers. The siege continued, night and day, for an interminable amount of time. While those inside the fortress were secure, the attack never let up.

The pile of ashes grew higher, some swirling so thickly in the breeze that eventually, like a heavy fog, it began to obscure the view from the windows and of those who were manning the weapons within that they would close the windows to avoid being struck by the stones and other dangerous objects the enemy sometimes threw. While heavy rains cleared the air enough for the defenders to use their weapons successfully, it didn't wash the ashes away quite as expected, instead the rain seemed to harden the ash into higher and higher piles. Many wounded fell on these piles and the sight of their obvious suffering was difficult for those inside the fort to bear. They would sometimes watch in horror as stone dwarves or hoblins, or other attackers would climb over the writhing bodies of the wounded only to hit the force field and be turned to dust.

Eventually only those required to stand lookout and occasionally man the guns or crossbows even bothered to view the destruction beyond the walls. The remainder stayed well away, content to spend their days drilling and practicing for combat and enjoying the serenity of the cafes, bars and recreational areas.

For many in the fortress, the siege was virtually forgotten and that is how it remained as the days passed and the carnage continued. From time to time, the ramshorns would repeat their threats that earth was theirs and the humans did not belong and were destined to die at the hands of ramshorns' minions when they eventually broke through the wall.

Since these telepathic messages were weaker the farther one was from the source, many began to spend their time in the interior area far from the outer walls except when they were called to duty.

Despite the enormous size of the internal quadrangle and the massive dimensions of the building surrounding it, they seemed to grow smaller and more confining as the siege continued. Many felt more and more as if they were, in reality, prisoners of the ramshorn and the other diamonics who had yet to participate in the action. A great many of those who had lived outside the fortress in the long since overgrown experimental stations and small communities felt this way. Many of these were the ones who had deliberately sought out the solitude of the countryside and had wanted no more than to live in a small community. They could not help but feel trapped. While the population of Fort Spa did not compare to that of a large city of origin earth, for some it was still overwhelming.

There were even mutterings that they should accept the Ramshorn's offer and leave this world behind and take their chances with somewhere new. The vast majority of those who felt this way were dubious of the Ramshorn's sincerity. The computer agreed with the latter, estimating that a very small percentage, perhaps no more than two or three percent of the humans would make it to the transfer point. Those that passed through would likely find themselves in a world far more inhospitable than this one, making even the most favorable estimates for survival perilously close to zero.

The six first and their close aides and senior team members were gradually coming to understand that for morale's sake, the siege needed to be broken. To that end, they began working on plans to go out and challenge the hostiles. It was being made quite clear by the steady flow towards self-destruction at the force field that the ramshorn minions' strength was in their sheer numbers and not their tactical sense. The real enemy, the diamonics, continued to remain hidden while allowing their minions who lacked real intelligence to continue without pause, their relentless and always fatal onslaught. While the diamonics, whose strength was their psychic abilities might well be driving this based on the psychological affect it would have on those within the fort, the issue concerning the human defenders was the huge and steady number of assailants making it dangerous to leave the fort.

The question the first six and the others faced was how to reduce the enemy numbers. Reduced numbers would mean fewer attackers, less stress on the force field and the opportunity to carry the battle onto the Ramshorn's turf. They could send out combat teams with explosives and destroy many of the enemy before they got to the wall. Those carrying out the raids would be placing themselves at serious risk while even if successful would not significantly affecting the hordes of attackers.

For any kind of success, the raiding parties would have to get to those generation sites where the hostile forces were bred, or generated, or however they came into existence.

Patah's team set the computer to backtrack various species of attackers to see if these generation sites actually existed. If they did and could be located, then helicopters and even light planes could go up while staying within the walls so not to be at risk for destruction by harpies or spectra or, the Wampyra at night.

With cameras mounted on them, they could send back pictures of the distant surroundings to the computer processors that would then merge them with satellite pictures the computer was able to draw on to find any generation sites analyzing for numbers, origins and heat signatures.

Patah's knowledge of the Wampyra suggested that the fems and sires, while giving off little heat would show up in lightless underground caverns that could be determined by the numbers of offspring leaving each night.

They hoped that similar areas just as likely to be well hidden would similarly reveal breeding sites for stone dwarves, hoblins, trolls and others.

Although heat signatures proved difficult to pick up illustrating a significant difference in physiology between humans and the various hostile entities, the computers were able to pinpoint areas where there was significant activity marking the emergence from several mountains of stone dwarves and Wampyra. While a large swampy region very close to those locations showed hoblin and troll activity.

Having determined several breeding locations, at least two for Wampyra, three for stone dwarves and one large swampy area that hoblins and trolls had created like beavers in a location where mountain streams merged to flow into the lake.

The harpies and the specters bred in mountain eyries, A few well-placed percussive shells from the cannons mounted on the fortress roof would radically reduce the numbers of the neurofeeders and the acidic screamers. The harpies did not seem to be anywhere as numerous as most of the others. Spotters had seen perhaps fifty or sixty of them and of those harpies, some may have been counted more than once. The specters, too, seemed to be slow breeders. The humans and their allies being inside the fortress behind the force field were unreachable. The fact the specters were unable to feed probably contributed significantly to their diminishment in numbers. The werewolves had a very small population and breeding took many months. The werewolves who went to the wall, were large enough to be easy targets for the defenders. Those that remained tended to travel in pairs and although they were deadly one on one, they would be easily by passed with the help of spotters on lookout towers that had been built in key locations on the fortress roof and in the helicopters, the original and the far more sophisticated two built by Shanira and her team.

Having located the breeding sites, each of which could be seen to be quite large, the humans with the assistance of the main computer and its colossal data base, needed to come up with an effective means of disrupting and eliminating these sites either permanently, or at least long enough for them to engage and defeat the diamonics.

Combined teams working on the disruption tactics decided that for the stone dwarves, the best way to take out their breeding sites would be with highly concussive explosives. These should fracture the subterranean stone sending it crashing into the caverns and the breeding dwarves. Those who survived, if any, would be trapped and even with their ability to cut through stone would be a long time negotiating their way out.

The Wampyra, being susceptible to light, would likely succumb to high flash explosives that opened their breeding caves to daylight, along with incendiaries that gave off a light very similar to daylight. Percussive shelling would then cut through the rock and preferred soil necessary to the Wampyras' breeding.

The breeding and mustering grounds of the hoblins and the trolls required a very different approach. According to the computer hoblins and trolls bred in shallows pools within the swamp. The newborns of both species were protected by an egg-like shell that kept them from drowning until they were strong enough to break through and leave their watery birthplace. It would take perhaps two days before they were strong enough to break out. By then the recently born trolls and hoblins were miniature adults that grew rapidly once free of the shell. Each dam could produce two dozen or more offspring over several days.

The computer's heat and motion overlays revealed a hotbed of activity in the swampy areas the hoblins and trolls had created by blocking several streams. Since the newborns were deposited randomly throughout the swamp, explosives could not hope to do significant damage to the breeding area. The swamp was large, and any large-scale explosives would have to be brought in and spread around by hand. The team members would have to be precise in laying out the explosives and that would be difficult to do without encountering resistance.

Since the breeding ground assaults needed to be synchronized to provide the necessary window of time to carry out a successful offensive to break the siege.

The materials had already been assembled for the assault against the Dwarves and Wampyra.

The faye, who were primarily nested in trees close to the breeding caverns, could be quickly dealt with using airborne chemical dust that would kill many and paralyze many more limiting their ability to retaliate. The hoblin and troll breeding area remained the primary conundrum for the planning team.

The need to come up with an effective way to shut down the troll and hoblin breeding grounds was very important. They were larger and had a malicious intelligence that made them more dangerous to the humans and their allies than many of the other hostiles. Their breeding grounds needed to be considered a prime target. The question was, how.

The planning team wracked their brain for the answer. How is a swampy, widespread breeding area destroyed within a very limited time frame to coordinate with the other breeding ground assaults that were already equipped and ready to go.

Frustration was at a maximum after several days of trying to come up with something. "Let's break for a while," suggested Brunell, getting up from his chair and heading towards the door.

"Damn it," came a voice from somewhere in the room, "I just want to turn the heat up on that swamp and hard boil the little beggars."

Brunell stopped at the doorway and turned around, "You may have something there!"

"What, heat up the swamp and cook 'em?" asked someone.

"Yeah.... No. not exactly, but I have an idea. I know the biology teams at Logan Station and Bradley Station were both working on experiments with flash freezing. Let's get them down here and find out what they know."

"Freeze them rather than cook them. That sounds interesting," said the one who had spoken earlier, "let's see what they have to say."

Although the progress of the experimentation on flash freezing was cut off with the arrival of the specters, they were able to round up seven of the biologists and builders who were leading the experiments. They had a lot to tell, their plan was not to destroy life, but preserve it by flash freezing seeds and other items for long and medium term storage. They had had as many failures as successes and their freezing bins were small and the swamp was large, but they had some suggestions that got the planning team going.

The objective now was to find a way of flash freezing the swamp and assuring the destruction of the young hoblins and trolls, the breeding parents and any others that might be in the swamp with them. They had to develop something that would quickly lower the temperature of the water over a wide area while incorporating materials that would incapacitate and destroy the breeders and the newborns either on freezing or on melting. Those not killed or debilitated by the freeze, possibly some of the young in protective shells would be subject to a chemical that would erode the shells and cause them to drown.

The plan wasn't fool proof but since it was the best they had; it was decided to go with it.

With the help of the computer and the planning team that included members of both Brunell's and Jolinda's teams' knowledge of chemistry Shanira's team's skill and developing a delivery system, the fast freeze missiles were prepared. They looked like sleek winged canisters and would be deployed by way of modified grenade launchers. The carrying distance of the canisters depended on the size of charge in the launchers that would set them spinning towards their destination like an origin earth Frisbee. This would give the insurgency team an opportunity to set up fairly close to each other while some targeted near areas and others the farther ones. On contact with the surface of the water, concussive caps would mix the chemicals that would immediately and radically lower the temperature of the surrounding water to well below freezing to a waist high depth. With proper deployment, the entire swamp would fast freeze killing most of the enemy in contact with the water and the bulk of the newborns. Others that might remain in alive in their eggshell–like coverings would be immobilized until the swamp began to thaw at which time another chemical would spread to dissolve the shells of those remaining.

Computer mock-ups estimated an eighty to one hundred percent success rate. Along with the simultaneous assaults on the other breeding sites, this would eliminate the reinforcements for those already storming the fort, crippling the siege and opening the way for insurgency teams to carry the battle to the enemy.

With all designated assault teams equipped and ready for the attack on the breeding sites, the final step before the actual attack was to train in simulated conditions to get safely to the attack sites, carry out the assault as planned and return quickly to the fort and safety.

As to exit and entrance points, a number of bolt holes, already present, with well concealed exits outside the force field and enough distance from the wall, would bring the teams out well past the bulk of the enemy who were focused on getting to the walls of the fort.

The force field that seemed to have no end either up or down would be as effective against subterranean attacks as at the wall at ground level. The force field had no effect on the humans or their allies, and a brief check would quickly tell them if the enemy had found any of the bolt holes. In that case, they would move to another.

As preparations were being finalized, Jolinda and Patah began to question the morality of this venture. The concept of destroying breeding seemed to them and to the others, including the non-human allies was reprehensible to the sensitivities of all within the fort. Driven by Jolinda and Patah, the debate over the planned attacks lasted several days. The crux being, could these unborn and young creatures be termed innocent when within days of their birth, they would gleefully join the ugly and fatal assault on the human sanctuary.

At the height of the discussions when it seemed an impasse had been reached, the artillery attacks on the fortress began.

No member of the ramshorns' minions armed or unarmed could penetrate the force field, but stones and other projectiles could. The enemy had developed a frightening innovation, catapults. These catapults, while simplistic in design could hurl huge pieces of granite culled from the mountains and carried by groups of the larger enemy to the weapons lined up just beyond the trees from the fort.

The walls might be impregnable, the windows and doors shatterproof, but inevitably those on the catapults would find the range to lob huge boulders onto the roof and into the interior grounds. Those in the fort, especially those manning the guns and crossbows could get hurt, or even killed and their weapons destroyed.

Of course, the hardware would be immediately replaced, but bringing it back up to the roof would eventually become taxing. The injured and dead were not so easily replaced.

These new enemy weapons would have little effect on the siege, but would change it, adding to the already spreading frustration of those who felt imprisoned in the fort, despite its massive size.

The catapults were slowly making progress in finding their range, still killing far more of their own while doing no damage yet to those beyond the force field.

The stalemate over the morality of attacking the breeding grounds was quickly resolved and the assaults given the go ahead.

A tactical decision was made shortly after that the attacks on the breeding grounds would go ahead, but not until teams had been properly trained and sent out to destroy the catapults. While rocket fire from the helicopters were able to take out one or two catapults, the fact that they were placed among the trees made the difficult targets even with the sighting systems on board. Ground assault teams would be more likely to assure elimination of the current crop of catapults.

To maintain the element of surprise, the anti-catapult teams would begin as an advance guard for the teams proceeding to the breeding sites. They would then break off to attack the catapults while the breeding site teams would make their way through the stands of forest around the lake towards their objectives. Two howitzers back in the fort's interior were loaded and calibrated to carry out their part of the breeding site assaults.

Raphael led the team that was heading for the swamp. Their primary target was the many hoblin and troll newborns and the breeders in the swamp. If they failed, their secondary target was a small enclosure at the mouth of the river. There a small number of trolls had deposited their newborns.

Raphael's team gave little thought to the secondary target. They were determined to take out the swamp and leave the troll enclosure to the big guns.

Brunell led the team to the Wampyras' birthing place while Maricel led one of the anti-catapult squads. The remaining teams were led by second awakened and among them were a few non-human allies who had shown exceptional leadership qualities and combat skills.

The initial movement of the teams down the tunnels to the bolt holes was uneventful. The only remarkable discovery was a location in one of the tunnels where some of the wall had collapsed just beyond the force field. The collapse had opened up a tunnel that some of the Stone Dwarves had dug to get through to the fort. The computer had assured them that there was no way of digging under the force field. Several piles of ash and a number of Stone Dwarve axes at the deadly threshold was proof that the force field was truly as effective below ground as it was above.

A quick inspection of the dwarves' tunnel showed that it was long deserted and the entrance at ground level pretty well overgrown and closed. The decision was quickly made that the team in that tunnel could proceed to their assigned exit point and with only that short delay the sortie teams were through to the bolt hole and ready to get underway.

When the word came that it was a go, the various teams proceeded quickly and efficiently through the concealed exits, securing them when they were out and leaving them ready for a quick return.

The bolt holes were strategically placed so as to minimize accidental contact with hostiles. There were no accidental encounters, and the teams were able to move undetected to their launch sites. They set up their equipment and signaled their readiness with a triple tap of their microphone heads on their helmets. When all were ready, command sent the simple instruction to their headsets, "go."

The attacks proved completely successful. The element of surprise and the slow response of the enemy allowed the raids to be carried out without a hitch.

Catapults were blasted to pieces. The main birthing habitats for the Wampyra, Stone Dwarves, faye, hoblins and trolls were destroyed along with virtually every one of the creatures within them.

All the assault teams were able to make it back to the fort unscathed except for Raphael's and his team. Because Raphael's team was assigned to carry out an attack with an unproven weapon, they were assigned a secondary target, the smaller troll nursery near the river. Their initial set up was between the main target and the secondary target to expedite movement from one to the other, should their first assault fail.

As it was, their attack on the primary target turned out to be even more successful than expectation. Their escape route back to the fort, however, was circuitous. On their way back, they became the first of the human and allies to encounter diamonics, the vicious and cruel second level diamonics, the tricorns.

The encounter happened innocently enough. Raphael and his company approached a wooded area fronted by a small clearing. They were elated at the success of their attack on the hoblin and troll breeding sites, but fortunately still alert. One of the team noticed some movement at the edge near the clearing some distance ahead.

Long-range binoculars allowed them to identify it as a tricorn. They had all seen countless pictures of the different diamonics and recognized it immediately.

They knew from the regular announcements inside the fort that tricorns, like their fellow diamonics, were fierce fighters that had some form of parapsychological ability.

By that time, it had spotted them. They raised their weapons and began their approach. Reaching the clearing Raphael's team was astonished to find themselves confronted by a large number of tricorns, some bearing tridents, some with spears and others with battle axes. Raphael signaled them to withdraw and take up a defensive position. Although it appeared pretty hopeless, the tricorns seriously outnumbered them, they dug in and prepared to defend themselves. The best Raphael and his team felt they could do was bring down as many of the diamonics as they could before succumbing to the diamonics' overwhelming numbers. Taking shelter behind anything they could find, a tree trunk, a log, several fallen rocks, and sparsely scattered thickets, Raphael and his men were prepared to face the enemy.

The tricorns, weapons raised, advanced, expecting the humans to run away. Instead of running, Raphael's team stood their ground and began to shoot at the advancing enemy. Surprisingly, their bullets seemed to have no effect on the advancing diamonics. A large group of tricorns swarmed towards one of the closest of Raphael's team who fought valiantly but with rifle and pistol did not seem to be putting a dent in the enemy forces until he dropped his pistol after being pierced by a trident. He pulled it from his body and out of the hands of the tricorn. He quickly turned it and lunged at his attacker who fell to the ground mortally wounded. Almost instantly the tricorns surrounding him vanished.

Moments later, a random bullet hit an axe bearing tricorn and as he dropped his axe and began to fall, the other axe carrying tricorns that were it immediately disappeared. The remaining tricorns turned as one and raced for the woods.

Despite the number of ferocious attackers, they had faced, the casualties were few.

The one who had been struck by the trident was protected by the heavy clothing intended to protect him from the cold as the swamp froze over had minimized the effect of the thrust leaving only superficial wounds. On the other hand, the tricorn that had been stabbed with his own trident was turning to ash as was the axe bearer. There was no sign of any of the others.

Something very strange had happened. The other trident bearers and axe carriers had not run away; they had simply vanished. There was no rush on Raphael or his team's part to analyze what had happened. The made their way as quickly as they could to their exit point vigilant and prepared should they be attacked again.

It wasn't until they were back in Fort Spa with the other teams being debriefed that they joined the others in trying to understood what had happened.

They called on the computer to confirm that the tricorns could create such illusions.

Raphael's team had in reality been rushed by three tricorns clearly believing that their illusory numbers would panic Raphael and his team and send them running to Fort Spa to sow seeds of fear that vast numbers of the far more dangerous diamonics were around ready to attack any human they could find outside the fortress.

The humans, however, had not acted as expected. They held their ground and now they knew that the diamonics, at least the tricorns, did not likely have anywhere near the numbers that the other hostile creatures had and depended on their parapsychological ability to make it appear that there were many more of them than there really were. Raphael's team had provided some worthwhile, even heartening news for the others.

The computer, too, offered some interesting and heartening news. The successful destruction of the breeding sites had already shown a significant reduction in the numbers of hostile attackers advancing on the fort.

Conditions had changed and now the humans and their allies could carry the battle to the enemy, both real and illusory.

Although the Wampyra, Dwarves, hoblins and others were still intent on the destruction of the humans, their numbers had been radically reduced and the catapults destroyed. Individually they proved no match for the larger and more heavily armed humans and the far more intelligent non-human allies who fought with them. With the threat of hostile activity greatly reduced, the assault teams from the fort were going farther afield, meeting less and less opposition.

It seemed as if the battle was winding down for many who had been confined for so long in the fortress.

Some of those who had lived in the outer communities and experimental stations began to talk about returning to their homes. Many were taking the opportunity to spend time outside by the lake and nearby woods. They were sensing victory over the forces of darkness for the first time since awakening so long ago. They felt carefree and were, unfortunately, a little too careless.

The computer had told them that they wouldn't really encounter the diamonics until the war was nearly won or lost. They had encountered diamonics, at least Raphael's team had and came away victorious. The battle planners and senior leadership were not quite so sure. The felt that there could be more to come, and the computer was adamant this was this was the case. They had not achieved victory yet.

It was difficult, however, to curb the enthusiasm of the majority of the second awakened who saw the respite in the battle as the end of the war. They were anxious to get on with things. Those who had lived in the experimental stations, especially, were impatient to get back and get everything in their communities up and running again.

Much to the dismay of the strategy and planning committee and security advisors, residents of the outlying communities began to join up with the reconnaissance and clean up teams that were heading in the direction their particular stations or villages. No hostiles had been seen for many days, so they felt secure in doing so. Several of the outlying community groups had already gone out with their recon. teams as guides.

Brunell's team was preparing to set out to scout the distant foothills. There was one particularly large community that had been established out that way and so there was a large number of those lived there before the siege that wanted to travel back to their homes with the team.

Brunel was not too happy with this, but he knew that there was no way of putting them off. It forced him to increase the number of team members to provide suitable security for the sizeable group that was joining him. They left the fort early in the morning. On exiting, Brunell sent a number of his team ahead to serve as spotters and vanguard. Three more would follow up behind. Four more members of the team paced several meters apart to the left of the rag tag group while Brunell and several others kept to the right. Brunell had also sent a number of his team to join in with the group of returnees. Most of these were slated to remain with them at the community and it seemed important that they have some personal contact with those they would be protecting.

The road, although badly overgrown was relatively obstacle free and by mid-afternoon they were approaching the last forest stand before the fields and buildings that marked the destination of the returnees. As they approached the stand of trees, that's where they saw them. Yesterday's group that had already been returned to their nearby village and where they now should be, had apparently decided to gather at the forest edge to greet their fellows who were with Brunell's team.

Some of those with Brunell, upon seeing those lined up, apparently to greet them and began to run toward them. The team was uncertain as to what to do as this was a completely unexpected development. They looked to Brunell as the towns folk rushed to join the previous day's cohort. He signaled to his men to try and stop them, but they paid no attention to them in their excitement to greet their fellow villagers and hear what news they had to share.

Those at the front ran past the forward guard who immediately turned toward Brunell for guidance. Brunel indicated that they should stay with them as best they could. They proceeded to move ahead with the surging crowd.

As the group of those with Brunell's team reached the others something seemed to change. Instead of exchanging greetings, the ones at the edge of the forest appeared to be attacking those rushing to greet them. The seemed to be carrying some sort of weapon, but Brunell and those team members close to him could not see what weapons those previously resettled seemed to be using. Whatever they were, those they attacked fell quickly and did not get up.

Those who had assigned to mingle with the community group were at a complete loss. In their confusion, they didn't know if they should shoot or not. They looked back toward Brunell, but he was as badly shocked as they were at the strange turn of events.

The resettlers that Brunell had been asked to escort during his reconnaissance mission were falling quickly. From his position, he could see the bodies on the ground. Then he became aware that he could see many of the fallen joining the attackers and turning on their fellows. Seeing the duplicates of those already fallen suddenly join the assault against their own community members, he realized they were diamonics using their powers of illusion to disguise themselves as humans. Survivors from those Brunell and his team had been escorted, turned from the others and began to run back to the safety of the team. Seeing this, he immediately gave the order to shoot. And called for backup.

While some of the hostiles slipped back into the forest stand the others continued to chase the ones trying to get way.

The range and the speed of the chasers made it difficult for the shooters to be very effective. The helicopter carrying Shanira, and the rescue team entered the air space above the panicked community members and the uncertain team member attempting to engage the diamonics still projecting their illusions of being human. Brunell's team's bullets were having some effect on the attackers. Some fell revealing their true identities. There were several monocorns and one or two tri-corns. The attackers were not few in number and the attack continued and it became more difficult for Brunell's shooters to separate the enemy from the friends.

Brunell could hear the "chop, chop, chop," of the helicopter rotors in the distance, sounding like and orchestral movement rising to crescendo. It was as if a climactic moment in a movie was about to unfold.

With his back to the copter, he waved his arm in salute then raced to join his team members and join battle with them. He felt confident that reinforcements would soon join him and make short work of the enemy. As he joined the fray, he could see those who had slipped back into the forest standing near the trees on the forest edge. Seconds later the steady sound of the helicopter changed. Looking back, Brunell could see the copter was running a pattern of evasive maneuvers although the sky around it was clear. As it passed overhead, it went into a sideslip tipping it almost ninety degrees to the ground. Brunell knew immediately that that attitude was not sustainable. Above his head it rocked in an attempt to catch air and right itself.

While Brunell saw clear skies around the copter, he didn't see what the copter pilot and those on board saw. They saw five fire-breathing dragons surrounding them. They dived towards the helicopter shooting flames through their nose, then would pull up to go around again. This was the reason for the evasive maneuvers the pilot was taking and what ultimately brought the copter down. The sudden and surprising arrival of the dragons was threatening and to those on board seemed real. Even a suspicion that they were encountering an illusion could not overcome the suddenness of the attack and the very realistic visual effects.

As Brunell watched in horror, the movements became more erratic and the tail boom dropped, catching a tree and throwing it into a disastrous autorotation slashing into friend and foe alike, sliding along the ground into the trees making a direct hit on those hiding at the edge of the forest. Immediately the dragons disappeared. It then slid its nose in between two large trees and came to a full stop, its fuel tank beginning to smolder. In the brief moments, it took for this, the fighting ended, and the attackers quickly faded into the underbrush.

Brunell could see Shanira trying to pull the members of her team from the wreckage. As Brunell raced to help her, she pulled the last of her team out as the helicopter burst into flames.

A few of the survivors of the carnage were wandering aimlessly among the fallen, shouting names and crying. Humans and wounded diamonics were intermixed. Some were trying to get up. Some help was being offered to the humans and the few allies among them.

The tricorns and monocorns were left untended. Most who remained had been seriously injured by the falling copter. Any human attempting to assist were threatened with claw, tusk, or horn. Many were in the process of turning to piles of ash. They would never really be able to gauge the number of diamonics to perish in the encounter, but it was, by far, the largest death toll among the humans and their allies.

Two team members had been killed along with 32 community returnees while a number of others were nursing a variety of wounds.

The experimental station they were hopping to restart would stay empty and unproductive for a considerable amount of time. While the survivors needed to return to the fort to heal and regroup, teams went out to bring back the other groups that had gone out to their home villages earlier.

Some of them did encounter diamonic attacks coming in the guise of friends from neighboring communities. The word had got around quickly, stay in well-defended shelters and don't trust anyone from outside the village or station, and diamonic attacks were met and repelled with minimal loss of life, unfortunately the result was similar for the diamonics.

Back at the fort, the planning and strategy group were facing a dilemma. They needed to send teams out to confront the enemy and reclaim the valley, but they could not risk them falling afoul of the diamonics and their illusions and open themselves up to disaster.

Each team when away from the fort needed to be doubly alert for anomalies among villagers or with the environment in general and get in touch and consult with the command group immediately. The computer had generated three dimensional real time maps of the entire valley. Any out of place copse of trees or piles of rock or any other geographic feature would be identified immediately. Those on foot would be immediately ordered to retreat and the anomaly would come under fire from long-range weapons.

The environmental illusions while disturbing could be dealt with. It was the psychological impact of illusions involving humans or their allies that was the most difficult for the reconnaissance teams to deal with.

It was easy to call in a missile strike, or fire a mortar, or lob grenades at stationary environmental anomaly. A group of apparently lost humans and allies, or a group seemingly under attack did not make easy targets even with ninety percent or better certainty that they were diamonic illusions designed to lure and entrap humans.

Besides these attempts to lure reconnaissance crews into ambush, the diamonics would use illusions to disorient and confuse teams. Who would find themselves under attack by fire breathing dragons, hideous charging monsters, masses of serpents or clouds of faye. No matter how well prepared one was, stepping into a very real looking mass of different sized and vicious looking snakes were seriously disconcerting, despite the fact that their boots encountered no twisting, squirming creatures. Teams experiencing illusions of injured or suffering fellows could not resist attempting going to their aid only to find themselves under attack by the very ones they sought to help. The command team realized, as apparently did the diamonics that these encounters were the hardest to resist.

The nature of the battle began to change again. It looked as if the diamonics were gaining the upper hand using the human need to help their fellows in distress. This became the diamonics most effective weapon luring even the wariest into range of the tridents, axes, and clubs. While the humans and their allies were still able to put up a strong defense fighting at close quarters, too many of the teams were returning to the Fort in disarray, carrying their wounded dragging their dead. They had been instructed to carry back their dead to the fort whenever possible. The diamonics had proven to be contemptuous of the human and allied dead hanging them in trees in the most horrible and provocative manner. Anyone from the fort coming upon one of these scenes would be horrified and dismayed.

The stories were circulating at the fort and morale was lower than at the height of the siege. A sense of hopelessness was growing, especially among the humans.

The discovery that would turn the tide of battle against the diamonics came accidently.

One team that had stayed out in the field too long, finding nothing was on its way back to the fort when they came across a forest fire. They figured that it was an illusion, but the sight of the surrounding flames was enough to scatter the team. One member of the team, remembering the way they had been able to detect and destroy the specters wondered if he might see something through the fire with his night vision goggles. The goggles he put on, however, were the Octogel goggles. As soon as they covered his eyes, the fire disappeared. In fact, all he could see were some very pale heat signatures among the trees some distance away. When a fellow team member grabbed his arm and tried to pull him away from the flames that seemed to be engulfing him, he immediately shouted back that there was no fire and pointed to his goggles. The other put on his night vision goggles and although he could see the flickering of flames there was an unreality to them.

"Do you see," shouted the first to have donned the goggles to his fellow as he turned him to look to his left, those faint heat signatures; they're not any of ours."

In fact, the other, with his night vision glasses could see the heat signatures among the trees better than the one with the Octogel. What they both could see that the fainter heat signatures were moving closer to the brighter heat signature of some of the team members. Aiming their rifles at the lesser heat signatures, they began to shoot. Several of them fell to the ground, the fire immediately disappeared for those not wearing goggles while the two watched the remaining lighter signatures slip off into the forest.

As the team began to assemble there were informed of the positive effects of the night vision visors and the Octogel goggles.

The team returned to the fort having lost none of its members and passed on the information about the goggles. Maricel and Shanira along with Patah and several other of their second awakening fellows along with Forestman and two other Sasquatch that had demonstrated incredible technical skill worked day and night to modified the goggles so they could be used comfortably and be effective in seeing through the diamonics illusions in a daylight environment.

Now when teams left the fort on patrol, they were equipped with the new visors and ordered to keep them on or near at hand. The would learn that humans and some allies glowed red, other non-human allies might glow different shades of green and orange while invariable the hostiles, diamonics and others invariably showed up in glowing shades of grey or silver. The complex spectrum range of the lenses while revealing individual enemy did not pick up their illusions and the diamonics and their allies were soon on the run.

The computer, the tech team and the command group all agreed that this was the time for an all-out assault on the diamonics and allies that were still around. While the destruction of the breeding sites had been successful beyond their wildest dreams and very few of the diamonics allies had reappeared.

The diamonics greatest strength, their power to create illusion was now no longer a viable tactic. The humans and their allies now had the ability to spot the individuals making their invisibility screens, also a product of the diamonics ability to create substantial looking illusions, useless. This forced the diamonics, who were now beginning to experience serious losses on the battlefront to withdraw to the foot of the steepest mountains that made up a little less than one quarter of the valley wall.

There, they used massive boulders and shallow caves in which to hide from the humans and their allies. In effect, the siege had now reversed as the diamonics and their allies found themselves trapped between the wall of mountain and a formidable force of humans and their allies, all well trained soldiers and tacticians, gathered under Raphael's leadership.

Using a loud hailer connected to a number of speakers around the diamonic's defense zone, Raphael called out for them to prepare to negotiate surrender.

"Never!" came the booming voice of the Ramshorn and as if this was a signal, a large assortment of diamonics came over and around the scattered boulders that marked their defenses and rushed from the caves in a fierce attack. Their surprise attack was a desperate one and to some extent it was effective. Some humans on the front lines were injured and even one or two killed before Raphael's forces donned their visors and made a counter-attack.

This was the diamonics last-ditch stand. There was no subterfuge, no illusions, just a fierce determination to fight to the death, something the well-armed humans and their allies could easily provide.

Raphael immediately ordered his forces to pull back and if possible not engage the enemy. With the order, hold all fire." The front row backed quickly behind the second row bringing some of the enemy with them. Each of the members of the second row was carrying a huge shield. Immediately on command they dropped the shields and stepped back. The shields began to link and rise putting a super hard wall between themselves and the rest of the attacking diamonics.

While the diamonics who had come through with the first line were quickly dispatched the first diamonics to the wall ran into it and began to climb only to discover that like the force field protecting the wall of the human fort, it generated a similar field and was a fatal barrier for the diamonics and other hostiles. They were instantly incinerated. Unlike their minions, the diamonics behind them immediately stopped and backed away.

"It's working," called Raphael into his communicator mouthpiece.

Back at the fort, this was met with a collective sigh of relief. Shanira who, over the past two seasons had been working with the computer and its database to develop the force field shield and had constructed the prototype, Raphael was using pounded the air with her fists. Even the computer-generated hologram seemed pleased.

Using his powerful megaphone again, Raphael began to speak to the diamonics, his voice as loud and dominant as the Ramshorn. "Before you begin to look for a way around this wall, know that it will be no use to you. Our weapons are more powerful and have a far greater range than yours. We are able to counter your illusions so, if you continue to fight, you will lose, and countless numbers of your people will die needlessly. I have an offer.

Across the valley, the dimensional gate is still open. We will permit you to send some scouts through to check the world that lies beyond it. If they find it satisfactory, you and all your allies and minions will proceed there and leave earth to us."

The diamonics melted back behind the huge boulders and into the shallow caves that were their defenses. There were no more attacks, but no word either. A day passed with no movement on the other side. Then near dusk the following day, a group of about 30 diamonics representing the various orders, led by a tall ramshorn approached the human's barricade.

One of the shields dropped and Raphael, with Maricel at his side stepped through and up to what they knew was a lesser but still important ramshorn. "What is your answer," asked Raphael.

"We are they surveyors of the new land," said the ramshorn, "our duty is to go through the dimensional gate to the world beyond and determine its worth as a home. Once the determination is made, and if it is satisfactory, we will return to make plans for our exodus. If it is not satisfactory, we have not given up claim to this one."

The last statement proudly spoken by the ramshorn was chilling to Raphael and Maricel who, along with their fellows were tired of the carnage and wished only for peace. Without comment, however, their designated escort group stepped out to guide the diamonics to the dimensional gate. Visors down and weapons ready, the escorted the diamonics to the gate and stood aside. The diamonics hesitated for only a moment then the surveyors proceeded through the gate and vanished from the escorts' sight.

The escort group would remain for a great many days awaiting the return of the diamonic scouts. The wait was long and tedious for both sides. Some humans, feeling that the diamonic surveyors would not return began to urge for an all-out assault on the diamonics' position. Behind their boulders and in their caves, the diamonics were reinforcing the arsenal of weapons, bows and arrows and mini catapults, the ones that had showed themselves most effective against human defenses.

One morning after a great many days, almost unnoticed, the gate shimmered and there stood the lesser ramshorn and two of his fellows, a tri-corn and a mono-corn.

Raphael, Maricel and Patah had been standing by near the gate and when informed of the return of the ramshorn, rushed to greet them.

"Where are the others?" shouted Raphael.

"We will return to the Ramshorn to present our findings," was all the ramshorn said.

Later the humans would learn that the remaining surveyors were preparing for the arrival of the diamonics and their minions and that two had died searching some distant caves. The conclusion regarding them was that they were careless.

"What is your opinion of that world," asked Patah, "will it satisfy your people?"

"We have no opinion," said the ramshorn, "the only opinion is that of the Great Ramshorn whom I must speak with."

He made no response to Maricel's question, "What did you see there?"

Eventually they would learn that it was a valley similar to the one they were in, only described by the diamonics as more spectacular and regal and the mountains more colossal and the lake larger and deeper. For the diamonics, this grandeur better represented how they felt about themselves and their leader.

At the invitation of the humans and their allies, the one the diamonics termed the Great Ramshorn and his retinue came under human escort to meet the three returned from the world beyond the dimensional gate.

After the meeting and a lengthy discussion among them, one of the tri-corns from the Great Ramshorn's retinue came to the three first awakened who still remained close by. "The Great Ramshorn will give his decision at first light," he intoned.

With their human escort, they returned to where the remainder of the diamonics and their minions awaited them behind the security of the huge boulders and in the shallow caves.

As dawn broke over the land, the anticipation was agonizingly high among the humans and their allies both at the fort and among those standing guard at the dimensional gate. Raphael's special forces at the shield wall watched the place where the diamonics and their minions were hidden with special interest, wondering if the diamonics would choose to leave peacefully or would the war of final destruction begin.

The answer came very shortly as the Diamonics, led by the Great Ramshorn and his residue left the shelter of the boulders and the caves with several thousand followers to make their way to the dimensional gate.

"We will go, for the greater good of our own," exclaimed the Great Ramshorn as he stood before Raphael, Maricel and Patah, "But first you must build a canal from the lake to the gate so that our brothers of the water can join us."

This was the first time that anyone among the humans and their allies had heard about 'brothers from the waters', but if a canal would get the diamonics and their minions to leave the earth, the canal would be built. It was, in fact, completed within several days. The Ramshorn indicated his approval and with his retinue entered the gate,

The humans watched in amazement as vast numbers of diamonics, and their minions seemed to appear from nowhere to follow. Day and night the exodus continued. The four orders of diamonics, ramshorn, tri-corn, mono-corns and imps, were followed by clouds of faye folk, Wampyra throughout the night, spectra, hoblins, harpies and trolls. There were many the humans recognized and a whole variety they didn't, serpentine creatures and dragon-like beings and many more. They were being drawn to the gate from every part of the earth.

The Great Ramshorn was true to his word. Every sort of unnatural monster followed him through the gate. For days upon days they came, disappearing through the shimmering dimensional gate. When the last creature lumbered through the gate, it's surface burst like the skin of a bubble revealing a short cave. Then, as suddenly as it had disappeared, the gate returned.

The human's and their allies who had cheered loudly as the gate had burst were now quite disconcerted. They feared that this might mean that they remained vulnerable to sneak attacks by the diamonics or their minions moving secretly back and forth through the dimensional gate.

For the moment, the Great Ramshorn had been true to his word, but the devious and evil nature of the creatures could not be discounted. A decision was made by the planning team back at the fort that a reconnaissance group of mixed human and nonhuman allies would penetrate the gate and bring a video probe through to the world on the other side to see if there was a buildup of hostile forces nearby.

If the quick surveillance of the reconnaissance team didn't spot any threat, the video probe would remain behind on their return, linked to the computer to gather and analyze data should an enemy build-up on the other side of the gate occur.

The returning scouts reported a far different, less spectacular world than the diamonics had described. Computer analysis suggested that except for some earth like animals, there seemed to be no intelligent life present.

The mountains were low and rounded hills and the terrain filled with old growth forest. A science team went through and launched a small camera satellite that revealed that as far as intelligent life was concerned this world was a bare and virgin version of their earth.

After much deliberation, it was decided that the world appearing at the other side of the dimensional gate was a different one from the world to which the diamonics and their minions had gone. Shortly after the deliberations were made, some of the leaders of the non-human allies presented a proposal on behalf of their fellows that they, too, would pass through the dimensional gate to the world that was waiting there and bring those other non-human creatures that had remained neutral during the battle for earth with them.

The agreement was made and once again there was a parade of beings passing through the dimensional gate. Except for a very tiny group of non-humans, some of the elven and the Marefolk whose friendship and association with the humans was very close, the non-human allies and the neutrals had made their way to a new world and a new life. The numbers departing were huge almost equivalent to that of the diamonics. The Marefolk, the wood elves, the peaceful green dwarves, the mountain elven and so many others the humans had not encountered made their way to the dimensional gate. Many farewell tears were shed as loyal friends prepared to part.

Except for the very few non-human companions, the humans were left alone on legacy earth. The long-lived and slow breeding Sasquatch remained as did some others whose heritage was closely tied to origin earth. Perhaps those like them had secretly shared that earth or were similar enough to those that did that they bore closer kinship to the humans than to the non-humans. Those like Forestman and some of the others whose intellect and skill matched the humans and could contribute to the first and second awakened and all those who would follow remained close to their human friends. Many others not tied to a specific group or individual vanished into the mountains and forests.

The compulsion that had brought the second awakeners to the valley and Fort Spa was gone. Those remaining members of the villages and station communities were finally able to return home while others decided to leave the valley and find a ready-made community in which to settle.

Just as this was about to happen, the Fort community experienced its first human birth. Jolinda was delighted to finally use her skills for bringing new life into the world. From this time on, population would expand naturally and, indeed, other births followed shortly and continued to happen.

For the many who left the valley as for those who remained, there were new things to be learned, particularly what to do with these tiny newborns that looked more like Stone Dwarves than humans. In short order, they began to grow, and the question of education became important. Whole new sets of skills would be called upon as unlike the awakened, these small ones did not share the innate knowledge and specialties that had guided them.

The first awakened and some of the leaders of the second awakened remained in Fort Spa. Surviving many generations, they remained there ready to instruct and guide.

Over time, humanity grew to create the legacy earth that those who while scraping off the last vestiges of their own humanity had hoped for in constructing it. As those pan-dimensional entities in their last human act the construction of their legacy in that dark dead region of the universe that held their origins ever wonder if the humans of legacy earth, in their turn to evolve into pan-dimensional beings, would construct their own legacy earth.

Also by Mick MacNeil

Purgatory: Making the Champion
Legacy Earth
Spooked